Nikki

Books by Henry Kane

A KIND OF RAPE 1974

DECISION 1973

THE MOONLIGHTER 1971

A Kind of Rape

A Kind of Rape

HENRY KANE

Atheneum NEW YORK *1974*

Library of Congress catalog card number 73–91625
ISBN 0–689–10596–7
Published simultaneously in Canada by McClelland and Stewart Ltd.
Manufactured in the United States of America by
H. Wolff, New York
Designed by Harry Ford
First Edition

To B.G.

WHO WOULD BELIEVE IT?

You do solemnly swear, each man and woman by whatever he or she holds most sacred, that you will be loyal to the profession of medicine and just and generous to its members; that you will lead your lives and practice your art in uprightness and honor; that into whatsoever house you shall enter, it shall be for the good of the sick to the utmost of your power, you holding yourselves far aloof from wrong, from corruption, from the tempting of others to vice, from any act of seduction of male or female; that you will exercise your art solely for the cure of your patients and will give no drug, perform no operation, for a criminal purpose, even if solicited, far less suggest it; that whatsoever you shall hear or see of the lives of men, women, or children which is not fitting to be spoken, you will keep inviolably secret. These things do you swear. Let each man and woman bow the head in sign of acquiescence. And now, if you will be true to this, your oath, may prosperity and good repute be ever yours; the opposite, if you shall prove yourselves forsworn.

The Hippocratic Oath

A Kind of Rape

I

NUDE except for the flimsy kimono donated by the stage manager, she waited nervously in the recessed wing, the last for the audition, the last of six. Number 5 was out there now with Raywick. "From me to you," the stage manager had said. "Like a bonus, honey, from me to you. The last one on, she leaves the lingering impression. So I spotted you last because I happen to think you're the best of the bunch for this nothing part. And that's the truth, believe me."

She believed him. Because this one, certainly, was not on the make. Not trying for points with the usual, dreary, repetitive routine. This little man was not hot for the lady's body; openly and beautifully, and proudly, he was homosexual. So, for once, no ulterior motive. No bull. No con. No charming chatter to lay the groundwork, a normal nuance in theatrical circles, for the bedding down of an aspiring actress; a quick trick in the feathers and then g'bye baby, take care, I'll see you.

Not this one. In him, somehow, she sensed compassion. This one knew of the horrors.

"Easy does it," he whispered, small, bald, smiling beside her. "You've got the looks, the body; hell, you've even got the voice. And, honey, remember, you don't have to be a great actress. You are very goddam beautiful, which in this case should wrap it up. One scene. The opening scene and a shocker; I mean he hits the audience right away with both of you naked. But it's really a tiny scene, a bit. You say your lines; and then you're through for the night. And you can say the lines, kid. I heard you, didn't I? You just say them for them like you said them for me and you're in the bag. Right?"

"Yes."

"And if you don't know the lines, okay. You can read. I've got your sides right here. You can take them onstage and get into bed with him, and read."

"I know the lines. I've memorized them."

"Good. Never hurts. Shows them you're in there on the ball. Good intentions, you know? But if you futz up on the lines, don't panic. I can always come out there and give you your sides. What I mean—this trip, it's not a memory test. What I'm trying to say, if you lose a line, don't freeze, don't faint, don't screw yourself up."

"You're very kind."

"Not kind. Just working on my job, is all. Like the man said, the play's the thing. That's my job of work, the play. Hell, I screened you people, didn't I? And in my opinion, for this lousy little role you're the best, and you match up real good with John Raywick. And don't ever worry about Mr. Sex Symbol making a grab. They all do, don't they?"

"Well . . ."

"Not John. A very married man. Two kids. A homebody; square as a box. Never fools around. Tell you something else, make you laugh. Mr. Sex Symbol, he's got piles. You know, hemorrhoids. Not too bad. Like chronic. But he's afraid to go in for an operation. Okay. The hell with John. You're not here for John Raywick. You're here for the people out front there—the director, the author, the producer. And when you walk out there naked, already you'll have them locked. Then just do your bit. Say your lines and you'll knock them dead."

He slapped her rear. Convivial, altruistic, nonsexual. Like a coach slapping the ass of a basketball player. "You know why we're talking, honey? To keep you loose and easy. Like a little gossip, like John with the hemorrhoids; that don't hurt, you know? Helps keep you loose and easy. Which is the way I want you." The little man grinned up at her. "Sweetie, out there you're gonna justify me. You're my pick, remember? You are my choice."

"Thank you, Sid."

"What for? Nothing to thank me. I work at my job."

Sid. His name was Sid. No surname. There had never been a surname. Sid. That was clear in her mind. His name and the day. Today was Friday. Sid and Friday. All else was a jumble, an intricate jumble in back of her mind, as he talked to her, and continued talking to her, to keep her loose and easy.

Sue had called on Monday. Fat Sue, her agent. Successful Sue, whose sickness was food. Crazy Sue, who smoked cigars. Dynamic Sue, a beautiful person, a leveler. "Forget it, luv," Sue would say. "An actress you're not, and you're never going to be. So why don't you get that buzzing bee out of your bonnet? I've stuck you in stock, and off-Broadway, and off-off-Broadway, and I've watched you, and you're not there. Simply, it ain't there, baby. Everybody can't have it, and you don't. On the other hand, you're gorgeous, absolutely divine, and you've got a damn good head on those shoulders. So why don't you settle, for Chrissake? Latch on to a rich one; Christ, they're out there looking for the likes of you. Get married to a richie-bitchie, have babies and things, and become a patron of the arts or something."

And so at long last she had become convinced, the urge beginning to dwindle. Forget it. Forget the dream. Stop fooling yourself. Three years, and every Broadway audition had been a failure. Heck, they ought to know, no matter you blindly refused to accept. That you do not have the flair, the fire, the talent. Small parts in summer stock, yes; and off-Broadway, and off-off-Broadway; but that had been it. "A beauty you are, an actress you're not. Honey, get wise," Sue would say. And so finally, sadly, reluctantly she had begun to plan for a different career. School again, but a vocation. Steno and typing. Executive secretary. And move up from there.

But this Monday on the phone Sue had sounded excited.

"I've got a thing here, right up your alley. If you want to give it a try, I don't think you can miss. Made to order for you. Could be you can postpone executive secretary." A quick laugh. "Honey, I know you're still burning with your crazy hangup. I think you're nuts, but I'm an agent. I know you can just stroll through this part; hell, it's you; you don't have to be an actress. These things happen once every blue moon. This part is you. I know I can satisfy the producer, but it's up to you. On the other hand, there *is* a problem."

"What?"

"Tell you when you get here. How about two o'clock?"

And at two o'clock, with none of the usual waiting outside, she had been ushered directly into Sue's office.

"Sit down, Clare. Let me tell you what we have."

Just like that. No formalities, no amenities. Sue Robbins, who had been through all the wars. Crisp, quick, kind, but brusque. Short-cut tousled hair. No makeup. A face like a battlefield.

"What we have is a winner from the word go." Tapped a red-bound script. "A new play by Paul Rafferty. Produced by

Donald Franklin. Directed by Arthur McLean. Starring John Raywick and Beatrice Smith. A million dollars' worth of talent right there." She shook her head. "Boy, would I like to have a couple of units of this one. No chance. All gobbled up. Mostly by Anthony Ashland, the chief angel here, chief investor. More money added to his mint. Ashland. You know? The lawyer . . ."

Sue was stalling. Not like her. Why?

"No," Clare said. "I don't know."

"Probably the most important criminal lawyer in New York."

"What would I know about criminal lawyers?"

"The hell with it. The play. About a philandering husband who gets his comeuppance in the end. The hell with that, too. What's important to us, the opening scene. Rafferty sets up his guy right there. A beautiful little scene, very effective. It's morning. We're in the bedroom of Raywick's home. The wife is out of town. So Raywick was out *on* the town. Slightly bombed, he picked up a sweet little chick in a romantic pub, a singles bar. A quite innocent little chick. I mean not a bum, not a barfly—a lovely young girl. But he works his points, the charming bastard, and takes her home and screws his nuts off."

Sue moved forward. She laid her ample bosom over the desk and clasped her hands. "Opening scene. The morning after. In the sack, in his home. He is sober, he is satiated, he is disgusted with himself *and* the girl. So he gets her out of bed and gets rid of her. Cutely, but firmly, and to the girl's utter bewilderment. Rafferty's written a brilliant little scene there. But it's the producer, the wily Don Franklin, who's guaranteed a long-run hit. Because it's Franklin who's persuaded John Raywick to do, for the first time in his career, a nude scene. Can you imagine? The great John Raywick naked onstage. Honey, when this gets out, there'll be a hundred thousand housewives buying up tickets in advance."

That was when it had begun to come to her. She understood why Sue had been stalling.

"Two," she said. "Two nude onstage."

"Correct." Sue unclasped her hands, leaned back in the swivel chair. "Honey, you're the girl. This once, you don't have to act. Rafferty wrote—you! Deep inside you're a timid one, an innocent—perfect for the part. And the way you stack up, perfect as a foil for Raywick. The right height, and you're crazily beautiful. And you're blond and he's dark, they'll love that. Dramatic, you know?" A squint. "Does it bug you to be naked?"

"I—I don't know."

Sue lit a cigar, a long thin cigar. "Honey, I'm the one been after you to quit the acting business, right? But I'm an agent, and I know where people fit. For this role you don't just fit; I'm telling you it's *you*. No acting; you won't have to act. So I'm being practical—for me. For you, I still say quit the acting business, but quit after this one, and like that you'll go out in a blaze of glory. So lemme ask again. Does it bug you to be naked?"

"Honestly, I don't know."

"Why the hell should it? You're young, you're mod, you've got the bod. Honey, if a John Raywick is willing to perform in the buff—why not you? And you came real close the last time, remember? Four months ago on Christopher Street. What in hell was the name of that disaster? *I Will Travel with You.* Featuring that other great actor, your boyfriend Charlie Ennis."

"He's not my boyfriend. And his name isn't Charlie; it's Charles."

"Your friend Charles. Who was as much a disaster as that play was a disaster. Ran ten days, which was ten days too long." She puffed the cigar. "Learn from Charles, baby. A misfit, a no-talent, but hipped, driven. And the poor bastard will go on like that—a shitty bit part here and there—until he gets old and ugly. Happens to be a damn good-looking kid, but that's all there is for him in the acting business. And there are so many of him, the poor hopeless bastards. Honey, listen to Sue. Learn from Charles."

She wanted to scream; controlled herself.

"I've learned. And you helped me to learn. So why am I here?"

"Because I'm an agent. I'm practical. Because for this lousy little frig-bit, you're the perfect peg for the hole. And because I know you're still panting for that one Broadway turn. Okay, here it is. The blue moon happened. Rafferty wrote you! He wrote Clare Benton. And when he sees you and hears you, he'll damn well know it. So happy-happy for you, your last grasp at the dream. But don't you dare change your plans to quit. Grab at the blue moon. Get the part and enjoy. But after that—out, finished. Blaze of glory and done."

So? Why didn't she get up and walk?

Why didn't she say: "I've learned. You taught me. To hell with blaze of glory. Thank you, no."

But she did not get up and walk, did she? Because the remnants of dreams hang on.

"Nude," Sue was saying. "You came close in *I Will Travel with You*. You were the one sensation in that catastrophe. When you came out in that sheer black peignoir, there was one hell of a gasp from the audience. And that was it for the whole damn play. One gasp. And you were it. That you have, my lady. The looks, the body. So please don't go coy on me. If you want to turn this down, if you're already quits—fine. But don't do it because of nude. Not in this day and age. Honey, if a John Raywick is willing to do a scene balls naked . . ."

* * *

The initial audition had been on Wednesday. Morosco Theatre. Nine o'clock in the morning. Sue had predicted there would be many girls. There were. At least seventy. "Don't let the crowd get you down," Sue had said. "Most of them won't even be actresses. On this type of call, a lot of models come out." One of the stage manager's assistants had collected their résumés, then directed them to the seats, and they sat there like playgoers. There were three busy assistants, one man and two women. The stage manager, a bald little man, was dressed in sneakers, jeans, and sweatshirt. He never did introduce himself but they heard his name from the assistants. Sid.

At quarter to ten, Sid, onstage, clapped his hands and kept clapping until the murmuring in the seats ceased. "I'll take them in tens," he said to the male assistant. "I want ten bio's at a clip." The assistant counted off ten of the sheets. He gave them to Sid, who faced the audience.

"When I call your names, you will please come up here. You will take off your clothes and walk around. That's all I want you to do. Take off your clothes and walk."

From the first batch of ten, he selected none. They walked, he looked. Then he said, "Thank you," returned their bio's, and they got dressed and went away. From the next batch he selected two. And from the next, five. And from the next, one: Clare Benton. And he continued calling names, and girls continued coming up, but he kept the selected ones naked onstage. Smart Sid. He waved them toward folding chairs, unfolded to sit on, and some of the girls sat, and some stood, but the embarrassment began to dissipate. When you are naked among other nakeds, you become, in time, like cattle. Nothing. The nervousness peels away.

At the end, there were thirteen naked girls onstage.

"Okay, ladies," Sid said. "Nothing against any of the others. Everybody beautiful. But some were too old, and some too young, and some did not match physically for John Raywick. Okay, now we'll try for readings. No sweat, kids. This is just for voices." He snapped his fingers. A female assistant handed him two scripts. He gave one to one of the girls, retained the other. "I'll play Raywick," he said. "We're just going to read."

The readings eliminated seven more, and now there were six, one of whom was Clare Benton.

"We're down to the nitty-gritty," Sid said. "You're it, kids, but you're not yet anything, because I'm only the screener. The real audition is Friday, four o'clock. On Friday you'll play the scene with Raywick himself. And out front you'll have the producer, the director, the author, et cetera, and they're the ones that make the pick. But that pick is gonna be one of you." He turned to a female assistant. "Give them their sides, Martha."

Martha gave each of them two sets of the sheets that comprised the scene.

"Duplicates," Sid said. "Give one to somebody—your mother, your sister, your husband, your sweetheart—and do the bit with them. To get real acquainted with the scene, you know? You don't have to memorize; plenty of time for that in rehearsal. But get acquainted with it, so you know what you're doing. Okay, ladies. Thank you. You can get dressed now. I'll keep your bio's."

The girls began to dress. Sid came close to Clare. "Stick around," he said softly. "I want to talk to you." And after the others were gone, he said, "Honey, you're my Number One. I think you're it. Of course, what I think don't really matter, but for me you're the best of the bunch. So study hard, but don't overdo, don't try to playact, just be yourself. Your looks, your body, your voice, your manner, the way you read the lines—you're Number One."

Her heart thumped wildly.

"Thank you," she managed to say.

"Nothing to thank, nothing personal. The play's the thing, and that's my job."

"Thank you, anyway."

He smiled, squeezed her arm. "Okay, all right, you're welcome. But please. I would hate to build you up for a letdown. You're my pick, but who the hell am I? No. Check that. Correction. Fuck modesty. I know what it's all about. You figure to cop this part. Study. Get acquainted with the scene. And on Friday you just be yourself."

She had stumbled out to the glare of the autumn day, heart thumping. Hailed a cab and rode home to Barrow Street. A little one-bedroom apartment in a darned fine building in the West Village, but, wow, the rental. Two hundred and eighty-five dollars a month. God, the price of rent in New York City.

And in the little kitchen, water in the kettle for tea. Wanted to call Sue, but was still too excited. Made the tea, drank half. Quit the kitchen and in the bathroom swallowed a Valium. Took off clothes, showered, pulled on cool pajamas. Lay out on the couch in the living room and in time the Valium began to work. The thumping grew numb. She called Sue and told her.

"You're in," Sue said. "I tell you, you're in. The stage manager! Very important in the whole screwy machinery, and you and I, we both damn know it. For the bits, they lean heavy on the stage manager. But lemme warn you, kid. The chauvinist pigs. He'll probably try for a waltz in the sack. You turn him down, he'll find some excuse to roust you out. You know how it is with the pigs."

"No. He's gay."

"Oh, beautiful. Honey, you're really in! Now you just do what he said. Study. Get ahold of Charles and study."

"Yes."

"And keep in touch."

"I will. Bye, Sue."

Hung up and called Charles. The service answered. Of course. He was working. Between roles he was a salesman in Bloomingdale's furniture department. She left her message, went to the kitchen, and made tea again.

He called at six o'clock. She told him some of it quickly, and he said he would be there at seven. He came at a quarter to seven with a bottle of wine. She made bacon and eggs and they ate it with the wine and talked. He was a good guy, sweet and true, but in fact he had been the final blow; even more than Sue, he had helped, however unwittingly, to terminate her career—her alleged career—as an actress. Sue had put it pithily—leave it to pragmatic, outrageous Sue—and Clare Benton remembered every word precisely. "Take a good hard look at Charlie Ennis," Sue had said, "and maybe you'll begin to understand what in hell I've been preaching. Charlie Ennis, a perfect example. A hopeless case. A living example of sheer inadequacy. Self-traduced by the fury of the dream."

Yes.

Charles believed himself to be an actor. He wasn't. He stank. And everybody knew it except Charles. And again Clare Benton could quote the redoubtable Sue Robbins. "Honey, the mind is like a mirror; it fools the shit out of a hell of a lot of us. People looking in a mirror see what they *want* to see, but most of the time it ain't, goddamit to hell, what others see. Which explains why so many old bags still think they're young and beautiful."

Yes.

Charles Ennis, actor, did get roles—minor roles—every now and then, because he was young, attractive, tall, and rangy. And lately there was even money in the bank, residual money, because, making the rounds, he had fallen into that crazy TV commercial, the one for Volkswagen that they kept repeating.

She had met him four months ago, during the ten-day run of that silly little play, and was seeing him on and off but nothing serious. In fact, he bored her. She liked her men older. What men? Nobody. Nothing. A few insane entanglements—once even with a man she knew to be married—but always in time she dropped them, discovering that they were phonies. What was it with her? A propensity for self-destruct? A lack of capacity for love? A natural affinity for phonies? Or, dear Lord, was *she* the phony?

"All right, here we go," Charles said, and drank down wine. "Let's get at it, babe." Good Charles, sweet Charles, boring Charles; he worked with her until they were both exhausted. "I'm going to take tomorrow off," he said. "Clare Benton in a Paul Rafferty play! Man, that could finally be the break. And in our business, babe, that's all anybody needs. A little luck. A break." (Charles's song always, his constant ineffectual litany: all you need is luck, a break. Sue could tell him different, and by now so could Clare. There is also that other small matter, my friend. Talent.) "We're going to keep hammering away," Charles said, "until you're letter-perfect, one hundred percent letter-perfect."

He stayed over, and sometime during the night they screwed, and they slept late, and early in the afternoon he took her out for brunch, and then back in the apartment they worked, he with his script and she with hers, and hours afterward they neither of them needed the scripts. Not only did she know her part by heart, but he knew Raywick's.

And in the evening they did it again, and again and again, and he said, "You're letter-perfect, babe. One hundred percent letter-perfect. Now go to bed. Get yourself a good, long night's sleep. Tomorrow's Friday."

He went home. Sweet Charles went home. He did not stay and she knew why. A good, long night's sleep. Without interruption. No sexual combat. Sweet Charles, he was on her side, he always meant well for her. So? Why did she despise him? Because he was dull. Feckless. He was a nothing. And her adoration, an inner sickness, flamed only for those who were something.

But what was she? She knew what she was. Nothing!

Went to bed. Early. Tried dutifully. But of course she could not sleep. Turned. Twisted. Dozed in the snare of momentary nightmares. And then got out of bed and drank down a couple of Seconals. Yeah, man. Yeah, Charles. Yeah, everybody. In New York, you learn. You can create your own ups and downs. For up, there is Dexie. For down, there is valiant Valium. And for a good long night's sleep, there are always a couple of Seconals.

And now it was Friday, late afternoon. In a wing of the Morosco Theatre. Clare Benton nude within a flimsy kimono. A small man quietly jabbering beside her. And Number 5 out there onstage with Raywick.

Felt a touch at her elbow.

"Start getting ready," the small man said.

Number 5 came to them in the wing, a tall brunette with a slithering walk. Smiled at Clare. "Good luck," she said, and disappeared.

"Not yet," the small man said. "The poor bastard, he needs a little time. Like respite, you know? But you can start jogging inside, sweetie. Start revving up the motor."

She looked out toward the stage, bleak under the harsh light, empty except for a bed, a chair, and Mr. John Raywick, naked and handsome, perspiring, and so obviously weary. His bathrobe was crumpled over the back of the chair, and on the seat of the chair were cigarettes, a lighter, and an ashtray.

He sat on the edge of the bed, knees spread, pudendum dangling. He lit a cigarette, scowled toward the darkness.

"How many more?" he asked. "Christ, Don. This is one bitch of a chore."

"One," a deep voice answered. "You've been marvelous, John. Please hang in there. Just one more."

Raywick sighed, shrugged. Inhaled a last drag. Squeezed out the cigarette, swung into the bed, and pulled up the cover.

From the seats the deep voice called, "Okay, let's have her."

"Here we go," the small man whispered. "Gimme." He pulled the kimono from her, flung it away, and bent and kissed her left buttock. "That's for luck," he said, and danced onto the stage.

Sidney Menchikoff knew exactly who was out there in the dimness of the seats in the twelfth row. The producer, the director, the author, and the big money man. Donald Franklin, Arthur McLean, Paul Rafferty, and Mr. Anthony Ashland. And each of them with clipboards to which were attached copies of the bio's.

"We have here now Miss Clare Benton," he announced. "No i in that, gentlemen. This Clare is without an i."

"Okay. Let's have her."

"Yessir. Coming at you, Mr. Franklin. Gentlemen, I give you—Miss Clare Benton."

Menchikoff bowed and walked off.

The nude girl emerged to the glare of the stark-white light and Tony Ashland sat up in his seat.

"Sweet Jesus," he breathed.

"Sid goes to pattern," Franklin said, and stroked his jowls. "Saves the best for the last. This one's his choice."

"My choice too," Ashland said.

"You haven't heard her yet."

"Who needs to hear?"

"We do."

"Your business. Not mine. Me, I'm only slumming."

"Dirty old man," Franklin said.

"True. This time, correct."

True. Correct. A release—in a way, a lark—this viewing of naked girls. He had been on trial for twelve solid days, and was still on trial, in that damn manslaughter case. But it was coming to a close. On Monday he would put on his last witness, the psychiatrist, and that would be it. On Tuesday the summations, on Wednesday the judge's charge, and then up to the jury. Today, Friday, the judge had unexpectedly adjourned court early, and at two o'clock Anthony Ashland had been back in the office, restless, nervous, at loose ends. And had remembered that today at four Don Franklin was auditioning for that first scene. And had called and told Don he would attend. "I can use the recreation," he had said. "I'm your chief angel, pal, your archangel. An archangel, once in a while, is entitled to a private burlesque show."

"Archangel, you're a DOM," Don had said. "Love to have you. See you at four."

They had provided him with a clipboard and he was one of four in the twelfth row: they working, he enjoying, but even more impressive than the naked girls was the confluence of the numbers.

Confluence of numbers.

Four o'clock—four men.

Twelfth row—twelve days on trial.

Was somebody up there trying to tell him something?

He was a great man for omens, numbers, hunches, intuition, astrology, ESP, and all things occult, but he was a nonbeliever. That was a part of his vaunted charm, his friends would tell him: his ambivalence; Mr. Anthony Ashland at pinnacle, his friends would tell him: mature, respected, but a walking dichotomy. And he did not disagree.

His heart went out to fate, destiny, karma, matters unknown and unknowable to present-day man still primitive, but his brain rejected his heart; his cross was the rock of skepticism. "Proof," he would say to his sympathetic believer-friends. "I have an open mind, but a man like me—my training, my background—I require proof, a scintilla of proof, something! I cannot live by faith alone. Therefore I am a nonbeliever, and I hate it. Would that I could accept the myth of Christ's resurrection. Then, by God, I would not be a lawyer practicing in the criminal courts. I would be a monk in a monastery."

He was enjoying—one of four in the twelfth row of the Morosco Theatre—the knots in his stomach beginning to loosen. It was pleasant to look upon pretty girls naked as Eve, and interesting to hear them express the selfsame lines in such divergent ways, means, manners, and voices. Of course at the end, after the long-term period of rehearsal, the girl selected would speak the lines by rote, precisely as directed by Arthur McLean. But for now it was pleasant to watch and interesting to listen—until this one. Sweet Jesus, she was superb. And for Anthony Ashland it was no longer quite pleasant. Shocking, rather. Galvanizing. Like being struck, of a sudden, by a goddam thunderbolt.

Superb. Blue-eyed; blond hair glistening. High cheekbones, soft hollows beneath. A face like a nun, peaceful, placid; the voluptuous body an agonizing contrast. But more. More than that beautiful innocent face; more than that supple, white-skinned, firm-fleshed body. Something. An aura. A chemistry. He felt her in his loins, and it amazed him. Tony Ashland, fifty-four years of age. He had been there. Often, in his lifetime. White-skinned, black-skinned, he had been there, and they no longer stirred him from afar, not this way.

But this one did. However astonishingly, this one did. None of the others, of course. A pleasant procession of lovely nudes. A recreation. Relaxation. And he heard himself chuckle, a small laugh at himself, ironic glee. He was puissant, sexual, and for his age a potent lover, but right now right here he was not his age; right now right here in the dimness of the twelfth row, he was thrown back to boyhood, strangely young and furtively adolescent, as he pressed a clipboard against a rampant tumescence. . . .

The girl up there did her thing, by far the best of the lot, by far the best of any possible lot. A gem, Tony Ashland thought: Sid Menchikoff deserves a bonus for discovering her. Perfect, this one. Perfect for the role Paul Rafferty had written. The voice, the manner, the superb naked beauty, the unconscious hesitation in delivering the lines, that impact of innocence that Paul had talked about in conferences in Don Franklin's office, that inherent naïveté flowing across the stage to the audience of four in the seats. But was he, Tony Ashland, partial? Affected by personal opinion? Prejudiced because of the physical reaction now beginning to diminish under the clipboard? No! He had sat in as angel in other shows. He knew—he could feel, he could sense—the satisfaction among the professionals here with him now in the twelfth row.

And even John Raywick up there, the bit finished. An actor, John Raywick, in the best sense of the word: experienced, cool, knowledgeable, a pro, the play's the thing, a craftsman. He was smiling up there now, John Raywick, the ennui out of his face. And he did with her what he had done with none of the others. He made a little bow, took her arm, and nakedly escorted her to the wing where Sidney Menchikoff would get her dressed and send her on her way.

Obviously, John Raywick had cast his vote.

* * *

"Okay," Don Franklin called. "Let's get some houselights on, please."

The lights came on; John Raywick returned to the stage. He slung on his bathrobe but did not go off for his shower. He was still smiling as he trotted down to the people in the twelfth row.

"She is it," he said. "Up to that one, I figured we're going to have to do a whole new audition. But she is it. What's her name?"

"Benton," Franklin said. "What do you say, Paul?"

"It," Paul Rafferty said.

"Artie?"

"Get her," McLean said. "Who's her agent?"

"Sue Robbins."

"Are we agreed?" Raywick asked.

"So it seems," Franklin said.

"Good. Otherwise you guys would have a fight on your hands."

"No fight, baby," Paul Rafferty said.

The professionals talked while Tony Ashland studied the bio clipped to the board. Information meager. Name, Clare Benton. Age, twenty-four. No husband, no children. Born, Minneapolis. Graduate of the University of Minnesota. Majored in Drama. Address and phone number, the agent's address and phone number, the list of credits, and that was it.

"Look, guys," Raywick was saying. "Come back with me while I shower and dress, and I'll take you all out for a booze."

"Skip me," Don Franklin said. "Got to work."

"Me too," said Tony Ashland.

The others went off with Raywick.

Ashland said, "When do you sign her?"

"As quickly as possible. Monday morning."

"Could you make it Monday afternoon? Late Monday afternoon?"

Franklin cocked his head. "Oh?"

"I'd like to be there. But I've got court on Monday. Could you make it, like, five o'clock?"

Franklin's head straightened, but the frown that narrowed his eyes was a query.

"She really hit you, that Benton."

"Like the proverbial ton of bricks. The vibes, as they say in the today parlance. Happens."

"Couldn't happen to a nicer fella." The frown disappeared. "And a hell of a break for the gal. I mean there's no bigger, no better, no more eligible bachelor in this whole damn town than Mr. Tony Ashland."

Mr. Tony Ashland smiled. A lawyer, he was a stickler for definitions. A bachelor is an unmarried man. In his case, however, "widower" would be the more precise term. He had been long married, although never technically faithful, but those had been his younger, more sprightly days. His Alice had died two years ago, of natural causes. He did not particularly mourn her demise—we all must go—but he had to admit, however reluctantly, that her death had created a void. He was a man who needed a woman to cater to his creature comforts. The one offspring of the marriage, a daughter, was an interior decorator who had married an Australian osteopath and lived in Melbourne. The last time he had seen his daughter, and his son-in-law, and his two grandchildren, had been at his wife's funeral. No objection, Your Honor. She has the right to her civil rights and liberties, Your Honor. Tony Ashland was nothing if not an unoppressive parent, and he was a militant advocate of filial emancipation. He was against the coercions, the links and ties of family chains. He did not believe that the pleasures of sexual intercourse produced, perforce, slavebound progeny. But *quid pro quo,* my dear, as we say in the courts. This for that.

Tit for titty. Parent and child. Once you were grown, I acceded to you all of your exclusive rights. But as a consequence, the logical reverse is mandatory. *Quid pro quo*. Freedom both ways. I do not pull the father ploy on you; therefore do not pull the daughter ploy on me. No interference, you know? Like the old man, rich as goddam Croesus, is getting old, getting wild, getting a little nuts, reaching up there toward the climacteric, and we have to try to do something about it. Don't you dare, baby. Tit for titty, as we do not say in the courts. I have not impinged on you, my Melbourne stranger; don't impinge on me. And furthermore as you will learn if you live long enough: fifty-four ain't that damn old at all. . . .

Now Donald Franklin was looking at his watch.

"Late. The Robbins office probably closed. I'll try anyway; then try her at home. Don't you go away, my friend."

"I won't go away, my friend."

Donald Franklin went away. Tony Ashland stood up, stretched his long legs, and paced the aisle. In a few minutes, Franklin was back, and he paced alongside Ashland.

"No soap," he said. "Office closed, and nothing at home. The service. She's out for the evening, bless her lesbo soul. I'll get her at home tomorrow morning."

"I'll need a little leverage, Don."

"Oho! What now, master?"

"I want you to tell her that I turned the trick. That you and your people were evenly divided between her and—one of the others. But that I cast the deciding vote. That I persuaded you. That I—me—I was all out for her, and that because of me she got the job."

"It won't work."

"It'll work."

"Tony, you're forgetting. She's going to meet all the people."

"I'm not forgetting."

"The male star, the playwright, the director. They'll tell her that she was unanimous. Including me."

"Let me ask you something."

"Ask."

"What would they tell her if she were not the unanimous choice?"

Franklin stopped pacing. Ashland came back to him.

"Master," Franklin said, "you are the master. You've got a lawyer's brain."

"If not, I'd be a producer of shows."

"Touché, bastard. You're really all-out gone, aren't you?"

"First time in a long time."

"All right, I'll do it, kid."

"Thank you, kid."

"See you five o'clock, Monday, my office."

"Only an act of God will prevent me."

"Yeah. You and God."

"Me and God," Tony Ashland said.

Again, this time in the gloom of late afternoon, the extravagance of a taxi. And all the way to Barrow Street, the heart crazily pounding. *I can't believe it. Something will happen to make it all null and void. I cannot believe it!* But Mr. John Raywick had kissed her forehead in the wing of the Morosco Theatre. "Child," he had said, "under what bushel have you been hiding? Where have you been all of our lives?" And Sid the stage manager. Sitting on a stool, grinning like a fool, while she was dressing. "In like Flynn," Sid had said. "Go home and *plotz* on that gorgeous ass and wait for the call. Because if you don't get the call, my name ain't . . ."

Tea in the kitchen. Fright in the soul. Aching gnawing of vague depression. Stiffly sitting at a kitchen table. Creating tolerance. Establishing forbearance.

If it does not happen, I will not crack. What is it, anyway? It is not an acting job, and I am not an actress. No actress. That I have finally learned. That I know. Driven into me like a stake. It is a bit part, a nude scene, in a Paul Rafferty play. I happen to fit the bit—or so, at least, they seem to think, Mr. Raywick and Sid the stage manager. But what about the others, the bigwigs out there in the seats? Suppose they think otherwise? Then to hell with it. What is it, anyway? My last hurrah is what it is. Interlude before executive secretary. Hail, Sue. Blaze of glory.

She drank the tea. On a hard chair in the kitchen, both hands clasped about the cup, she sipped at the tea as though performing some mystical magical ritual. Finished it all the way to the bottom. Rose up from the chair, took the teabag from the saucer, and dropped it into the neatly plastic-lined, automatically top-covered chrome garbage can. Then conscientiously carried cup and saucer to the sink, washed them thoroughly, and laid them on the drainer. Wiped her hands on the kitchen towel and folded it back into place.

The living room was dark. She did not switch on a lamp: the rectangle of light from the kitchen was sufficient. She pulled off clothing, chortled, thought: Here I go again. That's all I've been doing of late. In and out of clothes, and parading nude. Not nude this time. No parade, no audition, no good-luck kiss on the ass from Sid, no kiss of encouragement on the forehead from Mr. John Raywick. Alone, thank God, in my lonely pad on Barrow Street. Big actress returned from Broadway audition. Sighed, stretched, shivered; then, in panties and bra, lay out on the couch, one leg high on the backrest, and listened to the music of the steam softly hissing from the radiator. I will not crack, she promised herself. No matter what, I will not crack. I am prone, I admit; inside me I'm a sad one, quick to despair. But once is enough. I did it once, and Lord was I glad to come back to the living. And remembered, in the soft music of the hissing steam. Her one affair with a married man. Dr. Jason Goldstein.

Jason Goldstein. She had loved him before she had ever met him; that is, she had loved the name. Jason Goldstein. Jason of the Goldstein Fleece. Her gynecologist, a tender old man whose teeth clicked, had retired to the warmth of Florida, and immediately of course she had been bereft. In our modern-day world—yeah, man—a girl deprived of a gynecologist is like a mainliner deprived of a hypodermic. Panic! First off, the need for the Pill; and then the many other matters. The Pap test deal, the regular checkups for bumps in the breasts, the fungus stuff that happens, and that other itching thing with the jaw-breaking name she could never remember ("honeymoon disease," they smilingly called it), and while you're in the stirrups, a probe for a smear so we know you're not unsymptomatically gonorrheal, and while we're at it, my dear, a bit of blood for a Wassermann.

An actress friend had recommended Jason of the Goldstein Fleece, and she had been taken with him at once. Tall and thin, with soft eyes and gray-flecked temples, he reminded her of Dad back home in Minneapolis. Dear old Dad, a dentist with all the modern equipment, a quiet, timid, gentle monster, beloved of children; slow, patient, considerate, he was great with children. Dear old Dad, a man without vices except Canadian Club, which, in small doses, he sipped all day and never got bombed. There were still kids, some grown up now, back home in Minneapolis, who believed all dentists smelled that way: an antiseptic, faintly alcoholic odor from the mouth.

And then one evening she had been Dr. Goldstein's last patient and he had offered to buy her a drink and she had accepted. Very pleasant. He was a thoughtful man, a learned man, cute in his way, with a dry sense of humor: an attractive man. Two weeks later he had called her at home, hesitatingly but specifically requesting a date, and again she had accepted, and darned well knew what she was doing: he was a married man. He had driven her in his doctor-type black Caddy to a little place in Brooklyn that served exquisite lasagne and he had drunk much of their dago-red and talked about life with wife, the four kids, the house in Great Neck, and the boredom of routine routine routine.

But it was all routine, wasn't it? Once their affair had begun, he came to her apartment every Thursday night, letting himself in with his own key, and bringing two bottles of wine, one a semisweet Hungarian and the other a sparkling Burgundy, but always the same brand name and always the same vintage year. And they would drink wine, cuddle, talk, watch TV perhaps, and then go to bed, but promptly at two o'clock he was up and off for home. She had wondered what his wife thought of his late Thursday nights, but dismissed it as none of her business. On occasion, not a Thursday, he would drive her to Brooklyn for some of that crazy Italian food; and sometimes they went to a movie, but not to the ones that had the lines waiting outside. And so it went for several months, and then there was that doctors' convention in June in Atlantic City.

He had prepared her in advance. He was ostensibly going alone, no wife, no children, but he was taking Clare Benton. It would be a form of vacation, a full month; one of his assistants was taking over his practice for that period.

They had registered as husband and wife in a small, offbeat, far-from-the-boardwalk, old-fashioned hotel, and he spent his afternoons with the doctors in the convention halls and his evenings with her, and weekends they swam in the sea.

Her malaise had commenced in bed.

He was a man of set patterns, and every morning at ten, Clare Benton beside him in the wide double bed, he would call his wife and they would talk—God, about everything. His low-cholesterol diet, her migraine headaches, the kids, the dogs, the house, the pool, the lawns, the garden, the new screens for the storm windows, the new pump to keep the basement dry, her brother's newly discovered duodenal ulcer, her poor mother's galloping senility, and Jack Tate, that unholy bastard of a hard-drinking advertising man, who had packed up and walked out on his wife of fourteen years, and divers other Great Neck social chitchat. And all the while Clare Benton, stomach writhing, was there in bed with him, and often (morning copulation being the Atlantic City pattern) he would hang up on his wife and enter into his mistress. Oh, the phony. An animal like all the rest. A nothing. Another beast indulging carnal appetite. No feel, no soul, no depth, no tender sensibilities. No give, no flow, no love, no real attachment. Not to the wife, not to the mistress. God, he could have managed it so easily had he cared. And properly. Simply could have asked her to leave, to go down and have breakfast or something, and she would have understood. Or he himself could have gotten out of the damn bed and made the call from some other phone. But not dear, compassionate, middle-aged Dr. Jason Goldstein, lying there at ease, skinny-legged, amiably chatting, tacitly insulting wife *and* mistress. Like all the rest of them. A superficial. An easy-mouthed sweet talker, sucking satisfaction, but insulated down deep at core, a male-selfish, coarse and vulgar. Another phony.

And so in the thirty days of June it drew to finish, and when they drove home, a Saturday, she knew it was over, and on that Saturday the torpor had set in. Not new: the dull, blank, hopeless helplessness. All the way since adolescence, these fits, this nadir, these bouts of dry-eyed depression. But this one was the worst, and bore in as the days passed—Sunday, Monday, Tuesday, Wednesday—and on Thursday she swallowed twenty Seconals. Why Thursday? If you want to kill yourself, you kill yourself. Why do you first comb your hair, fix your face, slip into your prettiest pajamas? And why do you do it at seven-fifteen on Thursday, knowing he will come at seven-thirty? What stresses are struggling inside the unconscious, pulling in different directions: the desire for death, but the need for life.

He had been good. Solid. A brick. Found her on the living-room floor. Roused her, slapped her, rubbed her, walked her until the ambulance came. Rode with her to the hospital and remained until they were through with her; she was released in his custody, but the facts on the record were not quite true. The record had it that she had taken the pills, then frantically called her doctor, and he had quickly come.

That night he remained with her, first phoning home and telling his wife he had an emergency, and he had called on her every day for a week, until he knew she was out of it.

But the affair was over. Both ways. More, in fact, his way. There had been no lengthy discussions, recriminations, explanations. She no longer wanted him but never told him; on the other hand, he no longer came, no more Thursdays, and she did not blame him, not at all. He needed a neurotic girl friend, a potential repeat suicide, like he needed a large hole in his head. In his middle fifties, sedately married, four children and a house in Great Neck, he was too smart to risk the possibility of a wide-open scandal.

Ancient history now. Long past now. Sixteen months. But Jason of the Goldstein Fleece was still her doctor, making the dry wry gynecological jokes when he did the internals, and he was still writing her scripts: the pills for contraception, the Dexies for up, the Valium for down, and the Seconals for sleep.

The ringing phone jarred her from reverie. A double ring, simultaneous: there was a phone here in the living room and an extension by the bed in the bedroom. Reaching over her head, she found the receiver and took it to her ear.

"Hello?"

"Hi. Sue here." Sounds of music mutely in the background. "Out for the evening, but I'm dying to hear. How'd you make out?"

"Good, I think." She told her about Raywick.

"Beautiful," Sue said. "Beauti-ful! Now listen to me. My hunch, Franklin's going to call me early Monday. So you stick around on Monday, stay put. I'll call you the minute I hear."

"I won't budge."

"You all right?"

"Fine."

"Honey, you don't sound—"

"I was kind of dozing."

"Right. G'bye. Have fun. I'll be in touch."

"Bye, Sue."

She hung up and the darned thing was ringing again. No, not the phone. The downstairs bell. She clambered off the couch and pressed the button and stood there; then the upstairs bell rang. She peered through the peephole, saw Charles Ennis, and opened the door.

"What's with all the darkness?" Charles said.

"Oh." She clicked on the overhead light.

"And what's with the striptease?"

She giggled, embarrassed. "Be with you in a minute." Trotted to the bedroom and returned in a housecoat. "I was napping." And regarded him. "My," she said, "don't we look spiffy."

"Spiffy." He laughed. "That's so old it's new." He shook his head. "You can take the girl out of Minneapolis, but you can't take Minneapolis out of the girl."

"Not new either, my boy." And they were both laughing.

"All right, dude," she said. "You look sharp as a blade."

He did. Formal, almost. A dark suit, a white shirt, a dark tie, and a vest.

"I'm the booby prize," he said. "You're going to get all dressed up and we're going out to a fancy place for a fancy dinner. We're going to do a little howling around this town, babe. Hell, I can afford. Hooray for Volkswagen."

"Booby prize?" she said.

"The bastards pushed you around, didn't they?"

"Not really."

An actor's eyebrow moved upward. "How'd you do?"

"Not too badly, I don't think."

He actually looked disappointed. Feckless Charles, the champion of the downtrodden. Charles the injustice collector. It was always *they* out there, pushing *us* around.

"They hire you?"

"They'll let me know."

He looked happier. "Sure they will," he said. Commiseratingly. "Of course they will. They should live so long, the sons of bitches. Okay, you'll tell me about it when we eat. Now start getting decent. I want you real fancy tonight. Spiffy."

She showered and dressed and they went out to Jimmy Weston's and ate shrimp cocktails and steaks, and talked, and listened to the music. And then they went to the Half Note for the heavy beat of the jazz, and drank up a small storm, and came home bombs away, and undressed, and he took a joint into the bed, a single cigarette. "Hash," he said. "But hash from heaven." One cigarette. He knew her. Not big for grass. A few pokes and that was it. They smoked, and made love, and once he said, "You're the greatest, babe. You are the greatest!" And then he was asleep, snoring. And she lay there, her eyes open in the darkness.

The greatest. It is to laugh. A fraud, a fake, but a fake

who knew every move; she had had the most fulsome of praise from the most horny of experts. I'm a lady of long experience, gents. All the way since early high school days. They taught me back there, and I improvised upon their teachings, and improvised on the improvisations. She knew how to please a man, and knew how to pretend the man was pleasing her; she gave them *macho* in bed; she gave them the balls of a bull. All pretense. God, if she was able to act out of bed like in bed, then Sue Robbins would never have had cause to complain.

Twenty-four years of age and never in her life an orgasm. She knew all about orgasms, from talk with the girls, and from talk with the boys, and from the explicitly explanatory (with pictures) sex manuals, and from all the ubiquitous porno literature. But it had never happened to Clare Benton, who knew how to pretend. Oh, she gave the hateful bastards balls. *Machismo.* Every man a bull. She gave them all the power they ever dreamed about, and more. Moaned, groaned, howled, hissed, squealed, churned, pumped, whirled, and reached a screaming crescendo at each putative climax, but it was all phony. As phony as they were phony, with all their sweet talk, the sweating bastards. Because all they really wanted was the flesh, the body, right, man? The breasts, the mouth, the tongue, the vagina, the anus. Anything else, gentlemen? If I were a monkey with hair on my chest, there wouldn't be that hard eye contact, would there, and none of that soft sweet talk, right, gentlemen? Oh, I know what I have, but that is all I have, and it kills me. A vessel. I am a vessel. A goddam vessel.

How lousy. How sad. How nothing.

She turned, lay ass to ass with Charles Ennis, and slept.

The phone woke him. He sat up, scowling, licking his lips for wetness. Looked at the clock. Ten-thirty. Looked at

Clare. Sound asleep. Looked at the phone and pursed his mouth. He was worldly wise, Charles Ennis, aged twenty-six, sophisticated. The gentleman does not answer the phone in the lady's apartment.

He shook her and she came awake. He pointed at the phone.

"The hell with it," she said and closed her eyes.

It stopped ringing. Then started again.

"They think they had a wrong number and they're giving it another try," Charles said. "Saturday morning, it ain't a social call, babe. Hell, maybe your father died."

"They wouldn't know where to reach me."

She sighed, sat up.

"Jeez," he said. "The most beautiful pair of boobs in the Western Hemisphere."

She grappled with the phone, took up the receiver. "Yes?"

"In," Sue said. "You're in."

"What? Wha—?"

"Not only do they want you, they're dying for you. Don Franklin, he just called me here at home. We've an appointment at his office, five o'clock Monday. You be at my office at four. Honey, are you there?"

"Yes."

"Well, *breathe,* for Chrissake."

"I'm half asleep."

"Rough night?"

"I was out late."

"Okay, go back to sleep. When you wake up, it'll hit you like a piano falling. We sign the contracts on Monday. I'll call you later."

Clare Benton hung up, sat there.

"What's up?" Charles said.

"That was Sue."

"So?"

"I—I got the job."

"You got the—*what?"*

"Monday we sign the contracts."

He stared at her. For moments it refused to penetrate. Then he whispered, "Holy cow." Clare Benton. Broadway. John Raywick. A Paul Rafferty play. "Jesus," he said. "How come you just sit there?"

"I'm numb."

"Jesus, this we got to celebrate."

Grabbed at her, kissed her. Pushed her over, mounted her. But for once she lay like stone, unpretending, unresponding. God, they're all alike. Even feckless Charles. Celebrating *her* celebration by using her.

God! Dear God!

2

ANTHONY ASHLAND awoke at seven o'clock Monday morning, alert and refreshed. He had had five hours' sleep, but five hours was sufficient for him. Six was his maximum. As his physician had once explained: "We all go by our internal mechanism. Eight hours seems to be the norm, but it swings both ways. At one end of the spectrum, there are those who actually require ten hours; at the other end, there are those who do splendidly with four. More would render them stale and languid, they would be overslept. You're a five-hour man, Tony, and I envy you. I'm eight hours. That gives you three hours more than me for the living of life. Every day."

Tony Ashland padded to the shower that started warm and ended icy cold; then he toweled in front of the mirror that was one entire wall of the bathroom, and smiled at his reflection. Not bad for fifty-four. No hanging flesh, no paunch: all tight and sinewy. He was six feet tall, weighed one hundred and seventy pounds, and had neither gained nor lost in the past twenty years. Three times a week he did an active stint in the gym, and at least once a week he put in eighteen holes of golf.

Shaving now, he was not displeased with the face in the small mirror over the sink. A ruddy complexion. Black eyebrows. No wrinkles except up there by the eyes. Well, hell, why not? At fifty-four you're entitled to your crow's-feet. He chuckled. Gives you character. The only real sign of age was the snow-white hair, and in fact it was no sign at all. A family trait. He had turned white at thirty-five, and so had his brother Frank, one year younger than Tony. And the old lady had had white hair as long as either of the boys could remember. They did not know about the old man. The old man had walked out when Tony was five and Frank four, and had never been heard from again. But the old lady was still alive, living in a house that Tony had bought her in St. Petersburg, Florida, and it was the old lady who had held them in line. They could have gone wrong, damn wrong, in the neighborhood where they were reared, South Bronx, a hotbed even then for dope, numbers, loan sharking, prostitution, and pimping. But the old lady had stayed right on top of them.

"I am a Jew," she would say. She worked in the Morrisania Hospital as a nurse in obstetrics. Not a nurse, really, not an R.N.; she had no diplomas. But in the neighborhood she had done a great deal of home midwifery, and was a skilled and appreciated assistant to the obstetricians in the Morrisania Hospital; today she would be called a paraprofessional. "A Jew but not a Jew," Mama would say. "I am a lapsed Catholic, which leaves me out on the limb like nowhere. But them Jewish people, I understand them. Smart. I ain't talking about the religion, I am talking about the tradition. The one big thing they got going for them—education. The one way they know to get their kids out of the fuckin' muck—education. Sam Smilowitz. a goddam consumptive spitting blood, presses pants in the back of that goddam cleaning store, dying there by degrees, but his son goes to Columbia College. Smart. Them Jews are goddam good people, smart. And that's the way it's gonna go in this cockroach house. School. I work my ass off, I put in overtime like Saturdays and Sundays, but my boys are gonna be goddam Jews, they're gonna go to school. Forget the crap games, the easy money, the poolrooms, the pushing and dealing. School. Education, goddam you. You are not going to be street bums or I'll kill you with my own goddam hands, may the Lord Almighty forgive me."

And she had had her way, the doughty lady, clapping her sons over their heads when she found them in the poolrooms, ranting, raving, preaching, but finally reaching them; she did get to her sons, that glorious ineluctable harridan, inspiring them. After high school, they went to college. Nothing fancy: City College; and at night they drove cabs to support themselves and to help at home because Mama could no longer put in a seven-day week at the hospital.

Tony Ashland had gone from City College to St. John's Law School. Frank Ashland had gone from City College to the cops, at a time when college graduates were a rarity on the cops, and, taking tests, had moved up quickly. By the time Tony Ashland had graduated, *summa cum laude,* from St. John's Law School, Frank Ashland was a lieutenant in the NYPD and had sufficient political muscle to land Tony a job in the District Attorney's office, where the older brother, one year older, quickly proved his mettle as a trial lawyer, and in four years Tony Ashland was the star of the staff. And then, his reputation established as a prosecutor, he resigned to go into private practice as a defense attorney.

Today the old lady in St. Petersburg had a right to be proud of what she had wrought. Her younger son was the First Deputy Police Commissioner of the New York Police Department, and her older son, far richer, was probably the most prominent criminal lawyer in the entire United States.

In the spacious bedroom Tony Ashland dressed carefully, his mind teeming. But it was a selective mind; he had trained himself not to permit the confusions of overlappings. Foremost was a personal matter, his astonishing reaction to the young woman auditioning for Paul Rafferty's play. Well and good, but dismissed. He would pick that up at five o'clock in Don Franklin's office. Next was another personal matter—actually, Duncan McKee's personal matter—but Duncan was his closest friend. That, too, was arranged, at least in its initial aspects. The full report was on the desk in his study, and Duncan would be here to discuss it tonight at eight. Thus, the personal affairs temporarily relegated, his mind was clear to concentrate upon the People v. Clifton Arvel, and upon Dr. Reuben Grayson.

But first, orange juice.

He was a creature of habit and, as the departed Alice used to say, some of his habits were certainly eccentric. On working days, rising at seven, he ate breakfast in two installments. Orange juice and a vitamin pill at home. Then a walk to the office. There were two cars in the downstairs garage—a Bentley and a Jaguar—but he always walked, unless the weather was inclement. An early morning constitutional, but a short walk in fact. The offices were at 477 Madison Avenue, near Fifty-first Street. The apartment, a duplex at 825 Fifth Avenue, was near Sixty-fourth Street. And, since he always arrived at the office between seven-thirty and eight, there was sufficient time for the second installment of breakfast, and time—utterly alone—for working, thinking, the cerebral marshaling of the forces before, at nine o'clock, the office personnel began to drift in.

It was a beautiful morning, cool and sunny, and he walked briskly, reviewing Arvel. The old old story. Love and stuff, the eternal infernal triangle, and the abysmal animal passions of man.

Clifton Arvel, age forty-seven, a manufacturer of children's toys—Arvel's Marvels—was married to a beautiful young woman, age thirty-six, who had met a beautiful if impecunious young man, age twenty-six, and she and the young man had entered into what is called in a courtroom an improper relationship and what is called outside a courtroom a fucking cheating affair. Cliff Arvel, a huge man, old-fashioned and jealously possessive, had begun to suspect, and had hired people to check, and his people had conclusively confirmed his suspicions. A forthright guy, Arvel had gone to the young man's apartment for face-to-face confrontation and civilized talk. The civilized talk had degenerated to an abusive dispute, and the abusive dispute had further degenerated to the abuse of uncivilized fisticuffs. Arvel had hit the young man on the chin, and the young man had toppled, the back of his head striking an obtrusive point of a sturdy coffee table, and the enormous amount of gore thereby produced had instantly returned Clifton Arvel to his good senses. He had attempted to aid the stricken young man but had swiftly learned that the young man was beyond any attempts at aid. The guy was dead. (A fractured skull had been the Medical Examiner's testimony in court, properly supported by the autopsy X-rays.) But—a strong point in Clifton Arvel's favor—he had immediately, from the young man's apartment, called the police.

Briskly walking in cool morning sunshine, Anthony Ashland thought about plea-bargaining, so roundly and soundly condemned by the law-and-order purists. He agreed. Too many lazy turntable-judges, too much of that easy revolving-door justice. Too damn many criminals, in the slovenly application of law in the inferior courts, sent back to the streets to pick up their accustomed patterns of crime. But plea-bargaining exists for a purpose, and has its proper place in the jurisprudence, and Clifton Arvel was a perfect case in point.

A cheating wife, an outraged husband, an unintentional death—that's what plea-bargaining is all about. Yes, Your Honor, in the strict sense of the law a crime was committed and Cliff Arvel committed the crime. But this is not a hardened criminal, not a criminal at all. A human being, an animal like all of us, he punched a man in the heat of passion. So the District Attorney should sit in conference with defense counsel, and then deliver the guy before the judge on a lesser charge. Defense counsel pleads him guilty and says his piece about mitigation and mercy, and the D.A. says his piece about the law being the law, and the judge comprehends the substance of both pieces and declares the defendant guilty but gives him a suspended sentence, and like that both sides are satisfied, and the poor bastard goes home free to live with his conscience for the rest of his life.

But Clifton Arvel, starting off with one point in his favor, had, unfortunately, two points against him. One: he was rich and famous. Two: the District Attorney was an ambitious man and a potential candidate for Governor. The trial of a Clifton Arvel would naturally be sensational and would produce the run of publicity every politician seeks, the newspaper headlines and the sanctimonious press conferences; a conviction would be that much lagniappe. And so a grand jury had returned an indictment for manslaughter, and Arvel was now on trial, and the poor bastard could be put away behind bars for at least five years.

But not if Anthony Ashland could help it.

Technically, the prosecution had a case. Technically, an assault resulting in death, no matter that the death is accidental, is manslaughter. And the prosecution did have Arvel's uncontroverted confession that he had in fact willfully assaulted his wife's lover. But that, despite the courtroom tricks and pyrotechnics, was all the D.A. did have.

Anthony Ashland had everything else. He had a client who was well-spoken, quiet, distinguished, cultivated; a client who had been cuckolded: there was no question about any of that. The wife, contrite now and desperately trying to save her husband, had admitted to the affair with the beautiful young man. And the unwritten law was on the defendant's side; the unwritten law which was no law at all, although many a layman believed that a spouse who kills the mate's lover is not guilty by reason of justifiable homicide. Not true, as the judge would properly charge the jury. But Anthony Ashland, wise in the ways, knew that an unwritten law did exist in the collective mind of a jury, a self-identification, an innate sympathy for the sexually cheated; the trick was to give them a legal loophole for a verdict of acquittal. In this case, the legal loophole was the defense plea of temporary insanity.

On the witness stand, Clifton Arvel, examined by his counsel, had laid the groundwork for that plea (beautiful testimony that would be highlighted in summation), and none of that groundwork had been eroded despite the District Attorney's fiery cross-examination. "I saw red," Clifton Arvel had truthfully sworn. "My mind went blank. I lashed out at him before I knew what I was doing. I am not a fighter. Even as a kid I was not a fighter. I never struck a man in my life. Honest to God, I didn't know what I was doing."

It was there in the record, perfect uncoached testimony, and today the psychiatrist's testimony would give it legal life; the loophole would gape wide open for the jury to skip through. Anthony Ashland, wise in the ways, knew he would have a quick acquittal. Because of this particular psychiatrist.

In point of fact, Anthony Ashland could not take the

credit for this coup. He had never imagined that Dr. Reuben Grayson would consent to come to court and take the stand in a case with which he had no personal concern; he would not have dared to request of Dr. Reuben Grayson that he come as a qualified expert, for a fee, to answer hypothetical questions. Grayson had been Duncan McKee's idea, an insane idea presumptively futile, but Duncan had accomplished it, and Grayson would be in Ashland's office today at eight-thirty, and at ten o'clock they would be in court, and the District Attorney would positively go livid in astonishment when he saw whom Anthony Ashland had enlisted as his psychiatric expert witness.

In the lobby of 477 Madison Avenue the uniformed starter said, "Good morning, Mr. Ashland."

"Good morning," Mr. Ashland said. "How goes it?"

"We have our ups and downs," the starter said.

"Yeah, that we do, don't we?" Mr. Ashland entered the indicated elevator and pressed the 44 button.

The doors closed, the elevator ascended swiftly, and at the forty-fourth floor the doors opened directly upon the carpeted reception room of the offices of Anthony Ashland, Esquire, Counselor-at-Law. He had the entire floor, and he needed it. Aside from the numerous clerks and secretaries, he employed six lawyers, each with an office of his own, and four investigators, with offices of their own, and a librarian and a library staff. The library was as vast as any attorney's in the state, a necessity, a tool as vital as a researcher's microscope. The legal law shifts and varies and changes daily, and you had damn well better keep up with it. Two of his lawyers were his courtroom assistants, the other four were legal researchers and briefmen for appeal, and the investigators were investigators. Abraham Lincoln had said it first, and Clarence Darrow had said it in his own words, and the come-lately hotshots said it in other words but as though they had invented it. "A trial lawyer must win his battle before he goes to court: thorough investigation and thorough preparation." Louis Nizer had added to that. Substantively: "A trial lawyer's chief capacity is his ability to think on his feet." And Anthony Ashland had added to *that*. "No matter what else his gifts, a trial lawyer has to be an actor, a consummate actor; his stage is the well of the courtroom."

He pushed through the leather porthole swinging doors into the inner waiting room, paused a moment, and sighed. He had one hell of a nut here; the overhead was enormous: the rent, the principal employees, and all the little folk—secretaries, pages, messengers, filing clerks, and on and on. But then he smiled. Proudly. He could damn well afford it, and he had earned it all on his own. Anthony Ashland here, fifty-four, self-made, the top man of his heap. His fee for a consultation was two thousand dollars. If he accepted a case, the retaining fee was five thousand dollars, come what may. And for his appearances in court—and as a busy trial lawyer he appeared in court virtually every day—the fee was two thousand dollars *per diem*. The hell with the overhead: he could afford. At their last financial meeting, his accountant had summed up his net worth: six million dollars in stocks, bonds, real estate, and other investments and holdings. Not bad for a kid from the South Bronx whose first earnings had been registered on the clock of a cab. Rich. But on the other hand, poor as compared to Duncan McKee. On the third hand, that comparison was odious, without disrespect to Duncan. Duncan was a worker and a damn good earner, but Duncan had had an initial catapult denied to Anthony Ashland; Duncan was a scion, an American aristocrat; a beneficiary of millions, early on, by inheritance.

Now he pushed through the leather swinging doors at the rear of the waiting room, turned left, and walked a long corridor to the kitchen. Correct, a kitchen. The offices contained a fully equipped kitchen, and also contained a fully equipped bedroom and bath for sleeping over when necessary.

In the kitchen he put up water to boil, ground his special-ordered coffee in the bean. Laid two slices of whole-wheat bread in the toaster. Prepared his coffee, made a ham-and-Swiss sandwich on whole-wheat toast, sat at the kitchen table for the second installment of his breakfast, and commenced a new concentration: Dr. Reuben Grayson. Without really knowing anything about the good doctor, he was well acquainted with the man, as who in all this country wasn't?

Dr. Reuben Grayson, until two years ago known only to his own, but today a national celebrity. The guy had written a book. *Sex Without Snobbery.* Another simplistic sex book, candidly graphic, the psychiatrist talking down to the layman. This one, however, was somewhat different because of the author's style: his approach was wry, humorous, tongue-in-cheek. But in Tony Ashland's opinion, and in the opinion of the professional critics, it was in no way exceptional; another sex book in the vast plethora of the genre. Nevertheless, *Sex Without Snobbery* quickly rose to the top of the Best Seller List, and it remained on top for sixty-four weeks, and was purchased by a paperback house for two million dollars. Even the title was transformed to cash: Five Star Levine Productions bought it for a film for six hundred thousand dollars. *Sex Without Snobbery,* a single book, had made its author a millionaire, a fact which he cheerfully admitted.

But it was not the book that had done it: it was the author.

Publishers are wont to send their authors on a grand tour of the media—radio and television—for the purpose of exploiting their work. Frequently they fizzle; dull, didactic, pedantic, they do more harm for their books than good. But on rare occasion the reverse is true. For whatever the reason—looks, charm, wit, quirks of character—a small minority become star performers, celebrities in their own right, and in consequence their books skyrocket on the sales charts. (In the publishing world, the three "S"es are still legend: Segal, Stillman, and Susann.) Dr. Reuben Grayson was already another such legend.

Smooth, charming, attractive, outgoing, at one moment sternly professorial, at another naughtily lubricious—but always, when necessary, flashing that ingenuous little-boy smile—Dr. Reuben Grayson was an instant success on the boob tube. And success, naturally, mounted upon success; he was sought after and clamored for. He appeared on talk show after talk show, afternoon and late night, and even on the early morning cooking shows, and always, casually, he plugged *Sex Without Snobbery,* which began to sell in the bookstores like hot franks in the baseball parks.

In short order, the good doctor burgeoned to renown as a boob-tube personality; he became a national celebrity and thus came within the ken of Duncan McKee, a television producer who owned afternoon game shows and evening sitcom shows. Duncan also owned a syndicated talk show, wherein he himself was the star performer, that had twice earned the TV Emmy because, though ostensibly a bland and smiling interlocutor, he was in fact an incisive inquisitor.

Since they were both based in New York City, Dr. Grayson had frequently graced the Duncan McKee Show, and had become a friend of the McKees—Duncan and Rosemarie McKee—which is how Anthony Ashland had made the acquaintance of Dr. Reuben Grayson, who often attended the McKees' soirées in the company of his lovely lady friend, Ms. Christine Talbert (herself a famous name and media personality; *the* Ms. Talbert of the Women's Movement).

Duncan had a high regard for Dr. Reuben Grayson, aside from business, aside from the fact that the doc was spectacularly Nielsen-soaring when announced as a guest on the Duncan McKee Show. Duncan believed the guy to be a true intellectual and a brilliant psychiatrist, and Tony Ashland had a high regard for Duncan McKee's opinion.

A week ago, at a McKee party in the town house on East Seventieth—Rosemarie conspicuously absent—Tony Ashland, prompted by Duncan, was discussing the Arvel case with Dr. Reuben Grayson and Ms. Christine Talbert.

"What about Reuben as your expert witness?" Duncan had asked.

That, of course, had thoroughly astonished Anthony Ashland, Esquire. Psychiatrists who testified in court were in fact a motley crew, however well qualified. The prosecution had their psychiatrists, and defense counsel had theirs, each testifying against the other for fees ranging from two hundred dollars to five hundred dollars a day. But none was ever a Dr. Reuben Grayson.

"The doc wouldn't be interested," Ashland had said.

"Why not?" Grayson said.

"Would you, Doc?"

"Yes, I think so. Once. I've never testified in court. I think I'd like the experience. When would this be?"

"My figure, next Monday. Could you clear your decks for next Monday?"

"I can do that. Once. But there can't be a delay."

"There won't be a delay. I'll fit you in even if it's out of turn."

"Then you have me, Mr. Ashland."

"For how much?"

"Nothing. A favor from me to my friend Duncan's friend."

"No sir," Ashland said. "Nothing ain't good. Charity doesn't work in court. On cross-examination you'll be asked, and a nothing fee won't sit well with the jury. They'll ask themselves—Why nothing? What's wrong here? Why nothing? People respect fees. Hell, I know. People are my business."

"So are they mine."

"But not in a courtroom."

"True. How much, Mr. Ashland?"

"For you, a thousand bucks. The jury'll love it."

"I hate to put you to that expense."

"Not my expense. The client pays."

"Done," Grayson said. "How do we work it?"

"I won't intrude on any of your time—until next Monday. If you can be at my office Monday morning at eight-thirty, we'll have an hour to talk. Sufficient. And then at ten o'clock—court."

"All right. Eight-thirty next Monday morning."

And right then Anthony Ashland had experienced sympathy for the District Attorney. Because now Anthony Ashland would cancel his prior-selected psychiatrist, his loophole for the jury, his expert to answer hypothetical questions that would establish temporary insanity. And in place of that psychiatrist he would present—Dr. Reuben Grayson.

Grayson would be a treat for the jury, a trick of the defense, but perfectly legal. Dr. Reuben Grayson, a national celebrity instantly recognizable, was the boyish smiling sweetheart of the tube, a doll of a guy, and the prosecution would be helpless; even the mildest cross-examination would be resented. Hell, who could fight Jesus Christ as an expert witness on religion? Or Mahatma Gandhi as an expert witness on fasting? Or Albert Einstein as an expert on physics? The District Attorney, spiked by ambition, was going to wind up with his just desserts, ignominiously defeated, because somehow the fates decree and luck happens. A crazy throw of the dice, Your Honor: the coincidence of incident. Just because Dr. Reuben Grayson happens to be a grateful friend of Duncan McKee, and Duncan McKee happens to be a close friend of Anthony Ashland, therefore Cliff Arvel, a jealous husband who manufactures toys for the pleasure of children, will go forth scot-free, out of the toils of the law, acquitted of the charge of manslaughter for which he would never have been indicted except for the venal inducements of an ambitious D.A. It had been an easy case in the first place and now it was that much easier. Arvel was as good as out right now.

Strange, the quirks of fate? Lovely?

Yessir, Your Honor. Beautiful.

Anthony Ashland finished his second installment of breakfast, went out to the reception room, sat in the girl's chair, and at eight-thirty-five the elevator opened and there he was.

"Good morning, Doctor."

"Morning, Mr. Ashland."

They shook hands and Ashland led him through to the large, all-windowed, soundproofed office. He indicated an armchair for the doctor and went round to the high-backed swivel chair. The huge desk top was neat and uncluttered; at its center lay a shiny-black attaché case.

"First off, Doctor. I want to thank you for being prompt."

"I'm rarely late for an appointment." A quick flash of smile. "Although this one's real early for me."

A hell of a good-looking guy. Tall, trim. Wavy dark hair, deep dark eyes. A clean jaw, a cleft in the chin. Figured great in court: a smooth baritone voice and excellent diction. A serious-looking guy, but there were laugh crinkles at the corners of the eyes, and there was always that quick, winsome, little-boy smile.

"And so to work," Ashland said. He opened the attaché case, extracted a long legal pad, and took up a pen. "I'll need some background. To qualify you on the stand. Let's begin, if I may, with your age."

"Thirty-nine."

"Married?"

"No. Hold it a moment." He lit a cigarette. "Look, in order to save time, why don't I give it all to you in one fell swoop. Should I omit anything pertinent, please feel free to ask."

"Fire away," Ashland said.

"Bachelor of Science from Yale. M.D. from Johns Hopkins. Residency in Manhattan State Hospital. I'm a psychiatrist and also a board-certified psychoanalyst. I no longer use psychoanalysis in my practice. I find it too long and too wearisome for the patient as balanced against the results obtained. I am"—the quick charming smile—"a modern-day shrink, a face-to-face psychotherapist who utilizes whatever the psychiatric tool available to get the patient over whatever the hang-up as quickly as possible. I've been in private practice for thirteen years. At my age—what with the requisite schooling—that may sound a bit outlandish. It isn't." Again the smile. "I was, if I may say, a child prodigy. I was graduated from high school, first in my class, at age sixteen, and was accepted at Yale first crack." He extinguished the cigarette in an ashtray on the desk. "My office is at 840 Park Avenue. I reside at 330 East Thirty-third Street. Any questions, Counselor?"

"Not a one. As I suspected, you're going to be the best damn witness ever laid his hand on the Bible." Ashland put the pen away. "Now, then, Dr. Grayson. We talked about the Arvel case at Duncan's house. You know the bare essentials, and that's enough. A wife was fooling around, and the husband found out. He confronted the lover, they argued. The husband lost his head and belted the guy. Repeat. The husband lost his head. When you lose your head, it's temporary insanity. I have tried, literally, hundreds of cases along this line. Temporary insanity. That's not permanent insanity. That's insanity at that moment. Right, Doc?"

"Could be," the doctor said.

"That's all I want from you, Doctor. That it *could* be." Ashland reached into the attaché case, drew out a paper. "I'll now read to you what I shall read to you in court. From the transcript of the court stenographer's minutes. This is Clifton Arvel's testimony, unshaken in cross-examination." He read: *"I saw red. My mind went blank. I lashed out at him before I knew what I was doing. I am not a fighter. Even as a kid I was not a fighter. I never struck a man in my life. Honest to God, I didn't know what I was doing."* He laid the paper aside. "How's that sound to you, Doctor? Please remember you're the witness for *our* side. Hypothetically, Dr. Grayson. Temporary insanity?"

"Yes."

"Let me add this, off the record. I know the man; he's a personal friend. Clifton Arvel, toy tycoon. A fine man, a philanthropic man, a lover of beauty, a collector of antiques; certainly not a killer." Ashland tapped at papers in the open attaché case. "Herein contained are the lengthy, carefully prepared hypothetical questions I shall put to you. There's no purpose to read them to you now; we'd be here until noon."

"I understand."

"But I must prepare you, however perfunctorily, for the tough grind of the District Attorney's cross-examination. On the other hand, since it *is* you, he might go easy."

"Prepare me, Mr. Ashland."

The doctor smiled. A rise of lips, a flash of fine teeth; the ingenuous boyish grin that had enraptured a nation. He sure knows how to use it, Ashland thought. A pleasant accident of the facial muscles. He can turn it on and off like the beam of a headlight.

"You tell the truth," Tony Ashland said. "Don't try to fence with him. The simple truth. That I talked with you at Duncan's, gave you the facts of the case, and you consented to come as my expert witness. We had this conference here, an hour's conference. I did not prepare you with the hypothetical questions. We talked, just as we *are* talking. Are you being paid for your time in court? Of course you're being paid. A thousand bucks. Simply the truth, Doc. Don't let him trap you into fencing with him, because then he'll have you in his bailiwick and you have got to lose. Okay, that's it." Tony Ashland placed his papers in the attaché case and snapped it shut. He looked at his watch. "We have time. Turnabout is fair play, Dr. Grayson. Ask me any questions you wish."

"When will I get out of court?"

Ashland laughed. "I figure you'll be our only witness today. The hypothetical questions, which must cover every legal aspect, are damned long, and then there's your answers. And then there's the cross-examination, and then, probably, there's my redirect. I'd say you'll be out by three o'clock, because Mr. Justice Aaron Linwood runs a very loose ship. The Criminal Part of the New York Supreme Court is supposed to go from nine in the morning until five in the afternoon, but not with Mr. Justice Linwood, an old-timer. He never starts before ten and he always ends at three or before. He's a lazy bastard, but a damn fine judge, one of few, a scholar of the law, a legal mind. Next question, Dr. Grayson."

"We still have time?"

"Time."

"Tell me about Clifton Arvel. Tell me what really happened."

"Sure. Happy to oblige, Doc."

They talked. Until nine-thirty. Then Tony Ashland took up his attaché case.

"We gotta go now, Doc. My people, my two courtroom assistants, are waiting for us, double-parked in front of the building."

He took the doctor by the arm and they went out to the elevator, and Tony Ashland, long-experienced and wise in the ways, knew that this case was over. It was now goodbye Mr. District Attorney and hello Mr. Clifton Arvel. Because what I'm holding by the arm, Cliff, is the bombshell that will explode you to freedom. You were entitled in the first place, but now we can all go home. We have the media. We have TV. We have, on your behalf, a national celebrity who wrote a book.

That's life, Your Honor

3

CLARE BENTON came early to the office, too early. Quarter to four. She was informed that Miss Robbins was busy. "Yes," she said. "I'm ahead of schedule."

Sat alone in the waiting room, Paul Rafferty's lines drumming through her mind. Since Saturday, that had been the solace for her nerves. She had discovered a kind of witchcraft, a litany for serenity, a tranquilizing self-hypnosis: repeating and repeating, singsong, her lines in the play. God, she knew them backward.

Now suddenly Sue appeared. Surprisingly, Sue herself. In the waiting room. A different procedure this day. Ordinarily a girl would come out for the client. Today it was Sue. In person. "I was locked on the horn, sweetie. Long distance. For a freak of mine for the movies. I'm all yours now. Come along, dear."

In the inner office Sue was all smiles; she looked marvelous, her bulky figure svelte within a stylish suit that Clare had never seen before. And a pink, frilly, feminine blouse. Her hair, normally a tumble of disarray, was neatly coiffed, and there was a touch of makeup on her face.

"Sit down, honey. Time, lots of time. We'll be at Franklin's office at five on the dot. Excited?"

"Yes."

"Me too, by damn." Slid into her chair behind the desk. "I'll tell you what I have to tell, and then we'll get out. A quick drink somewhere. To calm the nerves. Okay?"

"Whatever you say."

"Oho, do I have to say! We've got them by the well-known shorts, sweetheart. Franklin called me this morning, early, ten o'clock, and we talked like for a half hour, and I wormed a hell of a lot out of him. They had nude trouble, is what they had. The whole play was cast except for their nude. Seems they had a series of private auditions, recommended actresses, but nobody was satisfactory. So they had to put out the full call, and they found you. Now they start rehearsals quick—next Monday. How's that sound?"

"I—don't know."

"To me the sound was money. I like the guy, but I'm an agent, not a Samaritan, and not a father confessor. So I was about to ask him for three-fifty, when he comes up with four hundred." She peered across the desk. "You got a sponsor there, baby?"

"Nobody."

"You give that faggot of a stage manager a fast cocksuck or something?"

"Nothing."

"Well, when the producer offers four hundred for a bit part—true, it's a nude—and has already stated they want to go into rehearsal on Monday, then I'm in the driver's seat, you know? So what can I lose to try to up it, you know? So I ask for five hundred. Figure maybe I can settle for four-fifty.

And if he balks, of course I'll grab the four. So guess what?"

"What?"

"He comes across with the five with never even a hassle. Honey, that should keep you in wheat germ and fancy panties for a hell of a long time, because that's your salary for the run of the play. Five hundred bananas a week, and that's the contract we're going to sign in his office at five o'clock." Sue stood up, came round, and squinted down. "You sure you don't have a sponsor there?"

"Dear God, who in heck would I have?"

"Right. Honey, this I can tell you, like straight from the shoulder. For five hundred bananas a week, you must have mesmerized *some*body there. Okay, beautiful nude. Let's go have that drink now."

Donald Franklin's office was on Forty-fourth west of Broadway, and, despite their good intentions, they were late. They arrived at five-fifteen. "Sue Robbins," Sue said to the receptionist. "Mr. Franklin's expecting us."

"Yes." The receptionist pointed. "That corridor. First door to the right."

The door was closed. Sue knocked.

"Come in," a deep voice called.

"Here we go," Sue whispered and opened the door.

At first Clare Benton did not see the other man. She saw the one who rose from behind the carved mahogany desk: a big man, heavyset, with a double chin and loose jowls; he had a face like a sagging sweater. He was up there in his sixties, horseshoe-bald with gray fringes. He was not wearing a jacket; his striped shirt was rumpled. But he had a fine, big, wide smile.

"I was getting worried," he said. "I just called your office."

"The damn taxi," Sue said. "Crosstown, we went like molasses."

And then they heard the other voice, rich, clear, resonant.

"This time of day, the traffic is impossible."

He stood up from a couch at a side of the large room. A most impressive man, tall, slender, beautifully attired in a dark suit, white shirt, and gold-speckled tie. A full head of white hair like the mane of a lion. But a young, vigorous face. And large gray eyes under smooth black eyebrows. A lion. Leonine. That was the impression. He made her think of a lion.

"Mr. Anthony Ashland," said the man behind the desk. "Miss Sue Robbins. Miss Clare Benton."

Sue fairly whimpered. Clare had never heard her this girlish.

"Mr. Ashland! Oh my, this is a pleasure indeed."

"My pleasure, Miss Robbins."

"While we're about it," said the man behind the desk, "I wish somebody would introduce me to my actress."

Sue waggled a finger. "You mean you two never—"

"As far as Miss Benton is concerned, I have been no more than a disembodied voice crying out from the wilderness of the dark seats."

"Honey, meet your producer. Mr. Donald Franklin. The best in the business."

He laughed. "She says that to all the boys." And he reached out to Clare and they shook hands. Heartily. He had a warm, firm handshake. "Congratulations," he said. "And now let's get to business, people. Please sit down, everybody."

Everybody sat, Mr. Ashland on his couch.

Mr. Franklin opened a drawer of his desk and produced contracts.

"Three copies," he said. "I've already signed them. They now require your signature, Miss Benton, and then we distribute them. One to you, one to Sue, and one to me."

Sue took one, leaving the other two on the desk, and

scanned quickly, flipping pages.

"How about you, Miss Benton?" Franklin asked. "Don't you read your contracts?"

"Never. They're gibberish to me. When it comes to contracts, Sue's my lawyer."

"We've a *real* lawyer here. And there he sits in all his grandeur. Anthony Ashland, Esquire."

"I wouldn't dare presume on Mr. Ashland."

"No presumption at all," Ashland said.

"Not necessary," Sue said. "I'm done. Sign the papers, baby."

"You're a quick read," Franklin said.

"What's to read?" Sue said. "It's a standard contract and I know the form. My interest is the typed-in stuff, and the typed-in stuff is a hundred percent. Sign away, Miss Benton."

Clare signed. Sue stuffed two copies into her commodious knapsack bag, and handed the original to Franklin. "Thank you," he said, and returned the contract to its drawer, opened a humidor, and lit a fat cigar. "Now that we're all signed and sealed, I can let you in on a little secret. Off the record."

"Secret?" Sue frowned.

"It was Mr. Ashland who turned this trick."

Furiously Sue said, "What trick? What the hell's going on?"

"No trick," Ashland said.

"Boy, that Sue," Franklin said. "She's fast to jump."

"Look, Donny, I'm an agent. The other side of the fence, you know? I don't trust producers. Not even you. Now what the hell trick? And why in hell do you have a lawyer here?"

"Easy, Sue. Your hostility is showing."

"Okay, so I'm hostile." But she was subsiding. "Simply, I don't like tricks."

"My fault. An unfortunate phrase. Forgive me, and my

compliments. You're a damn good agent, always protective of the client."

"Butter me up, Donny." She was all subsided, smiling. "I love it."

"Now that's my Sue again. My dear friend Sue."

"Oh, this one should be in the diplomatic corps. Okay, Donny-boy. So what's your secret?"

"It's got to be off the record."

"Why?"

"I don't want internecine warfare."

"I don't know what in hell you're talking about, but now I'm curious. Okay, I promise. Off the record."

"It was Tony Ashland who selected Clare Benton."

"He—did—*what?*"

Franklin puffed, blew out a thick cloud of smoke.

"Quite amusing, really." He looked toward Clare. "You see, Miss Benton, our distinguished attorney is also our most distinguished angel. Our money man, our chief investor. It happens he was present with us in the seats during your audition on Friday." He puffed the cigar. "Well, we of the theatre were evenly divided. Half of us, including me, were in your favor; the other half favored another of the young ladies. It was then that Tony intervened. In substance he broke the tie, cast the deciding vote. And when you're the chief investor, your vote carries solid weight." He smiled toward Sue. "Thus, in effect, it was Tony Ashland who made the selection."

"Not at all," Ashland said. "With or without me, sooner or later, you'd have gotten the part, Miss Benton, because you're perfect for it. My intervention merely made it sooner. In my opinion—and Don agrees—you actually bring an additional dimension to the role, an innate grace, a charming diffidence. And, if I may be so bold, you're a superbly beautiful young woman."

"Thank you."

But now Sue Robbins was grinning lewdly, her previous girlishness vis-à-vis the lawyer entirely abandoned.

"Oho," she said. "So *you're* the sponsor."

"Beg pardon?" he said.

"Welcome aboard," she said.

He shrugged, smiled, stood up. "Ladies and Mr. Franklin, our show being entirely cast now, I've arranged a small celebration. Over at Sardi's. Took the liberty to reserve a table. Point of fact, a table for six."

"Six." Franklin chuckled dourly. "Ah, the millionaires. We are only four, and I'm not going. But he reserves for six."

"Two more," Ashland said. "A gentleman who testified in court for me today, and his lady friend. They're going to a cocktail party, a literary-type cocktail party, up on Central Park West. But he promised, first, to join us for a drink." A small frown. "Why not you, Donald?"

"Got to labor in the vineyard." Franklin glanced at his watch. "People coming." Smiled. "Don't look so sad, Tony. I'm sure the ladies don't also have labors."

"No labors, no pains," Sue said. "We'd love it, Mr. Ashland."

He looked toward Clare. "Miss Benton?"

"Yes, thank you," she said.

Like a dream, a waking dream ecstatic. In her three years in New York, she had been to Sardi's twice, and each time she and her escort had been exiled to a table in Siberia. Not today in the company of the leonine man. Today captains snapped to attention, and the maître d' hurried forward.

"Good evening, Mr. Ashland. We have your table, sir."

"I'm expecting people. They'll ask—"

"They're here, sir. Arrived a few minutes ago. This way, please."

He guided them to a corner table, VIP up front, and—waking dream—she immediately recognized both the persons already there. The man stood up. She had seen him often on the tube: Dr. Reuben Grayson. As, often, she had seen the seated lady. Ms. Christine Talbert, a beauty who had once been a Playboy bunny, a famous writer and feminist leader, and presently the editor of the magazine *Flare.*

Ashland did the introductions. Everybody sat and ordered drinks. And chatted vibrantly—except Clare Benton. Because—as she darned well knew—she was awed. A famous lawyer, a famous psychiatrist, a famous woman-leader-writer—and little old Clare Benton and Sue Robbins. Of course nothing fazed Sue Robbins. Nobody, but nobody, impressed her. And if they did, she did not show it. Except back there in Mr. Franklin's office, when she had been introduced to Mr. Ashland. But that had passed quickly enough, hadn't it? Now Sue was smoking a little cigar, and sipping a martini, and chattering blithely. Dauntless Sue, invincible. *God, I wish I could be like that.*

Mr. Ashland was saying: "He was in court with me today, and he killed the people."

"Who is he suing?" Sue asked.

"Not suing," Dr. Grayson said.

"My Ruby has no cause to sue," Ms. Talbert said.

"He was my expert witness," Mr. Ashland said.

"His expertise is sex," Sue said.

"I ought to know," Ms. Talbert said, laughing.

"Doc," Sue said, "what do you really know about sex?"

"He knows it all," Ms. Talbert said.

Dr. Grayson said, "What do any of us really know about sex, Miss Robbins?"

"Without snobbery," Sue said. "You're the expert. *Sex Without Snobbery.* To me that's a nothing title. Meaningless."

"But catchy." The doctor smiled that famous little-boy

smile. "It sold a hell of a lot of books."

"Not the title," Sue said. "You. You peddled it, Doc, and this is the era of electronic peddling. And you're the greatest peddler of them all, Doc, because you're beautiful."

"Speaking of beauty, physical beauty," Christine Talbert said. "The most beautiful, close up, I've seen in years is Miss Benton here."

Bitchily Sue said, "When it comes to female beauty, *you're* the expert."

Bitchily Talbert said, "I believe I detect a faint odor of possessiveness. Is she yours, Miss Robbins?"

"She's my client."

"Is that what they call it these days?"

"Girls," Dr. Reuben Grayson said. "Now now, girls."

"Girls!" Sue laughed. "You just said a no-no, Doc. Ms. Talbert had a long article in the last *Flare* about men demeaning women by calling them girls."

"I was being pejorative," Dr. Grayson said.

Pejorative, Clare thought; I don't even know what in heck that means.

"Christine," Mr. Ashland said. "How's Rosemarie?"

There was still bitchiness in her voice. "You should know, Tony."

"Should I?"

"She's your best friend's wife."

"I haven't see too much of her lately."

"Your loss."

"I admit that. Have you?"

"Seen much of Rosemarie? I certainly have."

"May I restate the prior question, Your Honor. How is she?"

"Flourishing, our Rosemarie. Flying like a flag."

"I'm glad."

"Yes, you are, aren't you?" She checked her watch.

"Ruby," she said to Dr. Grayson, "we've got to go." And smiled at Anthony Ashland. "It's been charming, Tony, and thank you. But we've gotta git."

"Just one thing."

"For you—anything."

Ashland shook his head. "A lot of flack today."

"I'm sorry. You misunderstood. I mean it. For you—anything."

"What I wanted to say, Your Honor. I spent most of this day with your gem, your Ruby." He gestured toward Grayson. "That's you, Doc. What I want to say—we should—us—get together more often."

"Good." Gently, Ms. Talbert patted Mr. Ashland's cheek. "Have you finally begun to understand my peculiar infatuation with the guy?"

"Yes ma'am," he said.

"Leave it to Chrissie here. I'll arrange." And to Grayson. "So now, dearest gem, we must *go!*"

"G'bye, everybody," Dr. Grayson said.

"You're beautiful," Sue said.

Anthony Ashland suggested a new round of drinks. Sue accepted. Clare declined. "Ladies," Ashland said. "An embarrassment. It's time for dinner, and so it shall be, except without me. I've an urgent appointment at eight o'clock, all the way across town. Theatre district, the damned traffic; I can't risk being late. Therefore I'll have to leave at seven, and that's only twenty minutes from now."

"A date?" Sue said.

"No. A business appointment. At my home." He sighed. "So, if you please. You ladies will order, and I'll grab a fast *nosh*. Then I'll leave you to, I hope, a pleasant and leisurely dinner."

"I'll miss you, Tony," Sue said, flirting.

"Will you miss me, Miss Benton?"

"Of course, Mr. Ashland."

He waved, and a waiter approached with menus.

"Just two menus, Harry. For the ladies. They will have dinner. I'll have a crabmeat cocktail; then I've got to run. You'll arrange the tab on my monthly statement."

He took out his wallet, extracted a bill.

"Thank you," Harry said, and deftly folded the bill with one hand and with the other gave the ladies their menus.

The ladies studied, and Anthony Ashland sipped his Scotch sour. I have got to make my move, he thought, and I don't quite know how. And inwardly he chuckled. Somehow her effect is to regress me to the gaucheries of adolescence. Not only is the mature Mr. Ashland puerilely passionate in the trousers, but he is skittish about the pragmatics of asking for a date. And doesn't even know for when. But for whenever—*do* it, for Chrissake. Even the most jejune of adolescents knows enough to strike while the iron is hot. This iron is not quite hot; lukewarm would better express it. Then strike, goddam, while the iron is lukewarm. But for when?

Tonight there was Duncan. Tomorrow in court the summations, and in the evening there was the appointment with Rosemarie's analyst. Wednesday was the judge's charge, and after court he had the first of two days' long-delayed client consultations at the office (which would stretch far into the evening). On Thursday he expected the verdict, and then the second of the day-to-evening consultations at the office. And on Friday night there was the appointment with Ritchie Crayne which he himself, personally, had arranged this afternoon.

Court had adjourned at two-fifteen. Dr. Reuben Grayson, as Ashland had expected, had been a sensation in court, and a splendid expert witness on the stand throughout the long direct examination. The District Attorney had virtually thrown in the towel; his cross-examination had been brief and polite and tentative, and Anthony Ashland could not fault him; had the D.A. attempted abrasive tactics, he would have totally alienated a jury already substantially lost to him. There had been no redirect by defense counsel, and at two-fifteen the judge had rapped his gavel and recessed until tomorrow at ten.

They had driven uptown together, the doc promising to come with Christine for a drink at Sardi's, and Ashland continuing to Jack LaLanne's Health Spa at Eighty-sixth Street, where Ritchie Crayne, famous since that article in *Flare,* was employed as a physical-education instructor.

He had asked for Crayne, waited in an anteroom, and there Crayne had joined him.

"Sir." A healthy, big-toothed smile. "What can I do for you?"

"I'm Anthony Ashland."

The smile disappeared. "*The* Anthony Ashland?"

"I should like to think so."

"Well." The smile was back but it was no longer a professional show of teeth. A smaller smile, quizzical now. "Rosemarie speaks of you often. She's very fond of you, sir."

"Mr. Crayne, we need a meeting, you and I."

"Isn't that what we're having, sir?"

"This is a preliminary meeting. What I have in mind is a long talk, and certainly not during your working hours. The talk I have in mind might prove"—a shrug—"shall we say beneficial to you?"

No more smile at all. But a pleat up there at the brow; a furrow of interest. "When and where would you like this meeting?"

I've got him, Ashland thought. Hell, I can *smell* cupidity.

"I'm in court on trial, and thereafter I'm jammed up with appointments. My first free time is Friday. How about Friday evening at my home?"

"Who'll be there?"

"Just you and I."

"Will you be representing somebody?"

A shrewd young man. Well, good.

"Yes," Ashland said. "Duncan McKee."

"Friday what time?"

"Your convenience."

"Nine o'clock all right?"

"Excellent."

"What's the address?"

"Eight-twenty-five Fifth Avenue."

"I'll be there, Mr. Ashland. Friday at nine."

"Just one more thing."

The bland professional smile was back. "Sir?"

"Important," Ashland said. "I wouldn't mention any of this to Rosemarie. Nothing, not a word. I suggest this for your own benefit, Mr. Crayne. If you talk, you can upset your own applecart. That would be stupid. I don't think you're stupid."

"I'm not stupid."

"I know. I've read about your vaunted IQ."

"Miss Talbert did a great article, didn't she?"

"Great," Ashland said. "And I'm depending on that IQ. Nose clean, Mr. Crayne, and mum."

"I promise."

"I want to hold you to that promise—for *your* benefit—until our conference on Friday. After that, you can talk your head off if you wish. I don't think you'll wish."

"Right. See you on Friday, Mr. Ashland."

"Good day, Mr. Crayne."

All in shape, Ashland thought, on his way to Don Franklin's office. This kid would hold his tongue, awaiting developments. Sweet Jesus, from long experience, don't I know the type? Hell, I can smell them a mile away, and this one's smell was suffocating: the redolence of avarice. But I had to know, from close up, face to face, whom I was dealing with. Now I know, Duncan, and we're in the bag, and I can also assure you, right now in advance, that he won't breathe a word to Rosemarie. Not a word. Not one fucking word.

The ladies dabbled at their appetizers and Anthony Ashland ate his crabmeat salad. Then he touched his napkin to his lips.

"Got to run. Miss Benton, I'll call you."

"Oho." Sue's eyes were wicked. "The sponsor speaks."

"Wrong, Miss Robbins. I am not a sponsor. Rather an admirer, very much struck, who, however lamely, is trying to get around to asking the lady for a date."

"Wanna know something, Tony? I believe you."

"Wanna know something, Sue? I don't care if you do or you don't. I should like to add, further, that this is not a situation that requires you to represent your client. So, if you please, I'd appreciate if you don't intrude."

Sue was grinning, beaming.

"Mister, you are something else!"

"Miss Benton," he said. "Are you, possibly, free this Saturday evening?"

"Yes," she said and felt herself, of all things, blushing.

"Can we—er, have a date?"

"Yes," she said.

"Good. Thank you." *Awkward as a goddam adolescent.* "I'll call you during the week and we'll talk. I have your phone number"—he smiled—"and all else of minor information from your biography." He stood up. "So then. *Adiós, muchachas,* the man must go to his appointment. Enjoy your dinner."

Sue enjoyed, Clare did not. Sue ate ravenously; Clare picked. Sue said, "I was testing the old bastard and he sure came through with flying colors."

"Testing! Dear God, you were brutal."

"Honey, you're my lamb and I'm the shepherd. I simply wanted to know if this was another sponsor looking to spread a pair of young legs in the feathers. If so, okay. But I wanted to know, so that you could know what it was all about. He ain't."

"Ain't—what?"

"Baby, I watched him, close as a cat on a mouse. This one, this once, ain't. He's not looking for a fast grab in the hay. He is smitten. Like love, you know? I tell you, this guy is smitten! Honey, listen to Sue. If you play your cards right, you can rake in the whole frigging pot."

"What in heck are you talking about?"

"I'm talking about what you came here for. New York, New York, the big apple. Forget actress. Actress won't ever happen. But you can make it."

"Make—what?"

"Honey, that was Mr. Anthony Ashland, free, unmarried, a widower, and a multimillionaire. And I tell you, I feel it in my bones—you really hit this guy hard. I tell you—listen to Sue—for you he's available, he is marriageable. Sounds crazy? It ain't. Did I ever say it to you before? And there were plenty big rich motherfuckers after you. This one's different. For whatever reason of his own, he's ready, and you're the one he's ready for. I *tell* you. Feel it in the bones. And these are old bones, baby; never failed me. I tell you, you can have it all—wealth, ease, society, the whole international jet-set whirl. I feel it in the old bones. I tell you, baby, if you just play your cards right . . ."

Embarrassed, Clare tried to change the subject. "God, this has been a day!"

"Great day," Sue said.

"Like nothing that ever happened. Clare Benton from Minneapolis—suddenly cheek by jowl with Manhattan's golden people. Mr. Donald Franklin himself. Then Anthony

Ashland. Then Dr. Reuben Grayson and Christine Talbert. Wow."

"Yeah."

"He's very sweet, that Grayson. Nice. Real nice. Even nicer than he comes over on TV."

"A beautiful man."

"But she—TV's no good for her."

"Honey, that gives them what they need. National exposure. If not for TV, she'd be another bigmouth in the Movement. Instead, she's the hoity-toity editor of *Flare*."

"The darn tube doesn't do her justice. She comes over tough and hard. In person she's much softer, and prettier and younger."

"A dyke."

"Pardon."

"She's a dyke."

"I've heard the rumors, but you know how it is. The minute anyone gets anywhere, there go the rumors. I mean, Talbert, she's so *feminine*."

"A dyke."

"How do you know?"

"Because I'm a dyke. Dykes know dykes."

"Sue, I've argued about that."

"What?"

"People saying you're a lesbian."

"Why? Because I never made a pass at you?"

"Could be."

Sue grinned. "That's because I'm a good kid."

"Look, if you'd rather not talk about—"

"I damn want to talk about. We never have, and it's time. First our relations, you and me. You're a square, you're straight; who needs it with you? Honey, there are plenty of my own people dying for a pass. I happen to love you, you're a doll, period. You're out of my particular league, and God bless. But that bitch of a Talbert, she's *in* my league. Dykes know dykes. Now the hell with Talbert. And the beautiful Dr. Reuben Grayson. And everybody except you. I love you, baby, I really do. But like a mother hen. Like as if you were my own kid; you're such a helpless little bastard. Hell, the way I've preached to you—as if you *were* my own kid. Some kind of goddam maternal instinct. Sue Robbins—that's to laugh. Do you want to laugh, luv?"

"No."

"All right. Mother hen here. And mother hen suddenly sees a wide-open spot. My bones tell me there's a guy flipping his balls for you, and the guy only happens to be Mr. Anthony Ashland. Baby, like that you can retire undefeated. You can get out of the ring before you accumulate the scar tissue. You can get out of the fucking competition while you're still young and gorgeous, and live happily ever after. Could be my bones are lying to me. If so, it would be the first time. So let's go along with my bones, call it intuition. My bones say this guy is in there with serious intent, whether or not he himself knows it yet. I think—however preposterous it may sound at this point—that there's a chance for marriage here. Crazy? Baby, I've come up with crazier ones, and they've worked out. So let's talk about you. The hell with Talbert, and the hell with Grayson—let's talk about you. Let's try to map out a campaign. Let's talk about you and Mr. Anthony Ashland. . . ."

4

IN GODDAM NEW YORK, he thought, it is always topsy-turvy. Criteria topple, standards fall, somehow the mad city does you in. When you leave yourself time in expectation of heavy traffic, there is no traffic. But an off-hour and you're in a hurry, then from somewhere a snarl of traffic finds you and ties you up like a sailor's knot. Serendipity dwells outside of New York City. This evening, no traffic. Reluctantly leaving the ladies, he had quit Sardi's at seven o'clock because Duncan was coming at eight. But—a swift smooth journey, no traffic to speak of—and he was home, ruefully, at quarter past seven.

Home. An immense duplex, especially immense for a man alone. The lower floor had a drawing room, a dining room, a library, a study, a recreation room, a billiard room, and the kitchens. Upstairs were the bedrooms, the guest rooms, and a small kitchen for snacks.

He went up for a quick shower and a change to slacks and

sport shirt and all the while his mind was on the girl. He was hit bad, and he knew it. Hell, he was old enough to know. (No fool like an old fool?) There had been girls before Alice, and during Alice, and after Alice, but to be hit like this—a totally new experience. Sweet Jesus, doesn't the long-distance runner *ever* slow down? At fifty-four this sort of thing simply doesn't happen.

But it damn well *had* happened, and in some recondite way, delightfully bewildered, he was enjoying. Love at first sight—ridiculous? Of course, at that first sight she had been bare-assed naked. So what? There had been other faraway nudes before her and nothing, no effect. But immediately this one had hit him where he lived. He remembered in amazement his rigid erection under the clipboard in the twelfth row of the Morosco Theatre. A hard-on, from stage to seats, in a man of fifty-four? He laughed aloud.

No question she was extraordinarily beautiful (at least to his taste), but beauty alone is not the mystical mainspring that sets the genitals to quivering. There has to be more. Something. A chemistry. Vibrations. An especial reaching into. (Karma?) A certain one for a certain other, no matter the discrepancy of age. Each to his own, and own to each. All right, so much for the physical. But contact can destroy that physical reaction; a reprehensible personality can be the guillotine that instantly severs sexual attraction. He had therefore arranged to meet her. And the meeting had made it worse. Or should that be—better?

He was in love, goddamit. His strong, old, male heart went out to her. Youthful and modern, he was at core old-fashioned: the male-male, the protector, the provider, the avenger, the guardian of the cave. He abhorred a loudmouthed woman, a shrew, a virago; he abhorred the present-day fashionably foulmouthed woman; he abhorred—although cynically was constrained to conceal—the militant likes of a

Christine Talbert, no matter that he agreed with her principles. He had been a fighter, long before Christine Talbert, for equal civil rights and civil liberties for women. But he could not accept the extreme of the Women's Movement philosophy: that a woman was a man. A woman was *not* a man, and a man was not a woman; instinctually, and certainly physically, they were different. Certainly a woman could accomplish as much as a man, and in fact a woman could rule a man by ruse and wile, but she cannot cross over or she must fail; the atavism of animal instinct must prevail; the male, however civilized, was still the guardian of the cave.

Okay. All right. The hell with philosophy. We go for what we go for, and I have always gone for the very feminine female, and this one is it, isn't she? That diffidence onstage was not an act; that was she. Sweet Jesus, how goddam sweet. No filthy crap coming out of her mouth like a toilet bubbling back from bad plumbing. Quite the contrary. Quiet, reserved. Hell, who could believe it of a young and beautiful woman in this era of the twentieth century—actually shy. He recollected the blush that had suffused her face when he —dumb guardian of the cave—had gawkily asked for the date. So okay, Pappy, but hold on to everything. Perhaps you are, insane as it sounds, in love; in love, goddam, with a stranger. Therefore hang in there; one step at a time; protect your flanks—you are fifty-four years old. Despite your preposterous hard-on in the Morosco Theatre, and the creeping feeling in your loins in Don Franklin's office, and your delight with her among her creature people in Sardi's, you are not, definitely, going to leap before you explore.

Now in his study he locked her out of his mind; this was Duncan's time and Duncan was entitled to the full concentration. He looked up at the wall clock. Twenty to eight.

Opened a drawer of his desk for the investigator's report, and heard himself laugh again. Wrong. She must still be lurking in the recesses of his mind. Because the report was *on* the desk, not *in* the desk.

The open drawer showed him the pistol and he gave it a small salute. Pistols. He had a loaded pistol in the drawer in his study, and a loaded pistol in his desk in the library, and one in the drawer of the table beside his bed, and another in his desk at the office. All legal; all with permits, of course. He was a criminal lawyer and frequently dealt with hardened criminals, and although most of them adored him, some didn't. That was one reason for the pistols. The other was New York, the city of his birth, which in recent years had become a jungle, and when you live in a jungle you must arm yourself against the possibility of attack by beasts. He closed the drawer, tapped fingertips on the report; then he crossed to the bar, poured a Drambuie, and settled into an easy chair.

Duncan McKee. Troubles. Matrimonial troubles. Duncan and Rosemarie McKee of the Beautiful People. Duncan and Rosemarie, the burnished and the beautiful, the chic and the splendid, the givers of the most dazzling of charity balls, the elegant patrons of the arts, the high-society jet-set travelers. They owned a town house in New York, and a beach house in Southampton, and a hedge-enclosed house in Beverly Hills, and apartments in Rome, Paris, and Copenhagen. Duncan was forty-nine; the vivid Rosemarie was forty-three; and they were husband and wife for eighteen years with never the faintest whit of jealousy or marital difficulty. They had foreclosed that in advance, the sophisticated McKees. Forerunners, they had established an open marriage before "open marriage" became a term in the language. They had each been married once before—each, in fact, to a jealous spouse—and they themselves had lived together for a year preceding their marriage. And even during that year they had each had occasional sexual affairs, each with the other's consent. That had been a fundamental tenet of their marriage, freedom to engage in outside sex, and for them it worked: it had been a hugely successful, exuberantly happy marriage.

And they had been forerunners in another matter, again before their time: population explosion. Neither had wanted children and therefore Duncan had submitted to a vasectomy long before vasectomies became the subject for titillating articles in popular magazines.

So? What in hell had happened?

Duncan, in his recent confidential talks with Tony Ashland had set it back—the remote cause—to about a year ago. At that time Rosemarie, however lightly, sometimes even jokingly, had begun to talk about desiring the experience of giving birth to a child. Duncan had listened, laughed, and dismissed it. But she had continued, less lightly, less jokingly, and he had begun to get worried. Was she flipping her wig? Was she being affected by drugs? She was a user, but not an addict, of the soft drugs: pot, peyote, the amphetamines, and of late she had discovered—fashionable these days—cocaine. Or, possibly, was it a temporary aberration due to change of life?

"Is she in her menopause?" Tony had asked.

"I don't know."

"Well, hell, you could ask."

"You're not her husband, my friend. Rosemarie clings to youth. You don't bring up menopause with Rosemarie. Taboo—unless *she* would bring it up. She never did."

"There are other ways to discover."

"There goddam are. And I did."

"Now you're my Duncan. How?"

"Had a private talk with her gynecologist."

"Smart. So?"

A private talk. A discussion of marital problems. The wife, in her forties, was suddenly talking about the experience of pregnancy, the birth syndrome, motherhood. The husband, even if he agreed—which he didn't—could not comply; he could not father a child, he had long ago had a vasectomy. Was this a thing with her because of change of life? Was she in her menopause?

No, the doctor had said. Not at all, Mr. McKee. Physically, not at all. In my opinion she will not go into the physical manifestations of menopause until her late forties. But there are, at the very early beginnings, years before, certain premenopausal signs, slight endocrinologic changes. In Mrs. McKee's case, at this time, they are so slight that no hormonal therapy is in the least indicated. However, Mr. McKee, yours is not at all an unusual problem. At this time of life, many women who have never before borne a child—usually, if you'll forgive me, neurotic women; and they're the most interesting, aren't they?—these women at this time of life suddenly evince an overwhelming desire to bear a child. An unconscious psychological torment; they realize they are nearing the end, that it's their last chance for procreation. But it passes. The husband must be patient. In time they come back to their good senses. Be patient with her, Mr. McKee.

"Were you patient?" Ashland had asked. Right here in this study, only four weeks ago. By then Rosemarie had been gone for a month. And for that month, Duncan had suffered in silence.

"Up to a point," McKee said.

"Then?"

"It got out of hand."

"This was last year?"

"Yes."

"What happened?"

"She kept talking about it, and I finally exploded. The first serious argument of our married life. Don't misunderstand. Not that I wasn't able, that I don't have the sperm to produce a child; I mean no self-guilt involved. Simply I didn't believe she could properly handle it. Neither of us. Too old, too set, too rigidly formed in the manner of our ways. Christ, what in hell would we do with an *infant?*"

"Okay, take it easy. So? Then?"

"It was absolutely insane. I told her, made it spotlessly clear. She didn't bring it up again, and I thought it was over."

"Did you talk to her shrink?"

The shrink was Dr. Arthur Sawyer and she was in analysis, the rich woman's casual twice-a-week analysis, for six years. Twice a week, that is, when she was in town.

"No," Duncan McKee had said. "A husband can cross the line to the gynecologist, but never to the wife's shrink. That's foreign territory, and you're the enemy. Furthermore, as I said, I thought it was over."

"But now it's really begun."

"If you think a discussion with Sawyer will help, you're going to have to do it. As the friend of the husband whose wife has walked out."

"I'll handle it, friend. All of it. One step at a time."

Tony Ashland stood up from the easy chair, added more Drambuie to the pony glass, and sat on a high stool by the bar.

Duncan believed it had germinated a year ago as a new quirk in Rosemarie's complicated psyche. All right, we accept that. Now we move it up closer. Six months ago. And at that time Rosemarie was still utterly uninvolved. The linchpin had been a young man by name Ritchie Crayne.

Six months ago New York had had another foolish contest, this one inaugurated by an advertising agency promoting a push-button-type shaving cream. Its putative purpose was to discover Mr. Most Attractive New Yorker. (Now, who in hell would enter this kind of contest?) It was not the usual Mr. America contest that featured muscle-bound male behemoths with huge biceps and sinew-striated buttocks. The purpose of *this* contest was to uncover the most normally handsome male within the purlieus of New York City, with the most normally handsome body, and they sure did uncover him. The winner, hands down and chest up, of the Mr. Most Attractive New Yorker was Mr. Ritchie Crayne, a physical-education instructor for Jack LaLanne. His prize was a thousand dollars in cash, a case of push-button-type shaving cream, and his signature on a general release that gave the agency the right to use his photo in their advertising campaign. And that was some photo, Your Honor. Uncovered in sexily bulging, tight-to-the-thighs swim trunks, the guy was only gorgeous: blond, tall, lean, and lovely. Of course, in time, the campaign petered out, and so would Mr. Ritchie Crayne have, except for Ms. Christine Talbert and *Flare* magazine.

Ms. Christine Talbert.

Christine was Rosemarie McKee's closest friend, albeit Christine was ten years younger. Rosemarie had always been strong in the Women's Movement, and Christine was its most dashing, most vocal, most talented, and most beautiful advocate; the now famous Ms. Christine Talbert, editor-in-chief of *Flare*. And the biggest money-winners of *Flare* magazine were the McKees. All, in fact, unintentional.

Four years ago, Christine had come up with the concept of *Flare*. At that time she had already written two solid books and was a contributing editor to *New York* magazine. Christine's idea had been a magazine by women and for women and solely staffed by women. She had interested some excellent creative talent, and some excellent investors, and only then had she talked to her richest friends, the McKees. She had insisted that if Duncan McKee would put up some real money, she could entice away her good friend Audrey Chappell, the lovely lissome lesbo who was assistant to the publisher of *Time* magazine at a salary of seventy-five thousand a year.

Duncan McKee had listened hard. He had liked the idea because he was morally on the side of freedom for women. He had also liked the idea because he thought it could work: Ms. Talbert had underscored her prospectus with some powerful females who were willing to give up surefire jobs to come into *Flare.* But for him the fulcrum was the lovely lesbo lady, Ms. Chappell, whom he knew to be a hardheaded businesswoman. If Chappell was willing to sacrifice her seventy-five a year, aside from the enormous fringe benefits, to take the risk of *Flare,* then he was willing to endow it with a few bucks of risk capital. His few bucks was a million dollars. *One million dollars!* On the part of Duncan McKee, it was in fact a philanthropic gesture; if it went bad it was a tax loss. Ms. Chappell had come in as publisher, Ms. Talbert had been instated as editor-in-chief, and *Flare* had immediately soared, an instantaneous success. As is writ in all the annals: money goes to money; the McKees, the chief stockholders, were reaping a new and unexpected harvest.

Okay, so much for *Flare.*

Back to Ms. Talbert and Mr. Ritchie Crayne.

After the guy had won his Mr. Most Attractive, Christine had decided to do an interview with him for a piece for *Flare.* She had contemplated a tongue-in-cheek derogation, a satirical article on the immodesties of silly males, but it had developed differently, because the guy had turned out to have an IQ of 190—which she had verified. That number set him apart, and changed her original concept for the piece. The man was up there in the rarefied atmosphere of the genius types, yet he was a phys-ed instructor at Jack LaLanne's. What about other males with genius IQs? That sent her off on a spate of research and she learned a hell of a lot. Some of the genius types had acquired renown and high estate, but many of the others—nothing. One was a cable-car operator in San Francisco, another a porter in a hospital in Detroit, another a taxi driver in Cleveland, another a sanitation worker in Seattle, another a hopeless drunk in Chicago.

The article in *Flare* had not been a frivolous, down-the-nose piece; it had been, on the contrary, a long and serious piece, its theme that a genius IQ does not necessarily assure material success. But its focus had been Ritchie Crayne (with glorious photos) and its title had been *Mr. Most Attractive New Yorker.*

And so once again Mr. Ritchie Crayne had surfaced as a temporary celebrity. The swiftie magazines did things on him, and the New York *Post* did a personality piece, and a segment of the syndicated Duncan McKee Show had been devoted to him. For a time, he was the hottest item on the lists of the sophisticated party-givers, and he had achieved the pinnacle within that ambience because he had once—once!—even been invited to a bash at the apartment of the most élite of the sophisticated party-givers, a gentleman with the curious name of Truman Capote (which always somehow, to Anthony Ashland, sounded like a dessert named after a President).

And it had been at one such party, three months ago, that Mrs. Rosemarie McKee had met Mr. Ritchie Crayne, and one month later she had walked out on her husband and gone to live with Ritchie Crayne. And for four long weeks thereafter Mr. Duncan McKee had done absolutely nothing about it; hell, nobody even knew that they had parted. And then a month ago—finally—he had come to his friend Tony Ashland.

"I don't know what in hell to do," he had said. "If I make any precipitate moves, I'll involve her in an open scandal. That won't be fair to her, at this time of her life. I tell you it's her fright of that goddam menopause; she's a little nuts. At this moment she wants a goddam baby, and she knows I'm damned set against it. Which is why she walked out, and refuses even to communicate with me. And of course she picked a perfect specimen to father this temporary madness of a baby that's on her mind. This Ritchie Crayne. Physically a perfect specimen, and mentally a genius IQ. Oh, she knows her genetics, my crazy Rosemarie. Christ, Tony, what do I *do?*"

They had talked.

"One step at a time," Ashland had said. "And our first step is Ritchie Crayne. Who in hell *is* this Ritchie Crayne? He's our nub, my friend. He has to be our point of focus. In time I'll talk to her shrink. Leave it to me; I'll handle this whole deal. But Number One is Ritchie Crayne, and that could take some time. But you took your goddam time before you came to me; now just hang on to your pants, my friend. Leave it to Tony."

"Do I have an alternative?"

"Do you?"

"No."

"Thank you. But why in hell did you wait this long?"

"I—I love the woman."

"So the hell do I. Okay, I'm taking over. From here on out, it's my job. Your job—hang on to your pants and sweat it out. Like the gynecologist said a year ago—patience, Mr. McKee."

"I'll be eternally grateful, Tony."

"I don't want to hear that kind of crap," Ashland said.

The next day he had recruited his chief investigator, Ralph Hanson. If Hanson could not do it—it could not be done.

"I want it *all* on this Ritchie Crayne. Drop anything you're working on; pass it along to your assistants. You're now heart and soul on Mr. Crayne. Bug, tap, bribe—I want the whole story. Whatever you have to pay people to help, pay. I want to know the size of Crayne's *putz,* if you think it's necessary for your report. Go anywhere, do anything; expense account unlimited. You're the best in the business and you've got carte blanche. I don't care if you break me on this thing, but I want the whole story on Ritchie Crayne. From the day he was born right up to now."

And the whole story was lying on the desk, eighty-seven closely typed pages, neatly stapled within an innocuous blue binder. Sweet Jesus, would Duncan McKee be struck by surprises.

The downstairs buzzer sounded. Ashland answered.

"Mr. McKee," the doorman said.

"Send him up," Ashland said.

A Wasp of Wasps, Duncan McKee. Impassive, impressive. The figure ramrod straight; the attire, as always, elegant. The bony square-jawed face, tight-skinned, disclosed nothing of the man's suffering.

"Hi, pal," Ashland said.

"I'm on time, I hope."

"Right on the button." He took his topcoat, hung it away, led him to the study, gestured toward the bar. "Have a drink, my friend."

"Thank you."

The drink was the giveaway. Duncan drank bourbon and soda. Selecting a tall glass, he filled more than half of it with bourbon, added ice, but no soda. He drank a good deal of it.

"Tomorrow," Ashland said, "I've a dinner date with Dr. Sawyer."

"Good. But that's tomorrow. As you would say—one step at a time. Tonight I'm here for Crayne."

"I saw him this afternoon."

"Oh?"

"I'm one of the few of our circle who's never before met him."

"So?"

"We had a chat this afternoon. Up at LaLanne's. I wanted a vis-à-vis. Wanted to size him."

"How'd he size?"

"Good, I think."

"What's that mean?"

"I think he can be handled."

"How?" McKee poured more bourbon, but added soda. He hooked himself up on a bar stool, pulled an ashtray near. He produced his cigarettes and lit one.

Ashland carried his Drambuie to the desk.

He sat in the leather swivel chair, placed the blue-backed sheets on his knees, and swung around to face McKee.

"The report," he said.

"Yes, that's why I'm here."

Ashland flipped pages. "Richard Crayne. Age twenty-nine. Born Los Angeles. Graduated Los Angeles High School. The college is UCLA. Top of his classes all the way. That IQ is correct. One-ninety."

"And he winds up," McKee said grimly, "a lousy physical-training instructor."

"I have stranger things to report." Ashland turned pages. "Richard, who prefers to be called Ritchie. Arrested twice. Both times Los Angeles, both times no convictions. First time, age twenty. A raid on a stag party where males were giving a lewd exhibition. Case dismissed—insufficient evidence. The second time, age twenty-two. The charge is sodomy and impairing the morals of a minor. A boy of fifteen made the accusation. But when the hearing finally rolled around, the complainant failed to appear. Case dismissed. Our man has a clean record."

"Who the hell cares about his record."

"The point is—he's gay."

"So what? Let's not fall into the trap of that old, pinched myth. I mean there are plenty of gay guys who have satisfactory heterosexual marriages. *My* point is, gay or not, he must be perfectly capable of performing sexual intercourse with a woman because—"

"Not Ritchie Crayne," Ashland said.

"How the hell do *you* know?"

"Ralph Hanson." Ashland held the report aloft. "Hanson," he said. "The best of the best. Hanson bought, bribed, dug into records, paid handsomely for information, talked to everybody who had to be talked to, and what we have here is the total, in-depth biography of Ritchie Crayne. Our man is *not* acey-deucy, he is *not* a switch-hitter, he can*not*—I said *not!*—make it with a woman."

"You're crazy! That's the only reason she's with him, I tell you. She has picked him—a marvelous physical specimen and a guy with a hundred-and-ninety-IQ brain—to father her child. If he can't make it with a woman . . ."

"It's goddam perplexing," Ashland said.

"Or your Hanson isn't the paragon you think he is."

"No, sir. In his business, he's the paragon. I would stake my life that Ritchie Crayne cannot fuck a woman. Perhaps she's with him as a friend. Perhaps she's taken *him* on as the baby she wants."

"Not at all. Her madness of the moment is the whole birth syndrome. She desires the full experience of pregnancy."

"Perhaps you're wrong."

"I know I'm right."

"Duncan, there's no question they're having an affair." Ashland sighed. "I cannot comprehend what in hell type affair it is, but I believe I know why he is submitting himself to it."

"Why?"

"Money."

"Not Rosemarie," McKee said. He sipped bourbon and soda. He punched out his cigarette and lit another. His one real vice was cigarettes. An addict. A chain smoker. "Not Rosemarie," he said. "She would not pay for services, cash on the barrelhead. Not beautiful, narcissistic Rosemarie. Not the type. Would not—could not—demean herself to buy the guy."

"Perhaps that's why it's been going on this long. Perhaps, subtly, he's playing the angles."

"What angles?"

"Money." Ashland returned to the blue-backed report. "Ritchie Crayne, the genius IQ who majored in phys ed. At twenty-four he moved from LA to San Francisco. Then Las Vegas. Then Miami. A couple of years ago he junketed around the capitals of Europe. Last year he came to New York and went to work for Jack LaLanne. Then the Mr. Most Attractive New Yorker. And then Christine's piece in *Flare.*"

"We were, I believe, talking about money."

"Ever hear of Spencer Poole?"

"Who?"

"Sir Spencer Poole."

"You mean that British financier?"

"That's who I mean."

"Of course I've heard of Sir Spencer Poole."

"The *Flare* article, and the subsequent publicity, brought Crayne to Poole's attention, and the old guy came up with a brilliant idea. A new health spa in London. The Ritchie Crayne Health Spa. He crossed the big blue ocean and talked with Ritchie Crayne. If Crayne could put up fifty thousand dollars, the old boy would put up three hundred thou, and they'd go into business in London, England. He gave Crayne six months to get up his ante. And that's about the time Mr. Most Attractive and Mrs. Rosemarie McKee joined forces as an exclusive team—each for whatever the one wanted from the other."

"Christ, I tell you she wouldn't pay it out on the line like that."

"She hasn't," Ashland said. "In a way, on the other hand, she has. The guy used to live in a one-hole room in the Dixie Hotel. Now they live in a husband-and-wife suite in the Croydon. He couldn't possibly pay for that. He earns three hundred a week in LaLanne's. What with all the withhold takeoffs, it amounts to nothing for a guy who likes to live right, and Ritchie likes to live right." He consulted Hanson's report. "At the time he got together with her, he had twelve hundred dollars in his savings account, and his checking account balance swung between four hundred and eight hundred. Both accounts are the same, which means—you're right—she hasn't, yet, contributed cash loot. But she has bought him gifts from Tiffany, and gifts from Cartier, and he does have a whole new expensive wardrobe."

Ashland tossed the report to the desk. He swung around in the swivel chair, making a full circle. Abandoning his Drambuie, he clapped his thighs, stood up, came to McKee. He went behind the bar, poured a Scotch on rocks, drank. Then, smiling, he faced his friend—the bartender behind the bar and the customer on the high stool.

"Duncan," he said softly, "I know what you've been thinking, and that's what I've been thinking, and we both have the connections for it. I believe we now have an alternative."

"What have I been thinking?"

"We can destroy the son of a bitch. He took away a man's wife—then he has to know he's left himself open to any kind of retribution, and he would goddam deserve it. We can have his nose broken, his eyes gouged, that whole pretty face smashed up forever. I know that you've been thinking about it, and I have, and the only reason neither of us has suggested it is that we both know that *she* would know where it came from."

"Yes," McKee said.

"I talked to him today. I think he'll go for the alternative."

"Which is?"

"Fifty thousand bucks. I'd swear that's what he's been after her for, dangling the angles. Duncan, I talked to the son of a bitch today. I didn't present it, of course, but I hinted, and he came up for the bait with his mouth wide open like a hungry fish. What the hell is fifty gees to a Duncan McKee? Hell, a spit in the river. Without ripples. You can put it down as a loan, and it winds up for the IRS as a bad debt."

"Who says it'll work?"

"I do. I think it will. He's coming here to talk to me on Friday night."

"Will I be here?"

"No. I don't want to risk personality clashes. And on Friday it won't just be talk. We're going to close a deal." A sip of Scotch. "Now this is what I'd like you to do. I want your certified check, made out to him, for fifty thou. And I want his plane ticket to London." He thought for a moment. "For next Wednesday. Thus, we—Ritchie and Pappy—will settle up on Friday. Then he has four days to get ready before, abruptly, he skips. Technically he's in shape. Passport's in order."

"How do you know?"

Ashland waved toward the desk.

"Hanson's report. You'll take it home with you. Very interesting reading. I've another copy at the office. Let's see, now. Schedule. Tomorrow I see Sawyer—kind of preparation for my dealings on Friday. Wednesday and Thursday I'll be in the office, after court, till late."

"Eight?"

"Late. So you get the stuff to me at the office—the check and the ticket—on either of those days."

"May I ask a question, Counselor?"

"Be my guest, Mr. McKee."

"Suppose he doesn't quite skip? Suppose he takes off with my money *and* my wife?"

"We'd be fresh out of alternatives, wouldn't we?"

McKee squinted, inclined his head.

"He'll be warned," Ashland said.

"Of what?"

"We're neither of us children. Nor is he. He has, as we say in the law, the right of refusal. But once he takes your money, then the contract is closed. We have performed, and he *must* perform, or he's dead. He'll hear that warning, straight and clear. If he tries to screw it up, if he tries a swindle, quite simply he's dead."

"Literally? You mean—"

"Duncan, don't go coy on me. I came up from the streets and you came up with a golden spoon in your mouth, but when the chips are down, you're just as tough as I am." He sighed. "It wouldn't be a simple matter. Our people would have to do it in London, and it would have to be—an accident. It wouldn't do at all—would it?—for her to have any suspicion that we were behind it."

Now he raised his hands high, wriggled them. "But nothing like that is going to happen." The hands descended. "He's going to give her the heave-ho, walk out cold, and that's when you'll make your move to take her home. Duncan, I've seen the guy, talked to the guy, smelled him out; I know.

Fifty thousand dollars—that's his chance of a lifetime. That's why he got *with* her. She's his opportunity, and he's in there pitching. Now it comes to him from the husband's side. Could be that was the pitch in the first place. Could be he figured that out in advance. Could be he's playing the old gypsy backfire game. Hell, he's the boy with the IQ brain."

"Not him. You," McKee said. "I'm going to go along with this because *you're* the IQ brain. You're the goddam smartest man I've ever known."

"Well, thank you, friend."

"I mean it."

"Okay, I accept it."

McKee smiled. First time this evening.

"What *is* your IQ?"

"Haven't the faintest," Ashland said.

"Never been tested?"

"Wouldn't submit to that kind of test."

"Why not?"

"First I'd have to know who devised the test. Then I'd have to know the particular mood at that moment of the tester. And then I would have to know who would be the evaluators of the test. Put the variations of those combinations into a computer and you'd come up with something that had a long string of zeros after it."

"And the zeros would be a nullification."

"Correct. I'm not a believer in psychological tests. That, of course, makes me a nut. When you rub against the grain, you're a nut. Christ, in his time, was believed to be a nut."

"But you don't believe in Christ."

"I goddam do. In Christ the man, Christ the rebel, Christ the preacher, the thinker, the philosopher, the poet."

"Then you believe in nothing."

"Lord, how small-minded the religious can be. What do you mean *nothing?* I believe in Jesus Christ, a marvelous man. I believe in you. Me. People. Evolution. I believe we progress like an inch per millennium. I believe that in a few million years—if our species is still around—we'll be out of our swaddling clothes and start toddling, still fairly insensibly."

"Christ, you're the pessimist."

"I think I'm an optimist."

"Who started this?"

"I don't know."

"Let's get off it."

"Yes."

McKee lit a cigarette, departed the bar. He went across to the desk, sat in the swivel chair, took up the blue-backed report, turned pages, read, turned more pages; read intently.

He looked up. Shook his head.

"Your Hanson insists he can't *possibly* have physical intercourse with a female."

"And he gives you unimpeachable sources, doesn't he? He interviewed Crayne's closest friends, gay-world intimates. And from all the way back. Los Angeles, San Francisco, Las Vegas, Miami—and here in New York. And note they don't say it about all gay people. They admit that *many* of them swing both ways. But they're unanimous about Ritchie Crayne."

"Then what in hell do they do?"

"Who?"

"Rosie and this unanimously certified one-way fairy."

"Search *me.*"

"I'm searching you."

"I'd have to go back to my original premise. Maybe she's adopted *him* as her baby."

McKee's brief laugh was bitter derision.

"No, sir, not on your life. I know my Rosie." He slammed down Hanson's report. "Jesus Christ, what *do* they do?"

5

AT ELEVEN-FIFTEEN at the Croydon Hotel, she emerged from the tingling shower, rubbed briskly with a thick Turkish towel, then snapped off the shower cap and shook out her hair. This season she was a redhead.

Hands over head, she did a full pirouette in front of the tall mirror, and smiled. She was proud of her youthful body, a girl's body. The smile broadened; well, a full-breasted girl, *zoftik,* but there wasn't an ounce of extra fat anywhere on her body: 38-23-38. Them's pretty good numbers, boy. And the ass is firm, and the thighs are firm, and the firm tits protrude as though invisibly bolstered, and the smiling face is a girl's face, but the face is another matter. The body was all hers, well kept, well nourished, massaged and exercised; the face was Dr. Robert Banner's handiwork. She had promised herself a face-lift at age forty, before the wrinkles really began, and she had kept her promise, and the doc had done a wonderful job. There were times—when she was putting people on, strangers—that she took ten years off her age, and nobody blinked an eye.

She brushed her hair, and suddenly giggled at the full-length reflection—remembering Duncan. The delta of curly pubic hair was exactly the color of the hair on her head. The head was done at Kenneth's; she herself touched up the silken fur at the mound of Venus. "Fastidious, my Rosie," Duncan would say. "With her, the collar and cuffs always match."

Dear Duncan.

Brushed her hair. She had been visiting with Christine, but at the stroke of ten-thirty, she was up and gone and back to the hotel because lover-boy (unless by chance they were out on the town) went to sleep precisely at midnight. And was up precisely at 8 A.M. He was a stickler for the salutary procedures, was lover-boy, a health fiend, an exercise freak, and a devout vegetarian.

And queer as a three-eyed monkey.

My lover the *faigili.* Is it not to laugh? That gorgeous hunk of man, utterly useless in sexual combat with a woman. But before she had known, she had become obsessed with him: the perfect father for her child. Lord, those photos—Mr. Most. And handsome as the devil. And an IQ of 190.

And then she had learned that he was gay; nevertheless *he* had persistently pursued their friendship and she had therefore decided he was homo-hetero, and had posed a question to Dr. Arthur Sawyer. "Can homosexuality be inherited?"

"Ridiculous," the doctor said.

That's all she wanted to hear. All the rest she knew. Brains and beauty were hereditary, a matter of the genes and the chromosomes, and it was not until she had moved in with her perfect specimen that she learned he was monstrously incapable of connection with a woman.

He had permitted her kisses (he was trying, the poor

dear), but his lips had gone dry and his stomach had gurgled; had she not desisted, he would have puked. And had tried other methods. Masturbating him at the mouth of her vagina —without success. The very touch of her hand on his penis made it retreat. But, like a heroic stallion, he courageously submitted to her diverse experiments, and they had finally discovered a means. He was reactive to her fellatio.

Lying on his back with his eyes closed, firmly closed (he was probably thinking of a male lover), he had responded to licking, to the blandishments of tongue-touch, his powerful thing coming up like lava from a volcano, and thus they had worked out their abominable means of artificial insemination.

Had he suggested it? Had she?

She did not remember, could not remember. Perhaps they had thought of it together. Abominable? Yes. Revolting? Yes. But wild! She had never dreamed of anything like it in her life, and she had believed she had dreamed of it all, no matter the fantasy. And the fairy bastard, once within the modality, even knew how to please a woman. Because he knew how to hold back his come. And thus, sucking his intransigent prick, she—a passionate woman—achieved orgasm after orgasm in the weird hideous excitement until at long last, finally, he condescended to ejaculation.

But why?

Why was he willing to undergo what for him was a stress entirely against his nature? She was not a stupid woman: this man had to have a motive. All right, what motive? The answer was easy. Money! What in hell else could he get from *her?* True, she paid the rent here in the suite, and paid for all necessities like food and such, and bought him expensive gifts, and insisted that he accept pin money, but a homo-stallion would not submit to these crazy indignities, foreign to his homo urge, for those kinds of peanuts. So? Did he need five thousand? Ten? She might have paid it out—*might* have—but he was wise, he had a genius IQ, he sensed her nature. He knew that if he made an exorbitant demand, such demand might flatten her, a denigration; she might—*might!*—turn around and walk out on him and there would go his possibilities of bonanza. So he was holding back; that brilliant IQ was working for him. If once he impregnated her, then he was the father of the child growing in her belly, and then she would be vastly vulnerable—and she damned well *would* be—and she would probably accede to whatever in hell he demanded. Was that his game? Was that the game he was playing, her fucking fuckless fairy lover?

She came out to him and was struck again, as always, by that astonishing, incredible body. He was lying nude on the bed, two pillows propped at his nape, reading *Flare* (which had of course, since "Mr. Most," become his favorite magazine). He was a gleaming man, hairless except for the beige bush at his crotch; a triangular man with broad shoulders that tapered down to narrow flanks; a sinewy man with long, graceful, rippling muscles. A tawny man who appeared to be lightly suntanned, but that was the natural color of his skin. He did in fact avoid the sun (as he frequently lectured her to do), because the rays of the sun, he direly insisted, immediately ruined the human epidermis, burned it, dried it, wrinkled and aged it.

He saw her, smiled, laid away the magazine. He sneaked a glance at the clock. Bastard, she thought, it's not yet your beddy-beddy time. "Lord, you're beautiful," she said. "I can never get over it. Mr. Most!"

"*You're* the most," he said. Gallantly.

And stretched his long legs, keeping them together, touching parallel, and dutifully closed his eyes.

She did not extinguish the bed lamp. She liked making love

in the light. *Love!* A tremor shivered through her and for a fleeting moment she tried to understand it. Anticipation of an esoteric venal ecstasy? Wrath at the screwy vagaries of fate? Or—sheer revulsion?

She flung away from tremors and into bed and straddled him, her knees open at the sides of his knees, and lowered her head, and commenced kissing his body, lightly: his shoulders, under his arms at the armpits, his chest, the nipples of his breasts, and down, the tip of her tongue writing lines on his belly, her teeth nibbling at his hips, and down—no hands, never a hand touching—to his smooth strong thighs, and then to the center of him, to that cock risen enormous as her tongue artfully licked, licking under, licking over, and then she had to rear back for a quick look at the gorgeous prick, the most beautiful she had ever seen, a cannon but superbly shaped, a rigid organ molded by some fantastic sculptor, a phallus that was a goddam work of art, and she plunged down on it, her spread hands on the bed giving her leverage, knees and hands giving her leverage as she sucked, sucked cock, eating him, engorging him, capturing all of him deep in her throat and then letting loose for air and then capturing, enrapturing again, but the son of a bitch up there held back, and she hit, and hit again, orgasm after orgasm, and now sucking cock and jaws beginning to hurt, she was perspiring, her sweat dripping down on him, but the contumacious bastard, the spiteful fairy bastard was still holding, and she was tiring but still hot, and then she hit the last one—Jesus Lord!—an excruciating, debilitating, enervating orgasm-*orgasm!*—and she was through, she was done, sucking cock mechanically now, waiting for him, taking the punishment he was meting out, and then at last she felt it beginning, felt the swelling in the veins of the prick, felt the rigidity harden to that iron-rigidity which was the moment before ejaculation, and then he let her have it, the cannon blasted, his hot come struck at the roof of her mouth and she could taste it, that metallic taste, and she held it, her throat locked; she held it all, her mouth full.

And now their strange play was at high point; before it wound down, it must reach up to climax. Now they were arrived at the pivotal, necessary, obligatory scene. Successful—the play was a hit. Unsuccessful—it was another hard-wrought, well-done, well-meant, perfectly rehearsed failure. They knew what it was all about, they knew it all. They had discussed it, researched it: they knew the biology. They knew how long sperm lived; they knew that the oral cavity contained mucus that was as benevolent to sperm as was the mucus of the vaginal tract. And so now they were sitting, facing one another, and his eyes were open. And she bent toward him until her mouth touched his, like a devil's kiss, and she spat his semen, the semen of his loins, into his mouth. And then she lay back, her legs in the air, spread wide open. And he knelt between her legs, as though in prayer, as though performing some obscene, occult, ritualistic act of worship, and the lips of his mouth touched the lips of her vagina, and he expressed his semen, spurting it into her hot cunt. And she lay there, on her back, legs up, like a stricken cow in the field, and lay like that, letting his sperm permeate her. Lay there, an animal motionless, but her mind churned.

Lord!

Oh, Jesus!

Who is this? Me?

Jesus Christ, how crazy can I get?

Brethren, one day I'm going to write a book.

God, will I be able to write a book!

Ladies and gentlemen, let me put it to you fairly. I ask you. Don't put me down. Or up. Just answer me fairly, as fairly as I ask. I can give you the bare facts. The lady is a little nuts. Menopause, you know? The first, faint, remote quiverings. She ain't there yet, and it's going to be a long time coming, but it seems there is advance notice, and it seems I got locked within this advance notice. Don't fault me, kiddies. One day it'll happen to you. But answer me fairly. What do you think? But think. Don't go at it too fast. Think, like, with compassion. Okay, the question. Don't call. Write me letters. All right, the question. Please answer in a paragraph of less than five hundred words. More than five hundred words, you will be disqualified.

What?

I'm prattling?

Sorry—this is my time of life.

The question?

Of course. The question.

Wanna know something? I forgot the question. But the answer has to be in less than five hundred words.

Hold on! Hold everything!

I have remembered the question. This is the question.

All right, then. Here we go.

Ladies and gentlemen—

What?

You don't think the gentlemen should be included?

They *must* be included. That's the law now. What's good for the goose is good for the gander or vice versa. Otherwise you are guilty of the crime of sexism. Or discrimination. Or abuse of civil rights, or civil liberties, or civil civilities. We are always abusing something, it seems.

The question? Oh, yes, the question. I want you to tell me, in less than five hundred words. I want your opinions, ladies and gentlemen, about what you think about *my* method of artificial insemination, as yet unsupported by controlled clinical research and not yet approved by the AMA.

Right? Okay?

What is my method?

Didn't I tell you?

I didn't?

Right, I didn't. Sorry, but I ain't gonna. So hang on to those letters, less than five hundred words or you're disqualified, for some other time. Because right now, me, I'm just too goddamned exhausted. . . .

Promptly at twelve, he turned off the light, and turned from her, and lay on his side, and was immediately asleep, breathing quietly and rhythmically. He never snored.

In darkness she lay on her back, straight out, legs down, her animal-rutting for the nonce accomplished. Sooner or later, Mr. Most, the perfect specimen, would create gestation within her, and then she would flee. Back to Duncan. And home, and her people, hers and Duncan's people: bright, exciting, seminal, stimulating. Not like this gorgeous *klutz,* her sleeping beauty, who turns off at midnight. She detested this IQ genius whose brawny brain was wasted within his nurtured preoccupation: health. That was his thing, this brilliant dull bastard: health. His health, her health, people's health, everybody's health, a very worthy preoccupation indeed, but shit for her. He did have things to accomplish for people, and his health thing would help people, but he was so fucking dull, so narrow-funneled within this driving need to make people eat right, and think right, and do right for their bodies.

That's all there was to him—this exclusive concern, this concentration on his body, and others' bodies, and vitamins and nutrients and jumping-up-and-down gymnastics. There was simply nothing else: he was a solitaire without facets. Perhaps it was to admire—this single-mindedness, this genius-devotion, dedication, tenacity of purpose—but not for her.

She was a woman of many interests; his one interest was health, and it had begun to bore her to distraction. They had nothing in common; even their sleep patterns were different. He was a day person, she was a night person, and when he slept she wanted to romp. And it was all Duncan's fault.

But she could not blame him, dear Duncan. She understood, although she did not approve. Which was why she had acted the way she did. Which is why she had left him. Because poor Duncan, this once, was inflexible. Adamant. His mind absolutely closed against her bearing a child. Therefore she had to do it this way. It was necessary to leave him, because living with him she could not lie; he would know she was being screwed, and to what purpose, and it would have been hell. This way was better; it was the only way. Once she was definitely pregnant, she would leave this bore of a gorgeous man, this health freak with the genius IQ, and return to charming, lively, lovely Duncan, and he would accept her. She knew Duncan. Once there was a child alive in her womb, he would not turn his back on her. Not Duncan McKee. Once it was a *fait accompli,* and knowing all she had gone through to achieve it, he would, however reluctantly—and perhaps *not* reluctantly—join in the adventure.

6

CLARE BENTON, thanks to Seconal, spent a restful night. Ten hours in bed. Like dead. Awoke at eight-thirty, her mind numb but vaguely snatching for memories. Nothing came. She yawned, stretched, lay there, and awoke. Overwhelmingly. The play! Signing contracts at Donald Franklin's. Mr. Anthony Ashland. Dr. Reuben Grayson. Ms. Christine Talbert. Dinner at Sardi's. Miss Sue Robbins.

Out of bed and into the shower. Turns the water from warm to cold, gasps, jumps. But good. Refreshing. Towels vigorously, cobwebs clearing. Brushes teeth and towels again in damp places. Talcs and slips into scuffs and housecoat. Tea and toast in the kitchen, and a vitamin C tablet. Looks at the clock.

Sue had said she would call early. Said she would try to clear her decks so she could have lunch with Clare and perhaps they would do some shopping. Said she would call either way, clear decks or no.

Last night Charles had called to come over. She had refused. Bushed. Exhausted. Too full of everything. But on the phone she told him about Donald Franklin, and the five hundred dollars a week, and the dinner with Sue at Sardi's. But made no mention of Anthony Ashland, Dr. Grayson, Christine Talbert; now she wondered why.

The phone rang. It was twenty to ten.

Not Sue. A man.

"Clare?"

"Yes?" Tentatively.

"Tony Ashland."

"Oh, hi."

"Hope I didn't wake you."

"Wide awake."

"I'm before court. Thought I'd call now. Might miss you later." A pause. "You've—been on my mind."

"I'm glad, Mr. Ashland."

"You're going to have to cut that out."

"I beg pardon?"

"Mr. Ashland. Funny. Sue Robbins quickly picked up on Tony, but you persist with the Mr. Ashland. I'd prefer it the other way round."

"Yes. All right."

"All right—who?"

"All right—Tony."

"See you Saturday. Remember our date?"

"Of course." A moment's hesitation. "I'm looking forward."

"First words of encouragement. You beginning to come out of your shell?"

"Do you think I live in a shell?"

"Somehow, yes."

"You're an intuitive man, Mr. Ashland."

"Tony."

"Tony."

"Say it again."

"Tony."

"Good. I'll call you. Got to go to work now. And just between you and me and Sue Robbins—so am I looking forward to Saturday. G'bye now. Got to run."

"Bye."

She hung up.

Sue called at ten-thirty.

Lunch. Sue Robbins with Clare Benton at the Sea Fare of the Aegean.

"Beautiful, beautiful, *beautiful,"* Sue said. "Anthony Ashland. Mr. Anthony Ashland, no less. Honey, we're not talking about some con-man *shmuck* with hot pants and a smooth line of gab. This is Mr. Anthony Ashland, God love us. Honey, do you know whom we're talking about?"

"Yeah, yeah." She laughed. "Mr. Anthony Ashland."

"Smitten, I tell you. Smitten! The old boy is smitten. Cripes, even more smitten than I thought he was smitten."

Still laughing. "What's more smitten than smitten?"

"Honestly—even me and my bones—I didn't believe that Mr. Anthony Ashland would call up the very next day, and like practically the crack of dawn."

"Twenty minutes to ten."

"Hell, that's crack of dawn."

"If you say—"

"Which is why we're here."

"Crack of dawn?"

"Shopping."

"You're confusing me."

"What's confusing about shopping? I've taken off the rest of the day."

"The whole day for shopping?"

"Anthony Ashland, baby. We have a project on our hands, and what with crack of dawn, it's even better than I thought. We're going to get you a wardrobe that'll knock his ass off. Just remember you're not going to be going out with a Charles Ennis or somebody. This guy is a major-domo, whatever the hell that is. I mean when you travel with an Anthony Ashland, in his circles, the places he goes, you've got to goddam *look* right. And you're going to goddam look *right.* Not for the play. For the play you don't even need a fig leaf, hah-hah. And for the play people, who in hell cares *how* you dress. But this guy is a horse of another color, and for him we're going to spend the afternoon at Bergdorf Goodman."

"Bergdorf! Who in heck can afford?"

"Baby, you're signed for five hundred bananas a week. But even if you weren't—this is Sue here. Remember me? I know all about your little nest egg."

"That's not for wasting on clothes."

"Not wasting. Investing. Hell, if you didn't have the money, I swear to God I'd lend it to you. Honey, we're shooting for a top prize and I feel in my bones—you know my bones—that you've got one real good hell of a chance to win the whole works."

"God, I only met the man yesterday."

"You're going to capture him, baby."

"Suppose I won't want to."

"Then he'll capture you. The old bones don't lie. One way or another, you're going to wind up Mrs. Anthony Ashland."

"You're crazy."

"Yeah," Sue said. "Like a fox."

Lunch. Dr. Reuben Grayson with Christine Talbert and Audrey Chappell at the Laurent.

"Ruby," said Ms. Chappell. "I think what I admire most in you is your bulldog pertinacity."

"Pertinacity." He smiled at her. A handsome woman. Late forties. Good teeth, lovely complexion, good figure. A mite too heavy, perhaps. A little too beefy about the shoulders. And a little too beefy in personality. Aggressive. Her manliness came through. "Pertinacity," he said. "That's a nice word, Ms. Publisher."

"Thank you, Mr. Doctor."

"What do you think, Chris?"

"Pertinacious," said Ms. Talbert.

"Is that good or bad?"

"I agree with Audrey. Admirable."

"But nothing will help you," said Ms. Chappell.

"I don't quite understand."

"Your persistent campaign will avail you of naught."

"That would look good as a line in *Flare*. But in conversation at lunch—nothing. Care to amplify, Ms. Chappell?"

"We're enemies, Ruby."

"Now that's *not* a nice word. Enemy implies hatred. Hated enemies don't sit around together, voluntarily, at a civilized luncheon."

"And with this great food," said Ms. Talbert.

"Don't go psychiatric on me, Doc," said Ms. Chappell.

"I'm trying not to, Audrey. We aren't enemies. There is no hate."

"Okay, all right, you son of a bitch." Good teeth gleamed in a quick smile. "I'll amend that. Not enemies. Competitors. Does that suit you better, Doctor?"

"Doesn't suit me at all, but at least the clearer language is more worthy of you, Ms. Publisher. I assume the object of this alleged competition is our Christine?"

"Not our. Mine."

"Eat, people," Ms. Talbert said. "The food is delicious."

"You did it yourself, Audrey," Dr. Grayson said. "You put us together. You introduced us."

"A business matter," Ms. Chappell said. "You got very

big with that *Sex Without Snobbery.* You began to command a big audience on those stupid TV talk shows when your name was announced in the newspapers. So I persuaded Duncan to put you two together—kind of a debate. It went off beautifully and I loved it. It produced a hell of a lot of publicity for *Flare,* and that was the purpose. The purpose was *not* for you to encroach on me. I'm laying my cards on the table, Doctor."

"Encroach?" he said.

"You know what I mean," she said.

"Enough," said Ms. Christine Talbert. "I have had it, lady and gent. I am I. I live my life as I please. And I'm not some kind of shuttlecock in your weird badminton game on this Tuesday afternoon. Now, cut. I owe nothing to either of you, and I fuck you both. So either we have some pleasant conversation here, or I pick up my ass and walk. Now how do you want it, lady and gent?"

"Pleasant conversation and delicious food," said Ms. Audrey Chappell.

"Enthusiastically, my sentiments," said Dr. Reuben Grayson.

Lunch. Duncan McKee with Philip Donovan, treasurer and comptroller of Duncan McKee Associates, at the Harvard Club.

"A company check for fifty thousand dollars," McKee said. "Certified. Made out to Richard Crayne. That's C-r-a-y-n-e."

"Right," Donovan said.

"A ticket to London, England. The reservation for the same guy, Richard Crayne. For Wednesday, a week from tomorrow. TWA, BOAC, I don't care if it's Air-India. London, England, for next Wednesday, and I don't want any hangups. If it happens to be tight, then lean on them. Pull whatever strings you have to."

"Right," Donovan said.

"I want the check and the ticket in my office tomorrow morning."

"Right," Donovan said.

Lunch. Anthony Ashland with Mr. and Mrs. Clifton Arvel at Angelo's.

"Mr. Ashland," said Barbara Arvel, "you were wonderful, truly wonderful. I just sat there with my heart in my mouth. And a couple of times I broke. Had to hold my hankie at my mouth to keep from sobbing aloud."

"That won't hurt with the jury," Ashland said.

She was petite, very pretty, but because of her hair she looked older than her thirty-six years. Either she tinted her hair gray, or it was prematurely gray and she did not tint it out.

"And this afternoon it's the District Attorney's chance?"

"His turn to sum up," Ashland said.

"Is it fair that he gets the last word?"

"It's the law. The prosecution has the right to open and close. But it's not really the last word. The last word is the judge's—when he charges the jury."

"When will that be?" Arvel asked. For a large man, he had a surprisingly soft voice.

"Tomorrow."

"And the verdict?"

"Well, now." Ashland smiled, laid a finger along his nose. "With any other judge, the verdict would also be tomorrow. But not with Linwood. He's a lazy guy. In the morning I'll be making various motions, and then my requests for his charge to the jury. So will the District Attorney. Then we'll recess for lunch. And then the judge will charge, and that charge will take a long time."

"Why?"

"I know the man, I know how he works; I've been in his

court many times. If he sends the jury out tomorrow, it could mean that he might have to hang around until late in the evening while he and all of us wait for the results of their deliberations. Not Judge Linwood. He likes himself too much for that. So he'll stall around, and then draw out the charge until deep in the afternoon. Then he'll become very sympathetic with the people of the jury. Certainly they should go out to dinner. And then after dinner it's already evening, and it would be an awful imposition to have them commence their deliberations that late. So he'll sequester them, have them put up at a hotel for the night. And then the next day, everybody ostensibly clearheaded and refreshed, the jury will go to the jury room."

"Then Thursday we'll have the verdict?"

"Should be Thursday."

"What do you think, Tony?"

Anthony Ashland leaned back in his chair. He knew Cliff Arvel for many years, a solid man, intelligent, a thinker, a philanthropic man. Alice had been very fond of him; had sat with him on many charitable committees, had often shopped with him for antiques: he was a dedicated collector. And often the Ashlands had had dinner at the Arvels' home (when Barbara was still a very young woman) and the Arvels had been guests to dinner at the Ashlands' home. In ordinary circumstances, Anthony Ashland, defense attorney, would decline to vouchsafe opinion. But these were not ordinary circumstances, because the client was Cliff Arvel.

"In the bag," he said. "They'll come back fast, and they'll come back with an acquittal. And I can't swell up and modestly preen that I brought it off. No. Check that. Correction." A grin. "I'll preen. Because I brought in Dr. Reuben Grayson who *did* bring it off. In my opinion it was in the bag before Grayson—any competent psychiatrist would have been sufficient—but the great Grayson, the idol of the boob tube, sewed it up for us. And the judge knows it, and the jury knows it, and I know it, and the D.A. knows it. You're in the bag, my friend. Or—more properly I should say—out of the bag."

"Some bag," the large man said softly. "A dreadful experience." He took the napkin from his lap and pressed it against the sheen of perspiration on the rosy fleshy face. He replaced the napkin. He smiled fleetingly, wanly. "I'm of another generation," he said slowly. "Of another school, an old school. I don't understand this present generation; I don't understand permissive, promiscuous sexuality. I believe in the sanctity of marriage, I believe in fidelity. Am I some kind of anachronism?"

"Each to his own," Ashland said.

"I want to talk of this once, and in your presence, Tony, and then, I promise, never again, no matter what verdict the jury returns." He glanced at his wife, and then back to Ashland. "I believe a woman, or a man, can fall out of love. Fine. I don't believe that people should be bound within a marriage. If there is a new love, if there is someone else—it happens. Fine. If my wife is in love with another, then all she has to do is come to me and tell me, and we end our marriage and she goes her way. But I don't believe in cheating. I don't believe a wife can sleep with another man, and then, without hellish guilt, come home and sleep with her husband."

"There are those who believe, and practice, precisely the opposite," Ashland said.

"As you said, each to his own." His glance again was toward his wife. "I will say this to you, Barbara. Now. In Tony's presence. You have backed me up at the trial, you've been proper, pragmatic, the repentant wife, and I appreciate it. Tony believes I'll be acquitted; if so, you've helped to that end immeasurably. But if I am acquitted, and you do want a divorce, you may have it, and I assure you of full pecuniary protection."

"No." Her eyes brimmed with tears.

"Then this last time, this once and never again, here in Tony's presence. A marriage can end. If either of us falls out of love, should I want another woman or you another man, then fine—we talk it out and we part. But no cheating. No disgusting, back-street cheating."

"Each to his own," Ashland said.

"Yes, Cliff, I promise," Barbara said.

Ashland looked at his watch. "So much for the letting down of the hair, the serious discussion. Time for the frivolous now. For the fun and games of a trial for manslaughter."

"The poor bastard," Arvel said.

"Pardon?"

"The poor young bastard, dead."

"It's courtroom time, kiddies." Ashland waved to the waitress. "The check, please."

At six-thirty, at home, he was showered, newly shaven, and freshly attired. His appointment with Sawyer was for seven. He was to pick up the doctor at his office and thence to La Caravelle for dinner. The dinner would be social; the pertinent conversation would take place right here. It was an old habit, and it was contrary to present custom. He was resolutely opposed to the business lunch and the business dinner: business interfered with the pleasure of dining and he had found that it also interfered with his digestion. Important conferences took place at the office or right here at home. Now he glanced at a mirror, adjusted his tie, locked up, and went down to Benjamin Morse in the Bentley.

A good kid, Benny Morse, a law clerk in Ashland's office. An enterprising lad who knew how to turn a buck; one day

Benny would be a rich man. (He reminded Tony Ashland of young Tony Ashland in his taxi-driving days.) It had been Benny's idea and a good one (for Benny *and* for Ashland). The lad knew that on occasion, for certain occasions, Ashland would hire a limousine.

"I'll be your chauffeur," Benny said.

"Thanks, but I don't need a chauffeur."

"I mean when you rent a limo. Hell, Mr. Ashland, you've got *two* cars. Why rent a third when you can rent me at the same price to be the chauffeur? And like that you'll have the personal touch."

An enterprising lad. Good for him. Benny bought himself a visored cap and Ashland paid him ten dollars an hour for the chauffeur duty, and thus Benny Morse could augment his income and did. For tonight Ashland needed a chauffeur. To pick up Sawyer. To have a car waiting when they left La Caravelle. To take Sawyer home after the conference at the Ashland residence. The Bentley was a sedan, and with Benny up front in the visored cap, it was a limousine.

Ashland climbed into the rear and slapped the door shut. "First stop, 160 Central Park South. I'll pick up a guy and we'll go to the Caravelle. You'll hang around out there till we finish dinner and then we'll go home, my home. And then you'll hang around again while the guy and I have a long talk. Then he'll come out and you'll take *him* home. Figures about midnight."

"Lovely," Benny said. "A money night for me."

"More power," Ashland said, as pleased as Benny that he would be earning an extracurricular fifty bucks for an evening of sitting around in the front seat of a Bentley.

The lad was a good driver, no lurches, no short stops, and Anthony Ashland, thinking about Dr. Arthur Sawyer, was comfortable in the unaccustomed rear of the quietly purring sedan. Of course he had done a check on Sawyer. A-1 professional standing; top-rated amongst his peers. Forty-five years of age. Twice married, twice divorced. A bachelor now and a stud-about-town. Very popular with the ladies. A humper type. Well, hell, why not? More power, Doc.

At La Caravelle, a restaurant with a snobby-patrician reputation, Mr. Anthony Ashland was greeted by name. And with smiles, deference, enthusiasm. He loved it. Because of the impression it *had* to make on Dr. Arthur Sawyer. It is good to be a made man. It is good to be *Mr.* Anthony Ashland, renowned, respected, a perdurable hero in a city that perennially and cannibalistically destroyed and devoured its heroes. Not Anthony Ashland. He was up there on a damned well-deserved pedestal, and nobody would ever knock him off; not until he became old, feeble, senile, and could no longer practice his profession, and even then he would not be knocked off; if ever he lived that long, he would crawl off the pedestal and retire. But here he was at zenith, at this time of his life acclaimed, feared, and revered, and tonight he loved it because fame produces perquisites, however unconscious, and he intended to take advantage of the unconscious perquisites with this lanky guy walking the restaurant aisle alongside him.

Lanky. And damned good-looking. Of course. A ladies' man, a stud-about-town, you're not apt to be ugly. Tall. Very tall. He judged him at six feet three. Wore his hair long, and sported a thick Zapata mustache that went down at either side of his mouth almost to the jaw. A character type, brown-faced and eager-eyed; a strong healthy specimen beautifully dressed in tailor-made mod, and he smoked Hebra Superior Manila cigarillos.

The captain guided them to an excellent table and they each ordered the same drink, dry martini, and Ashland made all the jokes and got cozy, but the guy held his distance, wary, the psychiatrist fencing the attorney, and the attorney decided a second drink would help; and the second drink did help, the guy beginning to warm, and the marvelous food helped further: Sawyer's barriers gradually diminished under Ashland's soft assault. They talked of politics, women, books, sex, the Supreme Court, and the stock market, and touched, but only a scintilla, upon Rosemarie McKee. That would come later at home in the study.

It was a fine dinner but, surprisingly, even better than the food, Ashland enjoyed the company. Surprisingly, because the first impression had been disturbing. He had never before seen the man—they had talked on the telephone—and the first sight back there at the office had been rather a shock. He certainly did not look like a psychiatrist. (But what does a psychiatrist look like?) The first impression had produced the stereotype of the coxcomb, vain, banal, egocentric: the exceedingly long hair, the punctilious mod clothes, the sweeping Zapata mustache, the Hebra Superior Manila cigarillos which he smoked with élan and flourish. It had boded for a dull evening, but the converse had become the fact. The guy was quick, deep, at moments quite serious, but even the serious moments were skewered with humor.

Ashland enjoyed. The dinner and the company.

Later, in the study in the duplex at 825 Fifth Avenue, Ashland said, "What would you like to drink, Doctor?"

"A bit of brandy, please."

He poured the brandy for the doc.

Poured a Drambuie for himself.

"Won't you sit down, Doctor?"

The doc sat in an easy chair.

Ashland remained at the bar.

"First," he said, "a small speech. After that we'll get down to cases."

Sawyer smiled, sipped brandy.

"I gave you an inkling over the phone," Ashland said.

"More than an inkling, Mr. Ashland."

"Doc, right now we're kind of in conference. You're here with me this evening because of Rosemarie McKee. Good friends of mine. I would say Duncan McKee is my closest friend and vice versa. They're in trouble, the McKees. I assume you know that."

Sawyer nodded.

"Doc, I'm a lawyer and of course I know all about privilege. The privileged communications between priest and confessor, lawyer and client, doctor and patient, et cetera. I want you to understand, right off, that I've no intention to try to coerce you into breaching any confidential communication. I trust that's clear, Dr. Sawyer?"

"Yes."

"On the other hand, there's much we can discuss without impinging on privilege. You can help me with my friends, Doctor."

"If I can, I will."

"Good. Thank you."

"By the way, let me thank *you*. I believe I neglected that. Thank you, Mr. Ashland, for a truly epicurean repast."

"That was a bribe, Dr. Sawyer."

They laughed. Sawyer sipped brandy.

"She's left him," Ashland said. "Do you know that?"

"Yes."

"Do you know why?"

No reply.

"Okay, Doc. I'm telling you—you're not telling me. She wants to have a baby. Duncan can't make a baby because long ago he had a vasectomy. And even if he could make a baby, he wouldn't at this period of their lives. He is definitely against her bearing a child. That's why she left him, moved out. That's why she's presently living with another man. Do you know any of this, Doctor?"

"All of it."

"She still sees you?"

"Regularly."

"Do you know whom she's living with?"

"No."

"No?"

"She preferred not to inform me."

"You didn't inquire?"

"In my business, Mr. Ashland, the patient imparts information voluntarily."

"You didn't press—?"

"We're not antagonists. I'm not an attorney cross-examining a witness."

"Then I'll tell you, sir. Genetically, she picked a perfect specimen. But the guy she picked happens to be a fairy."

"That doesn't surprise me."

"Beg pardon?"

"No breach of privilege, Mr. Ashland. But she once asked me—hypothetically, mind you—whether homosexuality could flow through genetically."

"Can it?"

"No. But in view of that casual question she once asked, and in view of what you have just said, it doesn't surprise me that the man she selected to father her child happens to be a homosexual."

"You don't know the half of it, Doc."

"Do you, Mr. Ashland?"

"All of it."

"Well, bully for you."

Laughter again. They were getting along. Ashland liked it.

"Doc, let me ask you. Hypothetically, mind you. What do you think of all of this?"

The tall man with the long hair and the crazy mustache and the crazy clothes unbent from the chair, rose up and went to the bar, replenished his glass, and returned to the easy chair. He sipped brandy, crossed his legs.

"Hypothetically?" he asked.

"Hypothetically," Ashland answered.

"Well, hypothetically," the tall man said. "A whim, a mood, a moment at this woman's particular time in life. Not unusual. It passes. If it passes before a pregnancy eventuates, it is not too bad. It skims through and can be easily handled. But if a pregnancy does eventuate, we can sometimes be in a hell of a lot of difficulty."

"This one picked herself a fairy."

"But, as you said, a perfect specimen genetically."

"Sure. But she didn't have to extend herself like that. Didn't have to reach out that far."

"Why not?"

"She had as good a specimen right there at her beck and call. And without any taint of homosexuality."

"Beck and call? Who?"

A lawyer's pause for effect. Then: "You! Young, strong, pretty, and a hell of a fine mind." A harsh note came into his voice. "That's a whole big thing these days, isn't it? The shrink and the patient fucking on the couch. Allegedly, a new form of therapy—right, Doctor?"

"What in hell are you talking about?"

Ashland pulled his lips against his teeth. He hated it, hated the sons of bitches. He had sat with too many clients in private consultations; he had heard too many horror stories, shocking, revolting, bewildering. And nobody did a thing about it, because they were all of them so damned afraid.

"It's a bug with me, Doctor."

"What bugs you, Mr. Ashland?"

"Reverse prostitution, the sons of bitches."

"Lay it out, Mr. Ashland."

"Come on, Doc. Feel free. Don't shit a shitter. You know damn well. Kind of subterranean but it's beginning to surface. The shrink screwing the patient and he calls it therapy. Hell, they've even got a name for it. The 'love treatment,' right? So there you are, and there she is with you all alone twice a week. An attractive woman and her handsome doctor, and the lady wants a baby and the husband cannot make it. So why does she have to go out searching? Why doesn't she give *you* a little nudge?"

"Because she damn well knew better than that!"

The planes of Sawyer's face hardened. He uncrossed his legs. He set away the brandy, lit a cigarillo. No élan, no flourish. His brow was furrowed and his eyes were bitter.

Ashland said mildly, "What did she know, Doctor?"

"We discussed it a long time ago."

"A baby?"

"No. The relationship between the psychotherapist and the patient. She knew my attitude as concerns this alleged love treatment."

"What is your attitude, Dr. Sawyer?"

"A psychotherapist who indulges in sexual intercourse with his patient is a rascal and a scoundrel. Please don't misunderstand. I'm not setting myself up as an apostle of virtue. This has nothing to do with morals or morality. People in close contact do have affairs, and I certainly have no objection. I mean people like . . . lawyer and client, or investor and broker, or executive and secretary, or . . . the optometrist who falls for the nearsighted girl he is fitting for glasses. You know? But never psychiatrist and patient. *Because the patient is sick.* In the head. In the soul. In the psyche. If she is seeing a shrink, she is mentally or emotionally ill. And therefore, perforce, not fair game. Have you ever heard of—transference?"

"Yes."

"May I continue?" Sawyer smiled, crookedly. "We're on a subject deeply disturbing to me. Sort of, my *bête noire*."

"Mine too, Doc. But please go on."

"Transference," Sawyer said. "In the ongoing relationship between psychiatrist and patient, a transference evolves—flowing from the patient to the psychiatrist.

"A long-accepted psychological term, transference is variously defined as an adoration, a veneration, a total trust and confidence, an unconscious substitution of the parent image, a leaning upon, a *love!* Quite often a patient in transference attempts to elicit sexual reaction from her therapist, but of course the ethical therapist avoids any such involvement, any physical sexual involvement.

"Transference, Mr. Ashland. An important, powerful, potent therapeutic tool to be utilized for the benefit of the patient—*not* the psychiatrist. Therefore if he reverses the procedure, if he takes advantage of transference, if he succumbs to sexual temptation no matter what his excuse of unorthodox therapy, then it crosses over the line of mere seduction."

"Damn right," Ashland said. "It's a kind of rape."

"I agree."

"An invidious kind of rape."

"I agree."

"I know all about transference."

"Then why did you let me run on?" But the frown was gone from his brow and he was smoking what was left of his cigarillo with élan and flourish.

"A patient in transference," Ashland said, "is beyond the capability of true consent. Aside from the fact that she *is* a patient, and as such patient she *is* a disturbed individual, she is in love, she adores, she accepts, she *believes,* and she will go along with whatever her father-master-guru suggests."

Sawyer laughed. "I love you, Mr. Ashland."

"The law has it, Doctor, that one who takes advantage of a person incapable of consent is guilty of rape. The patient of a psychiatrist is sick. Mentally ill, emotionally disturbed, have it however you wish. If the shrink fucks her, he is goddam guilty of rape."

"I agree."

"Invidious," Ashland said. "Because no such perpetrator has ever been indicted, and has ever stood trial for rape in a criminal court. That day will come."

"Why hasn't it come? You're the lawyer, Mr. Ashland."

"Because it would be damned devilish to prove. Almost impossible. Hell, there are no hidden cameras; there is no *real* evidence; in court it would be the patient's word against that of the psychiatrist. Whom would a jury believe? The sick girl or the sane psychiatrist, who would insist that the sick girl is indulging in wish fantasies, that she is hallucinating. Whom would the jury believe? The poor bitch of an admittedly sick girl, or the suave sane psychiatrist, the expensive doctor? But *once* I'd like to get one of these sons of bitches in court. Just once. Because, I tell you, *one* conviction, and all these evil bastards would cease this subterranean, *sub rosa,* obscene practice."

"But you're a defense counsel."

"I would go in on the side of the complainant, on the side of the prosecutor. *Amicus curiae.* Friend of the court. Oh, Christ, would I love to get one of those sons of bitches pinned down on a witness stand." Ashland sipped Drambuie. "But let me ask you this, Doc. What about the bastards that openly admit to this practice? Of course those admissions are insufficient to convict them in a court of law. But what about them? Hell, some of them have even written books on the subject. What about the practitioners of the love treatment?"

"They're really very few."

"What *about* those few?"

"Sick," Sawyer said. "Sicker than their patients. Just as there are some sick lawyers, so are there some sick psychiatrists. Succumbing to temptation, they rationalize it as therapy. But when I discuss it with them in seminars, and I press in, they retreat."

"Press in?"

"I believe the legal term is *reductio ad absurdum.* They insist their sexual indulgence is a therapy for the benefit of the patient. So I ask a few simple questions."

"Such as?"

"Suppose the patient, qualifying for this alleged type of intimate therapy, is seventy years old, crippled, and ugly. Would our therapist—and could he—enter into sexual relations with this patient? Or, conversely, suppose this therapist had eight patients a day, day after day, all beautiful and all amenable to this particular form of therapy. Would he screw all eight of them every day, day after day? They retreat, Mr. Ashland. Retreat to a mumble of psychiatric jargon, and I readily admit that my profession, probably more than any other profession, has erected huge screens of opaque, incomprehensible mumbo jumbo.

"Look," Sawyer said. "It can happen, however infrequently, that a shrink falls in love with a patient. He's human. Then all right. Then he ceases being the therapist. He ceases taking her money. He divorces himself from the doctor-patient discipline. He recommends her to another psychiatrist. And then on his own, as a private individual, and with the new therapist fully aware, he can woo the lady, and if he wins the lady, then it's a fair, and proper, and private affair."

"We're not talking about that."

"Damn right we're not." Sawyer pulled an ashtray near, thumped out the stub of his cigarillo. "Mr. Ashland, I'm interested. How come my *bête noire* is so obviously also yours?"

Ashland's mouth tightened. For a few moments he was silent.

"Dr. Sawyer," he said finally, "a lawyer is on the receiving end of even more confidences than a psychiatrist. I mean, by the very nature of his profession, the psychiatrist is limited as to the number of his patients. The lawyer, on the other hand, has, literally, hundreds upon hundreds of clients, and the longer the lawyer practices the more these clients increase, cumulatively."

He added more Drambuie to his glass, sipped. "I am a criminal trial lawyer; that is my specialty, but it is not exclusive. I represent many clients in many other matters: the drawing of wills, financial matters, matrimonial matters, contractual matters, and divers personal matters. And they come to me, frequently, for personal discussions of personal dilemmas. Do you understand?"

"Yes."

"That's how I've become cognizant of this covert activity, this subterranean practice of sex in the office of the shrink. I consider it reprehensible. A psychiatrist is a doctor and a doctor is sworn to the Hippocratic oath. But to hell with the Hippocratic oath. There is the inherent moral responsibility, the *distance* that the therapist must maintain in this delicate interpersonal relationship—"

"I agree emphatically."

"Increasingly over the past few years, distraught clients have discussed this with me—without the culmination of relief or result. I have urged them to file formal complaint, but I *cannot* in legal practicality—as I've already explained to you—assure them that the perpetrator will be convicted. And even if I could, they would still be reluctant. Dr. Sawyer, you have no idea how many cases of rape—physical assault by a total stranger—go unreported. Because the woman shrinks from the public exposure of this heinous act committed upon her. And in the matter of psychiatrist and patient, the poor woman shrinks even further. Incapable of true consent under the influence of the father-image master, she nonetheless feels she did consent. Nobody physically forced her. Sometimes they finally do break off from this father-image bastard master, but then they're even more psychologically damaged than when they came to him."

"Absolutely. I can personally testify to that."

"But *once,*" Ashland said. "Just once would I like to get one of these bastards into court. Win, lose, or draw—conviction or no—just once! Because the resultant publicity would scare the shit out of the rest of these love-treatment hyenas. They'd goddam think twice before they'd give in to themselves, before they'd indulge themselves in sexual gratification with the poor sick girl who thinks her consent is voluntary but who, in fact, is under that black-magic influence. They're no match. She's sick, and he's all the way over on top of her. He is the confidant, he owns her soul; he is the father, the mother, the wise, the almighty, the pundit, the master, the guru. He goddam knows, when he's letting loose his nefarious libido, supposedly with consent, that that is no consent at all, that the poor bitch is incapable of true consent. He's got her hypnotized, mesmerized—call it transference—call it what you will. But the son of a bitch knows it. He *has* to know it. He *knows* he's taking advantage. He knows he's breaching the rules of the game. In his heart he goddam knows he's assaulting the woman despite her purported consent. The son of a bitch *has* to know he's committing a rape."

"Easy," Sawyer said.

Ashland laughed. It had begun as a game; his purpose to soften up the doctor. But he had become hoist with his own petard. "Right," he said.

"I cannot agree with you more," Sawyer said. "But I hope

you don't fall into the trap of condemning an entire profession. They are, in fact, a tiny minority. Some are out-and-out bastard criminals. But those who practice that way, these unorthodox people, these love-treatment people, are fringe people; they are really very few and far between."

"Doc, let me tell you about a case, a rather recent case, and then we'll get off it. May I?"

"Please," Sawyer said.

"A father, a mother, a daughter. A family. Friends of mine from way back; I was present at the daughter's christening. Grown up now, nineteen, a lovely girl. Then suddenly something hits her. She goes into a tailspin. Depressed. Withdrawn. Quits school. Hangs around the house, hides in her room, doesn't go out. A home in Westchester. Scarsdale. The father and mother, of course, are terribly concerned. The kid needs help.

"So they cast about for a shrink. They pick a big shot, well known, a Manhattan psychiatrist, very expensive. I'm not mentioning names. The girl agrees to go. She goes. In a few months there's a decided improvement. But it turns out the shrink is fucking her."

"How do you know?"

"Not only fucking her, but he knocks her up. Knocked up, the girl confesses to the mother. The mother goes down to the shrink. He absolutely denies. If she's knocked up, someone else knocked her up. Certainly not he."

"How do you know he's not telling the truth?"

"There you are, Doc. Always—how do you know? Always—how do you know who's telling the truth? A rape, this kind of rape—any rape—simply isn't performed in front of witnesses."

"What happened?"

"The father came to me. We talked. The poor man was out of his mind, distraught. I asked him your question—how do you know who's telling the truth? His answer—that he knew his daughter. She wouldn't lie about this kind of thing. Furthermore, she wasn't going out, she had no boyfriends. I said to the father—let's haul this bastard into court. Let's, once and for all, bring one of these hellish things out into the open. The father's a strong man. He agreed. He went back to the daughter, to persuade her to go to the District Attorney's office and swear out a complaint. She refused. Frightened. Couldn't expose herself like that. Cringed. Wept. Refused. The mother understood. And finally the father understood. And when he reported back to me, so in hell did I understand. And that was that."

"What happened to the girl?"

"She killed herself." Ashland sighed, shuddered, drank down his Drambuie. "The poor kid killed herself. Drove into New York one day, parked the car, went into the subway, threw herself in front of a train. *And there wasn't a goddamned thing we could do about it.*"

Silence. Sawyer lit a cigarillo.

Ashland left the bar and paced.

Hands clasped behind his back, chin down, he paced. He had wanted to soften up the doc for the one pertinent question, but in the softening process he himself had become entrapped. But the lawyer in him liked it: he now had a respect for the man's opinion. Without respect, he might have vacillated, perhaps even consulted another. There was always the brilliant Reuben Grayson, a great star in the galaxy where this guy was only a small planet. On the other hand, Mr. Mustache here was *her* doctor, and who would better know? Anthony Ashland, outwardly bluff, sometimes brusque, was essentially a sensitive man. He knew what to do about Ritchie Crayne and was certain he could handle him, but what about Rosemarie? You don't throw out the baby with the bath water. His problem: Rosemarie. Which is why he had arranged the appointment with Sawyer before the meeting with Crayne. He believed in expert opinion. Certainly he was not a psychiatric expert, nor was Duncan, and although they both believed they were plotting a project for Rosemarie's benefit—suppose the opposite were true. He had not discussed this aspect with Duncan; the guy had enough troubles going for him. It would be up to the doc now. The expert was here in the room with him, and during this long evening the expert had qualified to Ashland's satisfaction. Which way he would jump would now be up to the doc. If the expert's answer was positive, Ashland was certain he could carry it off. But negative—he would have to abandon the whole damned project and *then* explain it to Duncan.

"Rosemarie," he murmured. "We're back to Rosemarie." He ceased pacing. "Doc, I should like to pose a question to you. Hypothetically, of course."

"Pose away," Sawyer said.

"The guy she's living with. Suppose, suddenly, he ups and blows. Suppose, suddenly, without any explanation at all, he walks out on her. Disappears. What about the effect on her?"

Sawyer looked up, his eyes shrewd.

He damn well knows what I'm talking about, Ashland thought. This doc is no dummy. He knows that Duncan McKee is a multimillionaire, and he knows I'm Duncan's friend, and he knows I'm a wiseacre big-shot criminal lawyer. He knows we can buy the guy off, or threaten him off, or blast him off.

"What I'm asking," Ashland said, "is in that hypothetical instance could there be a—deleterious effect upon the woman? I'm not talking about normal reaction. Rage, anger, disappointment. I mean—a truly deleterious effect."

"Truly deleterious effect," Sawyer repeated.

Is the mustachioed son of a bitch having fun with me? Mocking the old boy? I'll kick him right in his ass. I'll take him by the scruff and throw him the hell out.

He stood there. Stood his ground. Waiting.

Sawyer puffed on the cigarillo. In the cloud of smoke, his eyes were smiling. But the voice was slow and serious.

"Mr. Ashland, I'm about to breach privilege. A tiny breach." And now his mouth was smiling. "In these particular circumstances, I don't believe a tiny breach to be an unforgivable impropriety." And the smile disappeared. "I have mentioned whim. Mood. I don't remember whether I mentioned premenopausal syndrome. But I'm rather certain, you being you, that you know about that, too. This woman, at a moment however transitory, desires the motherhood experience. And for that reason, she leaves her husband. But if you have inquired—and I assume you have—then you know that most of her wardrobe is still in her home, her various homes. When she left her husband, she packed a few bags and that was it. And remains it. It is approximately two months now, but she has never returned for the rest of her wardrobe. That has its implications."

"Like?"

"Like she *knows* this is temporary. A mood, a whim, a moment. An adventure. But when it is over, she intends to go home."

"She's told you this?"

"Of course not. But the implications are clear, Mr. Ashland." The doctor smoked his cigarillo. "And now my tiny breach of privilege. To good cause, I hope. Please remember she has continued in therapy; she has not broken a single appointment. She's never mentioned the man's name, and only from you have I had definite word of his homosexuality. But I know—shrink and patient, Mr. Ashland—that she isn't happy with him. That doubts have begun to beset her. That she is now worried, uncertain. That, however unconsciously, she has begun her retreat. Of course it's difficult for her. She is mired in a morass she herself created. But in my opinion—shrink and patient, Mr. Ashland—I believe, however far removed it is from the ultimate act . . . I believe she is already on her way home."

"I want your opinion, Doctor."

"I've given you opinions, Mr. Ashland."

"I want an answer to one, single, pertinent question."

"State the question, Mr. Ashland."

"You say she's retreating. Okay, she's retreating. But she has not—yet—retreated. What happens if the guy ups and goes before *she* does? He suddenly gives her the air. He walks out. He disappears. What about the effect—now—on her? Would it hurt her, harm her, hit at the psyche, knock her out of the box, cause her, possibly, to break down?"

"Would you restate the question, Mr. Ashland? More succinctly?"

The mustachioed son of a bitch is having fun with me. Well, hell, why not? I've had fun with him, too.

"Dr. Sawyer, my question, succinctly, is this. If the lover walks out on the lady, would she, hypothetically, in your expert opinion, suffer a nervous breakdown?"

"Hypothetically, in my allegedly expert opinion," Sawyer said, "no!"

7

WEDNESDAY. Clare Benton. Rush rush rush. Crazy Sue. Lunch again. Then shopping shopping. Spending money like it grows on trees. But I love it. First time in my life I've really lost my head. Like it grows on trees. But such gorgeous clothes. Never in my whole darn life such gorgeous clothes. The nest egg is diminishing. No, not really. Like Sue says, you'll put it back from the five hundred bananas a week. Every week, week after week, five hundred bananas. Good Sue, fat Sue, sweet Sue. Taking time off from her business. Hell, it's a quest, Sue says. I'm going to marry you to a millionaire. Hell, I'm greasing my own wheel, sweetheart. And Sue laughs her fat laugh and smokes her cigar. Honey baby, you'll be my federal reserve, Sue says. Anytime I'm short, I'll be able to come to you to borrow loot. You won't forget me, will you?

I'll never forget you, Sue.

Now home on Barrow Street. Trying on clothes. Hanging

away clothes. Then tea in the kitchen. And the phone ringing. Ringing ringing. Never stops anymore. I live with a ringing phone. Mr. Ashland again? He called early today. Don't think of him as Mr. Ashland. Think of him as Tony. He has a beautiful voice. I love his voice. Runs to the phone. It is not Mr. Ashland. It is Mr. Franklin. Reminding her the rehearsals commence Monday and telling her what time and where. Yes, Mr. Franklin. Hangs up. And the phone is ringing. Sue. Inquiring if Don Franklin called. Yes, he called. Calm down, sweetheart, Sue says. Relax. Take it easy. How do you know I'm not calm? I can tell by your voice. Right, Sue. G'bye, Sue.

She wants a long warm shower. She wants to stretch out in bed and just lie there. The darn phone rings. She wants to scream. She answers the phone. She does not want to answer the phone. Let it ring, and the heck with it. But she must answer the phone. Because she's a very busy lady these days, a lady with commitments. She's an actress in a play. That's definite, with contracts signed and all. And she's going to marry a millionaire. Not so definite.

It's Joe Bryan. God, I forgot all about Joe. Are you all right, kid? I'm fine, Joe. I haven't heard from you, kid, I was beginning to get worried. You been sick or something? No, I'm just fine, Joe. Can you come to work tonight, Joe says. Oh no, she thinks. How stupid of me to forget Joe Bryan. God, how dumb. I was going to call you, she says. I've got a job. I'm signed with *Open Season*. You know, Paul Rafferty's new play. Well, that's great, kid. Beautiful. Congratulations. Joe laughs, a happy laugh. Paul Rafferty, no less, he says. Well, good for you, kid. Now don't you forget to remember to stay in touch with old Joe. I won't forget, Joe. Well, goodbye, kid, and congratulations again.

In the bedroom now. Naked, ready for shower. The phone rings. Oh no. I don't *believe* it. Hesitates. Let it ring? Just let it ring? She can't. Takes up the receiver and her heart plummets. It is Charles. She keeps postponing him, but he won't stay postponed. She needs to be alone. She's told him, but he won't listen. She doesn't like it, doesn't like herself, postponing Charles, good dear sweet Charles, Charles the injustice collector. Filled with fright, she is fighting it off; she doesn't need Charles to set the sad fires going again. She is enough of a natural pessimist without Charles. She has been on the good side, the happy side, brightened by Sue, by contracts in Donald Franklin's office, by the attentions of an Anthony Ashland, by shopping for extravagant clothes, by spending like it grows on trees, by the marvelous excitement of numbing exhaustion. She does not want Charles, feckless Charles, to bring her down. Boring Charles, handsome Charles. Charles the useless, grousing always, sustaining himself by hitting at sorrows, a dumb-dumb hopeless actor who floats above despair by happily beating his wings against despair. He condemns, he sniffs his haughty nose, he arrogates, he despises his betters, he puts down, and like that he stays up. And thus Charles will triumph in failure for all the rest of his life. But his blatant, overt, jocund, self-sustaining pessimism reaches into her morbid, tacit, quietly flowing, death-inspiring, deep, and different type of pessimism. He has acquired and burnished a trick, a device; feckless Charles will never be defeated. He hangs on to himself by happily howling against the fates, but, no matter unwittingly, he touches points in her that she knows should not be touched. And therefore at this time she has held him away, postponing, pleading fatigue. But he does not listen. He keeps on calling.

"I'll come over tonight."

"No."

"Something else cooking? You got something on?"

She wanted to laugh. Hysterically. She had nothing on. No clothes. She was standing naked. Which is how she became a signed-up Broadway actress. Which is how she got the job with *Open Season.* Which is why she had put her signature to contracts in Donald Franklin's office. Naked. The gorgeous body. It had worked for her from all the way back. The beautiful face, the gorgeous body. Everybody appreciated. Especially the naked body. Including Daddy. And also Dr. Jason Goldstein. I mean when the gynecologist picks you, when Jason of the Goldstein Fleece picks you, you really figure to be the cream of the crop, no? And now another phony who had seen her naked was after her, but at least this one, according to Sue, was a millionaire.

"No," she said into the phone. "No date. Nothing."

"Then let me come."

"No," she said. "Charles, can't you understand? I'm strung out. I'm falling-down tired."

"Tomorrow," he said. "And I'm not taking no. I'll come over right after work. I'll pick up some deli and we'll just sit around and talk. Babe, there's so much to *talk!* Christ, just to talk! Look, I insist."

"All right, all right," she said.

Wednesday. Duncan McKee. He himself is the messenger boy. He himself delivers the check and the ticket to Anthony Ashland, late-afternoon busy in the busy office. And uses a phone in the library to call Christine Talbert at *Flare.* And after talking to her secretary's secretary, and then her secretary, he finally gets through.

"McKee here," he says.

"Hi, Duncan."

"I want to remind you about tomorrow night. Supper. You, me, and Grayson, at Christo's. Ten o'clock. I'm calling you because I can't reach him. You know he doesn't answer the phone when he has patients. And I didn't leave my number with the service because I've been moving around today, all sorts of meetings."

"That's all right, Duncan. He talked with me. Called me for the same reason as you; to remind me. What's with all the reminders, for Chrissake? Tomorrow. At Christo's. At ten o'clock. Because you can't get away any earlier, busy with business."

"Our supper's also business."

"We'll be there, Producer."

Thursday. Clifton Arvel. Pacing in the corridor of the Criminal Court. Barbara, alongside, must hurry her steps to keep up with him. They are waiting. The jury is out, and they are waiting. Nervous. Pacing. Killing time. Ashland, in the corridor, is surrounded by assistants, cohorts, and well-wishers. The District Attorney stands alone, a distance away, smoking a pipe.

A bailiff emerges. Talks to Ashland. Talks to the D.A.

The D.A. knocks fire from his pipe. Ashland comes quickly to the Arvels.

"Jury's ready. Let's go."

In the courtroom they all sit in their accustomed seats. The judge is not yet on the bench. The spectators in the pews are noisy. Arvel looks at his watch. The jury's been out—it seems like a year—for an hour and a half. That's supposed to be a good sign. Tony had said the longer they're out the worse it is. For any defendant. Rule of thumb for the defendant: the shorter the time the better. An hour and a half is short. Very short. Is it *too* short? Has something gone wrong? He looks toward Tony for a sign. No sign. Tony's face is impassive. Looks toward Barbara. She is pale, her eyes frightened, her lips sucked in.

A bang on a door. The clerk calls, "Everybody stand."

The door opens. The judge, in his robes, enters. He sits. Everybody sits.

"Your Honor," the clerk says. "The defendant is present, defense counsel is present, the District Attorney is present."

"The jury has a verdict?"

"Yes, sir. So we're informed."

The judge looks at the bailiff.

"The officer will bring in the jury."

"Yes, Your Honor."

Now the jury files in and sits in the jury box. The clerk polls the jury, calling each by name, and receiving acknowledgment.

"All present, Your Honor."

"All right. Proceed."

"Ladies and gentlemen of the jury," says the clerk. "Have you agreed upon a verdict?"

"Yes, we have," says the foreman.

"Jurors, please rise," says the clerk. "Defendant, please rise. The jurors will look upon the defendant, and the defendant will look upon the jurors. Now, Mr. Foreman, what say you? What is your verdict?"

"Not guilty."

Barbara is the first to reach him, fairly leaping upon him, her arms around his neck, her lips missing his lips, and kissing his nose. She is openly weeping. And now Ashland is there, smiling broadly, and Barbara kisses him and pumps his hand.

"Oh, thank you," she cries. "Thank you, thank you . . ."

Thursday. Clare Benton. Six o'clock on Barrow Street. All quiet today. Peaceful. No ringing phone. No shopping. Laughs. Yes, shopping. But not for clothes. For food. With all her whirling and swirling, she had neglected. Felt like bacon and eggs this morning. No bacon in the refrigerator, no eggs. Scarcely anything. And in the freezer, one noble frozen steak.

She had shopped. Dear God, shopped! Three different trips, lugging. The grocer, the butcher, the baker. Not the candlestick maker, hah-hah. She was all stocked up now, even with cans. Bacon and eggs this afternoon—with French fries, yet. And an English muffin heaped with butter. Boy, would Sue's eyes bug out at that. Simple food, but enough for a horse. "God gives and takes away," Sue once said. "He gave you a crazy metabolism. Me He gave fat."

True. Clare Benton did not worry about diet. Ate what she liked whenever she liked and somehow burned it away. And sometimes *really* ate like crazy. Like today. Bacon and eggs and French fries and English muffin at one o'clock. And at three o'clock, tuna-fish salad. With lots of mayonnaise. Mayonnaise. She giggled. That's a word I cannot spell. However I try to spell it, it comes out wrong. A hangup. And even when I write it down, and look it up, and it's right—it *looks* wrong. Hangups. Everybody has hangups. And, brother, do *I* have hangups. Mayonnaise is the least.

Giggles again. Likes the sound. Good mood today; I'm in a good mood. But what was I thinking? Oh, yes. Food. Ate at one o'clock and ate at three o'clock—and I'm hungry. Honest to God, right now I'm hungry. Nerves. Must be nerves. All the excitement.

The bell rings.

Flies to the door, peeps through the peep thing. Charles. Tall and handsome, his right hand latched to a shopping bag. She turns the locks and opens the door.

Charles comes in, does a bow.

"Hi, stranger," he says.

"Hi, Ennis," she says.

"Always absolutely gorgeous. You never cease to amaze."

"Thank you, Ennis."

He holds the shopping bag high.

"I bring gifts. In a Puerto Rican suitcase "

"A Puerto Rican what?"

"Suitcase. Where do you hide, babe? How come you're the

last to know what's hip? That's what it's called these here days. Shopping bag. A Puerto Rican suitcase."

"Charles Ennis the bigot."

"Not me. I think Hispanics are living dolls. Also, I happen to love niggers."

"Yeah. Where were you born, Charles? And how come I've never asked?"

"You don't know me long enough. And as long as you've known me, you haven't seen me *often* enough."

"Where?"

"Atlanta, Georgia."

"That explains it."

"Explains what?"

"Why you call blacks niggers."

"Now she goes superior on me. Look, babe, it so happens Atlanta's the beacon beam of Southern liberalism. You Northerners just don't understand. Or Midwesterners. Or wherever the hell Minneapolis is. Where I come from, it's a term of affection. Hell, that's what the niggers call themselves."

"But you're not one calling yourself."

"It's affection, for Chrissake. But let's get off the ethnic kick. Let's get into, like—you hungry?"

"Starved."

"Come with me."

In the kitchen he emptied the shopping bag. Brought out pastrami sandwiches on Jewish rye, pickles, potato salad, and a basket-encased bottle of wine.

"Chianti," he said.

"I can see," she said.

"Wow, this motherfucking Mother Superior. Just wants to sit on me, all over me. And I take it. I don't know why I take it. Okay, eat up, Mother, and drink Chianti."

They ate, then took the wine to the living room.

"Let's see the contract," he said.

"What contract?"

"You signed a contract, didn't you? I *hope* you signed a contract. And I hope *they* signed a contract."

"Everybody signed."

"So let me give it a *blick.*"

"A what?"

"A glance."

"I don't have it."

"You don't have your *contract?* Oh, Jesus, those mothers. You mean they didn't give you a copy of the contract?"

"They did."

"So that's what I said. Lemme see."

"And what I said—I don't have it."

"Who has it? If it exists, *somebody* must have it."

"Sue."

"She's got her own. That's the way it works. But where's yours?"

"Sue has it."

"You mean she talked you into giving her *your* copy?"

"She didn't talk me. I gave it to her."

"And you don't have a thing to show?"

"I don't need anything, for God's sake. She's my agent, for God's sake."

"She talked you into it, babe. Whether you know it or not."

"God, why should she?"

"Because she doesn't really want you to know what's in it. In the small type. Jesus Christ, Minneapolis. You're naïve, babe. These agents are all barracudas. They're not working for you. They work for the mother-producers. Because without the producers they're up shit creek. There must be things in the small type—that they can fire you out on your beautiful can, without notice, without severance, on *their* say-so.

Christ, a contract like that—a Paul Rafferty play—you take the contract and bring it to a lawyer."

"What good would that do?"

"The mother-lawyer would protect you. Your interests. An outside lawyer. Not a lawyer mixed with a barracuda-agent. Jesus, why don't you be smart? A break falls in like from holy heaven. But you've got to be Minneapolis, right? Don't know enough to protect your own interests. They're going to fuck you, babe. I can tell you right now. Five hundred bucks a week. Who are you for five hundred bucks a week? Okay, till they get the opening-night notices. If the notices are good, the show's a hit. The people buy tickets. Then they'll ease you out on your lovely can, and get themselves another naked broad, not for five hundred clams, but for scale. And they'll pay off Sue, give her a nice fat bribe, and she will tell you it was the small type in the contract. Babe, I've been all around that mountaintop. You just listen to Charles."

He was wearying her. It had been such a good day, happy, until now. Now he was collecting *her* injustices. She knew. She had known. Which was why she had tried to avoid him, her good sweet handsome Charles. It was his need. His disease. He had to rap out, rant at *them* out there, and suck in the residue. Like blood for a vampire. A need. It sustained him.

"Okay, all right, the hell with it," she said.

"Lemme tell you. Lemme just give you an example. The mothers, the barracudas, the agents. When I got up here, when I first got up here, I wanted a small guy; I didn't want to get lost in a big agency. I got tipped to a fella who was himself a beginner. He's a big wheel now, out on the Coast. At that time he was a shit, a nothing. He had four clients, and I was the fifth. But he liked me. He kinda dug me, you know? So one time we're sitting around and he says to me, 'Charles, you're a lousy actor. No offense, but in my opinion you're a lousy actor. However, you're a beautiful-looking guy, you got a hell of a lot of sex appeal, and this is the business you picked to want to make it. I think it can happen. I think if there's somebody behind you, one thousand percent working for you, something can happen. Somebody who's willing to break his ass for you. Somebody who'll depend on you to be his living. There's worse actors than you who've made it big in films. Okay, Charles, this is my proposition. I'll give up my other people and devote myself entirely to you. For fifty-fifty, you and me, a lifetime contract. Fifty percent, and I'm all yours.' "

"What happened?"

"I gave him the air, is what happened. Can you imagine that barracuda? He wants fifty percent of me for life."

"But he'd be giving his life to you."

"A barracuda. A leech. A blood-sucking parasite."

"So where are you now, Charles?"

"What do you mean—where am I now?"

"You're selling furniture in Bloomingdale's."

"But I'm not giving away half my salary, am I?"

"Cut," she said. "Fade out. Next scene. Let's, please, get onto something else."

"You're so right," he said, and grabbed at her. They wrestled on the couch. He tried to kiss her, but her mouth was closed. He released her. "What the hell's the matter?" he said.

"Nothing."

"You're sore at me."

"It's not you. Me. Nerves. The play."

"Doesn't even *start* till Monday. Cripes, today's Thursday."

She did not mention Saturday. Anthony Ashland was a famous name. Charles knew all the famous names. He would lash out with disparaging cross-queries. She did not want to quarrel.

"It's just—I don't know. All the excitement."

He reached for her again. She resisted. He quit. They drank wine, chatted stiffly. Obviously the martyr, he sat far away from her, did not touch, and at eight o'clock he left. She felt guilty, but to hell with him. Leaving, he had been darned disgruntled. To hell with him. What in heck did he think she was? A groupie-houri for a handsome actor? A charity bum who gives her body for pastrami sandwiches and Chianti wine? She sighed, shivered, turned on the TV, and lay on the couch. The phone didn't ring. Not once.

Thursday. Ten-fifteen. Dr. Reuben Grayson. Eating with gusto. A marinated herring in cream sauce at Christo's. Christine dabbles at chopped liver. McKee has skipped the appetizer in favor of a second bourbon. "They're putting out a huge new edition of *Sex Without Snobbery,"* McKee is saying. "The PR talked to me. She would like to hustle up some new exploitation."

"Then why in hell didn't she talk to *me?"*

"She knows you're reluctant."

"Damn right." Grayson laid knife and fork on the herring plate, pushed aside the plate, tapped at his lips with a napkin. "Look, I'm not going out on a tour for the paperback house. I'm not going out on tours anymore, period. I don't have the time if I wanted to. I'm back in active practice. Happily. No more performer. Those days are over."

"Ah, the rich," Christine murmured.

He smiled at Christine, but stayed with Duncan. The man looked awful. Drawn. Fatigued. Was he drowning his sorrows in cunt? They had the best in the land at their command, he and Tony Ashland. Whenever they required. Call girls, but not quite. Semiprofessionals. Actresses, dancers, models. Secretaries, copywriters, cool salespeople in high-toned shops. Rounding out income, tax free, by occasional service to a discreet, élite clientele. At two hundred bucks a crack. But Dr. Reuben Grayson was not supposed to know that Duncan McKee had sorrows to drown. The Spartan McKee was not one to ventilate distress. Grayson knew from Christine. There are no secrets, Duncan. How had the man put it? Benjamin Franklin, the eighteenth-century Renaissance man. "Three may keep a secret, if two of them are dead." Christine knew from Rosemarie. And Grayson knew from Christine.

"No tour," McKee said. "But the full slot on the Duncan McKee Show, you and Christine as the only guests. One taping. You'll make the tour without doing the tour."

"Wise man speaks in riddles," Christine said.

"No riddle. Syndication. We appear on independent stations throughout the country, and at different times. A tour without doing the tour. Dr. Reuben Grayson on different days and different times shows up all over the country."

"Ah, the chauvinists, the sonsabitch chauvinists. Notice he mentions Dr. Reuben Grayson. Notice he does *not* mention Ms. Christine Talbert."

"Beautiful. Glad you caught me up on it." McKee laughed. "That's going to be the theme. Male chauvinism. Ms. Talbert lashing away, and Dr. Reuben Grayson zinging back at her as devil's advocate. And should either of you articulate people begin to lag, I'll be prepared with a set of combustible questions."

"Oh, I'll bet on *that,*" Christine said.

"You'll be able to ride out your pet peeves, Ms. Talbert. The fact that there are no female priests among Roman Catholics. The second-class status of women in the business world. The degradation of the male-dominated American housewife. Your belief that marriage as we know it is already on its way to obsolescence. The Great Debate, with two great debaters. Audrey loves the idea."

Goddam right she does, thought Reuben Grayson.

"National publicity for *Flare,*" McKee said.

It's more than that, my friend, thought Reuben Grayson. The extremist concepts of the Women's Movement are bread and butter for Audrey Chappell, and cakes and ale. She's a bull of a dyke who hates men, hates marriage; she even hates children, who for her are the living, walking, mocking symbols of male-female copulation. Not Christine Talbert. Of another stripe, our Ms. Talbert; her homosexuality is not the essential pit of the fruit, not a fixation at the core of the psyche. She is gay by choice; she does not abhor or exclude the male. And I am that male, Mr. McKee, locked in combat with Audrey Chappell, but on my part it's not some jingoistic competition. I love the woman. And I intend to marry the woman.

He lit a between-course cigarette, heard them talking, pretended he was listening, but he was thinking about the beginnings of Christine Talbert. Smith College. Brainy, beautiful, and into her own at a time in the culture when intelligent women were striking off shackles. She came out of Smith a fiery feminist, and not at all the type at that early time of the emancipators. Not a square-shouldered bull dyke fulminating of hate and inequality as a form of compensation. Not this one, a tall, small-curved, splendidly beautiful girl. And after that *Playboy*-bunny piece, she was risen in the ranks, an acknowledged leader.

". . . Christine Talbert," McKee was saying. "Always a feather in my cap. Remember you're right up there. . . ."

Grayson smothered his cigarette in an ashtray.

After the publicity of that *Playboy* piece, she wrote, talked, appeared, lectured. To raves and huzzahs from the gathering army of indignant women. And to insults and derogations from the articulate bastions of male-established superiority. But she *was* a leader, a forerunner and therefore a fanatic, and her eloquent rhetoric had carried her a long way beyond the actual battlefield and, as Dr. Reuben Grayson was able to recognize, she was now looking back, wistfully and regretfully (impelled by unconscious impetus), toward some of the conquered areas that should never even have been attacked.

The girl was growing older. She had once been adamant against marriage ("a trap engineered by the covetous male"). And had flamingly proclaimed that children born outside of marriage would be so much the better, untainted by the insidious subservience of wife to husband. ("Bastardy is the filthy term created by self-protective males who themselves created the so-called bastards.")

But that had been the youthful Talbert.

She was growing older. Maturing, mellowing. Beginning a slow, subtle retreat under the patient guidance of Dr. Reuben Grayson. At thirty-three, she was still a rebel outside the establishment, but coming around. Slowly. You can do your thing far more effectively, he would preach in quiet moments, *within* the establishment. Compromise is the trick of maturity.

She was coming. Slowly. But she wasn't there yet, not by a long shot.

". . . and we won't impose on your valuable time," McKee was saying. "One session, one taping, and that'll be it. I can arrange that we do it on a Saturday if you like. Or even a Sunday."

Their steaks arrived, sirloins for Grayson and Talbert, a filet mignon for Duncan McKee. They ate, Grayson unusually silent, somehow grumpy, morose, but Christine, quick to sense his mood, took up the slack, chattering cheerfully, a happy magpie.

Not happy at all, Grayson thought. She doesn't want to do this taping, but how can she refuse? She's a big wheel in the Movement, she's their star TV personality, beautiful, articulate. And Audrey, of course, would love it. For three reasons. First, Christine would be expressing Audrey's views. Second, the publicity for *Flare*. Third, and possibly most important for Audrey, a public debate between Talbert and Grayson could serve to divide them, and any such division would be right up Audrey's alley; perfection for Audrey would be a permanent division.

Not Christine. This was one appearance she would prefer to avoid. A full shot on the Duncan McKee Show. Ninety minutes. With Duncan McKee, smooth and shrewd, in the middle as the interlocutor. The guy was a showman, and this type of show required controversy. Duncan would poke where it hurt, without meaning to hurt, because he was unaware (who was aware?) of Christine Talbert's difficult backpedalings. She no longer staunchly declaimed against marriage, nor did she preach of the efficacy of illegitimacy. There were more important matters, *real* matters, to fight for in women's rights. But the old matters were the sensational matters and they brought in the phone calls and the letters, and raised high the ratings, and Duncan would not neglect them. And what in hell could Christine do about it except hypocritically affirm? Could she refute herself on open television? The crazies would come down on her like an avalanche. A traitor! A turncoat! The young Christine had painted the mature Christine into a corner and she could not crawl out, on open television, without besmirching herself *and* the Movement. A hell of a quandary, hey?

There was more. She was going to acquiesce to marriage with Dr. Reuben Grayson. It was far away and long off, a tiny glimmer of light at the end of a long dark tunnel. He knew it because he was the doctor, and he knew that somewhere in her it was beginning to stir. Without her actually knowing. But it was there, a knot in the psyche, sufficient for her to want to decline a debate with Dr. Reuben Grayson.

A fight. A public battle. And again painting herself into a weird corner. He knew she wanted to refuse, but how could she? Why?—Audrey Chappell would demand. Why, why, why?—her women would demand. Why in hell did you turn your back on this golden opportunity? A full shot, the whole damn show on the Duncan McKee Show?

Therefore, fronting for Christine, whether or not she knew it, he would have to do the refusing. Not pleasant. Rough. Duncan was a friend, close, a dear friend, and Dr. Grayson was no dope. Duncan was not doing it for him, or for *Sex Without Snobbery,* or for Christine Talbert, or for the Women's Movement. Duncan was doing it for Duncan; it would be a hell of a show and Duncan would advertise it in advance all over the country and it would garner him an immense audience. So how, and why, and for what reason do you refuse your friend? You cannot plead time. The guy was willing to do it on a Saturday, or a Sunday, and he would have to pay heavy premiums. Double-pay, perhaps triple, quadruple to the technicians; the unions protected the workers. So how do you refuse your friend?

It came to climax over coffee. Friend looked at friend and uttered a single word.

"So?"

The answer was no.

"Why?"

"A number of reasons," Grayson said. "But two will suffice. One—I'm simply not your man for this sort of thing. I am *not* what is euphemistically called a male chauvinist pig. I am not on the other side of the Women's Movement. I am *for* the Women's Movement, except for certain of their small idiocies."

"Idiocies." Christine laughed. "Listen careful, children, to the man. This here is the man. Man speaks. Me, Jane. He, Tarzan. We swing in trees."

"Two," Grayson said. "I don't want it. I have had it. I'm not an actor, a public figure, a TV type. I'm a doctor. I did it to push the book, to make money. And made more money than I ever dreamed. Hell, I've a bank now—a bank!—to handle my finances. But that phase of my life is over. I'm a practicing psychiatrist, period. That's my work and I'm devoted to my work, and that's all I want to do."

A beautiful man, this Duncan McKee. "Yes," he said, "I understand."

And that was it. The bony face showed no sign of disappointment. He channeled the conversation to other matters, smoked his inevitable cigarettes, and when it was time he called for the check. Outside he gestured toward his chauffeured car. "May I drop you somewhere?"

"No, thanks."

"Good night, then. Night, Chris. My best to Audrey."

He went away in his limousine and they went home in a cab. Grayson's home: 330 East Thirty-third Street. Bachelor quarters. Four large rooms, male-decorated. And there, in the living room, he kissed her lightly and left her, and she knew where he was going. To the kitchen, the refrigerator. Champagne. If he had one weakness, that was it. She heard the cork pop, and then he returned with the tall black bottle. He poured, for her and for him, and raised his glass.

"Long life."

They drank.

"Audrey'll die," she said.

"I turned him down. You didn't."

"She'll be awfully disappointed."

"Nevertheless, she can't blame you. Look," he said, "it's not the old days. Once upon a time, she fixed up what she calls a debate between you and me on Duncan's show. It wasn't a debate, it was a discussion. And only a tiny segment of the show was ours."

"She rues that day." Christine chuckled.

"You bet she does. Because she herself put us together. That is, introduced us." He lit a cigarette. "You're still hers. She still thinks she owns you."

"What do *you* think, Ruby?"

"Still hers. I think, when you're away from her, like now, you still consider it cheating. A form of self-hypnosis. The inertia of habit. You and she are a team and you loved it as a sexual rebel, and your world out there approves and accepts. But you've come a long way, and you're still coming. Which brings me back to my point. You're not the same person who appeared with me on that long-ago show. And this would be the *full* show. You're not quite the fiery militant anymore; you've toned down on certain matters. But on the show Duncan wouldn't let them rest, and I don't blame him. The full show. Ninety minutes of just us. He'd poke for the hot topics, dig for sensation. Out there in front of the cameras he's a showman. It's his job to excite an audience. Audrey or no Audrey, you damn well know you didn't want any part of it. You're thankful I turned it down."

She sipped champagne.

"Right?" he said.

No answer. Sipped champagne. Then suddenly yawned.

"Tired?" he said.

She smiled, set down the glass, stood up, began to undress.

He loved it. Christine Talbert unclothing in the presence of a man; and in the living room. There was a time she could not do it, not even in a bedroom: her heterosexual shyness an illness. She had come a long way, his feline woman, his cat of a woman, her movements slow, sinuous, her arms thin, her belly flat, her hips round, her stick-up breasts small, pear-shaped. He liked his women more curved, more buxom, but this was not a matter of like. He loved the woman.

He was thirty-nine. He had had many women, but finally

this one had come; finally he wanted to marry. He wanted this one as the damn legal-wedded wife, matron, matrix, mother of his children, family. Legal-wedded wife. Not yet—she was not ready yet. It was still a long way off, but he knew it was possible.

Naked, she stood motionless, her little smile cryptic, her eyes hot; then she turned and padded toward the bedroom, legs long, undulant ass enticing. He killed his cigarette, grabbed bottle and glass, and followed. She went through the bedroom and into the bathroom and he ripped off clothes and joined her under the shower and they laughed, soaped, washed, kissed, slithered, touched, and this, too, was new, comparatively new, a part of his patient teaching; until him, she had never bathed with a man, naked together in a streaming shower.

They came out and rubbed one another, toweling, and he went into the bed and she went into the living room. He poured champagne, sipped, lay pillow-propped supine, holding the cold glass on his chest.

In the living room she took a joint from her purse, lit it, dragged in a deep poke. One joint. Nothing for him. He did not smoke grass. Another poke in the living room, and then went back with the joint and lay alongside him but not touching. And not talking. She smoked.

The gentle man, the patient man, he drove her crazy with his lovemaking. She had never thought it could be this way. Not with a man. Bulls. Beasts. Rampant cocksmen. She had hated them, the raping, rapacious, ripping, pummeling animal bastards. The first real experience had been at college. Eighteen and a virgin, at a time when "virgin" was not yet a dirty word. Back home she had necked with boys, and played with boys, and enjoyed with boys, but had never been fucked. And as a freshman at Smith she had necked and played and enjoyed with boys, but, unfucked, had been labeled a cockteaser. (Cockteaser! God, she hadn't heard the word since school. Was it still in the language?) She had cockteased because she could not quite take them. Enjoying, she had not quite enjoyed. They were too quick, too rough, too brutal, too sweaty and grossly importuning.

And then in her sophomore year fate had decreed Frederick Eubank as her prof in English Lit. Fred Eubank, young, unmarried, with an underground reputation of bestowing honor upon the best of his bunch by bestowing himself upon her. A cachet. To be chosen by Freddie Eubank was like being chosen Miss America. As a freshman, she had heard the rumors of this royal collegiate mishmash, and had not believed, but it all turned out to be true. Because King Frederick chose her to be his queen.

They began to date, surreptitiously of course, but the word got out in the underworld of Smith College, and Christine Talbert became *Numero Uno*. She got fucked, of course; the king made short shrift of her nineteen-year-old hymen—to her utter displeasure. Because the king was similar to the vassals: rough, brutal, sweaty, gross. Either she was too small or he was too large: every time he breached her upslung thighs, it was as though the back end of a tennis racket was rammed up her cunt. But she took it and kept taking it; it made her cock of the walk and queen of the campus. She—she!—was being laid by Freddie Eubank and, bruised vagina notwithstanding, she was the imperious peer among her peers.

Nineteen. Christine Talbert. Big in her studies and big as a writer on the school paper, but biggest of all she was Freddie's secret queen, and it went on like that, it went on for a year, and never once in that year did she have an orgasm. But, nothing new. She had never had an orgasm. Not necking with the boys, or in solitary experimentations with herself. Until age twenty—unorgasmic.

Twenty. A junior at Smith. A queen because of King Fred. More. High in studies. Big as a writer. Dean's list, an A student all the way. But at twenty she got a new roommate and began to acquire a new philosophy. And also acquired, at last, orgasm. The roommate was Mary Walker, transferred from Berkeley, a hip thinker, an activist, a proselytizer, a feminist, a large, strong, energetic blonde who was thoroughly devoted to the general cause of the Women's Movement, but was as thoroughly devoted to the specific cause of lesbianism. Mary seduced Christine, and Christine experienced her first orgasm, and many orgasms thereafter, and Christine joined Mary's movement, and gave the air to King Fred, who found himself a new consort among his students of English Lit.

She continued to date boys, but did not sleep with them; she slept with Mary Walker until their time of graduation and then they parted, Mary to the West Coast and Christine to a job on a magazine in New York. And then had come that project as a bunny in the Playboy Club. She had been perfect for them, tall and sufficiently beautiful, with great legs and a good shape; the difficulty had been the boobs, small for a girl as tall as she. But she had passed the personality test with flying colors, and they loved the fact that she was educated, and when they got her into the costume she looked great (the boobs skillfully and sexily bolstered). Thus she passed muster and got the job and stayed with it, taking notes, for four months, and then she quit and wrote that article for the magazine—a three-parter—which depicted the sexist denigration of the female, the bolstered boobs, the exposed legs, the crotch-tight costume, the wagging tail sprouting from the cleavage of buttocks, the simpering service for the male customers. It was a sensation. And even more of a sensation was Christine Talbert on television: she burst on the public like a bombshell. The Women's Movement then had been lagging.

It was a time of the bra-burnings and those who burned burned the public: ugly, vicious, angry little women. And now this one appeared on the TV, lovely enough to have been a Playboy bunny, but strong as a feminist. It goosed the Movement, set it onto its skyrocketing course, and Christine Talbert was acclaimed as the hero. (Heroine?)

Thereafter it was all milk and honey. She met Rosemarie McKee and swirled amongst the millionaires. She wrote, and whatever she wrote was snatched up at beautiful prices. And traveled, always to acclaim, and lectured, always to beautiful prices. And met Audrey Chappell and swirled amongst the élite of the gay world. And then came *Flare,* and she was editor-in-chief, and the milk and honey flowed.

Audrey. Dear, devoted, fine as spun silk, and a wonderful lover. They were lovers, and known to be lovers within the cognoscenti of New York City. But New York City was not the world, and for the world Christine Talbert dated men. Because she was an anomaly. A throwback to other times, this militant feminist: it shamed her to be known as a lesbian. She insisted she was *not* utterly lesbian and persisted in dating men. In truth, enjoyed men. Even sexually. Enjoyed cuddling, kissing, clinging, holding. And on occasion even got laid, and hated it (until Dr. Reuben Grayson). Because they were all alike, the males, the hammering animals. No matter how sweet, how charming, how gentle in the wooing period, once they got her into the feathers, once in bed, they were excited, aroused, and the animal took over; they grabbed, they squeezed, pressed, bit, hurt, plunged; the back end of the tennis racket rammed into her (until Dr. Reuben Grayson).

She was, essentially, a passive, an oral-oriented passive. She was a taker, a receiver, not a giver; she lay back and took; she loved to have her cunt sucked, and responded with orgasm, but gave nothing in return. She comforted herself by thinking of herself as the eternal female, the vessel, the unaggressive receiver, and loved it that there were those who loved it to give (it is more blessed to give than receive). Mary Walker had loved to give, but Audrey Chappell was the consummate giver (until Dr. Reuben Grayson). Then why did Christine Talbert continue to seek out men?

The élitist of the élite gay world put her down with a deprecatory term: bisexual. Audrey, more kind, called her a switch-hitter. Dr. Reuben Grayson, kinder than Audrey, used a term applicable to all human beings: androgynous. She herself called herself AM-FM, but of late the AM was taking over from the FM: she enjoyed her gem of a Ruby even more than Audrey. Nonetheless it was cheating; Audrey suspected there was sex going on between Ruby and Chris, but Chris never once admitted it to Audrey. Why? Goddamnit, why? Why was long habit more powerful than new occurrence? Why was she frightened of this new ecstasy? Because, in fact, she was unsure. All these years of females and now this male. Inertia, he called it. He was marvelous.

It had begun like it had begun with all the others. He was a handsome, vibrant, intelligent male, and she was attracted. And he had begun like the others had begun. Dinner, a play, conversation in a supper club. Dates upon dates, no hammering, no plunging, no attempts at sex, all sweet and charming, the wooing period. And then one night he had taken her back to his apartment, and they had slept together, and he had not done a thing: they slept. The next time she was curious, but the same: bed and nothing. Was he impotent? Asexual? She dismissed that in favor of wisdom. The man was a shrink, a psychiatrist, and he knew who *she* was, and he was playing it cool, the male chauvinist son of a bitch. He continued to play it cool and her curiosity continued to prick; time after time, naked in bed: nothing, they slept. Until she made the first move, Christine Talbert the unaggressive; she touched him, ran fingers along his body, kissed him; and even then he had not seized, plunged, pummeled. They had necked, like kids, like her adolescents in the old days. Was he wise or was he sick? He was not sick.

Because at last, one night—by then she was thoroughly accustomed to being naked with him—*he* had finally kissed *her,* her mouth, neck, shoulders, breasts, gently, lightly, and then down along her stomach, her legs, her toes, and up, and along her thighs, and between her thighs, and at her cunt, and at that hidden hooded point within her cunt—*and, oh my God!* A tongue like the point of a red-hot poker, a tireless licking burning tongue, and hot sucking lips and teeth that nibbled softly. God, the man was the cuntlapper divine; superior even to Audrey Chappell. He was gentle but devious, artful, adventurous, extraordinarily skillful, and she came and came, rearing to him, orgasm after orgasm, and he did not let up until she was limp, sobbing, blissfully exhausted, and even then—she wouldn't have refused him—he did not use her for himself. He used himself. He jerked off. Masturbated. She had never before seen a man masturbate. On his back, openly masturbating. And then the geyser of semen sprayed high and descended on them, and he went out of the bed for a towel, and wiped her, and wiped himself, and flung away the towel, and doused the light, and took her in his arms and they slept.

And so it had gone with him, her remarkable male lover, date after date. First the long, excruciating cunnilingus, and then he masturbated, using himself so as not to abuse her. And again she had been confused. A nut? A deviate? A sexual eccentric? She had wanted to find out, and learned that this wise and patient man had wanted her to *want* to find out; she herself had initiated their first experience at coitus. Oh, he was wise, and patient, but damn clever. She had asked: "Don't you ever fuck?"

"Of course I do."

"You don't have a feeling to fuck me?"

"I'm dying to."

"Then why don't you?"

"I—I'm afraid of you."

"Don't be afraid."

No back end of the tennis racket. No plunging, no ramming. He had slid it in, gently gently, and had fucked her gently, slowly and gently, and she had begun to respond, for the first time in her life, arching up, receiving him, enjoying the feel of penis in vagina, moving with him until he came, his hot ejaculation flooding her cunt, and she loved the feel of it in her. No orgasm. Until this day no orgasm during coitus, but she loved it, she loved it all, because she loved him.

And now in bed she could no longer wait. Wiped out what was left of the joint in an ashtray, and touched him. He took a last sip of the champagne, set away the glass, smiled that sweet little-boy smile, turned, took her, kissed her.

Friday. Clare Benton. Noon. In bed, reading. Nervous. At four she has an appointment with Jason of the Goldstein Fleece. Not nervous about Jason. Nothing. Normal. The regular checkup, and prescriptions for pills. She is nervous about tomorrow, the dinner date with Tony Ashland, and nervous about Monday, the start of rehearsals. But why in heck be nervous about the darn rehearsals? Let the bigwigs be nervous, the real actors. She was nothing. One scene. One lousy, little, nothing scene, and she knows the part by heart, she knows it backward. She reads the book and doesn't know what in heck she's reading. The pages don't turn; no concentration. The phone rings; she is glad to lay the book away. It is Tony Ashland.

"How are you, dear?"

"Oh, fine. Great."

"No complications about tomorrow?"
"None at all."
"I'll pick you up at eight."
"Fine."
"That's not too late, is it?"
"Of course not."
"I mean for dinner."
"Of course not."
"Just remember, don't eat." He laughed. "Be hungry."
"I'll be."
"G'bye, then. I'm jumping in for my swim."
"Swim?"
"I'm in my gym."
"Oh."
"See you tomorrow. I'm really looking forward."
"Me too. Bye, Tony."

Hangs up, lies there, heart pounding. Not quite the way she wanted it; she had hoped he would ask her to meet him. On the outside. But he was coming here, her millionaire—Sue's millionaire—he was coming here to her lousy little apartment on Barrow Street. No, it wasn't a lousy little apartment. It was a nice little apartment. But, I mean, for a millionaire? And she is out of the bed, putting things away, already cleaning up for him, tidying. And her heart is pounding like mad. Thumping. And she leaves off tidying and goes to the bathroom, to the medicine cabinet, for a Valium.

At a quarter to nine on Friday evening, Anthony Ashland was ready for Mr. Ritchie Crayne. Attired in slacks, loafers, and white silk sport shirt, he lounged in the swivel chair by the desk in the study, reviewing the office copy of Ralph Hanson's report. He sighed and laid it on the desk beside the certified check and the airplane ticket, opened a drawer, took out the loaded pistol, and placed it near Hanson's report.

Hell, if the guy saw it and didn't like it, that would be just too bad. It was his home, not Ritchie Crayne's, and if he chose to keep a gun on his desk like a bibelot, that was his business, not Ritchie Crayne's. It was not there as a bibelot. It was there as protection. He was fairly sure of the guy, but he *was* going to insult him, and you never know which way a crazy cat will jump. Could be—possible—the guy might get violent. He was twenty-nine and a phys-ed health man. Anthony Ashland was fifty-four and a trial lawyer. In terms of fracas, they were unevenly matched, but a gun was an equalizer. He smiled, recollecting. That's what the hard boys used to call a piece in the old days—the equalizer.

He looked up toward the clock on the wall, and then, still smiling, leaned back in the chair and closed his eyes and thought fleetingly about Clare Benton. And shook it off. He shook her off. One step at a time, one thing at a time. This was Duncan's time and Crayne's time; not the time for enchanting ruminations. He remained in the swivel chair, eyes closed, resting but not dozing. The buzzer sounded.

It was the doorman downstairs.

"A gentleman to see you," the doorman said through the intercom. "A Mr. Crayne."

"Yes. Please send him up."

He waited in the foyer. And waited. Where in hell was he? Why the delay? Probably combing his hair in a mirror. Primping or something. Mr. Most Attractive, by your leave. Finally the bell rang; he opened the door.

"Hi," he said.

"Good evening."

"Come in."

"Thank you."

He led him through to the study.

Mr. Most Attractive, looking damned attractive, stood in the middle of the room. Stood there, eyes darting about, appraising. Stood confidently. Arrogantly.

"Very lovely," he said.

"Sit down."

The young man sat. Ashland sat in the swivel chair by the desk. He wondered if the darting eyes had taken in the gun. If so—no untoward effect. Mr. Most sat comfortably. Cool and contained.

"Mr. Crayne, I assume you know why you're here."

"You invited me."

"I assume you know why I invited you."

"You mentioned you'd be representing Mr. McKee."

The son of a bitch, cool and contained, was fencing with him. Well, sonny, this is *not* a fencing match.

"Mr. Crayne, we're interested in your affair with Rosemarie."

"We?"

"Duncan McKee and I. That's plural. We."

"I didn't know you were personally interested."

"So now you know." Irritation put a burr in Ashland's throat. His voice thickened. "My dear Mr. Most, if this were an ordinary love affair, then neither McKee nor I would presume to interfere."

"But you are interfering."

"Not an ordinary love affair."

"Says who?"

"You're a faggot."

The young man smiled. Big-toothed, healthy.

"Flattery," he said, "will get you nowhere."

"Not an acey-deucy faggot. A faggot faggot. No interest in women. You cannot make it with a woman." Abruptly Ashland took up the copy of Ralph Hanson's report. He turned pages and read rapidly. He read aloud of Crayne's arrest in Los Angeles at age twenty, and of his second arrest at age twenty-two. And turned pages and read aloud the names of gay-world intimate friends, friends in Los Angeles, San Francisco, Las Vegas, Miami, and New York, and read the statements of those friends and of Crayne's admissions to the friends, and the sum of it all was ineludible: Richard Crayne was a male incapable of sexual intercourse with a female.

The reading took a long time, a hell of a long time. Ashland's mouth was dry, he longed for a sip of Drambuie, but he would not leave the desk on which lay the pistol. Finally he was finished with this section of the reading, looked up from the report, and was pleased with what he saw. The gleaming smile was gone; instead the upper lip was gleaming—with beads of perspiration. And the handsome eyes were no longer arrogant; they were staring, bugged, downright respectful. The fencing match was over. Palpably—it was inscribed on his face—the young man realized he was out of his league.

"How we doing, Ritchie?"

"You—you're doing all right, sir."

"I'll do better." Took up the report, turned pages. "Your salary at LaLanne's, three hundred bucks a week. In your savings bank, your life savings—twelve hundred dollars. Your checking account, it swings between four and eight hundred bucks. That's no capital, no capital at all, to meet Sir Spencer Poole's gracious offer."

"Oh Jesus, you know that, too."

"I know it all. Now let me have it straight out, my friend. Let's level here, you and I. For whatever reason Rosemarie picked you, you took up with her in the hopes of hitting her for that fifty gee. Your chance of a lifetime. Right or wrong?"

"Right."

"And thus far you haven't been able to make it. You're no dummy, you're the man with the IQ. You know when you can and when you can't. You've been living with her, studying her. And up to now, you know you can't. You can't hit her for a straight-out, flat-out fifty thousand bucks. Right or wrong?"

"Yessir. Right."

Ashland tossed Hanson's report to the desk, took up the gun, and leveled it at Crayne.

"I can kill you, Ritchie. Right here and now you can be dead, and all your ambitions dead with you. And I can get away with it." With his thumb, he released the safety catch. "Like this," he said. "You stole my friend's wife. I asked you here in order to try to bribe you—to release my friend's wife back to him. You were insulted, you attacked me. I defended myself. With a pistol, legally permitted to me. I fired, you died. I'm Anthony Ashland—not some hoodlum on the streets. I tell my story, and they believe me. Like that, this whole thing can be finished. You're dead, I'm vindicated, and McKee's wife returns to him. But we're too civilized for that method of reprieve, aren't we, Mr. Crayne?"

"Are we, Mr. Ashland?"

"I think we are. Don't you?"

"I—I don't know."

Ashland stood up. Carrying the gun, he went to the bar. Laid the gun on the bar and poured a Drambuie. Left the gun on the bar, settled in an easy chair, and sipped the liqueur. This kid was in the bag, a docile kitten; all the rest was mop-up. He had further to impress him, and then get him the hell out. Rosemarie was already home.

"There is a second method," he said. "McKee and I discussed it." The smile was back on the young man's face, but it was a pallid little smile now. Bless the high IQ. It is good to know that the antagonist knows he is far and away out of his depth.

"Second method like what?" Crayne said.

"McKee is a powerful man in this town, with powerful friends. We discussed the utilization of these particular friends. Two or three of them might run into you one evening." Ashland shook his head sadly. "To awful detriment. They'd break your legs, Mr. Crayne, and break your nose, and slash you, possibly blind you. You'd wind up a wheelchair case, and for the world it would be another mugging on our rotten streets. We decided that, too—unless you were utterly unresponsive to our talk here this evening—would be uncivilized."

"What, sir, is civilized?"

"Duncan McKee is civilized." Ashland sipped the Drambuie, left it, stood up, and paced. "McKee is a businessman, he thinks in business terms, and somehow he admired your business acumen. You're a gay guy who cannot make it with a woman, yet somehow you captured *his* woman, for *your* business reasons. He liked it. He liked the push and go. Objectively, he admired. And therefore he came around to a third alternative. Which leaves you not dead, which I could have accomplished for him, and leaves you not a wheelchair case, which his powerful friends could have accomplished. It leaves you, in fact, a rich son of a bitch."

Ashland was a trial lawyer. He knew how to do his thing dramatically. He strode to the desk, lifted the check, and deposited it in Crayne's hands.

"A certified check for fifty thousand dollars. McKee's token of appreciation anent your business acumen. Now listen to me, son. Listen to me good, and listen hard." He plucked the airplane ticket from the desk, and tossed it into Crayne's lap. "This is the story, and it has no sequel. You've got the fucking fifty thousand bucks you're after, courtesy Duncan McKee's whim. And that's an airplane ticket for you to get out of this country on Wednesday. Clear?"

"Yessir."

"Stand up."

The healthy young man stood up.

"Shake hands with me, you little son of a bitch."

They shook hands. Ashland spat on the palm that Crayne released. "I think you're a shit," he said. "My impulse is to belt you right in the mouth. But I'm being civilized, under Duncan McKee's auspices. You've got your money and you've got your ticket. Now this is the contract. Are you listening?"

"Yessir."

"You'll pack up and you'll blow—without a word to Rosemarie McKee. And never, for the rest of your life, any word. If ever there's any contact between you and Rosie—it's your story that you packed her in, you just couldn't stand her anymore. And never—ever!—any word that McKee bought you. Because if any such word comes to Rosie, it can only come from you. And if that happens, at any time, no matter where you are, I promise you—you're dead. Do you understand that, Mr. Ritchie Crayne?"

"Yes."

"Dead."

"Yes."

"I want that very clear. I want you to repeat after me, 'I'll be dead.' "

"I'll be dead."

"Okay. You've got your money and you've got your ticket and you know our contract. That's it." He took him by the arm and hustled him to the door. "G'bye, Mr. Crayne. Good luck. Now get out of here." He opened the door. "Out. Before I vomit."

"Yes. Thank you for everything."

"Out!"

He pushed him through, slammed the door, and turned the locks.

8

AT EIGHT O'CLOCK on Saturday, dressed and shiny, and happy, she was ready. Nervous, yes. But happy. It had been a good day all day, and a beautiful day, bright and sunny. Last night had stunk. In bed early, she had read until tired, but then—no sleep. Tossed and turned. And finally to the bathroom for Seconal—two!—but they had worked like magic. Slept like a top. And awoke clear-headed, no drag, to sunshine on the blinds. And felt good. Good! She knew it would be an up day.

She had cleaned the apartment, cleaned like crazy, until it was sparkling spick-and-span. And then—sweaty, hot, dusty—a shower, and then into the tub, imbued with bath oil, and lay there resting, languidly soaking. An up day, a good day, and she knew it would be a grand evening. As Sue would say, she felt it in her bones.

And then out of the tub and rubbing with a towel, she thought about liquor. The gentleman was coming a-calling; certainly the lady should offer a drink. Scotch. She remembered in Sardi's he had ordered a Scotch sour; she and Sue had had martinis. And so in the kitchen she opened a cabinet and inspected her meager stock; well, not so meager, she thought. Lying on their sides, three bottles of wine. And upright, a bottle of Scotch, unopened. Also upright, a bottle of gin, half full, and a bottle of vodka, half full. That was it.

And looked in the cookbook—in back of the book under "Beverages"—to see how to make a sour. An ounce and a half of whisky, three-quarters of an ounce of lemon juice, a teaspoonful of fine granulated sugar. Shake in ice and strain into a glass prepared with a slice of orange and a cherry. She had oranges—but no lemon, no fine granulated sugar, and no cherries. But suppose he wanted a martini. Well, heck, at least she didn't have to look in the cookbook; she knew how to make a martini. But there was no dry vermouth and no olives.

So she had pulled on jeans and a sweater and gone out into the bright afternoon, and everybody loved her. "You always make my day," the man in the liquor store said. And the grocer, a little old man, had smilingly murmured, *"Bella, bella, bellissima,"* when she paid for the lemons, the box of confectioner's sugar, the bottle of olives, and the bottle of maraschino cherries.

And now at eight o'clock, the apartment spotless, the drink ingredients sitting on the kitchen counter, she was ready, all dressed up in Bergdorf finery. And sneaking glances in the mirror. And loving the clothes. And loving herself, for a change. A good day, a happy day.

The downstairs bell rang and she froze, rooted, paralyzed; in the mirror her face was pale. Then she moved. To the button, and pushed hard with her thumb. And at the door she opened the locks and waited. And the bell rang, and she restrained herself, counting up to five, and then opened, and there he was—tall, distinguished, a beautiful man.

"Hi. Come in."

He smiled, entered, looked about.

"Pretty. A very pretty place."

"Thank you, sir." Did a little curtsy. Her heart was hammering. "Would you—like a drink?"

"We'll save that for another time. I don't want to be late for our reservation."

"Yes."

Perfect. When it's a good day, it's a good day. She was so darn nervous she probably would have mixed the drink all wrong. Or spilled it all over her new dress.

"At the risk of being repetitive," he said.

"Beg pardon?"

"You're absolutely breathtaking."

"Thank you, sir."

She got her wrap (Bergdorf's) and they went out and he led her to a gleaming Jaguar—a Jag!—and gallantly helped her in and went round and they took off.

"It's been a lovely day," he said.

"Just beautiful."

He talked about the weather, and lightly about other light matters, and she appreciated. A good man, a smart man, wise, sensing her nervousness, easing her past it. Thank you, Mr. Ashland.

"Hungry?" he asked.

"Famished." But, in truth, no appetite at all.

"The Four Seasons," he said. "Do you like the Four Seasons?"

"Of course."

She had never been there in her life.

The Four Seasons was large, sumptuous, spacious, glittering, and at the table, the waiter hovering, Ashland inquired as to what she wanted to drink, and when she hesitated, he said, "How about a Gibson?"

Thank God she knew what a Gibson was. Sue sometimes drank them. Same as a martini, but with a pearl onion.

"Love it," she said.

The Gibson was delicious, smooth, ice-cold, and she drank a lot of it quickly, and it helped, warming her, dissolving some of her nervousness; but then the menus were presented, and she was confused, and the good sweet wise man charmingly made suggestions and she avidly accepted them, and it was the best darn food she had ever eaten, and even as she ate her appetite returned, and a good deal of that was due to him because he kept her mind off herself with a running monologue of chitchat and gossip. He talked about *Open Season*, and of the peculiarities of the playwright, and of the peccadilloes of the lady-star, Beatrice Smith, and of the eccentricities of the producer-man, Donald Franklin, and it was only during dessert that he brought it around to her.

"Monday's rehearsal, isn't it?"

"I'm scared stiff."

"Nonsense," he said. "Just keep in mind yours is a small role and you're damn perfect for it. The big troubles and the rewrites will come with the major people in the major scenes. I'll give you this advice, though. During the early days, when your heart is still up there in your mouth, then out of the theatre and in your personal life—concentrate on your hobbies."

"I don't have any hobbies."

"None?"

"Do you?"

"Well, golf. Do you play?"

"I don't know what golf is all about."

"I'll teach you. No, I mean, one day I'll get a pro to teach you."

"Is it necessary?"

"You'll love it."

"I shoot."

"You what?"

"Shoot." She laughed. "Not since I've been in New York. Shoot, you know? Handguns. Pistols. Target stuff. It was my father's hobby, pistol shooting, and he taught me from the time I was a little girl. I am—I was—good. A darn good shooter."

"Me too." And *he* laughed. "We're on common ground. Me too, a pistol shooter. I belong to a gun club, and I'll get you to join. Definitely. We'll shoot together."

"Well, well," she said. Naughtily. Happily.

And so in the dark of the evening they left the Four Seasons and he took her to the Rainbow Room (so different from the Four Seasons), sixty-five stories high in the sky, dimly lighted, romantic music softly playing. They were ushered to a secluded table and there he ordered sparkling Burgundy, by brand name and vintage year, and they drank the full-red wine, and she grew drunk—happily, sentimentally, romantically drunk—and they danced to the soft slow music, and her hand around him could feel the hard muscles of his back, but her nether regions felt another hardness, his penis at the crook of her thighs, and she moved forward to it—as he moved back and held back. But she did not permit him his respite. She moved forward to him, arching her lower torso forward until there was contact again, and somehow spitefully (death wish?) hinged herself upon it. God, he was an old man but his thing felt thicker, longer, harder, hotter even than Charles's. She wriggled against it, moved subtly, salaciously—but why? Why? She was a little drunk but not *that* drunk. She was attracted to him, definitely sexually attracted, but why suddenly was she so much out of character, pressing in on him like some kind of warped nympho? Why? Why? Death wish? What was she trying to prove? Was she trying to make him come, an involuntary ejaculation, during this crazy, romantic, soft-music, perpendicular fornication? Was her damned inferiority trying to prove some insane superiority? Or was it all death wish? Was she, in advance, trying to destroy something she knew could possibly be good? But she did not let up, could not resist the drive of impulse, continued to move, wriggle, close, subtly, and felt his thing there at her crotch, and liked it, enjoyed—it made her hot—and suddenly realized that if he *did* come it would soil her expensive dress.

He did not soil her dress. The dance ended and she was silent as he led her back to the table and there he ordered more wine, and he poured and they drank, and finally began to talk, somehow heart to heart, about themselves.

He told her, reminiscently, about his young days, his taxi-driving days, and about his mother, who was still alive, and about his brother Frank, who once also drove a cab but was today a Deputy Commissioner in the New York City Police Department, and about Alice and terminal illness and death two years ago; and a wistful note crept into his voice and for the first time to anyone, to this girl, a stranger, he talked about loneliness, and then quickly switched away from that and told her about his daughter, who was married to an osteopath and lived in Melbourne.

"Funny about families," he said. "There are all sorts of families, some tightly knit, some not. My family, we're devoted but separate." He sipped wine. "Devoted but separate. My mother—I see her on occasion when I'm in Florida. We do talk on the phone, but that's about it. My daughter—the last time I saw her was at my wife's funeral. And my brother Frank—right here in New York, a married man with five kids—we get together maybe—maybe—once a year. What about you?"

"Me?"

"Minneapolis. The home of Honeywell."

"Yep. Honeywell."

"Also Pillsbury."

She laughed. "You know it all, don't you?"

"I'm old enough to know. Do you know how old I am?"

"I don't care."

"I know how old you are."

"Oh?"

"From the bio. Twenty-four. I'm thirty years older than that. Thirty years!"

"You don't look it, you don't act it, you don't talk it."

"But I am."

"You know what they say about age. Different with different people. It just doesn't apply chronologically."

"Ever go out with a man my age?"

"Of course." Dr. Jason Goldstein was probably older; he certainly looked older (except for the mane of white hair). And this leonine man was far more handsome. "As a matter of fact," she said, "that's sort of been a thing with me. I, somehow, prefer mature men."

"A father complex?"

"Definitely not."

She was silent.

He poured more wine for her.

"How long in New York?" he asked.

"Three years. As soon as I got out of school and some things got settled—I took off."

"Why? Unhappy at home?"

Again she was silent.

"That's usually the reason," he said. "I mean when a youngster leaves home that quickly."

She could not tell him the truth. She had never told anyone.

"You're forgetting I wanted to be an actress."

"Not forgetting. I was never told."

"I'm sorry. That was my hope, all the way since high school days."

"So you up and went." The gray eyes looked at her shrewdly. *"Were* you happy at home?"

"Not especially."

"How big a family?"

"Just my father and myself. Mother died when I was four. My dad's a dentist and does very well. He never remarried. He—well—he brought me up. I never needed for a thing. We were, I mean, quite rich. A nice house in a fine suburb. Traded in his car every two years. And a pistol-shooting hobbyist. And adored his daughter; never refused her a thing she ever wanted."

Warm with the wine, relaxed, somehow trusting this man, she talked about herself, her early days, her girlhood days, and talked the truth, frankly, omitting only what had to be omitted. Told him she had always been quiet, shy, somehow frightened, but beautiful, darn beautiful, and that very beauty in a way had been a curse. Because she had coasted along on it—the beauty. She had been an ordinary student—a disappointment to herself—because she had not *tried.* Flunked courses, and hated herself for flunking. She did not tell him she had screwed her way all through high school in order to prove herself to herself, and at the University of Minnesota the same thing: the beauty queen had humped the boys in her quest for conquest, her need for compensation, her balance against her mediocrity as a student, her need to prove herself to herself, but never any satisfaction, no orgasm to this very day. And not once during her long, wine-warm recital did she reach in for basics, for root cause: not once did she mention her father.

"Beauty," she said. "I hope to God I don't sound immodest."

"Of course not."

"A curse. I coasted on that. I do have a mind, but I never really developed it. I had darn good teachers in high school and darn good professors in college, but I did not take advantage. I majored in Drama because I was oriented in high school."

He laughed. "Would you do that over again for me?"

"A good-looking girl gets the parts in the high school plays. I got the parts. I probably stank but who knows the difference? That's when I got the acting bug. And in college, nobody discouraged me. I was the ingénue in all the school plays, and I loved the applause, and it's only when I came to New York that I learned I was nothing."

"You're not nothing."

"No talent. A dream, but a nothing dream. You saw my bio, Mr. Ashland."

"Tony."

"Three years of nothing."

"How do you—live? I mean, make ends meet?"

She giggled, sipped wine, stopped giggling, smiled.

"I didn't make Phi Beta Kappa at the U. of M., but I'm not dumb. Not really. Believe me."

"I believe you."

"Let's get back to Minneapolis."

"Right. We're there."

"My mother. Rich in her own right. A heck of a lot of money, and all in cash. Her will divided her money evenly; half to my father at the time of her death, and the other half to me when I reached majority, age twenty-one. So, at twenty-one, with all taxes and everything paid, I came into thirty-eight thousand dollars, cash money."

He whistled a mock whistle.

"A veritable fortune."

"And I wanted to get away from my father."

"Why?"

"Because I wanted to get away."

"Rebellion?"

"Call it what you wish."

"So?"

"So I came to New York to be an actress. But I didn't come with a pair of jeans and a knapsack. I came with backing. Thirty-eight thousand dollars was transferred to my bank here."

"Three years," he said. "How much is left in the bank?"

"Thirty-five thousand."

He whistled—not a mock whistle.

"Very good!" And squinted. "How did you manage that? I mean, I've seen your bio. Definitely not enough work, and definitely not enough pay."

"There's other work."

"What do you do?"

"On and off. Part time."

"Doing what?"

"Ever hear of Joe Bryan?"

"A common enough name. Must be thousands of Joe Bryans."

"The Mazda Club?"

"*That* Joe Bryan. Of course. I've known Joe since he was knee high."

"God, you know everything."

"Honey, I was born in this town."

Joe Bryan. Once the best damn dancer on all Broadway. But fate had hit him where he lived. In a tall building, an elevator cable had snapped and Joe went down with the rest of them, but it was worse for Joe than all the rest, because it finished him in his profession. Many bones were broken in both his legs, and when he was finally repaired he could walk but he could never dance again. He had got himself a damn good lawyer, Moe Levine, and Moe had got him a damn good settlement, three hundred thousand dollars, and Joe had gone into business with his three hundred thousand, and he had flourished.

The Mazda Club with the affable Joe Bryan as boss man. A bottle club, very necessary in New York City, where the drinking curfew was four o'clock, and on Saturday night it was three o'clock. New York was a thirsty town, and many of its wealthy denizens were loath to discontinue convivial drinking because the law tolled a curfew bell. Therefore a private club was in order, a bottle club, and Joe's was the best because it was the most exclusive. There were others, but Joe's was the best because Joe had the feel of the town and the prices he posted for membership excluded the hoi-polloi and even what is frivolously called the upper middle class. Joe catered to the society folk and the millionaires (who enjoy gamboling amongst their own), and there were sufficient society folk and millionaires (and their friends by invitation) to have hoisted Joe right up there into their own class; the Mazda Club had made a millionaire of Joe Bryan.

The Mazda opened when the other *boites* were beginning to close. The Mazda opened at 11:00 P.M. for late dinner, or supper, or what-have-you, and stayed open until 11:00 A.M., which was the next day, but nevertheless the Mazda broke no law. No drinks were sold after the legal curfew because when the bell tolled the Mazda was transformed into a private club, its members owning their own booze in their personal lockers. Thus no drinks were *sold* after curfew; the members were *served* drinks from their own private stock. It was a beautiful enterprise, perfectly within the law, and so it goes with karma. Joe Bryan's accident had been the incident that had catapulted an ordinary guy (shades of Mike Romanoff) from Broadway hoofer to boniface *extraordinaire,* international character, and millionaire. For twenty-two years, the

Mazda Club was New York's stellar bottle club, and it was still Number 1 in the town.

"Joe Bryan," he said.

"The best," she said.

"You're one of his girls?"

The Mazda operated like the Playboy and the Gaslight: the waitresses were beautiful girls in hip-length hose and scanty skirts.

"Part time," she said. "Joe is a darling man. Aside from his regular people, he puts on theatre people. Long ago, he himself was a Broadway actor; he knows how tough it can be when you're 'at liberty.' So for part-time work he hires theatre people, and when they do get a job in a play he's just as darn happy as they are. Of course they come back. How many plays are hits?"

"Lucrative, this work at the Mazda?"

"Very. The tips are enormous. A girl can earn a hundred dollars a night, sometimes more. We fill in when a girl is sick—I mean the regular girls—or goes off on vacation, or runs off with a guy, or on their nights off. I've been able to earn, sometimes, two or three hundred dollars a week—at times even more—but it's darn hard work and all-night work. It turns your life inside out, topsy-turvy. I was going to quit it for good."

"Why?"

"Because I was going to quit trying to be an actress."

"Why?"

"I finally realized I simply don't have the talent."

"What were you going to do? Go home?"

"Oh, no."

He looked at her. "When were you home last?"

"I haven't been."

He looked away, said softly, "You don't get along with your dad?"

She didn't answer. She sipped wine.

He smiled. "Feel free," he said, "to tell me to mind my own damn business."

She had some more wine.

"So what were your plans?" he said. "I mean—if you stopped trying for the actress thing."

"Back to school here. Vocational. Steno and typing. And then out into the business world. Executive secretary."

"With your looks and just a minimum of the skills, and a little experience—you'd be up there real quick."

"Well, thank you, sir."

"And meet new friends and—get married."

"I'm not so sure of that."

"Oh?"

"I've met new friends. Often. I've never wanted to get married."

"Ever in love?"

"Never."

"Boyfriends?"

"I've had my share."

Sweet Jesus, she was so damn beautiful. But restrained, reserved, and somehow sad. He wanted to lean over, kiss her. Not like when they were dancing. Christ, how she affected him. Not that kind of kiss now. Not lustful. Instead he took her hand, held it. "What is it with you, Clare?"

"What with me?"

"I, kind of—well, sense in you—an unhappiness."

"You're a darn good senser, Tony."

"Because your career didn't go the way you wanted?"

"No," she said in that hushed, quiet whisper voice. "It's me. Something deep down inside me. Never *really* happy. And at times I'm all the way down, but down." Her smile was small. "Once upon a time, I tried to kill myself. And that wasn't so darn long ago. Right here in New York."

"A love affair?"

"You're a wise man."

"You said you were never in love."

"Love affair doesn't mean love."

"Yes. You're a wise girl." He laughed, released her hand. "Don't look so serious about it," he said. "One suicide attempt among the young people these days seems to be par for the course. What happened? The guy disappointed you? Didn't live up to your expectations?"

"That is correct, wise man. But with me they never do. Maybe it's me; I don't know. But that's been my story all my life. The men I pick are wrong. Or maybe all men are wrong. Any man I've ever been interested in—turned out to be a phony." Her eyes were shining with the wine. " 'Phony.' It's a word with me. Probably doesn't at all express what I mean. But for me it—what's the word?—encapsulates. Phony. I'm not talking about the little ordinary boyfriends, you know? I mean people I've really been interested in. Like it's my fate. Always they turn out to be—phony."

"May I ask a question?"

"You've been asking questions."

"An important question."

"Sure."

"Perhaps premature. Not perhaps. Premature."

"What's your question, sir?"

He hesitated. Then he said, "Are you interested—in me?"

"Yes," she said. So damn simply. Bluntly.

"Why?"

"Honest to God, I don't know. I can give you the reasons, the phony reasons. The best reason is—you could be a great catch. You're rich. Sue Robbins says you're a millionaire. And you're available, you're a widower. But that wouldn't be a reason for me; I'm not that crazy about riches. Also you're very attractive, darn terribly handsome. But I've met terribly handsome men—without being interested. What's more important, I think, is you're strong—I feel strength!—and I *need* strength, because I, me, I know I'm weak. And you're powerful and famous, you're up there, you've made it—and I admire that terribly. But it's more, if you want the truth. Something"—she shrugged—"that one can't explain. A chemistry. Vibrations. Like when we were dancing before, there on the floor. I felt you, Tony, and I couldn't resist. I ground into you like some cheap harlot. Heck, that couldn't do me any good—my image with you. Sue would have shot me on the spot. But with you I couldn't help myself. I enjoyed it—I enjoyed you—and to hell with image. Sue would call it the self-destruct, the death wish. Did I kill myself with you? If I did, that's it. I can't put on. My one lousy pride—I'm not a phony."

"Vibrations," he said. "Chemistry. I think that's our story. Please let me turn it around, Clare. Let me do the vice versa. Me. I've met beautiful girls before—nothing. Young and beautiful girls—nothing. With you, for some reason—something. I wish to declare myself, right here and now. I'm interested in you—deeply, seriously—and I don't know why in hell I am. It's stupid, we're strangers, we don't really know a goddam thing about one another. But that's it, and we'll play it out from that premise. If it gets screwed up—so be it. But at least we know where we're starting from. Okay?"

"Yes."

"Just one more question. For the hell of it."

"I'm tired, Tony. I'm tired of questions."

He drank down his wine. He was smiling.

"Just this question and we wrap it up."

She grinned. "All right, let's wrap."

"Do you think I'm a phony?"

"I don't know."

"But what do you think? In your heart, what do you think?"

"I don't know. I'm not going to flatter you; I'm not going to play the easy game. It's always happened to me, and as I've said—maybe it's me. I hope you're not. That's the best I can say. You, I hope not. I hope to God—dear God, this once—not you."

He drove her home, parked the car, took her up to her door. She invited him in for a nightcap; he refused. He did not want to risk it. He might start pawing, he might even get laid; he did not want it. He was an old-fashioned man; even if he could get into her, he did not want to—not on this first date. He had to play it *his* way, and then his way would become hers. Young people were easy; he did not want it easy. He wanted to woo her, with respect, and win her, with mutual respect.

"I could see you tomorrow night," he said, "but Monday you start rehearsal. Suppose we do brunch tomorrow. I'll pick you up at two and I promise to get you back by five. That is, if you'd like."

"I'd love it."

"Good night, then."

"Good night, Tony. Thank you for a lovely evening."

"See you tomorrow."

At home, he could not sleep. Unusual for him. He was a good sleeper, quick to fall asleep. Not tonight. The girl whirled in his mind; she was so damn perfect for him. Not brash, not coarse, always a trifle hesitant, somehow an innocent. Chemistry. Vibrations. He laughed aloud. At first, at first sight, there at the Morosco, it had been sexual. Now it was more. She roused his maleness two ways, sexually and paternally. He would have to struggle with the sex; he did not want a quick lay, a fast affair; he wanted to avoid the trap of that syndrome. He was determined not to go to bed with her until there was a reciprocal understanding of serious intent—

or no bed at all. In the interim, for his animal lusts there were always his willing and beautiful semipro ladies for pay. Transactions. He meant nothing to them; they meant nothing to him.

No struggle with the other, the paternal. He wanted, right now, to lavish her, care for her, take her in under his wing. She pricked at his male strength, and he was strong. Everything about her touched chords in him, engaged his instincts, evoked puissance—her quiet voice, her delicate manner, her diffidence, shyness, sheer vulnerability—and that amorphous aura of unhappiness. Amorphous? No. He had asked and she had answered. *Something deep down inside me. Never really happy. And at times I'm all the way down, but down. Once upon a time, I tried to kill myself. And that wasn't so darn long ago. Right here in New York.* The poor little bastard.

But they were met. The karma, or whatever the hell, had produced them at this time of existence, one for the other. His needs fit within hers. She was the sheath for his sword, the glove for his hand, the anvil for his hammer. He had a need to take over, to take charge, to provide, to protect. And there she was, young, marvelously beautiful, but somehow drifting, helpless, alone.

So was he. Alone.

He turned the pillows, tried to get comfortable, and gave in for once, momentarily, to self-pity. Two years now. Rattling around alone in this huge apartment. That was not his way, his style, his experience; from his early days there had been Alice, the wife, the attender to matters that needed attending to while he was out there winning the bread—the social lady, the balance wheel, the home essence, the close, dear, necessary, intimate woman companion. Then sickness, and death. And a void. An emptiness. And a whole damned new life-style. Two years now. His friends, of course, had tried. Duncan, Cliff, Donald; even Rosie, Christine, Audrey, and so many others. Matchmaking. To fix him up. With a proper lady who could be the proper wife for the long-married man now a widower. To the avail of nothing. Ridiculous, his dear friends attempting to choose for him. And now suddenly. From nowhere. This one. Young, a baby. But he wanted her. Sweet Jesus, for wife, for close, dear, intimate woman companion. Wanted to take her in, care for her, lavish her, give her the whole damn full content of happiness. Live for her and give to her. Christ, I'm an old man with millions. Let's show her happiness. Let's turn the tables on her, the beautiful unhappy one. Let's give to her whatever in all her life she's dreamed about. Sleepily he laughed, and sleepily railed at himself. Tony Ashland the wise, the secure, the sophisticated, the cynical. Tony Ashland the top man in the criminal-lawyer business, hard, flinty, feared, and respected; Ashland the brain. Here I am, kiddies. Naked in bed, not yet asleep, but dreaming dreams. Here I am, Your Honor. This is I. Me. Naked. Tony Ashland in love.

9

MONDAY ON BARROW STREET. Eight o'clock and up and around. Not too nervous about the start of rehearsals and glad about that. Not nervous at all, really, because her mind was on Tony Ashland. God, what a nice man, a good man. Remembered Saturday night, the Four Seasons, the Rainbow Room. Beautiful, just beautiful, what a beautiful evening. And yesterday the brunch at Charley O's—beautiful. God, what a nice man, and a sexy man, darned attractive. But not a move. He didn't make a pass. Was he working points? Playing his cards his way? God, I hope not. If he had wanted, I would have given. But he does not seem to want. No flash fire, no quick bang. He talks about serious, serious; and Sue on the phone says that's the way it figures. He's a hip character, Sue said. If he was looking for hump, Sue said, he'd have laid you out and taken his chances. But not this guy. Honey, you know me and my bones. I saw this guy, I looked at this guy, I saw the way he looked at you. When he says serious—believe him serious. Smitten. I tell you he's goddam smitten. So you stay cool. Don't get wild. Listen to Sue.

Rehearsal. How to dress? First time for a Broadway show. And all the new Bergdorf clothes. Dress classy? Forget it. Dress the way you've always dressed for off-Broadway or stock rehearsals. Right you are, Ms. Benton.

Hungry. Grabbed some juice, tea, and toast; they'll break for lunch and that's when I'll eat. She knew from Sue: rehearsals would go from ten to six. At this empty theatre they'd rented on Second Avenue and Twelfth Street. They had it for six weeks. After that, Sue didn't know.

She showered. Slipped into jeans, a sweater, and sandals. Combed her hair, touched on light makeup. Made a face at herself in the mirror, but said a crazy little prayer. Then she went out to a rainy day and took a cab.

Busy. Dear God, it was busy. She arrived at ten to ten, but the darn place was busy with people, and more came and kept coming. As she knew from the script, there were nine characters in *Open Season,* but there had to be at least nine times nine, busy busy, scurrying around. Sue was there, and if Sue was there representing the most minor of the players, then the other actors' agents were part of the mob at this opening shot. Paul Rafferty was there with friends, and Arthur McLean with friends, and Donald Franklin with friends and flunkies. Sid was there—she finally learned his full name: Sidney Menchikoff—and Sid's assistants were there. The understudies were there, and the press-agent people, and the set designer, and the company manager.

Busy. Bedlam.

Sue introduced her to some of the other actors, and she sat with Sue in the seats, and Raywick came and said hello, and he introduced her to Beatrice Smith and to Smith's latest boyfriend, young and handsome. Smith was dark, lush, and sultry and, as everybody in the world knew, she was five times married and five times divorced and was crazy about very young men.

None of the actors were onstage, only the director, the playwright, the producer, and all the technical people—talking, talking. There was a huge oblong table with many chairs around it, and there were boxes and crates and stools scattered about, and there was a cot. The table held a mad variety of objects: a pile of scripts, a box of chalk, pads, pencils, a large thermos of coffee, mugs, a tray with a pitcher of water and glasses, a box of cough drops, a bottle of aspirin, a bottle of Jack Daniel's, and the set model. For most of the morning, the set model had their attention—discussions, discussions. Raywick told them that the set was being built in Brooklyn and that none of the actors would actually see it until their first run-through in Philadelphia.

They broke for lunch at one-thirty. By then the agents, the friends, the flunkies, and the press-agent people were gone. They ate in Ratner's—the actors, the playwright, the director, the producer, the stage manager and assistants, the set designer, and the company manager. They returned to the theatre at three o'clock and again the actors were in the seats, the others up on stage. Finally Donald Franklin stood up and came front and forward.

"Ladies and gentlemen, I should like to inform you of our—well—our itinerary." He consulted a sheet of paper in his left hand. "You will rehearse here for a period of six weeks. You'll have dress rehearsals here the last three days, for which, by your leave, we'll provide an audience. Then we go to Philadelphia. We arrive in Philly on November 4th. Forrest Theatre. We'll have run-throughs there—dress rehearsals within the permanent set for the play—on November 4th and November 5th; opening night is November 6th.

We close there on November 30th, and move on to Boston. Arrive in Boston, December 4th. Shubert Theatre. Run-throughs on December 4th and December 5th; opening for the paid audience on December 6th. We play there until December 27th. And then on to the Big Apple for make or break. We will *make!* Hell, already the advances are beginning to come through. A Rafferty play, with Raywick and Smith—we're in the bag, I hope, I hope, fingers crossed. Here in New York we've got the Broadhurst. I was dickering for it and I got it—the best damn theatre for our type of play. And at the Broadhurst we'll have *three* days for run-throughs—December 31st, Jan 1st, and Jan 2nd. And then—opening night! January 3rd.

"Now, if you please, I'll have our charming stage manager, Mr. Sid Menchikoff, pass among you and deliver to each of you a copy of our itinerary, so that you may make the appropriate notations in your personal diaries, and Sid will also deliver to each of you a spanking-new copy of the script of our play." He turned, did a little bow, said, "Sidney, all yours."

Sid came down from the stage, made the deliveries, and returned to the stage.

"And now," Franklin said, "I believe our illustrious director, Mr. Arthur McLean, would like to say a few words."

He retired to the table, and McLean came forward, front and center.

"A very few words," he said. He was thin, tall, loose, gangly. He had a no-nonsense, pepper-and-salt crew cut, a lantern jaw, a gracious smile, a quiet voice. You had to lean forward to hear him. "My first few words are two—forgive me. I've crapped up your day, people. And there's still a hell of a lot of crap I have to attend to up here. So, no sense crapping up the *rest* of your day. Go home, people. We'll start tomorrow. I promise I'll clean up this business shit if it takes all night. See you tomorrow morning at ten. Thank you."

Tuesday it was all different. No rain outside, no turmoil inside. She arrived at five minutes after ten, and was welcomed onto the stage, and at ten-thirty they were all seated at the oblong table, no busy-busy, no extraneous persons; only the actors, the playwright, and the director.

First McLean did the introductions. He introduced himself, and then introduced everybody to everybody as though they had never been introduced before, as though not one of them had even heard of any of the others. The stars were as casually introduced to the minor players as the minor players to the stars. "No scripts yet," McLean said. "I want you to know the story of our play and I want you to know the people of our play—who they are, where they came from, the whole schmear. And don't hesitate to interrupt me; ask any questions you like at any time you like. And if any of you want coffee"—he pointed to the huge thermos—"just help yourself. And if you get tired of sitting, stand up, walk, do whatever you like. Just stay with me, stay with the people, stay with our story."

Beatrice Smith poured coffee into a mug and lit a cigarette. McLean lit a cigarette and poured Jack Daniel's into a glass. Jack Daniel's—at ten-thirty in the morning.

Then he talked. It was fascinating. He talked about the people of the play—God, he gave their life stories—and actors asked questions and he answered the questions, and talked about the people, deeper and deeper, and actors walked and came back to sit, and asked more questions and were answered, and once Paul Rafferty said, "My hand on the Bible—this man knows more about my characters than I know myself." And only when all the questions were answered, when each actor knew who he or she was in relation to the play, did he begin to tell the story, things about the story that were in fact not in the script, the whole story, all of it, the beginning, the middle, the end—fascinating—and when at last he said, "I think it's time for lunch," Clare was shocked, and that shock was expressed by some of the others, at how fast the time had sped. It was two o'clock.

They returned to the table at three-thirty and now they opened their scripts. "We'll read," he said. "No acting. We'll read. If at any point any of you is confused, just stop and ask. If we can't explain, we'll fix. Also, another thing. If a line is tough for any of you, if it puts marbles in your mouth—stop and say so. That's why Paul is here. The creator sits alone with his typewriter and he writes his marvelous lines. But he cannot possibly know of the idiosyncrasies of the actors who will mouth those lines. If a line, a phrase, doesn't fit a mouth, Paul will fix it to that mouth. Which is only the start of this poor guy's agonies. The big fixes come when we block, when we have to cut for time, and when stuff doesn't work in front of an audience. Lord, how I sympathize with the passions of playwrights."

"Well, thank you very much," Paul Rafferty said. Dryly.

"In the interests of those who may not quite understand," John Raywick said, "I would like you to clear that word—passion. You don't mean passionate passion, do you?"

"No. I mean it in the ancient sense. Torture."

"That's what I thought," Raywick said.

"That's what I thought, too," Rafferty said.

Everybody laughed.

"Okay, people," McLean said. "Let's read."

They read.

The first, dull, dumb, flat, halting reading.

And so on this Tuesday the rehearsals began.

10

ON WEDNESDAY at the Croydon, the clock-radio came alive precisely at eight. Lover-boy swung out of bed and trotted to the shower. Rosemarie lay lazily, listening to the news. When he returned to the bedroom, freshly shaved and smelling of manly cologne, she clicked off the newscaster. She watched, lazily, as he tugged on tight-fitting shorts and commenced dressing.

"You know my schedule for today?"

"Of course," he snapped.

"Cross this morning, aren't we?"

"I'm always cross before breakfast."

"Crosser than usual. Something wrong?"

"Nothing."

"The job?"

"Pardon?"

"They pushing you around?"

"Nobody pushes *me* around."

"Yes, sir," she said. "Don't forget our date this evening."
"I never forget."
"Seven-thirty at Chris's."
"I'll be there, Your Highness."
She yawned. Schedule. An active day, thank the Lord. Christ, she was weary of this bland beautiful hunk of self-loving genius-type; wearied to death of this dumb, humdrum, unexciting, unimaginative, glutinous existence. Active today. At ten o'clock a beauty appointment at Kenneth's. At twelve a lunch date with Chris, who was taking the afternoon off. At two they were going to a matinée, a splendidly reviewed revival of O'Neill's *Desire Under the Elms*. And after the show—shopping. And then to Chris's apartment, where at seven-thirty lover-boy would pick them up for a dinner trio.
He was dressed.
He flashed his big-toothed, handsome, healthy smile.
"Take care," he said, and went away.
She called down for coffee and toast.

At noon she met Christine at the Côte Basque.
"Hi, luv," Christine said. "Always so damn beautiful, aren't you?"
"Kenneth's. What's your excuse for radiance?"
"Helena's. Yesterday. I'm glad it still shows."
They were led to a table, ordered cocktails, ordered food, drank, ate.
"How's Audrey?"
"Fine."
"Dr. Ruby?"
"Fine. To hell with me. You?"
"I'm bored shitless with the bastard. What do you hear about Duncan?"
"Had supper with him the other night. Me and Ruby. A business thing that didn't work out."

"How is he?"

"Alive and kicking. But looks lousy. Tight. He misses you, baby."

"And I miss him. Lord, do I miss him."

"What goes with Ritch?"

"I think, soon, I wash the fatuous bastard out of my hair. I think—he's served his purpose."

"Tell me. Oh, Jesus, tell me!"

Rosemarie smiled. Christine knew it all, but not all. Knew why Rosie was shacked with Ritchie, knew about Duncan's vasectomy, knew Duncan thought she was crazy to want a baby at this time of her life, and therefore knew why she had walked out on him. But she did not know of the tribulations of copulating with Ritchie Crayne. Did not know of the abominations for the purposes of insemination. Rosie believed Christine to be utterly homosexual, and therefore Christine could empathize with Ritchie Crayne, utterly homosexual, but if Ritchie was utterly homosexual—then where did he fit to make a baby for Rosie McKee? Chris was a friend, but Rosie could not confide even to this closest of friends of the weird bed antics with Mr. Most. (The only one she could ever tell would be Duncan.) Therefore she had subtly let on that Ritchie was AM-FM. Just as Chris subtly let on that *she* was AM-FM. As witness the fact that she kept her own apartment, did not live in with Audrey Chappell. And witness her relationship, a supposed affair for the straight world, with Dr. Reuben Grayson. Everybody puts on somehow. We all have our secrets.

"Jesus, tell me," Christine said.

"Pregnant. I think."

"Think?"

"I'm past my period, well past. And I've been regular all my life. But I'll know on Friday. I've an appointment with my genie-gynie for tests. If I'm pregnant, then that's it. I go home to Duncan. I walk out—with bands playing and banners flying—on Mr. Most. Lord, I've had him up to here!" Pushed the back of her palm against the bottom of her chin. "I'm absolutely dying of boredom. You've no idea what an awful prick that man is."

"Yes, I do. Chrissie here. Remember me? I'm the broad that did the in-depth interview. Okay. So good. Great. If he's served his purpose, you walk. And the bands are playing for you."

"They're not."

"Now what?"

"I'm scared to death."

"Naturally."

"It's more than that."

"Like what?"

"I—don't think I want a goddam baby."

"Oh, Jesus Christ."

"Forty-three. You're one of the few who know my age. By the time it comes, I'm forty-four. When it's six years old, I'm fifty. What in hell do I do with a six-year-old when I'm fifty? And hell I can die having a baby, a first baby, at forty-four."

"*Now* you think about all of that? Rosie, you're crazy."

"That's what Duncan said. That's what Sawyer implicitly said. Now you're saying it, and I agree. Suddenly, I—I don't want it. Sawyer said it was a whim, a mood."

"Perhaps this now is a whim, a mood. Or fright, or something."

"It's the goddam oncoming of menopause."

"Easy, Rosie. Maybe your genie'll say you're not even preggie. If not, okay, you're out. If yes, then maybe *this* mood will change."

"Maybe. Who knows? Me, I don't think so." And shrugged, shook it off, laughed, looked at her watch. "Let's get moving, Chrissie. Let's go to Eugene O'Neill. The way *that* guy writes, none of us has troubles."

The show was engrossing, the shopping successful, and then at Chris's apartment they washed up, rested, sipped cocktails, but at seven-thirty—no Ritchie. And at eight o'clock—no Ritchie.

"Something's happened," Rosemarie said. "He's not one to be late; certainly not *this* late."

She called the hotel. No answer at the suite.

"Perhaps he's been delayed on the job," Chris said.

"Then he'd have given us a buzz. We've been here since seven."

"They're open evenings?"

"Yes."

"Give them a call. Or should I?"

"I will."

She called LaLanne's. Nobody knew a thing about Richard Crayne. She asked for Mr. McCloskey. Mr. McCloskey was gone for the day. She hung up.

"Who's McCloskey?" Chris asked.

"His supervisor. But he's on the day shift, like Ritchie. Nine to five. Something's happened. An accident or something."

"He carried identification, didn't he?"

"Of course."

"Then there should be some word at the hotel."

"Or, whatever happened—happened there. At the suite. He figured to go home first, to pretty up. Perhaps a heart attack. A seizure, something. It can happen to the healthiest, can't it? Come on. Let's go find out."

At the desk at the Croydon, she inquired if there were messages for or about Richard Crayne.

"Nothing at all, Mrs. Crayne."

That's the way they were registered: Mr. and Mrs. Richard Crayne.

"Thank you," she said, and they went to the elevator and upstairs she opened the door and they entered the sitting room. Quiet, peaceful, uninhabited. But the bedroom was a turmoil, an upheaval, an insane farrago of disarray. Every drawer of the three chests was yanked open and intimate items of clothing, her clothing, hung out in a bizarre jumble. Underclothes—panties, stockings, bras—and nighties were heaped in frilly hills all over the floor. One of the chairs was overturned. Hangers—wire hangers and wooden hangers—were strewn indiscriminately, on the bed, on the floor, on chairs. The high doors of the two walk-in closets stood wide open.

Christine said, "Wow!"

Rosemarie went toward a closet, tripped over one of her housecoats, disentangled herself, continued, looked into the closet.

"His clothes. All gone. Oh, the son of a bitch."

Chris inspected the other closet.

"How many bags did he have?"

"Four."

"Come here."

Rosemarie came. Chris pointed.

"There they are. Four bags."

"Not his. Those are mine." And began to laugh.

Chris righted the overturned chair, sat in it.

Rosie sat in another chair. And laughed. Long. Gratingly.

"Easy," Chris said. "Let's not get hysterical."

"Oh, the son of a bitch, the son of a bitch." And the laughter began to wind down. "Looks like my fucking rooster flew the fucking coop."

"Well, that's the way you wanted it."

"Me?"

"You were going to walk. So he did it for you. So it becomes *his* embarrassment rather than yours."

"That's one way of looking at it."

"There's another?"

"Pride, Chrissie. Pride! If I walk, I'm leaving *him*. But *he* walked, the son of a bitch. Took up his ass and walked out on Rosie McKee." Wrath made a tight splotch of her mouth. "And if I'd have walked, I'd have told him, informed him, eased him; I wouldn't leave him with his cock in his hand. Oh, I tell you, lemme tell you, your Mr. Most is a measly, cowardly, evil little son of a bitch." She was quiet. She sat there. Then she said softly, "What do I do?"

"Just what you intended to do."

"But what I intended—would have been my way."

"Look, let's first of all clean up here."

Not difficult. They picked up and put away, closed drawers and doors, and in short order the room was placid, serene.

"At least he wasn't a crook," Rosie said.

"Meaning?"

"He didn't take anything of mine."

"What would he do with anything of yours? He's gay—but not a transvestite. At least as far as I know. Or—was he?"

"No."

"Let's go eat, Rosie. We'll eat, relax, talk plans. How about it?"

"You're a damn good kid," Rosie said.

They found a restaurant, ate, found a liquor store, and came back with a bottle of Scotch. They drank, slowly, but a hell of a lot, and in time they were both slightly sodden.

"Tomorrow I go home," Rosie said.

Chris said, "I'll stay over."

"You don't have to, baby."

"I want to. I'm not going to let you stay here alone. Tomorrow I'll help you pack, and I'll see you home."

"What about work?"

"I'll call the office in the morning."

"You're good."

"Let's get comfortable."

"You're a damn good kid," Rosie said.

They removed clothes, removed makeup, showered, donned housecoats, went back to the sitting room, drank, turned on the TV and watched a late-night talk show. At one o'clock they went to bed, both naked, both looped, and Rosie hoping. She enjoyed lesbo love, but had never had love with Christine Talbert. But she had never been naked in bed with Christine Talbert. She lay there, her heart beating fast; they lay ass to ass, warm body to warm body, but nothing happened, and in time she heard Chrissie snoring drunkenly, and in time resigned herself to a celibate night. A damn good kid, she thought. But disappointedly.

The clock-radio woke them at nine-thirty.

"My tongue," Chris said, "feels like a lumped-up wad of cotton."

"You and me," Rosie said.

"Coffee," Chrissie pleaded.

"You betcha," Rosie said.

"And you know what?"

"What?"

"You won't believe it."

"What?"

"I'm hungry. Starving." Giggled. "I must still be a growing girl."

"If that's it, then me, too. Goddam famished."

"So call."

"Just hold your water, luvvie."

"Oh, Christ, them were the wrong words." And Chrissie scurried to the bathroom, and Rosie called down for breakfast, a huge breakfast—juice, eggs, bacon, toast, and pots and pots of coffee—and Chrissie came out of the bathroom, and Rosie went into the bathroom, and Chrissie called the office and told her secretary she would be late, sometime in the afternoon.

They ate, with zeal, with gusto, ate like a couple of starving Armenians, and poured in loads of coffee, and then commenced the packing, and in the middle of the packing Chrissie said, "Call."

"Duncan? No. I'm going to be a surprise package for friend husband. Whenever he gets home, there I'll be for him, surprise-surprise. And if he throws me out on my voluptuous ass, I wouldn't blame him. What do you think?"

"He won't throw you. I don't mean to call Duncan. LaLanne's. Let's hear what *they* have got to say."

"Yes. Right. Good idea. You get on the extension horn, out there in the sitting room."

"Oh, you're a devious woman."

"Yep, that's me. A fucking, pregnant, premenopausal, devious woman. Get out there on the horn."

Rosie called, asked for McCloskey. McCloskey came on. "Yes?" he said.

"May I talk to Richard Crayne?"

"He's not with us anymore."

"Since when?"

"Who's this?"

"Christine Talbert," Rosie said. "A friend of Mr. Crayne's. I wrote an article on him for *Flare* magazine. Perhaps you know of it."

"Oh, yeah, sure, of course, Miss Talbert."

"I tried to reach him at his place. No answer all day

yesterday and nothing this morning. So I'm trying LaLanne's. He told me you're his supervisor."

"Yes ma'am, that's me."

"Not with you anymore?"

"He quit."

"When?"

"Yesterday morning. Walked in, said it was an emergency. Picked up his things, picked up his check, and blew."

"To where?"

"Search me, ma'am. I asked him. He said—parts unknown. That's what he said, ma'am."

"Any reason? Anything?"

"Nothing. Parts unknown. That's all he told me, that's all I know."

"Well, thank you very much, Mr. McCloskey."

"Anytime, Miss Talbert."

Rosie hung up and Chrissie came in.

"Parts unknown," Rosie said. "The beastly, wretched, evil little son of a bitch."

"The hell with him."

"Let's finish the damn packing. I can't stand this place. Can't wait to get out of here."

Downstairs at the desk, she paid off and checked out. A cab took them to the four-story house at 20 East Seventieth, where an elderly housekeeper helped with the bags. She was a silent, wizened Danish woman, fifteen years in their employ, accustomed to the erratic peripatetics of the McKees. She and her husband, the permanent caretakers, resided in a fully equipped, private, secluded basement apartment of their own.

Bags disposed and housekeeper gone, Rosie offered drinks, coffee, whatever.

"Nothing, thanks," Chris said. "Look, if you'd like me to stick around—"

"No. You've been so damn good, a perfect doll. I've imposed enough."

"Nonsense. What the hell are friends *for?*"

"You've been a brick, friend."

"Why don't you call Duncan?"

"No."

"I don't like to leave you here alone."

"Won't be here long. I've an appointment with Sawyer at three. And, sister, this is one time I really need that man. So you run along. Go to work. I love you and I thank you."

"Keep in touch."

"You bet."

She arrived at 160 Central Park South at ten minutes to three. Early. Unusual for her with the shrink. She was rarely on time, often quite late. Today, early, she turned the knob and entered into the silent waiting room. Nobody there of course: three o'clock was *her* appointment. The door to his office was closed. Naturally. There was a patient in there with him. She sat in a leather-upholstered chair, picked up a magazine, turned pages, put down the magazine, lit a cigarette.

He was a nice guy, a good guy, a bright guy, and also a damn gorgeous guy, and of course, early on, she had tried to make him. Nothing. And had kept trying. Had told him it would not be a cheating thing, that adultery was not adultery with the McKees, that they constantly slept with other people, and loved one another nonetheless: loved one another even more. But nothing. No move. He did not give an inch. And she had invited him to one of her swinging parties, had warned him it would be a crazy orgy, had laughingly tempted his refusal, but he had accepted and *she* had been shocked. And had demanded explanation. Nothing to explain, he had said. He was a modern-day shrink; he had no objection to entering into the background, the home life, the family ambience of a patient. (Although lately they had stopped calling their customers patients. Nowadays they were calling them clients. It's all in the verbiage, isn't it? The unconscious implications. If you're a patient, you're ill, sick, you're bleeding, you've got holes. Client is different. Client gives you stature. But Doc Sawyer to this day kept slipping; frequently he called his patients clients, but all too frequently he called his clients patients. Well, hell, Doc, you're so damn right. We are not clients. We're patients. If we're regularly visiting a shrink, we're sick. Not clients. Patients.)

At the party he had been a wheel, snorting coke with the best of them, and playing with the girls, but not once with her. And their next session had been entirely devoted to that. And he had laid it out for her, clearly. A shrink who plays with a patient is a degenerate. Their very relationship gives him an unconscionable edge. There is transference: sooner or later every patient wants to screw the shrink. But the shrink who takes advantage of his advantage is committing rape, a subtle form of rape, but rape nonetheless. The client is incapable of rational consent; she is caught in the transference phenomenon, trapped within a self-spun hypnotic web of admiration, magnetic attraction, veneration. Of course, if the man is in love with the woman, that's another matter. He discontinues the shrink-patient, therapist-client relationship, and lets it all out on its own, come what may, good or bad. But any shrink who screws his patient while the patient is still a patient is a rapist taking advantage of the powerful, subtle, inner-lust workings of transference. "These are difficult ratiocinations," he said. "In our case, please let me try to do it from the bottom line. You're a very attractive woman, but I'm not in love with you. That presents our situation, clear and concise. Either you understand what I'm saying and accept what I'm saying or we must terminate. Up to you. How do you want it?"

It took time. Session after session of this very discussion.

Until she did understand. It came through and she understood and loved the guy, no longer lusting after him. And respected him. This was a damned good, straight, right guy. (But, Lord, she would have loved to have had him. Once. Just once. A session in bed.)

Now she tapped out the cigarette, automatically reached for the magazine, stopped herself, clasped her hands in her lap. She had been seeing him twice a week regularly, although occasionally skipping a session, all during the affair with Ritchie, but had talked of none of it, and he had not pressed. At the beginning, she had dutifully done the ritual confessions: the obsessive desire for motherhood, Duncan's vasectomy, Duncan's objections, her leaving home, her moving in with a lover, and then she had turned it off. No discussions of Mr. Most's homosexuality, no talk about the rococo acrobatics in pursuit of insemination—

The door opened.

A young man emerged, slammed the door. His face was red, his eyes swollen. He glanced at her, quickly looked away, marched out stiffly.

She stood up, opened the door, entered, closed the door behind her. He was at his desk, talking into the telephone. He waved to her. She sat. He finished his conversation, hung up.

"You're very early."

"Yes."

"First time," he said.

"There's always a first time."

"Forgive me," he said. "I've another few calls to make." He made his calls, then sat back in his chair and smiled.

"How are you?"

"I stink."

"You look good."

"I think I'm pregnant."

He said nothing.

"I—I don't think I want the baby."

"Are you pregnant?"

"I've missed a period. I'll know tomorrow. I've an appointment with Kaplan. I'm going there tomorrow for tests." Then she blurted, "He walked out on me. The son of a bitch walked."

"Who?"

"Lover-boy. My perfect specimen. Packed up and ran. For no reason. I mean no argument, no words. There has to be something wrong with a man like that. A latent evil. Or some innate insanity. I mean you want to go? Talk. He didn't. Nothing. No warning. No explanation. Not even a note. There has to be something wrong with him. Inside. Inherent. And I can't risk it. I can't risk *him* as the father of my child. I won't have it."

Sawyer was silent.

"No," she said. "I'm lying."

"All of this is whole cloth?"

"No. No! It's me. Something wrong with me. Something radically wrong with him—but something damned wrong with me. The baby. It's there inside me, I tell you. But from the moment I began to suspect, I didn't want it. Christ, am I bonkers?"

He smiled, shook his head.

"No."

"Married eighteen years," she said. "I love the man. And look what I've put him through. And for what?"

"You wanted a child."

"And now, so quick, I *don't* want the child. Lord, I must be crazy. Am I?"

"Of course you're not."

"What do I do? You're the doctor. What do I *do?"*

He raised his hands, palms up, crooked his elbows and hunched his shoulders in the age-old Gallic gesture of *Mon Dieu, what can I say?* It made her laugh. That foreign posture in this all-American, mustachioed, mod man made her laugh. And it was good. It broke the tension.

More easily she said, "What *do* I do?"

"You're going to answer that."

"How?"

"You love your husband?"

"Eternally."

"He opposed this idea?"

"Implacably."

"And now you're in doubt?"

"More than doubt. I don't want it."

"You've answered."

She lit a cigarette. Surprisingly, her fingers were steady.

"Steady," she said.

"Pardon?" he said.

"I'm confused. All I've put him through. And all I've gone through—you don't know the half of it. Lord, you don't know *any* of it. What I don't understand—is me. I left a husband whom I love and bedded down with a brainy, beautiful specimen who in fact bored me to tears—all because of an irresistible compulsion. I wanted to have a goddam baby—from me, born of me. And when it happened—I *think* it's happened—when the reality set in, the realness, then every argument that Duncan had presented became firm and cogent and irrefutable. That's what confuses me. How could I do the quick switch that fast? How could I be that damned irrational? Lord, I know I'm whimsical, perhaps eccentric, certainly unconventional, but I didn't think I was nuts."

"You're not nuts."

"Then what—"

"Normal. You're not the first, and you won't be the last. A classic case. We used to study about you in school." He lit a cigarillo, puffed, blew aromatic smoke. "A great many women, childless by preference, suddenly do a complete about-face in their forties; the desire to give birth to a child becomes an overwhelming passion. Fortunately, in most cases, it's a transitory passion. Either their circumstances don't permit, or their husbands are intransigent, or they themselves come around; in a sense, they come to their senses. Reality overtakes the dream, and the dream dissolves. That's Classic Case One.

"Classic Case Two. The passion persists and the woman has the child, sometimes with great difficulty. Classic Case Two breaks down into two subdivisions. One: the child is born and the woman is deliriously happy. Two: the child is born and *that's* when the dream dissipates. An unfortunate situation. Like locking the barn door after the horse is stolen, if you'll pardon the analogy." He shook his head. "There can be, and there frequently are, dire consequences both for the woman and the impulse-child." He smoked the cigarillo, smiled. "Now we come to Classic Case Three, and that's you. The dream rolls blithely on despite whatever the obstacles until that first shock of pregnancy—and that's when reality overtakes the dream."

"But I wanted it so badly."

"Of course you did."

"And now, so quickly, I know it's all wrong. Lord, it would ruin me, my entire way of life. Senses. I've come to my senses, damn right. And it has nothing to do with the man, his leaving me, any flaws in his nature; I was trying to fit in some sort of rationalization. It—suddenly—the whole damn dream—just—just—madness . . ."

"Keep talking," he said. "Let's get it all out."

In her office at *Flare,* Christine Talbert labored over projects until, suddenly, Audrey was there, grinning, hoisting the back of a thigh over a corner of the desk.

"You're a dear devoted servant, but take a look at the time."

Chris looked. "Jesus!" It was six-thirty.

"Knock it off," Audrey said. "Go home and get gorgeous. I just got a call from Jackson Peters. He's having some people over. He suddenly got an idea, impromptu. You know Jackson when he gets ideas, impromptu. He'll have everybody who's anybody; Jackie-boy throws the best bashes in this whole damn town. Especially impromptu. What time should I pick you up?"

"No good. I'm bushed." It was a lie. She had a date with Grayson. "I'm going to take some work home, and turn off the phone. I'll sit around with the work, and then I'm going to bed."

Audrey looked down at her, shrugged, got off the desk, and ambled out.

Chris sat there, hating herself. I made my bed, she thought, and it's a damn hard one to sleep on. Christ, a normal life in this atmosphere becomes abnormal. A date with a man and you've got to squirm, and hedge, and lie. Not just to Audrey; to all of them. Once upon a time—until Ruby—it was great that way; it was the way she had wanted it, a part of a pattern she herself had woven—Christine Talbert the radical of the Women's Movement. Shit.

For the record—for Audrey, for her own secretary—she flung work into a briefcase, got up, and got out. Going home, Audrey. To get, like you said, gorgeous. But not for Jackson Peters, et al. For Ruby Grayson. For a date at eight. At his apartment. Where he's going to do a cook-in.

She rang his bell at ten after eight. He drew her in, kissed her nose, took her wrap. "The menu as follows," he said. "A bit of caviar to tease up the taste buds. Shell steaks smothered in sautéed onions. Caesar salad *with* anchovies. And wine all the way. But first, me love, a cool and soothing cocktail."

He was a marvelous cook. The onions, slow-sautéed in butter, were touched up with truffles, a modicum of garlic, and a dash of cognac. The Caesar salad was simply out of this world.

"You're going to ruin my figure."

"Never. Which is why I don't too often seduce you—culinarily."

And then in the living room with champagne he said, "All right, out with it."

"What?"

"What you've been busting with all through dinner."

"Oh, these shrinks, these shrinks. They read your mind, these witch doctors."

She *had* been bursting with it. He was the only one who knew about Rosemarie's adventures—at least from Christine Talbert.

She told him. About their afternoon yesterday, and then Crayne not appearing at the apartment for the dinner appointment, and the call to LaLanne's, and their concern about an accident, and their going to the Croydon to discover that he was gone, bag and baggage.

"How'd she take it?"

"Devastated. Not that she gave a hoot for the guy. But pride. You know?"

"Yes."

"I got her out of there, took her down for dinner. We came back with a bottle and got bombed. Today she'd pack and go home, but I wouldn't leave her there alone. I stayed over."

"How many beds?"

"One. Why?"

"How'd you make out?"

"Oh, these degenerate shrinks."

"She's a handsome woman."

"Now stop it."

"How'd you make out?"

"I—was tempted. But nothing. Not Rosie. We're too far along the road, you know. Old friends, good friends, straight friends."

"The poor bitch." He shook his head. "All this time with the guy—a waste."

"Not really. Matter of fact, she was about ready to end it. He served his purpose. Mission accomplished."

"Pregnant?"

"So she believes. Tomorrow she sees the doctor for tests and stuff."

He raised his glass.

"Well, here's to Mama Rosemarie."

"No," Chris said.

"Now what?"

"She doesn't want it."

"Doesn't—"

"Reversed herself completely. Doesn't want a baby at forty-four. Doesn't want to be saddled with a child. Of course she can afford the best in help, the best of nannies, but that isn't it. The whole life-scheme. Too late. Suddenly realized. Not for her."

"Classic."

"Pardon?"

"I won't bore you with the psychiatrics." He came near, sat close. "In point of fact, I approve."

"Of what the hell?"

"The reversal. Her instincts. It's damned unnatural to have a first child at forty-four. Bad all the way around, especially for the child. An aging woman, childless, rigid within the patterns—not the most optimum situation. Can you imagine Rosemarie McKee at fifty, the smart sophisticated Rosie McKee, with a six-year-old underfoot?"

"Practically her words."

"Think about my words."

"Don't look so serious, Doctor."

"The words I've been hammering at you for so damn long. A family. A going-on, a completion. A continuum that's a part of God or nature or whatever the hell. Poor Rosie's desire-impulse—a cry from the deepest part of her soul." He stood up. "I love you, Chris. Which is why I've been after you, lecturing like some crazy persistent Johnny-One-Note. And now a case in point—your closest friend—rears up and hits you right between the eyes. You're young, you're still young. Christ, how sad it would be . . ."

At a quarter of nine, Duncan McKee entered his house, locked the door, strode the corridor toward the elevator, saw the light in the downstairs drawing room, angled off into it—and there she was. Rosie McKee in gleaming silk lounging pajamas, relaxed in an easy chair, a tall highball in her hand.

"Hi," he said. Awkwardly.

"I'm home," she said.

"Welcome home."

"For good. Never again."

"Thank you," he said.

The way he said it, she wanted to cry. He was not a humble man.

"I love you," she said.

He did not go to her. Better. More Duncan. He went to the bar.

"I love you," she said. "Only you. No one else. Ever."

He poured bourbon, added soda, drank.

"You look great," he said.

"Thank you."

"I mean it—great."

"I mean it—thank you."

"How's everything?"

She understood.

"Not tonight," she said. "We'll talk tomorrow."

"Yes."

Beautiful? Just like that—yes. After all these many weeks, no questions, no demands. Just yes. An affirmation. A comprehension. What a beautiful man. But he looked so tired, pallid, haggard.

"Running, running," he said, as though in answer. Of course it was an answer. "Since nine this morning, on the go."

"After eighteen years, there's telepathy."

"There was telepathy before the eighteen years. What now telepathy?"

"I love you."

She put down her glass, went to him, kissed his ear, bit his earlobe. "Upstairs," she ordered. "A nice long shower for the tired old man. And then a wifely massage to relax the old muscles. There's no masseuse like a wife-masseuse who knows how. How about that, sir?"

"Yes ma'am, ma'am."

They went to the corridor and to the elevator and upstairs to the bedroom and there they undressed and showered and then, her palms anointed with baby oil, she rubbed his back, kneading skillfully, and then turned him supine and worked the muscles of his neck and his chest and down and saw his erection and laughed and kissed it and he reached to her and turned her over and entered into her and she reared up, her legs around him, and it was good, Lord, it was good, dear Lord, after so long, how good to be fucked. . . .

In the morning, he called his office that he would be delayed. They had breakfast in bed and there she talked, told him all, her entire experience with Ritchie Crayne. He drew her to him, kissed her, held her.

"We'll have it, we'll have our baby. And I promise—"

"No."

Told him she didn't want it, told him why, and told him of her session with Sawyer.

"Could be, possible, I'm *not* pregnant. I'll know today. I've an appointment with Kaplan at two o'clock."

Dr. Peter Kaplan was of course the most prominent gynecologist in New York City. He practiced in a five-story brownstone on East Eighty-fourth Street. The lower floor contained the offices proper, the upper floors were a private hospital. She arrived promptly at two and was promptly ushered into the consultation room. He was a small man with a halo of white hair around a pink pate. He greeted her smilingly, offered a chair. They sat and discussed symptoms and he made notes. Then he led her to an examination room, worked over her briskly and efficiently.

"So far, yes," he said.

He took blood, took urine, turned the specimens over to a nurse, guided his patient to a private anteroom, gestured toward a magazine rack. "Be with you shortly," he said.

Twenty minutes later a nurse came for her, and she was seated again in the consultation room.

"It's positive," he said.

"I don't want it," she said.

Dr. Peter Kaplan sat back in his swivel chair. A first baby at forty-four is never a picnic. The over-forties, especially with a first, were in the high-risk group. Also, the husband had talked with him privately, had confessed he was sterile by reason of a vasectomy. A curious situation.

"I don't want it," she repeated. "It—it was an accident."

"But I have you on the Pill."

"I—uh—kinda screwed it up."

Also curious—since the husband's confession. An infertile husband, but the wife on a regular regimen of contraceptive medication. He sighed, sat forward. Life is complicated.

"I take it you're talking in terms of abortion, Mrs. McKee."

"Are there any other terms?"

"You've discussed this with your husband?"

"Of course." She smiled. A handsome woman. "Let me ask you frankly, Doctor. Is it safe?"

"You mean abortion?"

"That's what I mean."

"At this early stage, quite definitely."

"Safer, I would imagine, than having a baby at my age."

"You imagine correctly, Mrs. McKee."

"Then that's it, Doctor." She produced a cigarette, lit it. "All right, prepare me. Give me the gory details."

"Nothing gory. And in your particular case, at this very earliest stage of pregnancy, quite nothing at all. A quick, simple, bloodless procedure."

"All right. When do we do it?"

"When would it be convenient for you?"

"Right now," she said.

He smiled. She liked his smile. It made him look like a cherub. "Not right now," he said. He opened a leather-bound book, a diary. "Monday?" he said. "Can you be here Monday at eleven?"

"Monday's fine," she said. "What happens?"

"Beg pardon?"

"Details. Non-gory. But I would like to know."

He made a notation in the leather-bound diary, closed it, smiled the cherub smile. "A simple, nonsurgical procedure. Finished and done within fifteen minutes. My preference, you stay here overnight. Not necessary if you wish otherwise, but that's my preference."

"Then what?"

"You return to the normal tenor of your ways. For a week I'd like you to take it easy, but nothing special; I mean no spate of invalidism, you know? On the other hand, that week I wouldn't want you to go off on a skiing trip."

"How about sex?"

"The next Monday, you'll come in for a recall examination. Then you're discharged."

"How about sex, Doctor?" She squeezed out the cigarette, stood up, leaned over the desk, and said to him, shockingly she hoped, "I'm a very sexy woman, Dr. Kaplan."

The old boy didn't bat an eye.

"If the recall examination discloses no pathology—and I'm certain it won't—then two weeks from that day, which would be three weeks from our really very simple procedure, you may live your life however you wish."

"Right. Thank you, Doctor. See you Monday morning at eleven."

11

THE DAYS MERGED to weeks and the weeks slid by magically and it was a month now, a month and a week actually, five magic weeks of rehearsal, and Tony, and Arthur McLean, and John Raywick, the five most wonderful weeks of her life. Rafferty had been compelled to do a great deal of cutting; once onstage, the play had run too long. But it was in shape now, the rehearsals in great shape, and the show blocked. Blocked—she knew all the words. The purpose of blocking was to establish the moves of the actors—stand here, cross there, lie down over there, go to the phone there, sit on that, walk behind that, make your entrance there, exit over there—but it was all makeshift, it was done by chalk marks on the floor and by the use of props like boxes, stools, chairs, and a couple of scraggly cots pushed together to represent a double bed. No real furniture because, as McLean had once told her, if you use real furniture then the union insists that you must use real stagehands, and that small item could cost fifteen hundred dollars a week; there would be no true furniture until the commencement of the run-throughs in Philadelphia.

McLean. She was in absolute awe of that man; God, she could go down on her knees in veneration. What a director, what a marvelous director, but always smooth, calm, polite, equable; never once did she hear him raise his voice, but never once did he fail to get his way. No harsh orders, none of the usual director's stubborn commands, no put-downs, no arguments, no insistence, no sarcastic critiques. He would let the actors play the scene the way they thought, and then he would talk with them, discuss, sharpening here, contradicting there, elaborating, and then they would do the scene again, sometimes over and over again, stopping and talking and discussing, and then doing it over upon their very own suggestions; but the suggestions (as afterward they would ruefully but happily admit) were not their suggestions, but his, although at the hot moment they believed them to be their suggestions. He was in charge, and nobody else. For line changes he would privately talk with Rafferty, and Rafferty would make the change, but it was always McLean's change. The guy was the best. It was Rafferty's play, but the vision was all McLean. This quiet man was the boss man; he molded the play *his* way, and they all knew, even Rafferty, that it was out of Rafferty's hands. The words were Rafferty's and the concept was Rafferty's, but the playing out of that concept, the variations, the changes, the subtle shifts in emphasis, the enlargements of some of the characters and the diminution of others—the whole production, the whole darn point of view was McLean's. If *Open Season* was a success, the unassuming McLean would take no bows. But if it failed the brunt would be his and they all knew it, all the way from Sid Menchikoff up to Donald Franklin and including the most minor of the actors, who in fact had become the pet of the show, Miss Clare Benton.

The pet of the show. Probably because she was the

youngest and the most inexperienced. And had only one small scene and none of those lines had been changed. And did her bit the way McLean wanted it and that was it, and therefore she was not engaged in the scuffles and jealousies of actors whose parts were constantly shifting; and so when they wanted to bitch they came to her. And often McLean would excuse her early, but just as often she would remain in the theatre, watching, fascinated, as he quietly but firmly pulled the play together. And Raywick, when he was not onstage, would watch with her and explain what McLean was doing and why he was doing it. He was just great with her, John Raywick, he had become her father protector and, heck, even her escort; on his way home he drove her home, dropping her off on Barrow Street; that, upon his insistence, had become the pattern. Yes, no question she was the pet of the show, but especially she was McLean's and Raywick's pet, and she realized why—Tony Ashland. They were Tony's friends and she was Tony's protégée.

She saw him regularly: Friday night, Saturday night, Sunday afternoon, and sometimes Wednesday night. He took her to nightclubs, to plays, ballets, concerts, even to the opera, and to dinners at the homes of people or in the grand restaurants. And on Sunday afternoons they went to his gun club and she was darn good at target practice and he was proud of her.

No sex.

They had dinners alone and dinners with people: Rosemarie and Duncan McKee; the McKees and Beatrice Smith and friend; Diane and Arthur McLean; Sara and John Raywick; Florence and Donald Franklin; Barbara and Clifton Arvel; Christine Talbert and Dr. Reuben Grayson, and others, but most of them were old, so darn old, and despite Tony's presence she was uncomfortable—and with the McLeans she was absolutely numb. She was normally shy, and with Tony's people downright timorous, but in McLean's company her conversation was reduced to an occasional yes, no, um, uh-uh, and that was it.

Old. Not *old* old, but compared to her—old. They were up there in years, forties and up, wise, worldly, scintillating, clever and sophisticated; she was the kid, the baby in their midst, although they pretended not to notice. Thelma Ashland had noticed, and Clare Benton had loved it. Thelma was Frank Ashland's wife, Tony's sister-in-law, and they had gone out there once, to Frank's house in Queens, for dinner. Frank was just another guy, but Thelma was beautiful.

Thelma was a large woman—God, at least six feet, with arms like hams and a pair of breasts like watermelons—but a down-to-earth, laughing, happy Irish woman, and the dinner had been corned beef and cabbage (delicious) with cans of beer. Thelma had called her "child," and after many beers Thelma had said, "Child, what are you doing with an old bird like Tony?" And after many more beers Thelma had said, "Sweetie, I've gotta introduce you to my son. Tommy. He thinks he's something, an assistant prof at NYU, and the girls always chasing after him. But a beauty like you—you're a real beauty—you'd knock him right over on his ass. You know why? Because it's not only beauty, it's class. You got class, kid."

Thelma was not, quite, Tony's people.

"I can't stand her," he said on the way home. "Which is why I see them perhaps once a year. But each to his own. For Frank, she's the salt of the earth. For me, you're the salt of the earth. Frank loves her. I love you."

"Do you?"

"Your Honor, more and more am I convinced."

The intellectual Christine Talbert and the brilliant Dr. Reuben Grayson were much more Tony's people, and one night after the ballet and after hamburgers at P. J. Clarke's and after the chatter of prolonged good nights on the corner of Fifty-fifth and Third, they had ridden off alone in the Bentley, and on Barrow Street he had come up for a nightcap and she had said, "Sue says she's gay."

"So say they all."

"Then what's with her and the handsome Grayson?"

"In my days, it was called a beard."

"A beard?"

"When a married guy would openly go out with the lady fair who was his mistress, he would take along another guy, and then nobody would know who was who and what was what. The other guy was called a beard. Could be Dr. Grayson is Chrissie's beard, in a manner of speaking. If she doesn't want the outside world to know she's gay, she does the town with Dr. Ruby, and like that nobody knows who is who and what is what. Of course, Your Honor, I cannot state that with any real degree of certainty. I am not privy to the parties' sex habits."

Sex habits. The sex habits of these parties here in this apartment were nil. There was kissing, there was hugging, there was necking like a couple of kids, but there was no sex and she understood. (There was sex with Charles on the rare occasions these days when she permitted him to come with pastrami and wine and stay over.) But no sex, real sex, a hit in the hay with Tony Ashland, because, thank God, she had finally met a man who was not a phony. He was *not* a phony. He had declared himself and was waiting for her declaration. Love or nothing, he said. Permanent or the hell with it, he said. Either we have a life together or we go our separate ways. I'm an old-fashioned guy. I'm courting you, but I'm not pressing.

And no sex in *his* apartment. That night when he had casually invited her over, she had gone with trepidation. Not trepidation about being screwed. (She was by then in fact curious about his mettle in bed.) No, it was a different kind of trepidation, ambivalent. Was he like all the rest, but taking his time, playing a more subtle game? Would this one, too, finally become unmasked as a phony?

No phony. Not Anthony Ashland. Not yet, anyway. He had shown her through the fabulous duplex—"The guided tour," he said—and she had been truly impressed: the thick carpetings throughout, the fine paintings on the walls, the huge book-lined library, the billiard room, the recreation room that contained—go believe it!—a fully equipped soda fountain. "That's for laughs," he said, "but also for damn good ice-cream sodas." And he had shown her the pistols—not target pistols, these—in the desk in the study, in the desk in the library, and in the bedside table in the master bedroom, and admired her competence in handling them. They had had food, wine, laughs, music, and even a couple of crazy ice-cream sodas, but he had made no sneak grabs or sly propositions, not even by the inviting bed in the master bedroom. And then back on Barrow Street they had kissed, hugged, held, wriggled, but before it got out of hand he quit, gave her a fast fatherly kiss and departed. No phony. Not Tony. She was beginning to believe it. She was almost convinced.

And now on this Friday evening, in lovely late October, over dinner at the Quo Vadis, he said, "We've a party for tomorrow night but I don't know if you want to go."

"Why wouldn't I want to go?"

"This type of party."

"What type of party? Who's giving it?"

"The McKees."

She frowned, blinked. "Why wouldn't I want to go to the McKees' party?"

"It's a swinger."

"All their parties swing."

"This one's special. A *real* swinging party. Swinging. In the very modern sense."

"You mean, like, you know, an orgy?"

"That's what I mean."

She sat back. Was he testing her?

He said, "Have you ever been?"

"Never." And that was the truth.

"Would you like?"

Testing? Was he testing?

"What—like—I mean—what happens?"

"The McKees," he said. "Good people, dear people, beautiful people, real damn *people.* But their way of life—how shall I say?—unconventional. Open marriage, you know? The wife is permitted to screw around and the husband is permitted to screw around, and none of that takes the shine off their love. For one another. And they *do* love one another. Eighteen years. And it's a deep and abiding love, a damned perfect marriage. One would *kill* for the other, I'd take an oath. But in matters of sex, they're varietists. Open marriage."

"Do you approve?"

"Of what?"

"That type of marriage?"

He shrugged. " 'Judge not, that ye be not judged.' "

"I'm not asking you to judge. I'm asking—you personally."

"Me?" For a moment, sitting up stiff, he seemed affronted. "Me?" As though blustering against a blow.

"You," she said.

"Not me," he said.

"Not that kind of marriage for you?"

"Damn right not," he said. "I'm not criticizing, not judging others. But not for me. I'm of another school, an old school. Possessive. My wife is mine. I'd forgive her anything, but she can't fuck around. Hell, that way, I'm on the side of God, and I can quote you chapter and verse. Matthew 5:32. 'But I say unto you, that whosoever shall put away his wife, saving for the cause of *fornication* . . .' "

"You're a religious man?"

"I don't think so."

"But you quote our Lord God."

"I do," he said, "when it suits me."

"What happens?" she said.

"What happens what the hell?" he said.

"Swinging party. Who'll be there?"

"Nobody you know, except Beatrice Smith."

"And the McKees."

"The McKees."

"How many?"

"Fifteen couples, but that includes us. Without us, twenty-eight people."

"What happens?"

"They drink, they smoke, they snort, they change partners and screw their nuts off."

"Right out in front?"

"Some in front. Some want privacy. Most are married, changing partners. Some, like us, are boyfriend and girlfriend, changing partners. Everybody lives."

"Must they?"

"What?"

"Must everybody live?"

"Nobody forces anybody to do anything."

"Well, I mean, I thought if you came you had to go by the rules of the game."

"No rules. No games. Nothing. But whoever comes knows what kind of shindig they're coming to. They can do or not do. Nobody holds a gun to the head. Would you like?"

Testing? Testing? Was he testing?

"Yes," she said. "I've never been. I would like."

If he *was* testing, he might catch up with an awful surprise. She had never been, and did not know how she would react. But she would not put on—not Clare Benton—she would not dissemble. Perhaps the very fact that she was willing to go was already a disappointment to him. Well, then, that's just too bad, mister. This one here is *not* a phony. And, once there, it could be worse—for him—for his opinion of her. Because however it went, that's the way she would go. She would not hold back—whatever the impulse, she would not hold back—in order to show herself pietistic, in order to impress her millionaire wooer (if in fact he *was* a wooer for marriage, and not some sophisticated bastard who was playing his cards in a game she did not understand). She was not a self-lover, she did not love herself; she was a self-despiser, she hated herself because she knew what she was—a nothing. But her one pride: she was not a phony. However it went, that's the way it would go.

"I'd like it," she said. "I've never been. I've heard about these things, but never been. Tell you the truth, I've always wanted to go. I mean I've heard, people always tell you about orgy parties, but they always tell you about the parties that *were*. Me, I've never been invited to a party that *is*. Figures. Because who in heck am I?"

"Tomorrow night," he said. "Pick you up at eight-thirty."

The vast drawing room was softly lighted. Music from an invisible stereo was lush, soft, slow. People laughed and chatted, kissed, danced. Blue smoke swirled. The room was warm. A heavy fleshy odor pervaded, not unpleasant, a commingling of perfumes, perspiration, and pot. The long bar had bottles and glasses and buckets of ice, and snacks and cheese dips, and a large rectangular cigarette box that was filled with joints of grass. Clare took a few drags of a cigarette, gave it to Tony, but he laid it away. They danced, with each other, and with others, and then Rosemarie went out and came back with a crystal bowl and a shallow velvet-lined box which contained tiny, glittering, golden spoons. She set the bowl and the box on a table and people gathered eagerly, but held back: the initial ritual was the hostess's due. The hostess used one of the tiny gold spoons. Dipped it into the white powder in the bowl, raised the spoon, sniffed powder into one nostril, sniffed into the other nostril, moved off, and then the others snorted, many of them, including Tony. She knew of course what was in the bowl: high-fashion coke. She had never tried it, but she was darn well going to tonight. Somebody—Beatrice Smith's young man—handed her a tiny spoon and she knew what to do from watching the others. Dipped and sniffed, one nostril and then the other, and almost at once the drug produced effect. Dear God! Flying, floating, carefree, careless. A high inexpressible, ineffable. An ethereal, free-floating, mountaintop high, and yet an earthy, salty, sexual, erotic high. And right then the party turned wild, and Beatrice Smith started it.

The stereo had switched to *A Pretty Girl Is Like a Melody,* and Smith strode to the middle of the floor and commenced a graceful striptease, and people gathered in a circle about her and clapped their hands like tom-toms in rhythm to the music, and Smith tossed away clothes until she was stark naked, and then her young man was suddenly within the circle, and he strutted round and round about her, tossing off clothes until he, too, was stark naked, and took her in his arms and they danced together, and then he lowered her to the floor, all to rhythm, and opened her legs and went down on her. And now others were tearing off clothes—not all, not Clare Benton, not Tony Ashland—and people were making love, some in pairs, some in groups—and she sat there and watched, astonished, embarrassed, and, deep inside her, revolted. A naked man came to her and asked her to dance and she laughed and said no, but there was Tony on the floor dancing with naked Rosemarie McKee, Tony all properly attired; even his jacket was buttoned. And Duncan McKee, as properly attired as Tony Ashland, took hold of naked Beatrice Smith and they disappeared; and then naked Rosie took hold of Smith's naked young man and they disappeared; and others disappeared; but others stayed, some naked, some dressed, and the sex went on openly, even two men in a sixty-nine suck-off posture; and she went to the bowl again and snorted and Tony was there snorting with her, and they danced together closely, and she whispered, "I want you. Let's go home. Let's get out of here."

On Barrow Street, he undressed her, undressed himself, and took her to bed. "I love you," she whispered, high on coke, snuggling, snuffling, clawing at him.

"Do you?"

"What? What?"

"Love me?"

"I love you."

"I want to marry you. Is that clear?"

"Yes."

But he held off, holding her off, and she admired. It came through, coke or no coke. No phony, this one. Even here, now, naked in bed, he wanted it right or not at all.

"We'll get married?"

"Yes."

"I'm not going to rush you, Clare. We'll give it time and see how it works out. We won't take any final step until after the show opens in New York. And if you don't find me to be what you want, you can always back out. But for now at least I want us to be, in a sense, engaged. No one else for you, no one else for me. A trial period, in a manner of speaking. Do you understand?"

"Yes."

And so on that Saturday night on Barrow Street, bespoken, betrothed while flying on coke, Clare Benton and Tony Ashland clove to one another and fucked.

12

OPEN SEASON was a hit long before it came to New York. The reviews in Philadelphia were raves, and the reviews in Boston were raves. New York, of course, had a finger on the pulse. Not only was the incoming show a play by the twice Pulitzer-honored Paul Rafferty, with McLean as director and Raywick and Smith as stars, but the out-of-town notices were gilt-edged encomiums. *Variety* summed it up in an article headlined: STIX FIX HIT ON OPEN SEASON. "In the bag," Tony told her. "The advance in the till is already four hundred thousand, and it's still going strong."

He came out weekends, weekend after weekend in Philadelphia, and then in Boston, and she stayed with him in his hotel, and the cast knew about it, and nobody said a bad word. Nobody said anything except Beatrice Smith and all her words were good. "He's only a multimillionaire, sweetie. You're young and beautiful, but he's had them young and beautiful before. A guy like Ashland doesn't come running every weekend just to get laid by young and beautiful. Play it cool, baby. Play it nice and cool and you're liable to wind up with the whole damn jackpot. I tell you, the old boy's smitten." Smitten. Sue's word. That's what Sue had said right up front, right there at the beginning.

He was good, kind, solicitous, and absolutely not a phony. He had her, he had her exclusively; he owned her body, and she knew by now his rhetoric wasn't some kind of game plan for exclusive possession. He kept talking marriage and she was coming around to it. She admired him, she revered him: he was a doer, a maker, a shaker, a high success; he was all man. And he even had sex appeal for her. Big deal for her—sex appeal. But she enjoyed the feel of his hard body, liked the way he smelled, and his intimate habits pleased her. A maker, a shaker—that's what had always drawn her to a man, and this one could be the jackpot. And what was she? She was a nothing. No special talent, no arts and craft—nothing. She had always despised herself because she was not a maker, a shaker; she was devoid of talent and even drive; she was a nothing except for the accident of genes, a beautiful body and a beautiful face, and had traded on that all the way since high school, and now she could make the trade once and for all—bingo! She could (if he wasn't a phony) marry a millionaire—a fine, strong, powerful, dominant man—and her worries would be forever over. She would have it all: riches, ease, comfort, luxury, a direction in life, and a man to direct her.

He was quite the stalwart in bed. He was no Charles, who could do it over and over again all night, but Charles was twenty-six where Tony was fifty-four, and for fifty-four he was a darn resolute lover, certainly sufficient for her. Heck, the less he did it the better she liked it, and that had nothing to do with Tony Ashland; that had been her way all her life:

a vessel, a receiver, a pretender, a pleaser, but not an enjoyer. Tony enjoyed. Unlike her, he was a sexual animal, although old-fashioned, unimaginative, a straightaway banger, but a sturdy lover who did it good, did it long, and did it hard. No tricks; mostly the missionary position. But she did tricks for him; she knew how, knew the moves, knew how to make the sounds; in bed she was an actress who could win all the awards. And it pleased her to please him; he was a handsome man, a charmer, a learned man, a vivid and interesting man, but most of all a good man, clean, kind, sympathetic, not a phony, and in her own crazy way—no swirling madness, no head over heels, no bursting rockets—she was in love with him.

Christmas fell on a Wednesday, and he came to Boston on Tuesday afternoon to spend Christmas Eve and Christmas Day with her. It began to snow early Tuesday and kept on snowing: Boston would have a white Christmas.

They played to a packed house on Christmas Eve, and then they all repaired to McLean's suite where he had a tall tree gleaming with tiny lights and little bells and shiny balls, and there was a large old-fashioned bowl of potent eggnog, and they drank from thick mugs; and then lanky McLean stood on a chair and made a small speech in that quiet voice of his. "Christmas is a time for home, for homegoing, for family gatherings. But we are a working crew and therefore our dear ones have come to us and we are gathered." He raised his mug, smiled sweetly. "To my wife, Merry Christmas. To the other wives and husbands and lovers, Merry Christmas. To my actors and crew, you've been absolutely wonderful. To everybody—I wish you all a Merry Christmas!"

"Merry Christmas."

"Merry Christmas."

People embraced, people kissed, people wept.

It was a lovely party: a bittersweet sentimental party.

They walked in the Boston night, in the invigorating cold, crunching on snow, from her hotel to his, a short distance. She was carrying packages: she had stopped in her room to pick up his Christmas presents. She loved it in the cold, snow whirling; she clung to him, she chattered, animated, about the show, about McLean, Raywick, Smith, Menchikoff, the actors, the crew, the people, the trials, the tribulations, the ups, the downs, the fights, the loves, hates, seductions, affairs; they were truly a family, a tribe intimately intermingled: six weeks on Second Avenue and now almost two months a show on the road.

Upstairs in his suite their faces were red with cold; snow glistened on hair and eyelashes. They removed their coats, shook them out, hung them away. They wiped with towels, giggled, chuckled, grew warm. She gave him his presents, two presents, and watched him open the packages. One was a pair of gold cuff links, the other a pair of crazy silk pajamas outrageously striped in blue and gold.

"Thank you, thank you," he said.

And went to his bag and took out her presents; coincidently, also two presents. He gave her the first. She gasped. A marvelous, ruby-encrusted platinum wristwatch. She put it on. It fit perfectly.

"God, thank you," she said.

And gave her the second. A small velour box.

She opened it, and her mouth opened, and stayed open until she said, "Oh my God." A ring, an engagement ring. A huge diamond, it had to be five carats at least, but in taste, not garish, not myriad-faceted, an emerald cut.

"Oh my God," she said.

"Put it on."

She put it on, third finger left. Like the watch, it fit. Perfectly.

"How—how did you know size?"

"I'm a sneak," he said.

She flew to him, kissed him.

"We're engaged," he said.

"Yes."

"Engaged to be married."

"Yes. Yes."

He took her to a chair, sat her down. He made drinks, gave her hers, sat near her with his. He spoke soberly.

"I have plans," he said, "but of course they're subject to your approval."

She looked at the ring, looked at him. The ring was real, he was real. Not a phony. He was not a phony. All her life her cry had been—phonies. All her life they'd been after her blondness, her beauty, her blue eyes, her white skin, her tits, her ass, her cunt. All her life she had heard line after line, protestations of undying love, or charming flippant declarations of out-of-my-mind love, but always bull, always they were bullshitters; it seemed it was her fate that those she picked, those she selected, those to whom her heart went out—they were of a single stripe, high-up people, doers, achievers, movers and shakers but bullshit artists, suave and skillful fakers, classical phonies. But not this one; thank you, God. I don't think this one. My luck has changed, my planets have shifted, something. I think this one is real. I think at long last this one, this one whom I want—me, the sickie—this one to whom my heart goes out, I think—I hope to God—this one is real!

"Whatever you say," she said.

"Plans," he said.

"Whatever the plans."

"The show opens in New York on January 3rd."

"January 3rd," she said.

"We've got to go along. I mean, in a manner of speaking—go along. We can't let our personal lives totally interfere."

"I don't understand."

"I'm going to want you out of the show."

"No show?" She said it quizzically. Somehow blankly.

He laughed, drank. "I'm old-fashioned, remember? Not quite the type who would want his wife exposed naked on a public stage. Not, at least, when she *is* his wife. On the other hand, we don't have the right to screw up a whole production at this stage of the proceedings. Therefore, plans."

"Whatever you say."

"I'll talk to Arthur. I'll let them have you for a month after the New York opening. This show's going to be a hit, and once it hits, changes in minor personnel don't mean a thing. They'll have a month to find a substitute for Clare Benton." He took a little book from a pocket, opened it. "I've got it all down here—subject to your approval, of course. You'll leave the show on February 3rd. We'll be married on the fifth, and the next day we leave. I've already arranged to take off the rest of the month—all the rest of February. That's for the honeymoon. We'll go where it's warm, we'll travel—Spain, Italy, the South of France. Then we'll come home and settle in."

On Christmas Day they had lunch with Arthur McLean. She showed him the ring. "Well, good for you," he said. "Congratulations." He kissed her cheek.

"Arthur," Tony said. "There's something—"

"Excuse me," McLean said. "Honey," he said to Clare, "please remember not to wear it onstage. Our young lady from the singles bar simply couldn't afford a rock like that."

Always the director.

"Yes," she said.

"She's not going to be with you long," Tony said. "She's going to retire as an actress."

"Retire?" McLean frowned. "When?"

"A month from opening. February 3rd. You'll have a full month to work in a replacement. It's only one scene and Raywick, thank God, is a pro. He'll cooperate."

"Yes, a pro," McLean said dourly.

"We're getting married on February 5th."

"Yes, the fifth," McLean said.

"Christ, stop looking like the world just ended."

"Yes, yes," McLean said, rousing. "I'll send Sid back to New York today to start the ball rolling for a replacement."

"Today's Christmas."

"Right, you're right." He shook his head. "You've kinda knocked me off my pins. Yes, I'll send him tomorrow." He raised his hand to a waiter and procured a fresh Jack Daniel's. "Good luck, happy landings." He drank, turned to her. "We're going to miss you," he said softly. "All of us. Very much."

The company returned to New York on December 28th. McLean gave them three days off—the 28th, 29th, and 30th—to relax, refresh, revitalize, while the sets were installed and put into working order at the Broadhurst. On December 31st and January 1st and 2nd they would have dress-rehearsal run-throughs for final polishing and then on January 3rd—opening night. "What's dress rehearsal for them," Raywick said, "is *un*dress rehearsal for us."

"Yes, isn't it?"

Raywick laughed. "My one big joke that I was saving up. Nothing, right?"

"No, great," she said.

He kissed her forehead.

"We all love you, bride. Tony's a fine man, but he's getting one hell of a fine girl. We ought to know; for three months we've practically lived with you. You're a good kid, baby. The best."

"Thank you," she said.

On the evening of the twenty-ninth, Charles Ennis came to Barrow Street with a brown bag of pastrami sandwiches and a bottle of red wine. "I've been reading," he said. "You knocked them dead in the sticks."

"McLean," she said. "All McLean. That man is fabulous."

They were eating in the kitchen. She kept flashing her left hand, but somhow he did not seem to notice.

"All of a sudden McLean?" He chewed pastrami. "Since when do you put down a Paul Rafferty?"

"I didn't put him down."

"You said McLean."

"I say what I think."

"Hell, babe, a Paul Rafferty play *you* could direct and it can come up a winner. But don't put your money on it. Not yet. The review guys in the sticks, they're peanuts. It's the guy here on the *Times.*"

"There's more than four hundred thousand advance."

"Better than that has withered. If the guy on the *Times* puts his thumb down, you're all out in left field."

"Let's hope that doesn't happen."

"It can happen."

And then in the living room, with what was left of the wine, he suddenly saw. He grabbed her left hand.

"Oh, wow!" he said.

"Like?"

"Ashland?"

"Yes."

He released her hand. He drank wine, walked.

"Wanna know something, babe?"

"What?"

"I didn't think you."

"What?"

"Not you."

"What?"

"Flip out for the mess of pottage."

"What in hell are you talking about?"

"Clare Benton. Selling out. I didn't think."

"Stop it."

"The old old story. Legal prostitution. Selling out for the big head of cabbage, the *mucho dinero."*

"Get out of here, please. Go home, Charles."

"That's guilt, babe. When you're afraid to talk—guilt. May I say my piece?"

"Say what you like and then get the hell out."

He drank his wine, set down the glass. Hard. The glass broke. "I'm sorry," he said.

"That's all right," she said.

"How old is he?"

"Why?"

"How old?"

"Why?"

"You ashamed about his age?"

"Fifty-four."

"Christ, he's got you by thirty years. Lemme ask you. Would you dig him if he was a cabdriver?"

"He *was* a cabdriver."

"Would you?"

"He's not a cabdriver."

"He's a fucking bundle of money, is what he is. Legal fucking prostitution. Christ, in ten years your husband'll be a doddering old fossil. You'll have to wheel him in a chair.

And you, young. Christ, you'll be looking around for the likes of me to get your ass knocked off."

"Not the likes of you."

"I never heard complaints, babe."

"Get out, Charles."

"I'm getting. And lemme tell you. I'm not coming back. Not ever."

"You bet," she said.

And on the afternoon of the thirtieth she had lunch with Sue Robbins, a hoity-toity lunch at the Forum of the Twelve Caesars. She came late, Sue was already seated, and the first thing Clare did, seated, was fling out her hand impulsively and show the ring. "Jeez," Sue said, "that's a rock what's a rock! Jeez, how many carats?"

"I don't know."

"He didn't tell you?"

"I didn't ask."

"He didn't tell you?"

"Would he? Tony Ashland? Discuss carats?"

"Yep, right, I forget when I'm out of my league. Let's eat, baby." Sue took up the tall menu. "Let's get into this glorious food."

They ordered, they ate, they talked about the show—McLean, Rafferty, Raywick, Smith, the actors, the gossip—and only when the coffee came did Sue, smart Sue, switch it back onto the track. She lit a thin cigar and grinned around it. "I was practically one of the first to know. Sidney Menchikoff. Out of Boston and back in town, shaking us up for your replacement. When you getting married?"

"Feb five."

"A big wedding?"

"A judge in chambers."

"Reception?"

"No way. No big wedding, no reception. The nuptials in chambers and the next day we go off on the honeymoon."

"I hope *that's* big."

"Big. Travel for the rest of the month. Spain, Italy, South of France. We'll come home on March 1st."

"Honey," Sue said, "are you sure about what you're doing?"

Sue. This was Sue. Sue who had really started the whole darn thing, who had practically whipped her into it. Fat Sue the cynic, the wiseacre, the clever sophisticate. Now Sue was biting hard on the cigar and her eyes were deadly serious.

"Are you, sweetie?"

"What?"

"Sure?"

"What in heck are you talking about?"

"Sex. How're you fixed for sex?"

"I—don't understand."

"How does he do in the feathers?"

"None of your business."

"How long *will* he do—that's what's been on my mind. Hell, in a way I started this ball rolling, but now I've come up with reservations. One reservation, really, but it's the kind of thing that could in time create an awful mess. So, for *my* conscience, it needs talking." She smoked the cigar. "Honey, I'm on your side, all the way with you. That's why this needs talking—now."

"What, damn?"

"Sex."

"Here we go again."

"Christ, with you it's like flogging a sponge. But I'm going to keep flogging until we get this out." She grinned. "I've never been to bed with you, so I can't have any personal value judgment. Sex. And in this situation, you're the pivot point. I know you're a shy little creature and this kind of stuff embarrasses you, but we've got to get it out on the table—now. How do you burn in the sex department? High? Medium? Low?"

"I don't think—"

"Men," Sue said. "They wane as they age. He's in great shape now, but he's no boy, and he'll just keep on getting older, won't he? Could be at present he performs okay in the hay but—we've got to face it—in time he's going to slow down to a limp. Then what? I don't mean impotent; I mean not often. But if you burn high in the sex department, then you'll be in for a mess of trouble. Because—with that in mind—I've inquired about him. Old-school chauvinist, a possessor. Maybe he'll let you have a dildo, but he won't let you run. Different from his friend McKee. McKee would permit you to get all the outside nookie you wanted. Hell, I'm in the business, I know all about the McKees. But he's not McKee. He's Tony Ashland. It's something to get out on the table right here and now. I—somehow—have the responsibility, the feeling of responsibility, and therefore the right to ask. How do you burn, baby?"

"Not high."

"Medium?"

"Low. Sex, for me, not—really important."

"Well, all right. Great. Christ, why'd you make it so tough for me? Fine, beautiful, I'm out from under, no more worries that with my big mouth I did you in. You'll marry Mr. Rich and live high on the hog happily ever after, and me, I'm keeping February 5th open. Guess why."

"I know why."

"Who's going to be your witness in that judge's chambers?"

"You," Clare said.

January 3rd.

Opening night.

An opulent audience.

A hit. A smash hit.

When the final curtain came down, the applause was deafening. Deafening! McLean, of course, had arranged as to how they were to take the bows. First the entire company. The curtain came up on the company and the audience rose up from the seats, clapping. And the curtain went down. And went up on five of the major players, and the clapping continued. And the curtain went down and came up on Raywick and Smith, and the clapping continued and did not desist, and Raywick and Smith were compelled to take nine curtain calls—nine!—and on the ninth they dragged out Paul Rafferty and linked hands with him and the applause exploded to crescendo and there were whistles and screams and shouts of "Bravo! Bravo!"

And then the curtain came down and stayed down.

Backstage it was riotous. They were all there again as on that first day of rehearsal—actors, agents, friends, flunkies, press agents—but more than on that first day. Now there were newspaper people and photographers, and formal-attired celebrities, and grandiose VIP well-wishers, including the Mayor of the town and other worthwhile politicians, and Clare Benton danced around John Raywick and kissed him and kissed Beatrice Smith and kissed and hugged Tony Ashland. Only Arthur McLean and Donald Franklin floated above the excitement, somehow cool.

"Opening-night audience," McLean warned. "Friends, relatives, divers freebies, and that hard corps with the soft core—the society-folk first-nighters. I must admit, however, that tonight's reaction was high and away above the norm." He laughed. "Could be we've got a hit on our hands."

"We'll know soon enough," Franklin said. "Let's move it, people."

He had hired a fleet of limousines, and they filed out and

piled in, actors still with makeup on, and were driven to Franklin's apartment on Central Park West. McLean's wife and Franklin's wife—slender, gracious, both white-haired—were already there. It was a party and they were the co-hostesses, Diane McLean and Florence Franklin, laying away coats and directing people to booze and food. There was a liquor bar with a white-jacketed bartender serving, and a buffet bar piled high with food. People drank, people ate, people gathered about the televisions. Three televisions. The permanent walnut console was flanked this night by two small pull-about portables. All three TVs were on but the sound was off. The console was tuned to CBS, one portable to NBC, and the other to ABC. At news time, Florence Franklin turned up the sound, not too loud, but as each respective play reviewer came on—loud. And the loud reviews drew loud cheers.

The boob tubes had delivered three resounding ayes!

The TVs were turned off and the bartender grew busy. But then a phone rang and Franklin hurried through the sudden hush and lifted the receiver. Sid Menchikoff brought him a ball pen and a spiral pad.

"His private number," Raywick whispered to Clare Benton. "One of the bribed copyboys."

Franklin listened and wrote.

Clare whispered, "Suppose a bribed copyboy can't get it?"

"There are also bribed typesetters and such. Don is an old hand at this game."

Franklin listened, nodded, wrote, his double chins quivering. Finally he said, "Thank you." Hung up, put down the ball pen. He was smiling. His round face was red. He laid a finger along his nose and lowered an eyelid.

"We're in," Raywick whispered.

"Ladies and gentlemen," Franklin said. "That was the notice from the *Times*. It's good. It's *very* good."

He read it aloud from start to finish, and then read it more slowly all over again, and he was reading praise all the way: praise for the playwright, the players, the director, the sets, the lighting. There was even a line for the most minor of the players: "On occasion nudity is justified on the Broadway stage, necessarily justified as appropriate to the action of the play, and in her single scene in *Open Season* the spectacular Clare Benton is a divine exemplar of such justification."

The phone rang with more advance notice of notices, and after the last Donald Franklin said to the company manager, "Tomorrow you'll put two more people in the box office. We're going to have long and steady lines out there."

"Calls for a drink," said Beatrice Smith.

The bartender grew very busy indeed.

The succeeding days were filled with acting, shopping, moving, subletting, and acquiring a passport. The acting was her job (although McLean and Raywick, mornings, were engaged in developing her replacement). The shopping was for her trousseau (mostly traveling things). The moving was sporadic. She had in fact moved the night of the party at Donald Franklin's; she had gone home with Tony and thereafter continued to sleep at his apartment (and he, skipping a beat, had introduced her to the doorman and to other of the house people as the new Mrs. Ashland). There was little to move out of Barrow Street except clothes and some favorite artifacts, and she did that moving piecemeal. The subletting, with the consent of the landlord, had commenced with an ad in the newspapers, and that deal was quickly closed and included the sale of her furniture.

She picked up her passport on January 27th, quit the show on February 3rd, and on February 5th at four-thirty they were married in the chambers of New York Supreme Court Justice Mr. Abe Bremer, who terminated the ceremony by wetly kissing the bride. Her witness was Sue Robbins, Tony's witness was Duncan McKee, and after the nuptials in chambers they went uptown for dinner at the Côte, for which Tony insisted on signing, and then Duncan took Sue away, and Clare went home with Tony, and the next day they flew off for their honeymoon.

13

NEVER HAPPIER in her life. He took her only to the sunny places. Madrid, Barcelona, Valencia, Rome, Florence, Naples, Nice, Cannes, Antibes, Monte Carlo—no special itinerary, no schedule. They stayed where they liked for as long as they liked and moved on when they pleased, frequently by chartered plane as befits American millionaires. They stopped at the great hotels in the finest suites. (God, she would never forget the savory breakfasts on breeze-swept terraces under cobalt skies.) Days they swam, they boated, they surfed, they walked, explored-shopped, and whatever her whim he insisted she buy. Nights they ate in grand restaurants, danced and saw the shows in the famous nightclubs, gambled in the glittering casinos. The days slid into nights, the nights to days, the sun shone, the sea sparkled; the days and nights slid into weeks, and they ate, drank, lived, laughed, loved like crazy; and February slid into March and they came home to 825 Fifth Avenue, Mr. and Mrs. Anthony Ashland, and suddenly she was cold, like a portent, like out of sun and into shadow; suddenly a fright assailed her bones, a reminiscent fright. Her heart thudded.

It was, of course, the weather, or so she thought. March in New York, this early March, was brutal: snowy, sleety, gray, grimy, dirty. And during that first week at home she scarcely saw him; he was in court all day, working at postponed trials, and stayed late at the office, working at preparing for court the next day. And when he came home the poor guy was patently exhausted; he had a couple of drinks and dropped into bed, and then up at seven o'clock; he was an early riser. But after a few weeks the pressure was off and he was Tony again: good, kind, lavish, giving. He personally escorted her to the best stores in town, and arranged that she had unlimited credit, and if she did not shop enough, he scolded her. He bought her a shiny little Mercedes, all for her own, and now there were three cars in this family of two. And as the weather got good—brutal March gave way to a radiant April—he took her out to his golf club and paid a pro to give her full attention, and she caught on to it quickly; she was young and strong and supple, and in short order he was proud of her; she was a darned good golfer. But why not? When they played in a mixed foursome, who in heck did she play against? His friends. And they were old. He was old. Everybody was old. But in the clubhouse, at dinner or over drinks, they were *not* old; they were handsome, beautiful, charming, worldly; they intimidated her. Of course they did not mean to intimidate her, but she was the baby in their sophisticated midst.

That was it. She knew. Why the tremors had begun inside her again. No matter the paradise, always something. A new one this time, a new complaint inside her psyche. She was scared of his people; she tried to play up, but she was scared. They were up there, worldly-wise, comfortable, brittle, experienced, confident, capable, and she was a nothing, twenty-four years of age. And began to try, at least, to look older.

Wore less makeup, and parted her long blond hair in the middle, severely, and drew it up to an old-fashioned bun at the back of her head. And one night at dinner with the McKees at the Brussels, Duncan McKee said, "That new haircomb, makes you look like Betty Grable."

Who? Grable? Betty Grable? It did ring a little bell somewhere, but again these old ones lost her.

"Grable?" she said.

"Beautiful, sexy. The pinup girl of World War II."

World War II. That had happened before Clare Benton Ashland was born.

"Oh, yes, Grable, thank you," she said, and like that it went by.

Dinner at the Brussels. Always dinners. Dinners were a part of Tony Ashland's life-style, and the dinners drove her crazy, as so many of her other chores for Tony Ashland did. But he didn't mean to drive her crazy, the dear sweet man did not mean it. She had begun to enjoy the golf weekends (despite her fright of his friends) and she loved the target shooting at the gun club (that was every Wednesday now), but for all else, except for himself, he was driving her crazy. And the good, dear, sweet guy did not mean it.

He was a creature of habit, and his creature habits devolved the social amenities upon the wife. They would discuss what to do, but then *she* would have to do it, and how could she complain about these lousy little menial things that scared her witless, that frazzled her nerves, because she was a timid nothing, incapable, frightened to death of anything that was outside her ken? Just to call up for tickets, for reservations—a play, the ballet, a concert, the opera—and she would look at the phone as though it were a coiled snake, and would have to smoke half a joint to get up the nerve; or to call up, with authority, for reservations at one of his grand restaurants.

Most of their dinners were out, some were at home, but

the company dinners at home, where she was the hostess, gave her—a new thing—migraines. Their own dinners at home, alone, were disastrous, because she was a nothing. She could make tea, she could fry eggs, she could broil steaks, and that was about it; anything more elaborate, he would do. But for the company dinners she would have to call in a cook; he had provided her with a list of cooks. But the cooks, like his friends, terrified her; they were knowledgeable where she was ignorant, and she could sense their tacit contempt.

On occasion she saw Sue, but not often; Sue was outside the periphery of Tony's eclectic circle. His friends were judges, lawyers, business tycoons, rich and successful pinnacle people, and famous names like McKee, McLean, Franklin, Audrey Chappell, and Christine Talbert.

"Happy?" Sue would say.

"Of course."

Could she complain? About what? She was coddled and protected by a doting husband; she had a beautiful home, beautiful friends, beautiful clothes, a beautiful car, beautiful everything; she had it all, all her heart could possibly desire. What to complain?

She grew quieter and quieter, more withdrawn, as springtime melded into summer, and the old hopeless helplessness gnawed within her, and she hated herself. Never good with you, is it? Whatever it is, never good. Always something. Always something to make you hate yourself more. God, I'd like to sneak away. I'd like to go to sleep, and just sleep, sleep, sleep, like forever. Sleep forever—you know what that means. Well, fine. That would be best. The long sleep and you're out of it. No more troubles, no more worries, no more knowing that you're a nothing, because that's exactly what you are—nothing. You give nothing, you produce nothing, and you're frightened to death of everything, and no matter how good it is, you find a reason to make it turn sour. Right now you have it all, everything you ever dreamed, but you're running from it, running away, you want to sleep—sleep, sleep. Then go to sleep, goddam you. Easy. You can go to sleep and you're out of it, out of it all forever. You've got a big bottle of pills up there in the bedroom. Just swallow enough of them and you're out of it. But she fought. Somehow she fought herself, fighting for survival. And laughed. Laughed at herself, sometimes hysterically. Laughter became her crutch.

She could laugh with Tony, alone with Tony, happily. At the gun club, on Wednesdays—happy. And the golf, out in the open air with him—happy—even with the others around. But once with the others in the clubhouse—cocktails, dinner—then the bright face she put on was a heavy mask and the laughter was hysterical. Alone at home with him, beautiful. Like with fried eggs and sausages, beautiful. Because he was good, this man; a good man, no phony. Of course she was not in love with him—what's love, who knows from love?—but she adored him. And did not—*would* not—trouble him with her despairs, her pessimism, her terrors, her hopelessness.

It grew worse, it got worse, and the symptoms, this time, were different. Her hands trembled; they had never trembled before. She had to clench and unclench, furtively, to bring in the circulation; that helped. Alone, shaking her hands until they tingled, that also helped. And the occasional flashes of dizziness, and the occasional feeling of faintness—none of that had ever happened before. It went on, it did not let up, despite her bright face and her laughter. She kept it from him, tried her best, but he noticed—the hand-trembling. Once, one night in bed, he took both her hands in his.

"What is it?" he said.

"Nothing. An old story. Happens with me every now and then."

"You should talk to a doctor, don't you think?"

"I have. I've talked to my doctor. He gave me some pills. He says it'll pass."

Truth. She didn't lie to Tony. She withheld—fighting—the information of her slow, spiraling down toward the abyss of black despair, but concealment is not lying. She had talked with Jason Goldstein, had in fact expressed another new symptom: her feeling of wanting to cry, of having to bite back unreasonable tears.

"Not unnatural," Jason had said. "You're a sensitive kid. Marriage requires adjustment."

"I feel like killing myself—honest."

"You're not that stupid. You've married a rich man, you've shifted from your normal milieu, and of course all of that would have a traumatic effect even with a person older than you. Transitory, transitional. Believe me, it'll pass. Double the dosage of the Valium."

"How about the Seconal?"

"Never. Seconal's for sleep."

"Suppose it doesn't work?"

"What?"

"Double dose of Valium."

"I'm quite certain it will. Give it a few weeks, a month. Actually, it won't be the Valium. Nothing curative; merely a tranquilizer. It'll be you, adjusting, coming through. But the medication should help during the coming-through period."

"If it doesn't?"

"Then I'd suggest a bit of psychotherapy."

"God, that bad?"

He laughed, patted her arm. "Always melodramatic, aren't we? One doesn't have to be seriously ill for a bit of psychotherapy. Have you ever been in therapy?"

"No."

"Does the idea frighten you?"

"No, not really."

"Good girl." He stood up. "There you have it, Clare. The fact that you're fighting back, that's an excellent sign. I believe the double dose of Valium, taken regularly, will help you through. If not"—he smiled—"a good shrink'll do the trick in short order. Please believe me, there's nothing unusual about this. I've heard it time and again. A difficult period, adjustment period, initial stages of marriage . . ."

Some of the hand-trembling ceased, but the spiral down did not desist, and early in July, in Southampton with the McKees, she fainted flat out. They had returned to the house from the beach and the men were playing croquet on the lawn. She was in the recreation room with Rosemarie, who was stirring up gin and tonics, and she was just extending her hand for the drink when suddenly she sighed and passed out cold.

Next she knew, she was sprawled in an easy chair and Rosemarie was rubbing her wrists.

"Welcome back," Rosie said. "How are you?"

"All right, I think."

Rosie brought the gin and tonic. "Drink," she said.

She drank a good deal of it, quickly, ice tinkling.

"Ah, good," she said.

Rosie smiled down at her. "Are you pregnant?"

"No."

"Too much sun. Damn hot out there. And you weren't wearing a hat."

"Yes, that's it," she said.

And then that weekend with the Arvels in Nantucket when she was dumb, like struck dumb; if she said ten words during that whole weekend, it was a lot.

But later in July she seemed to improve. They went to Nassau for a couple of weeks, she and Tony alone, and it was all wonderful again; she was happy and sprightly, gay and talkative. But when they came home to New York the black depression set in again, bleak, despairing, hopeless. When she was not with him—golf, the gun club, some social event—then she clung to her room, did not go out: no shopping, no sunshine, no lunches with Sue. Once, she went to the bathroom, opened the cabinet, looked long at the bottle of Seconal; then she took it to the bedroom and hid it deep under clothes in a bureau drawer.

And then in August, there was the dinner.

They owed the Bremers a dinner, a cook-in dinner—Mr. and Mrs. New York Supreme Court Justice Abe Bremer. In June the Bremers had given a dinner for them, a belated marriage dinner, at the Bremers' town house on Eighty-fifth Street, and Tony said it was time for reciprocation. He set the date for August 5th; it fell on a Tuesday. "Anniversary," Tony said, and kissed her. "Six months to the day." Abe Bremer enjoyed the company of theatrical people and therefore Tony suggested the McLeans, the Franklins, and the McKees. "They're all in town," he said. "You'll give them a ring. If any of them can't make it, we'll substitute. Perhaps the Raywicks. Or Beatrice Smith and friend. And you'll get Michel for the cooking." Michel Antoine was his favorite come-in chef. "And for who to do the serving, let Michel suggest."

Next day she made the calls, Tony out of the apartment, the phone fearsome, a coiled snake, and her hands trembling. But she had prepared herself: a double dose of Valium topped with a long drink of vodka on ice. Made the calls to these important people and tried to hold her voice firm: she was twenty-four years old, going on twenty-five. First to Mrs. Abe Bremer—her name was Elsie—and then to Florence Franklin, and Diane McLean, and Rosemarie McKee, and they were all available and they all accepted. And then she called Michel for him to come the day before, Monday.

"Yes, Madame," Michel said. "Monday for Tuesday. I

shall be there at 9 A.M."

Nine o'clock in the morning. She knew why. Because *he* knew she was inadequate. He had cooked for them before, and he knew he would have to do all the suggesting and all the shopping. But for now, at least, her chore was done. She sat there near the phone, just sat there. Wanted another Valium but wouldn't dare. Instead, vodka. Got up and got herself another vodka on ice. God, I'm becoming a real drunk.

On Monday, August 4th, the bell rang promptly at nine, and she was ready, crisp in a white pants suit: the alarm had awakened her at seven-thirty. She led Michel to the drawing room and sat with him. No Tony. Of course no Tony. None of this was Tony's province.

"How many will there be, Madame?"

"Ten."

"An important dinner?"

"Yes."

He tapped himself, took out a small pad and pencil. He was dark, quite young, quite certain of himself—damned certain of himself, imperious.

"Madame has suggestions?"

"I depend on you."

"Oui." His smile was supercilious, his contempt obvious. He had cooked for them before. "So. If I may, I would suggest as follows. Pâté. My own. A creation of pheasant and wild duck. And then frog's legs from Florida, in the Michel fashion. For the main course—pièce de boeuf à la Flamande."

"What is it?"

"Beef, exquisite with savory sauce. And with the *boeuf* we will have soufflé potatoes, and salade Michel of escarole and beets, and the tiny tender baby peas. For dessert I will bake from New Orleans, crusty pecan pie topped with dollops of rich whipped cream. *Café noir,* and so it is it. Madame has suggestions for the wines?" His thin nostrils quivered.

"You're the expert, Michel."

"Oui. Yes. As Madame wishes. So now. For the pâté and the legs of the frog, a white wine; I shall acquire Moselle, Piesporter 1959. For the *boeuf,* a noble Burgundy—Corton, Clos du Roi 1955. For the dessert, we return to America. A rich port from New York State, which we shall place in decanter to be poured from decanter. So? Madame has further suggestions?"

Oh, the son of a bitch. The supercilious son of a bitch.

"How many will we need to serve?"

"Two." He knew her, this slender dandy of a cook, knew she was nothing, knew of her inadequacies. "Depend on Michel, Madame. I shall bring them tomorrow. Excellent young men, who also serve to assist the chef with the cooking. Tomorrow we will come, three, at ten o'clock. Dinner will be in approximation—seven?"

"Yes."

"So. *Bon.*" He put away pad and pencil. "I must go now for the shopping."

"Money?"

Now the nostrils flared. "I have sufficient money required. In time Mr. Ashland shall receive the bill for all. Shopping. Then I return, and I shall stay late. The preparations, and such cookings necessary today for tomorrow. So." He stood up, she stood up. His eyes moved over her. He smiled, inclined his head, made a little bow. "You are very beautiful, Madame."

"Thank you." A Frenchman. After all his snide little insults, finally a compliment.

"Pas de quoi," he said. "So. To go. And to return."

She showed him out, went back to the drawing room,

drank a vodka. And another. God, what's become of me? A new world, a morning drinker. After the third vodka, her hands ceased trembling.

They came on time, all on time, no waiting, at six o'clock on Tuesday, and Tony did the introductions, and stirred martinis in the drawing room, and the women talked, and the men talked, and at seven o'clock they entered the dining room, the table gleaming with crystal and silver, a long rectangular table. Tony had worked out the seating arrangement.

He sat at one end of the rectangle, she at the far opposite end. To his right was Abe Bremer, to his left Elsie Bremer. To Clare's right was Arthur McLean, to her left Diane McLean. To McLean's right was Rosemarie McKee, opposite Rosie was Duncan McKee. To Duncan's left was Florence Franklin, and opposite Florence was Donald Franklin.

The dinner was served and the food brought forth gracious compliments, as did the wines, and everybody ate heartily except Clare Benton Ashland. She pecked with one hand; the other, under the table convulsively clenching and unclenching to improve the circulation and stop the trembling. Then she changed hands, ate with one, clenched and unclenched the other. Somehow—and, as she realized, unreasonably—she felt rejected, alone, unprotected: so far away from Tony.

The conversation rippled gaily; fortunately she did not have to join, fenced off by the McLeans. To her right the garrulous Rosie engaged Arthur McLean; to her left, Diane was engrossed in Duncan McKee. Conversation. Brilliant, animated. God, they knew so much. About everything. And what did she know compared to them? Nothing. A baby in their midst, a babe in the woods. Timid. Frightened. Afraid to open her mouth. But she justified; she tried to justify. They were old, knowledgeable, worldly, experienced. And now Donald Franklin made a joke in his deep booming voice, and everybody laughed, and she laughed along with them, not knowing what she was laughing about.

Old. Once she counted heads, the white heads. Tony was white-haired, the Bremers were white-haired, Florence and Diane were white-haired. Old, all old. The Bremers were in their sixties, the Franklins in their sixties, the McLeans in their fifties, Tony in his fifties. God, the youngest of them was Rosie McKee and she was virtually twenty years the senior of Clare Ashland. So what? They were wonderful, marvelous, interesting people. Just what you wanted all your life. Not a feckless Charles Ennis among them. And you will learn from them, and grow with them; adjust. Time. That's all you need. Time. Time. Give it time. Her ears were ringing.

She ate, pecked, sipped wine, fought nausea, fought dizziness, fought away from her trembling hands. And finally the ordeal was almost over, they were at dessert, and she reached for the crystal decanter of port wine and toppled the bottle, and the red wine gushed all over Arthur McLean. *Oh, my God!* She jumped to her feet, he jumped to his feet, his clothes dripping. Rosie seized a napkin and commenced wiping him, and Clare Ashland stood there as though stricken, and heard herself moan, a low moan like from an animal, and then the tears burst from her, loud, sobbing, uncontrollable, and she turned from them, from all of them, and ran out of the room and up to the bedroom.

Soon Tony came. He took her in his arms, held her until the weeping abated. Held her even more closely now, as though to impart strength to the racked body, quivering, shivering. "Easy," he soothed. "Easy does it." And then used his handkerchief to wipe her face. "There," he said softly, and kissed her and put his fingers lightly under her chin. "Let's have a little smile, please." She obeyed. A grimace, wan, dreadful. He took his hand away from her chin. "Cold water," he said. "Wash, yes? Lots of cold water." She obeyed, moving stiffly, robotlike, to the bathroom. He heard the water, heard the splashing. When she came out, she looked better, much better. She had reapplied makeup and combed her hair.

"Honey," he said, "everybody, sometime in life, has tipped over a bottle." And laughed. "Think nothing of it. And no apologies necessary. Shall we go down now?"

"No."

"But—they're down there."

Her voice quavered. "I'm sorry I embarrassed you. And your guests. God, Mr. McLean."

"What embarrassment? No embarrassment. Nothing."

"You go, Tony. I—I can't."

He looked at her, studied her, nodded. "Don't feel up to it?"

"I—I just can't."

"Sure," he said, and smiled. "Lie down, take it easy, rest. I'll handle the downstairs situation. I'll get rid of them as quickly as I can."

She frowned, hesitated, seeming to seek for words. "You're good. You're the best I've ever known in my life." Hesitated. Then she said, "Tony."

"Yes?"

"In my own way, in my own crazy way, in the only way I know—I love you. Don't ever forget that."

"I thank you," he said.

"I thank *you,*" she said.

Downstairs they were still at table, drinking coffee, sipping port. Rosie said, "How is she?"

"The storm is over."

"But not yet the rainbow," Franklin said in his deep, sympathetic voice. "Evidently. Since you've come back alone."

"The poor kid," McLean said.

"Young. So darn young," the judge said.

"Lord, I'd love to trade with her," the judge's wife said.

"That trade would be all in my favor," the judge said.

Laughter. They laughed. And talked about the young and the old, and somebody quoted somebody about youth being wasted on the young, and they repaired to the drawing room with coffee and port and cognac and cigars and cigarettes; but the blight was on the party because of the girl upstairs alone, and Tony excused himself and went to the kitchen and dismissed Michel and his helpers, and poured himself a coffee, and sat at the kitchen table, sipping bitter sugarless coffee, knowing something must be done. She was ill. He had kept pushing it away, postponing, closing his eyes to the symptoms, hoping it was something normal, a natural reaction, a young girl married to an older man, a young girl suddenly snapped out of her accustomed background, ambience, environs, a young girl suddenly in the milieu of the millionaires, a new life, new responsibilities, the problem of adjustment, marriage—no! He had hoped, hoping it would pass, giving it time, hoping she would come up to it, blend in the natural course of the adjustment period, but now, finally, he himself had to face up. She was delicate, she was ill, she needed help, and that was *his* responsibility. He loved her. She was a fine kid, a delightful child, a sad one, unhappy. Well, it was time to shake up that psyche, time to bring in the experts, time to give her a goddam fighting chance to make a life of her life; and right then Dr. Reuben Grayson flashed through his mind. Perfect. A brilliant guy, a brilliant psychiatrist, not an old fuddy-duddy, and a guy she liked, admired. Yes, he would talk to her this very night; no, he would save it for tomorrow. He would do it easy, gradually; hell, all the damn rich women were in some kind of analysis. He would work it that way, roundabout; he would suggest and let her come around to it as though on her own. She liked Rosie; he would talk about Rosie and Dr. Arthur Sawyer. Or, perhaps better yet, he would have a private conversation with Grayson, discuss symptoms, solicit Grayson's advice as to how to approach her.

He returned to the drawing room, and there Duncan, sensitive Duncan, discreetly engineered the party's end. In the foyer there were handshakes, goodbyes, small chatter, but finally they were gone. He locked the door, bounded up the stairs to the bedroom, and at first glance could not find her. The room appeared empty. Then he saw her, lying on her stomach, on the floor at the far side of the bed. And saw, on the bed table, the empty bottle of Seconal.

He ran to her, knelt, turned her. She was pale, cold, damp. Her eyes were closed. A white froth of spittle bubbled at the corners of her mouth. He looked from her to the phone, back to her, frantically to the phone again. He released her, flew to the phone, dialed 911, told the man, gave his name and address. "We'll dispatch an ambulance immediately," the man said. And while there at the phone he called downstairs to the doorman.

"We've had an accident here. Ambulance coming. You'll let them up at once."

He hung up, ran back to her, slapped her, shook her; there was no response. Ran to the bathroom, filled a glass with cold water, poured it over her face. No response. Put the glass on the bed table, lifted her, walked her. Her feet were clumps, her knees did not bend. But she was breathing, she was still breathing, but badly: a shallow, rattling, gurgling breathing. Her eyes did not once open. What to do? What to *do?* He kept walking her, dragging her, up and down the room; he himself was panting from the exertion, hot, perspiring. Kept walking her, dragging. *Sweet Jesus, where were they? How long?*

Finally he heard the doorbell. He laid her on the bed, ran

down, and opened the door to a black woman with a little black doctor's bag in her hand. "This way," he said. "Quickly." He ran up the stairs; she followed closely behind him.

"What happened?" she said when she saw the girl on the bed.

He pointed toward the empty medicine bottle on the bed table.

"Goddam pills," the woman said.

She was crisp, alert, efficient. She felt for a pulse, then raised the girl's eyelids.

"Not good," she said. "You've got trouble, mister." Quickly she opened the little bag. "Get her sleeve up, mister."

While he pulled up the sleeve, she filled a syringe. Then she dabbed the arm with alcohol, and injected.

"Stimulant," she said. "Now get her up and keep her moving. I'm going down for the driver and a stretcher."

He got her up, kept her moving.

"Don't worry about answering the door," the woman said. "I'll click the clicker. Just keep her moving."

"Thank you," he said.

The woman went away.

He kept her moving, walking her, dragging. Not once did her eyes open.

The woman returned with a black man and a stretcher. They took her from him, handled her gently, strapped her onto the stretcher.

He rode with them in the ambulance.

At the hospital he waited in a hot, crowded, fetid anteroom, a green room with flaking paint, fluorescent lights, and wooden benches. It stank. Of unventilated August, of accumulated horrors, of all these sweating people sitting, haggard in the garish lights, hollow-eyed, sitting, troubled, waiting, anxious. Occasionally a name was called, and a person went out, and others came in, frightened-looking, sweating, ugly-anxious in the purplish lights. And now for the fourth time he went out to the desk.

"Ashland," he said.

"I know," the girl at the desk said tiredly. "They'll come for you when they're ready."

"Christ, it's over an hour."

"Nothing I can do, sir. When they're ready, they'll come."

"Yes, thank you."

He went back to the stinking room; there was no place left on any of the benches, no place to sit. He did not want to sit. He stood. Paced. Others also paced. And now a woman on a bench started to cry, stuffed a handkerchief against her mouth. The man beside her put his arm around her, whispered to her; then they stood up and went out of the room. That left two empty seats, but none of the pacers sat.

And then, at long last, a thin young man came into the room, a tired-looking young man, evidently a doctor; he wore white shoes, wrinkled white trousers, a T-shirt, and a wrinkled white jacket, open. "Ashland," he called.

"Me," Ashland said.

"This way, please."

He guided him through a corridor to another green room, paint flaking, and closed the door. A bare room with a small oak desk, an oak swivel chair, and three oak armchairs.

"She's going to be all right," the young man said.

"You sure?"

The young man nodded, winked. "Out of danger, as we say." Grinned with fine white teeth in the tired face. "Sit down, huh."

He went around to the swivel chair and sat in it heavily. It creaked.

Ashland sat in the armchair alongside the small desk.

"Moscowitz," the young man said, and extended his hand.

"Ashland," Ashland said, and shook it.

"Yeah," the young man said, and leaned back in the creaking swivel chair. He dug into the wrinkled white jacket, produced a cigarette, and lit it. Sighed. "I'm kinda resting, if you don't mind." Grinned with the fine white teeth. "I hope you don't mind."

"I don't mind."

"One beast of a night. Must be a full moon out there."

"How is she?"

"Copacetic." Inhaled cigarette smoke, let it dribble out of his nose. "You could have lost her, Mr. Ashland. It was nip and tuck there for a while. Cripes, we pumped the living shit out of her." Smoked the cigarette, grinned the grin. "That's one hell of a beautiful girl, your wife."

Christ, they notice. Nip and tuck. Could have lost her. Pumped the living shit. But they notice. It's a wild, weird, complicated life we live, isn't it?

"She's all right?"

"Perfect. She'll be okay." Took a handkerchief from a pocket, wiped his face. "Hot, huh?" A thin young man, but strong-looking. An interesting broken nose. Red-haired, with freckles. A scraggly mustache. "What was it? Seconal? Nembutal?"

"Seconal."

"Any of that stuff, fucking murder. And she wasn't kidding, your lovely lady."

"Beg pardon?"

"The blood work showed a hell of a lot in her." He scrunched out the cigarette in an incongruous seashell ashtray. "If she didn't swallow forty pieces, she didn't swallow a one."

"May I see her?"

"Nope."

"Why?"

"Rules." The swivel chair creaked, the young man sat forward. "And what to see? Nothing. She's sleeping."

"When?"

"Tomorrow."

"I want to get her to a hospital."

"This *is* a hospital."

"Payne Whitney."

"Now *that's* a hospital. I wish I could afford."

"I can see her tomorrow?"

"Of course."

"She can be transferred tomorrow?"

The young man nodded. "Figure two o'clock. If you figure two o'clock, I'll have her ready for you to sign out."

"Can you tell me—er, what her condition will be?"

"Groggy."

"A private ambulance?"

"If you can afford, that would be best."

"Is there anything, now, I can do?"

"You can go home, Mr. Ashland. And from the looks of you, I'd like to prescribe and I don't have to write a prescription. A couple of good shots of whisky. More than a couple, depending on your tolerance." The young man stood up.

Ashland stood up. "Take care of her, please."

"At least for tonight"—the grin was back—"as good as Payne Whitney."

"Thank you, Dr. Moscowitz."

They shook hands.

"She's gonna be all right," Moscowitz said.

At home he followed doctor's orders. Gulped a Scotch, gulped another, made a highball, and walked with it in the drawing room. Payne Whitney. No question, at least for this immediate period, she would require psychiatric hospitalization. But Payne Whitney wasn't easy, aside from the putative inordinate expense. To hell with expense, but can you get her in on such short notice? I'll get her in if I have to blast the place wide open. Anthony Ashland here—with powerful connections.

He went to the study, took pencil and pad, made a list of people who could pull the strings in this situation. But first, Duncan. Call Duncan.

He called, got through, told Duncan the whole damn story.

"Jesus," Duncan said.

"Payne Whitney. Tomorrow at two."

"Hold on to everything. Don't start with the list."

"Why?"

"Grayson. He's the biggie in that department. He knows all the people who know the people. You hang in there. I'll call you back."

He called back in ten minutes.

"Talked with Grayson. He says leave it to him. He's on the horn right now talking to people who know people and they'll reach people who know people—and get back to him. He says for you to sit tight. He'll call you as soon as he has definite word, one way or the other."

Grayson's call came an hour and fifteen minutes later.

"All in order, Tony. You're to call Payne Whitney tomorrow morning at ten. Ask for Dr. Ira Warsaw, he's chief of staff. He knows about the case; he'll be expecting your call."

"I'm going to move her at two o'clock. Does he know—"

"Everything. Your talk with him will be—merely the formal arrangements. As a matter of fact, he's an admirer of yours—your legal abilities. No problems, I assure you. Just the necessary formalities. But she's as good as admitted right now."

"Thank you," Ashland said.

14

SHE STAYED at Payne Whitney for ten weeks, and loved it. She grew to understand why soldiers re-enlist in the army; even why ex-convicts commit crimes in order to return to prison. Regimen and regulation. You do what you're told, you go by the rules, and in time your submission releases you to a strange self-ease, a contentment, a comfort, an odd, unvexed, preternatural serenity. Within the warm womb of establishment, you are cared for, carefree, insulated, protected. Your world is entirely run for you: no problems, no torments, no decisions to make.

For the first few days, she was still dull, dumb, withdrawn; gradually, she came out of it. Her room was lovely, the food was good; the doctors and nurses were cheerful, casual, insouciant, jokeful, splendidly unmelancholy, unwoebegone. For the first ten days, she was permitted no visitors, not even Tony; thereafter, during visiting hours, whomsoever she desired. She desired only Tony, and Sue Robbins.

Regimen and regulations. You went to bed at a certain hour, awoke at a certain hour, and in between the days were full. Three days a week, for three-quarters of an hour, you were closeted with your psychiatrist. She was among the élite: her shrink was the boss of bosses, the distinguished Dr. Ira Warsaw. Three other days a week, you had two-hour sessions of group therapy. On Sunday, the day the Lord rested, so did the shrinks. No therapy on Sundays.

Meals were served at precise hours, three times a day. In between you could snack all you liked, unless you were an obesity patient. And you were always busy. Exercises in the gym, arts and crafts under supervision, lectures by smiling pundits, music and singing, recreational games, different types of medication until they got you onto what they thought worked for you, blood tests by the medical doctors, psychological tests by the psychologists, and books to read from a wonderful library. Within three weeks the tremors in her hands ceased, the nausea passed, the dizziness passed, the crying spells passed, the whole darn depression passed. And after a month she was permitted to go out for walks with an attendant, and with Tony if he liked (and of course he liked). She loved it at Payne Whitney and thrived. Tony said, "They tell me you're doing very well indeed. And I can add something to that, but strictly from a layman's viewpoint." He kissed her. "You look better, and even more beautiful, than ever I've known you."

Privately, he had conferences with Dr. Reuben Grayson, approved and highly recommended by Dr. Ira Warsaw.

"She's amenable," Grayson reported. "Willing, after the Payne Whitney experience, to move along to personal therapy. Sometimes after hospitalization they're not willing, and that could present a problem. But she is willing and that's great."

"She thinks you're great. And Dr. Warsaw agrees."

"Humbly, I agree with them both." Grayson laughed.

"How are you fixed for time?"

"Lousy. Loaded up. But I do have a patient ready for discharge." He pondered. "And there's a woman who's been asking if I can move her to evenings. Clare comes out—?"

"October 8th."

He consulted calendar and diary. "Yes. I'll be able to give her three times a week, double sessions. Monday, Wednesday, Friday—five to six-thirty. Then at a quarter to seven, I'll take the other woman each of those days as my evening patient." He scowled, then smiled. "I won't get out of here till seven-thirty. With that kind of schedule, *I'll* be a candidate for Payne Whitney."

"I appreciate," Ashland said.

"Hell, if you can't do for friends—" Grayson lit a cigarette. "From my talks with Warsaw, from the little hints she's already imparted to him, I do believe I'll be able to help. And in short enough time. I'm against the long-term therapy, the old Freudian analysis, the four-year, six-year, ten-year bit, *ad nauseam*. I'm a face-to-facer, sometimes criticized as being unorthodox. What's orthodox? If I can't do it in a year, then hell, I can't do it at all. Double sessions three times a week, she'll be out on her own, out of shrinkland within a year, or I've failed. Look, I've had my failures; who in hell hasn't? If I can't do my thing in a year, then she doesn't belong with me. But I demand cooperation. Not only from the patient, but, in this case, also from the husband."

"I'll do whatever ordered."

"I'll order," Grayson said.

Payne Whitney. Regimen and regulation and medication. She felt good, and better and better. And during the last two weeks she was permitted to go home twice a week and sleep over; to go home twice a week, she assumed, in order to re-establish a gradual norm; to sleep over, she assumed, in order to prevent undue stress by getting laid. They did not permit the husband to sleep over at the hospital: Payne Whitney was not yet that modern. But she loved Payne Whitney and could, and would, recommend it with all her heart to whatever sickie—whatever poor bastard of a suffering sickie she would ever run up against the rest of her life. But they would have to be able to afford it. Because, as she learned from the more sophisticated patients—some of them returnees—the fees for the therapy and maintenance mounted up to terribly expensive figures.

She was due to be discharged on October 8th at four o'clock.

At three o'clock Anthony Ashland sat alone with Dr. Ira Warsaw in Warsaw's quiet, well-appointed, walnut-paneled office. The doctor was a large, heavyset, seam-faced man, utterly bald, with an aquiline nose and the eyes of an eagle.

"She's quite well," Warsaw said. "Ready—and, in fact, eager—to be transferred to Dr. Grayson." He opened a drawer, extracted a couple of bound sheafs of paper. "Our report, Mr. Ashland. One for you to turn over to the psychotherapist; the other for your personal files. You may read at your leisure, but at this time I believe a vis-à-vis discussion is imperative. Which is why I asked you here an hour in advance of discharge."

"Yes," Ashland said.

Warsaw lit a pipe, puffed.

"A most interesting case," he said.

Ashland said nothing.

"Sometimes," Warsaw said, "I skip this type of discussion. Nor do I generally hand over the reports to the next of kin. They would go directly to the therapist, upon his request. In this matter I'm proceeding differently. You're not quite the ordinary individual." He smiled. "It isn't often I have a really intelligent next of kin. But on occasion when I do, I believe a vis-à-vis discussion to be extremely beneficial for all the people concerned."

"Yes," Ashland said.

"We are dealing with a delicate, frangible psyche. A beautiful young woman, but oppressed with self-hatred, self-contempt. She believes herself to be worthless, which in itself represents a serious psychopathology. It is the reason she reveres success, successful persons, achievers—because she considers herself an absolute *non*achiever."

He puffed his pipe. "She has little or no confidence in herself; a case of arrested development. Not mentally, of course. Emotionally. Emotionally, she's still a child. But she's a grown woman. And that unconscious conflict has produced a syndrome of pessimism, desperation, depression."

He took up a report, turned pages. "A fear of men; somehow an unconscious loathing of men. Dr. Grayson, of course, will probe for the reason." Puffed the pipe. "She's never had a successful relationship with a man—until you. And the relationship with you triggered her back to the other—the child thing."

"I don't understand."

Turned pages. "This is your second marriage, I believe."

"Yes."

"How long married?"

"This marriage?"

"No, the first."

He had to think. "Twenty-six years," he said.

Warsaw looked up from the report.

"Mr. Ashland, we're approximately the same age, of the same generation. I take it your first wife was the woman of the house, performing all the necessary wifely duties, and thereby leaving you virtually free in your capacity as the breadwinner."

"Yes, that's correct."

"And I assume a similar pattern prevailed in this present marriage?"

"Well, yes, in a way."

"She couldn't handle it, Mr. Ashland. What for you or me would be a minor chore—for her would be a major matter, sometimes insurmountable. And as the pressure piled up, she broke down. Please understand, this is no criticism of you; you're not a doctor, a psychiatrist; you were merely"—he smiled—"a husband. A child, Mr. Ashland; emotionally, a child. Not yet a tree—a sapling; and a tender sapling must be cared for, nourished, nurtured. Therefore, now, when she returns, all pressures must cease. Not forever, of course; not by a long shot. But bit by bit, step by step. A child does grow up, but she must be nurtured. Dr. Grayson will discuss this aspect with you, and advise you."

"Yes, Doctor."

"There has to be cooperation—the husband, the therapist, the patient. We here have made a good beginning—actually medically. Drug therapy, it's like blindman's buff. What's effective with one individual may produce no results with another. Among other chemicals, we tried lithium carbonate, and with your wife it's worked like magic. Dr. Grayson will keep her on the medication, but of course she requires what we in the profession call talk therapy. Grayson's real job will be to build her ego."

He returned to the report. "This was her second suicide attempt. I take it you know that?"

"Yes."

"Suicide. What *is* suicide? *Why* suicide?" He laid the report on the other report, lined them up neatly, tapped his fingers on them. "There are so many theories. My ideas, they're all in here. I've elaborated, because one copy of the report is for your attention; you'll give the other to Dr. Grayson." He struck a match, relighted his pipe. "Rage, self-hate, desperation, depression—a mix that boils up to a wish to kill. Turned outward, the result can be murder. Turned inward—suicide, a self-killing, the killing of self."

"Just a moment, Doctor."

"Yes?"

"Are you saying she could be—homicidal?"

"We can all be homicidal."

"I'm talking about this particular case."

"I'd say no. There's no history of her turning outward. Always possible, of course. But so's that possible for you or me. Seems *her* rage and desperation turn inward—and the basis is lack of ego. That's going to be Grayson's job. To dig into that delicate psyche, to build up that fragile ego. Thereafter nature will take its course. The child will mature." He smiled, shrugged. "In my business we're fond of quoting the rule of Dr. James Blake—circa 1800—that one-third of all mental patients recover spontaneously."

"But what about *this* patient? Your opinion. I mean, you know—prognosis."

"I'm quite optimistic. She's not at all badly ill. I'm quite certain, given time, she'll come out of it solidly." He looked at his watch, slid the reports into a manila envelope. "Life, experience, even hard knocks. The gradual, inevitable nurturing process. She needs to grow up, Mr. Ashland, and I do believe, in time, she will."

15

SHE ENJOYED THE THERAPY. Heck, what was it with her? A weirdo? A freak or something? Who enjoys hospitalization? Clare Benton Ashland is who. Ten weeks at Payne Whitney and loved it all. Like one of the nurses said, that last day. "G'bye, baby, you've been a doll, I wish they were all like you. G'bye, good luck, you're an alumna now. Maybe they ought to give a certificate, a diploma, a sheepskin, you know? Ole Payne Whitney U. But the way you ate it up, I hope you don't come back for a postgraduate course." Loved it, and now, crazy Clare, she loved the therapy. At first she was shy, but little by little she opened up, because he was so darn wonderful. Sympathetic, empathetic, listened when she talked, but with such deep interest, as though she were truly a friend rather than a patient. And he was so darned handsome, so beautifully handsome; and so good and kind. For instance about the taxis.

Her sessions, five to six-thirty, were the worst time for

trying to get a cab, and if you called up for a radio cab, you never knew how long you had to wait. But even in so minor a matter he was considerate and helpful. He suggested she use her car, and when she protested about where she would park, he arranged car space for her in the garage of the building that housed his office.

And the matter of her dragging out the session beyond the allotted time. When you're immersed in talking about yourself, the ninety minutes telescope, and frequently, despite his body-language promptings, she was in there longer than her time period. And coming out, she regretted, because there would be the last patient, sitting, waiting, an elderly lady. And that always surprised her; somehow it had never occurred to her that old people needed psychiatric treatment. And, knowing him, she knew he would give the woman her full time and, since she was the last patient and had been kept waiting, a bit of additional time; and like that, because of her, Clare Ashland, the poor guy would be working deep into the evening. But never once did he mention it, never once did he criticize.

The three times a week became an important part of her pattern, like a rendezvous, like a date with a lover, and she looked forward eagerly, and she thought about him before, and thought about him afterward, and she found she was actually dressing up for him, worrying about what clothes to wear, and sometimes in bed, Tony asleep, she fantasized. . . .

After several private talks with Grayson, Tony Ashland changed his domestic life-style perceptibly, abruptly shifting away from the group dinner parties. They became a couple, an intimate couple; hell, like honeymooners. They went to plays alone together, and dinners alone together, and even the golf, while the weather was still good—a twosome. In the clubhouse they might have cocktails with some of the others, but that would be the sum of it. And, of course, the target practice at the gun club was always a delight for her. And at home he would do most of the cooking, laughing it up, experimenting. And *she* did cooking (they were like kids together) from a cookbook, from recipes, and if the result was unsuccessful, they would merrily dispose of the whole mess and send out for a Chinese dinner. And they went to movies alone together and wound up with hamburgers at a beanery. He kept the pressures off her and, shifting his own style, found he was enjoying it. They watched TV together, and spent hours battling over Scrabble. Yeah, Tony Ashland alone at home with his wife, playing Scrabble!

Of course they could not forever be alone. He went with her far more often to visit Frank because he knew she enjoyed Thelma's company. And knew she enjoyed Sue Robbins' company, and although he did not particularly adore Sue Robbins, he cultivated her, and Sue and friends were frequent visitors at the Ashland household. And when they did give small parties, they pondered the list together, and he kept it young (or younger than it used to be). Like the Raywicks. Or Beatrice Smith and her young-stud symbiotics. And other young people, like Benjamin Morse from the office, whom he gradually gathered unto the Ashland hearth.

It worked, somehow it worked, and although he did give to himself a modicum of the credit, he gave the full credit to Dr. Reuben Grayson whose head-shrinking art had so quickly produced volatile miracles. (Or was it Dr. Ira Warsaw and his magic medication? She adhered steadfastly; not once did she skip the prescribed capsule.) She bloomed, sprouted, grew, blossomed; she was gay, outgoing, cheerful, exhilarant, and yes, by damn—exuberantly confident.

It was she, in fact, who suggested dinners with some of his old friends: the Arvels, the McKees, the Franklins, and others, but never the McLeans; and it was she who suggested that they give a Christmas party, and when they made the list it was *she* who suggested the McLeans.

And the party, with the McLeans (first time since the bottle-toppling episode), was a roaring success.

And on the Monday following Christmas, at her session with Grayson, she reported a conversation with Arthur McLean at her Christmas party:

"It's so good to see you, Clare."

"It's been a long time, hasn't it?"

"Too long."

"Remember that night? When I soaked you in wine?"

"You ran away. You shouldn't have. Who hasn't been soaked in wine?"

"I wasn't well. On the verge. That night did it. I tried to kill myself."

"Welcome to the club."

"No. Not you. I don't believe it."

"Me. Three times. Thank God, I never made it all the way."

"How are you now?"

"In therapy. Always therapy. And pills. Therapy and pills—keeps me on even keel. How're you?"

"Therapy and pills. I think I'm on even keel."

"You look wonderful."

"You look wonderful."

"So it goes, my dear."

"Can you imagine," she said. "The great Arthur McLean. Three times, three attempts. Who in the world would believe it?"

"You're beautiful," Grayson said.

"Thank you," she said, and lowered her eyes.

"Come on. Get off it. Don't flirt with me. You know what I mean."

"What?"

"You're coming along. Your head is over the waterline. Can you imagine you—let's say you before Payne Whitney—openly admitting to an Arthur McLean that you attempted suicide?"

"No. I cannot possibly imagine."

"You'd have ducked. Bullshitted. Run around corners."

"Yes, darn right."

"But you didn't. You stood up to him and weren't ashamed."

"True, yes, I wasn't."

"Because you felt you were his equal."

"Me? Arthur McLean?"

"As good as he, as weak as he, as strong as he. We're all one family, Homo sapiens. Some are smarter, some are dumber, but all of us—every damn one—is filled with foibles and frailties. Some of us put on a good act, some of us don't. But inside, essentially, the core, the basic animal characteristics, the strengths, the weaknesses—goddam similar. But those that *think* they're weak *are* weak, and those who think strong are strong. Thank God, little, lovely, childlike Clare Benton Ashland is finally coming around to thinking strong."

"If I am, it's you."

"Not me. You. You're doing it and you're doing it beautifully. My function—to open up the vistas. To show you that essentially you're no better or worse, no weaker or stronger, no more frightened than I am, or Tony, McLean, or anyone else in this vale of tears. And it's beginning to come through. That lovely head of yours is holding above water. You're just as good as anyone else, and just as bad. We're all of us only lousy little human beings racked by nerves, frights, ghosts, guilts; quintessentially, down there at the basics, we're all alike. When we shit, we squat. All of us. From the Pope in the Vatican to the bum on the Bowery."

"Crazy," she said.

At home that night, his mind stayed with Clare Benton Ashland, and he was pleased with himself. The patient was progressing beautifully; of course, the medication was extremely effective. But medication without therapy is a glass crutch. Without successful therapy the crutch can splinter to dangerous shards. In this case the therapy was eminently successful, along the lines suggested by Dr. Warsaw: build the ego. It was clean-cut, somehow technical; the shrink was a surgeon, his scalpels were words. Incise until the psyche is exposed, cut away here, implant there, close, suture, let the wound heal, let nature take its course. It worked, and unexpectedly quickly. Because, highly suggestible, she was amenable to the words. Or perhaps this patient and doctor were suitable, compatible. Or perhaps, and most reasonable: an untreated chronic condition was finally under direct, acute attack. As is legend in a profession notorious for tenuous, subtle, long-drawn ministration, there is always the exception—generally a person never before in therapy—who responds with a unique, precipitate, fortuitous rapidity.

But there was more to do, more, more, much more, and he was shirking the quirk. Quirk. The ego was building, but the quirk stuck out like the proverbial sore thumb. Men. Males. The balls of the species. She feared, she hated, she loathed, she abominated: all unknowing, consciously unknowing. But their cheerful, occasional badminton game of free association starkly disclosed it, and the dreams she brought him were vividly filled with the symbols of male-loathing. But he let it go, turned from it, kept postponing. His rationalization: one problem at a time; the major matter in hand was to give her confidence, self-confidence, to build up that fragile psyche, to firm up the ego, to dissolve forever the self-contempt. But he damn well knew that the one entailed the other, that the sexual hangup was a part of the other, that unless he freed her of the unconscious male-hate there would never be a permanent platform for a sturdy female ego.

But he turned from it.

He kept postponing.

And the fault was not the patient's.

The fault lay with the patient's doctor.

He was holding off on the sex therapy because he himself was sexually entrapped. She was bewitchingly beautiful; Christ, she fairly *oozed* sex appeal. And he itched for her, romanticized, fantasized: she filled his dreams. He wanted her. His loins demanded, and he was already in hot pursuit. But he kept postponing, nagged within *his* psyche by the gut-rot, the dead-wrong, the enormity of the culpability. He postponed but knew it to be a delaying action, this avoidance of sex discussions with his patient, because once that door was opened he would plunge through; he would have her, he had to have her. The stress of desire was fixed, unremitting, a malevolent obsession, and there she was for the having, an overwhelming temptation and torture, three times a week alone with him.

But he enjoyed. Somehow enjoyed. Mordaciously enjoyed—the anticipation, the sex experience before it actualized, the delicious masochism of preliminary guilt, and none of it involved Christine Talbert, and properly so.

They were not sworn to fidelity, Ruby Grayson and Chrissie Talbert, nor did either of them demand fidelity. They were in love—love, love, goddam—and love is all that matters. Their aspects were broad: they were nonconformers and freedom fighters and not wedged within prosaic emotional strictures. He knew of her peccadilloes, her AC-DC predilections, and if she required an occasional bout of lesbo love (or any other kind of love) after they were married, that was approved in advance, a part of the life-style. They comprehended one another, accepted and respected the foibles. She knew he was highly sexed and a casual varietist. So what? They belonged to one another, inextricably paired, and all else was peripheral; a bang here, a bang there, flesh pleasure, carnal amusement, a bouncing around, a sleeping around, but superficial, insignificant. Yes, she knew that he fucked around, but she did not know that on occasion, rare occasion, he fucked around with a patient.

Rare. Rare occasion. Only when the loin-demands rendered *him* the victim. The doctor the victim, screwing the patient. But in such event he found purpose, he justified: the love treatment was integral to the therapy. But he knew different, damn well knew that this type doctor-victim was in fact the perpetrator, that justification could be a reverse conduit. He knew that a patient in transference was bereft of the normal palisades: defenseless, she revered, venerated the encompassing god image to whom she *needed* to give homage; if God desired, certainly the Virgin submitted—adoringly. But God was *not* God; he was a doctor-guy lustfully impelled, a human being committing a heinous act upon the living flesh that he himself had rendered innocent. But once he yielded to temptation, then he *had* to justify. It was a psychological truism that every criminal, after the fact, found reasons, however complicated, to assuage the roiling conscience: justification as a reverse conduit. And suddenly here at home, the redoubtable Dr. Reuben Grayson felt himself to be more common than the most common of criminals. Because now here at home, *before* the fact, he was already in the process of justifying.

16

HE WAS IN LOVE.

Anthony Ashland in love.

More and more, he was in love with his young wife.

And, even better, he had begun to admire his young wife.

Karma? The inscrutable involutions of the occult? Had the suicide attempt been a mysterious *pro forma* necessary for the ongoing progress of a May-December marriage? May-December—that was to laugh. May-December—I mean how corny can you get? May-December was a hyphenation in the language that had never once entered into his personal cogitations. May-December was a tired throw-cliché for the melodramatics of summations to juries. But it was a May-December marriage; right, Your Honor? Right, ladies and gentlemen of the jury?

And here it is, ladies and gentlemen, and on even keel, a thoroughly satisfactory marriage. Thanks to Payne Whitney, or Reuben Grayson, or Ira Warsaw—she was gay, buoyant, ebullient, laughing, happy, and of late tremendously involved, encaptured and enraptured with a totally new and laudable activity.

The 86th Street Aid Foundation.

A euphemism, naturally. But this is our time: we live in an age of euphemisms. A barber is a stylist, a beautician a cosmetologist. A lover living-in is a roommate. A hopeless harried spinster is a bachelor lady. A wheezing octogenarian is a senior citizen in his golden years. A naked group-grope is a touch seminar. Nobody dies: they pass on (may he rest in peace). There are no saloons; there are taverns, *boîtes,* and swinging (or swingless) bars. And no prisons; even the filthiest dungeon is a correctional facility. And there are no foundling homes, no orphanages; only aid foundations, social service organizations, placement societies, development centers.

The 86th Street Aid Foundation was a foundling home, an orphanage, and a damn good one. Abandoned children do not all acquire foster parents, and those who remain, an ever-growing host, must be clothed, fed, housed, schooled, and physically, mentally, and emotionally cared for. An eight-story building run by nuns, the Aid Foundation was one of Rosie McKee's charities, and every now and then, as the needs of her spirit moved her, she dropped in for tea and cookies and the nectar of expressed gratitude. On one such visit, she was accompanied by Clare and the latter was won to the cause; partially, like Rosemarie, as a money philanthropist, but, unlike Rosie, also as a worker.

Money was always a need of the nuns, but there was the additional need of clothes, toys, food, furniture, games, books, and the eleemosynary services of doctors, dentists, psychologists, teachers, nurses, and just plain people who could spare the time. Clare joined up, at first tentatively, then devotedly. She gave two full days a week, Tuesdays and

Thursdays from nine in the morning until six at night, and loved it. She read to the kids, played games with them, helped serve the food, cleaned and diapered the little ones, assisted in teaching the bigger ones, and when the weather was favorable she took groups to the zoo, or the museums, or on sightseeing hikes. The children loved her and gave her a name, and this evening in early April when Tony called for her, he heard the name the kids had pinned on her—"Saint Clare"—and he was heart-burstingly proud. It brought to focus what had begun to germinate in his mind, and that night at home he broached it.

"You're great with those kids."

"I love them."

"How about some of your own?"

"Some of my—"

He laughed, busied himself with making a drink.

"Why not?" he said. "You're young, I'm old, but not *too* old. A family of your own, Saint Clare. Hell, why not?" The laughter was done; his voice was serious. "There'll never be a problem about money. My present will leaves one large bequest to my daughter, but the great bulk goes to you, and there'll be enough for forever after, no matter how large a family. Also"—he sipped the drink, set down the glass, and now he was smiling—"you're not going to be a widow for a hell of a long time. Come with your lawyer, me love."

He led her to the library, pulled down a book. "Metropolitan Life," he said. "Actuarial tables. The life expectancies." He opened the book, found the place, ran his finger down the page. "See? Here. I'm now fifty-five." Moved his finger across the page. "Expectancy twenty years, and I'm going to go longer than that. Never really sick in my life, healthy as a horse, strong as a bull, and I come from long-life people. My mother's still around, hale and hearty. My old man walked out when I was a kid, but I bet he's still around unless he was killed in a fight or something. He used to boast, the old man, about the longevity of his antecedents. His father died at ninety-two; his mother at ninety-five. Same with my mother; her people lasted up into the nineties. And their grandparents—same deal." He closed the book, kissed her nose. "I'll father the family, and I intend to be around—Mr. Father Image—to rear the family. So?" He grinned. "How's about it?"

"I—I'm dumbfounded."

"Why?"

"I, just, well, like—never thought about it."

"Sure," he said.

Sure, he thought. When you're in analysis, or therapy—or whatever in hell they call it—you have to consult with the shrink. No objection, Your Honor. Dr. Grayson has worked wondrous miracles and I am with him all the way. Could be she isn't ready, not yet ready. If you say so, Doctor, all right with me. But in time—sometime—she *will* be ready. You're the brilliant psychiatrist, and I believe in the delegation of authority. In this department you're the boss; my spouse's delicate psyche rests within your capable hands. Up to you, Doc. Whenever you say. Her prospect of progeny is at your command.

"Sure," he said. "So, now, think about it, begin to think. No hurry, no hurry at all." Chuckled, pointed at the closed book. "We've lots of time, you and I."

Intrigued.

She was intrigued.

Crazy. All new. Intrigued.

She lay late, this Wednesday morning in April, Tony gone off to work, lay cool and comfortable in the massive bed.

Kids.

It had never occurred to her: kids of her own.

Kids had never occurred to her, her own or anyone else's, until her work at the Aid Foundation. And then, suddenly, a whole new world had opened to her. She had had no proximity to children, no experience with children until the Foundation, and she loved it, loved them and they loved her, a natural rapport, a whole new world.

Kids of her own. Intrigued, she'd have jumped. Except for Dr. Reuben Grayson.

Good Tony, dear Tony, wise and kind. *So, now, think about it, begin to think. No hurry, no hurry at all. We've lots of time, you and I.* Dear Tony, wise and kind and gently circumspect. Of course what he had meant was "Discuss it with the Man. If he thinks you're ready, and you agree, we'll start a family. If the Man doesn't think you're ready yet, I will of course abide by his decision."

But, in fact, the problem was hers.

Because, in fact, she was in her heart, ashamedly, disloyal to the husband whom she adored. She was in love with Dr. Reuben Grayson. Crazy? Yes, darn crazy. But do you take that final, total step—do you even begin to *think* about it, a family with Tony Ashland—when your fantasies have you leaving him and running off and marrying Dr. Reuben Grayson?

Love. Crazy. But *was* it crazy?

Sue had said, during confidences at lunch: "Watch yourself, kid. Don't lose your head. You're a bee in honey. You've got it all, you've got it made. And you really don't know a thing about Sir Shrink."

"I tell you I *feel* him. I—I know. . . ."

"Maybe you do, maybe you don't. Baby, if you weren't a little bats in the belfry, you wouldn't be going to him, right?"

"Yes."

"So do me a favor. Sue here. For me. Old Sue."

"What?"

"No half-cocked leaps. You've got it made, you've got it beautiful, you admit you adore the old guy. You say he's the best, and you admit if not for this nutsy bit about Grayson you'd be into the old guy one hundred percent. Right or wrong?"

"Right."

"So you just watch your ass, honey. Don't you dare burn bridges until you know just what you're doing. I want you to promise me, baby. You hear?"

"Yes, yes, I promise."

The conversations with Rosemarie McKee were less excitable, less frenetic, less overtly dissuasive, but paradoxically less reassuring.

"Dearie," Rosie would say, "we're all in love with our analysts, and each of us thinks we're the only one. Sooner or later it happens and they're delighted when it does. A tool in the trade, a need in the therapy; they even have a word for it. Transference. I believe that's it—transference. A kind of falling in love. Happens to all of us."

"But can't it sometimes really happen? Mutually?"

"That's what we all think because that's what we want to think. And they don't try too hard to talk us out of it because like I said—a tool of the trade."

"But like *I* said. Can't it sometimes *really* happen?"

"Possible. Everything's possible. And here we have some rather amenable circumstances, two very beautiful people. But I warn you, don't bank on your dreams; those dreams happen to all of us. I warn you not to try to live the dream; don't push it. Too *much* transference, active transference, could frighten the guy. He might pack it up, pack you in, send you off to another doctor. You're a baby, you're twenty-five, and at your age romance springs eternal. But just try to remember you're a patient in therapy, period. Look, the real thing's possible, everything's possible, but you listen to Rosie. Don't bank on it."

She didn't bank, but hoped. Hoped. Felt. There was something between them, she knew, she knew. And turned uncomfortably in the bed this Wednesday morning. Transference. A tool of the trade. The dreams happen to all of us. God, was she kidding herself? She understood about the involvement. Three times a week for practically two hours alone with a man, intimately discussing self. It generates a strange and encompassing passion; you look forward to those hours alone with your friend, your confidant, but a friend and confidant who is far wiser than you, who is trained to understand your kinks, caprices, conceits, vagaries, who is trained to comprehend and reason with and advise upon your purest delights as well as your secret obscenities, and in time this trained friend and confidant moves up in stature, rises up to a throne which you have created, and there he sits your king, your master, your pundit, priest, druid, guru, and your faith blends to him and you revere in awe: you listen, accept, obey. God, if he said she had wings she would darn well fly.

Out of bed now, nude, and into the shower. And then in a robe in the kitchen, tea and breakfast. But her mind remains enmeshed with her doctor-lover. Could she tell Rosie that the therapy was no longer pleasant (as it had been early on)? Rough these days, sticky. Her fault, of course, because when the talk turned inward to sex she became a nothing again, a frightened shit. And of late that had been it—sex—and he probed incessantly. And explained why. Explained her dreams and explained the correlations of the free association. Unconsciously she hated men, feared men, loathed the male—despite all of her remonstrances. And it was no longer face to face, because she was so damned ashamed when it came to sex. It was the couch-bit now. She lay out on the couch and he sat somewhere behind her, unseen, a disembodied voice. But he was smart, her king-master-guru. The couch worked. Her fear of men became evident—even to her.

Always, somewhere along the line, she discovered her male partner to be a "phony" and thus found reason to rupture the relationship. "Because that's the way you want it," he said. "You pull out because of that inherent loathing." And probed, probed, until she confessed she had never had any real pleasure in sex, had always pretended in order to please the man, had never in all her life experienced an orgasm. "Good, good," he said. "We're at it now. We're open for talk, for explanations, explications. There's an abscess somewhere in there, closed in, loitering, festering. We're going to get to it, you and I, lance it, open it, let the poisons out, and you'll be free. You're doing damn well. You've begun to believe in yourself as a person, which you goddam are. But this other thing screws you up. That's all we need now, to get down there to the root cause, and then you're done with it all; you'll be on your way on your own. You're not really a complicated case, Clare, believe me. Dr. Warsaw knew it back there at Payne Whitney, and I know it here alone with you. Two things. The fragile ego and the male-abhorrence, and they may be interlinked. Fragile ego—it's my hunch, and from what you've told me it's more than hunch—you were overprotected as a kid. The mother was dead; the father tried to be both mother and father. All right. We've worked on that. You've begun to come out—and the medication hasn't hurt. You've begun to believe in yourself; you're as good a person as anyone else. Now if we get to the other thing, you'll be clear. I don't care how in hell we get to it—but we're going to get! I'm against the twelve-year bullshit of analysis. I admit I'm unorthodox, I try every goddam method, but I want you out on your own as fast as possible. Root cause on the male thing. Somewhere down there you're hanging on, consciously or unconsciously, a closed fist squeezing a secret. We're going to open that fist, you and I. That's our job now."

Not unconscious.

Conscious. But could never bring herself to talk about it.

Time now. It was time. She was ready. Perhaps Tony's desire for children had triggered it. Perhaps her own desire for Dr. Reuben Grayson was the gun for Tony's trigger. No matter. Whatever, she was ready. Today! This very day. Today she would tell. And in the kitchen, tea and breakfast, felt herself melting, and steeled herself. Today. Today she would tell what in all her life she had been unable to tell. She would tell today about dear old Daddy, the quiet respectable churchgoer, the most splendid dentist for children in all of Minneapolis.

17

"So? How are we today?"

Patterns. In time all things fall into pattern; a repetition as though a ritual. She would leave the apartment at four-thirty, drive to the basement garage of 840 Park Avenue. Park the Mercedes in exactly the same spot each time, lock it, drop the keys into her handbag. Walk the exact same route to the elevator, push the button, wait, enter the elevator, push the 12 button. Emerging at the twelfth floor, she would look into the wall mirror opposite the elevator, smile at herself vaguely, adjust clothes, and walk the corridor to 12-C. Turn the knob and enter the waiting room; the door to his inner office would be open, and she would see him seated behind his desk. He was always there behind the desk. She knew that his prior patient had left fifteen minutes before and knew that in the interim he would call his answering service and make any necessary return calls. (The phone never interrupted during sessions: the turnoff wheel silenced any ring.) If he had any personal things to do, like going to the bathroom, he did them before she arrived.

Entering the inner office, she would close the door behind her. It was a large, quiet, high-ceilinged room with a deep-blue carpet and pale-blue walls and shirred curtains across the windows. His kneehole desk was mahogany, long and narrow. His leather swivel chair was tall and soundless. On the other side of the desk, directly opposite, was the patient's chair: a mahogany armchair with a leather seat and a leather back, and there were other such movable armchairs about the room. The couch was a leather chaise longue, wide and comfortable.

Pattern. She would say, "Hi," and seat herself in the patient's chair, her bag in her lap. Across from her in the swivel chair, he would be silent for moments, his face placid, even grave, but his eyes smiling as he studied her. Then: "So? How are we today?"

They would talk for perhaps fifteen minutes, small matters, her doings, her activities, her superficial concerns. She might ask questions and he would answer, but at length he would stand up and that was the signal. She would place her bag on the desk, slip out of her shoes, and go to the couch, and he would be somewhere behind her in one of the armchairs. He would poke, prod, set her off, and then she would do most of the talking. Sometimes her eyes were fixed on some tiny spot on the ceiling, sometimes her eyes were closed. Sometimes she fell silent, and he said nothing, and she would lie there like that, drifting, floating, as though hypnotized, and then his voice would come through, his stab of a question would startle her, and then another sharp question or two and she would be talking again.

Today in the patient's chair, she quickly told about Tony's desire for a family.

"What do you think about it?" he asked.

"I—I just don't know." She could not say what she wanted to say: *"I adore the man but I'm in love with you and I think you're in love with me and therefore I'm terribly confused."* No, she could not risk that. Not after Sue's firm admonitions. Not after Rosie's cool advice. Could not risk his terminating their relationship. Could not risk placid wrath, or deep concern that she was *that* crazy. Simply, she could not risk his sending her off to some other shrink.

"Would you like to have children?"

"I think, yes. Sometime. But now. So sudden. It never. I mean . . ."

He sat back in the swivel chair. He was silent.

"You're the doctor," she said. "What do *you* think?"

"I'm afraid, no. Not yet."

"Why not?" Explosive. As though *she* were on the offensive.

"I don't think you're ready. You damn well will be when you're out of here. But you're not yet out of here—because you've been fighting me. Clare, I tell you again what I've told you before. You're not a complicated case, not at all. You're a goddamned stubborn case, but not complicated. There's a double hangup, as Dr. Warsaw diagnosed. The feeble ego because of self-contempt—and the detestation of the male. You've done wonders on the first—"

"You did it."

"Not me. You. I merely suggested, but you came up out of it beautifully. Began to believe in yourself. Began to understand that if you're no better than anyone else, you're certainly no goddam worse. And the Aid Foundation—which I encouraged—proved it to you. You're great, they love you—you're Saint Clare. Beautiful. All beautiful along that line. But on the other—I have *got* to have cooperation. Once we clear that, you're out of here. You know me—I don't believe in the long-term bull. If we open that up, the male-hate, if we ventilate that—you'll be out on your own. Once we hit that root, then all we'll need is a few months of therapy and you're discharged. You'll stay with the medication so that you won't have the high-ups and then the low-downs. But you'll be fine, and on your own, and if you want kids—great. But you've been fighting me on the sex bit, the male loathing. Ducking, parrying, closing up like a clam—consciously or unconsciously. But I'm going to get to it, you're going to get to it—"

"Consciously."

"Pardon?"

"Never been able—to tell. I suffocate. Choke. I want to puke, want to die. But I know that's it. What you're after. What I haven't been able to bring myself to talk about—not even to you. But today, here goes. If I die. But I'm going to talk. I'm determined. Today—"

And *she* broke the pattern on this pattern-breaking day. Laid her bag on the desk, kicked out of her shoes, and stretched out on the couch while he was still in the swivel chair.

Closed her eyes. Heard him somewhere behind her.

"Yes," he said. "Tell me. Talk. Just let it come."

"She died. I was four. Mother. Me the only child." She did not recognize her voice. It was as though someone else were speaking in narrow, nasal, trembling tones. "I told you about my father—a nice man, religious, regular churchgoer, a dear dentist, everybody loved him. I was maybe six, seven, when I began to have those dreams. My father—father—fucking around with me."

"Fucking you?"

"Playing with me."

"Playing how?"

"Dreams. They were dreams. Always, even as a kid, I slept naked. My own room. Slept. Dreamed my father sneaked into the room. Naked. Sat on a chair near me. Touched me. With his left hand touched my naked body, and with his right hand he was jerking off. It was a dream, a dream, a horrible nightmare. And I kept it like that, a dream, because I needed it to be a dream. But once, once upon a time, I opened my eyes and I saw, and then I tightly closed them again, and it was a dream again. Can you possibly understand?"

"Yes," said the voice from somewhere behind her.

"It went on and on, all of my life, adolescence, youth, my father molesting me, touching, fondling while I was supposedly asleep. Jerking off. Once a week, twice a week, he was there in my room, naked on the chair, the left hand lightly sliding along my body, touching, squeezing, the right hand masturbating. And me with my eyes tightly closed, and him, the son of a bitch, he *must* have known I was not sleeping. And I never said a word, never objected, even when I was already grown. Who can possibly understand that?"

"I can," he said.

And he did. Because he himself, in early youth, had been violated.

She was panting, sobbing, crying.

"Never said a word. Asleep, I was always asleep, while my father used me to jerk himself off in the middle of the night. Who can understand the fright, the fear? It had started when I was practically a baby. Who can understand the panic, the anguish, the shame, the absolute need to pretend to be asleep? And yet, a funny thing, I felt sorry for the son of a bitch, I felt sorry for that poor, sick, driven man. But I got out as soon as I could. As soon as I was no longer dependent, as soon as I came into my inheritance, I cut and ran. Came to New York. And never again in touch. Never. He's never once heard from me."

In the armchair behind her—excited, aroused, phallus turgid, pulses pounding; her story thrust him back to his own youth, to carnal seduction, violation of an innocent by a trusted elder. The stories intermixed in his mind, exacerbating, inflaming libido, but he knew it had nothing to do with stories: it was the girl there on the couch, the flesh obsession, the overpowering animal desire. He had postponed, had kept postponing, but no longer. He would have her. Must. Here. Now. And immediately rationalized. Therapy. He could release her from her demons. But he sat there, motionless, as she continued talking, spewing, reviewing, repeating scenes, her eyes closed, her throat throbbing, sobbing; the abscess was open, the pus pouring. And now he pulled the chair close to the couch, touched fingers to her forehead. She opened her eyes.

"We're there," he said. "We're finally there."

"The son of a bitch, the son of a bitch."

Her face was contorted, wet with weeping and perspiration.

"Abreaction," he said.

"What?" she said. "What?"

"Abreaction. Do you know the word?"

"No." Her body arched, convulsed. The tears streamed.

"A psychiatric word."

"Oh, the fucking son of a bitch."

"Abreaction. We love it. Explosion of psychic tensions. Release—with affect—of repressed traumatic experience. I'm not one for the fancy psychiatric words. You know me. I prefer straight language with my people; hell, I've been criticized for gutter language, profanity. But, occasionally, necessary. Abreaction. You're in it, and I love it. But we're going further. Now. While you're in abreaction. Do you hear me? Can you hear me?"

"Yes. Yes."

"Psychodrama. Do you know *that* word?"

"Stop it. Stop it with words."

"Psychodrama. Another method for release. Unorthodox. I go with any method, at any time, if I think it will help. It will help now, while you're in abreaction. We're going to re-enact the experience. Now. While you're wide open for it. We're going to clean it up, clean you out. I want you to imagine you're back at home; in bed in your bedroom at home. Get up. Get undressed. And then lie there, nude, in your bed at home."

She obeyed; as though mesmerized, obeyed. One part of her, mesmerized, obeyed; the other part was alert to what she was doing and she loved it. Undressing for her lover. She had dreamed of undressing for him. But, down to panties and bra, she hesitated.

"All, everything," he said. "I want you naked."

The bra came off, the panties came off; God, she was beautiful. He sat there, a furnace, blazing in heat. He had seen her onstage, nude in *Open Season,* but up close she was ravishing, absolutely devastating. The milk-white skin, flawless. The breasts upthrust, pink nipples glistening. The concave belly. The thin dark slit of navel. The long legs. The high rise of hips. The gleaming blond delta at the fork of the full smooth-white thighs.

"Lie down. You're home in bed. Minneapolis."

She lay on the couch. Her eyes were closed.

"He was also naked, wasn't he?"

"Yes."

He stood up, tore off clothes, sat.

"Look at me. I'm your father. In your bedroom."

She turned her head, looked, closed her eyes.

"I'm your father," he said. His left hand reached out to her, caressed her breasts, fingered her nipples, moved down along her stomach, pressed against her pubis.

She sighed, moaned.

"Look at me," he said.

She opened her eyes, looked.

His right hand moved loosely up and down along his erection, simulating masturbation. "Was that it?"

"Yes."

"Did you like it?"

"What in hell are you asking?"

His left hand pressed at her pubis; an expert finger touched at the clitoris. She moaned. Her tongue wet her lips.

"As a child," he said. "Did you like it?"

"I—I don't know. Maybe."

"But as you grew up?"

"Hated. Despised." Her mouth writhed. "I hated the bastard."

"Yes." Both his hands were free now. The left hand did not touch her, the right hand did not touch him. "Yes. Taboo. Incest taboo. And you projected. Listen to me. The hate, the male-hate, the loathing. Unconsciously you projected; whoever the man that touched you was your father. Projecting, you rejected. Every man was your father, abusing you, violating. And so every man was a phony, and your sex was sexless, and there could not be an orgasm. Do you hear me? Do you understand?"

"Yes. I think—yes."

"We're going to go further. Abreaction—while you're in abreaction—all the way. A lover. You're going to have a lover, not your father. *Not your father!*"

And he was on the couch with her, naked to naked, embracing, kissing, his mouth on hers, hers on his, tongues lashing, and he moved down, licking her breasts, sucking her nipples, and down along her belly and between her legs, sucking her cunt, and her thighs enclosed his head, and she moaned, heaved, cried, screamed, and he opened her thighs and looked at her.

"Not your father. I'm not your father. Say it."

"Not—not my father."

"Again. Say it again."

"Not my father."

And his body moved up on hers, and his thick prick entered into her vagina, and she was living her dream as she rose up to him, receiving him, engulfing him ecstatically.

18

APRIL, May, early June, the weather lovely, the Ashland household peaceful, the lady of the house radiant, glowing, her life-style settled, her patterns fixed, her secret dreams bold and vivid, her imagination soaring. Weekends they golfed; evenings they went out to dinner, sometimes with friends. And of course there was always the gun club which she so much enjoyed, priding herself on her marksmanship, regularly outshooting him. Tuesday and Thursdays the Aid Foundation, and Mondays, Wednesdays, and Fridays she went to her lover.

During lunches with Sue or Rosemarie, she no longer talked about him. What was there to talk? They had been wrong, both of them, and he was now *her* secret. And there were no longer discussions with Tony about children. She had told him: "Not yet. The Man says not yet. Not until I'm discharged. But that won't be too terribly long."

"He's the Man," Tony said. "He's done damned all right,

and on him we depend. Like if he had legal troubles, I would be the Man, and *he* would depend."

She adored him, adored her husband, but she was in love with Dr. Reuben Grayson. And once, preoccupied with her own secret thoughts, but studying her handsome husband, he had said, "Why do you look so sad?"

"I'm not sad, Tony. I love everything about you. You're the best. Honest to God, you are the best."

He was. The best. Kind, good, the sweetest, the finest, the most compassionate. And therefore she would not trouble him with the soarings of her imagination, with the wild plans that coursed within her, with the future that was so inevitably coming forward; she wanted him happy until the darned last moment; until Dr. Reuben Grayson finally declared himself. He would. Oh, she knew he would. He was in love with her, he *had* to be in love with her, but he was waiting—until she was well. She knew, from Rosie McKee, he had no girl friends, no one except Christine Talbert, and she knew from Tony that Talbert was a lesbo, that her husband was Audrey Chappell, that Grayson was her "beard," that their thing was a friendship like male-male or girl-girl. He loved her. Her! Clare Ashland. God, with their goings-on he *had* to love her, but he was waiting—waiting—until she was well to declare himself, and then he would ask her to leave Tony and marry him and she would, she would. But not until then, until the full, open declaration, would she bring it to Tony, confess, tell, and she knew he would understand, her Tony whom she adored, this best of men, the kindest, the most deeply compassionate. He would let her go, no strings, no recriminations, and no matter his own abysmal hurt. She knew him, and was so darned sorry to have to hurt him. He would look at her long, ask her if she knew what she was doing, but once convinced, he would kiss her forehead, wish her luck, and let her go. God, she adored the man.

* * *

At the office on the twelfth floor of 840 Park, the pattern had subtly changed. There was first the face-to-face across the kneehole desk, the doctor-patient conversation, she sitting primly, her bag in her lap. But when he stood up, the signal for the couch, and she laid her bag on the desk and removed her shoes, she removed more than her shoes, she removed all of her clothes and lay naked on the couch and he came to her, came naked, and they made love, and then he left her there, disappeared behind her to his armchair, and they entered into the third phase of the new-type session, the vocal therapy; his short, sharp questions were daggers that cut into her, and she bled in talk. Today, a Monday in early June, she was talking about her father, talking in sympathy, talking about the poor bastard who had never remarried, who needed sexual release, who found it in stealthy advances upon his daughter, who must have suffered within himself terribly, and then she was off on other matters, personal matters, her eyes closed, her voice thin, talking flatly, slowly, as though hypnotized, as though self-hypnotized.

". . . I know you love me. I love you. I know you're waiting. Until I'm well. Beautiful. Us, together. Beautiful. I know you won't declare. Not yet, not yet. I do not blame you. Still sick. But when I'm well. You will tell me. We. Us. Together. Marry. I love Tony. In my own way, love. Adore him. But you and I. Different, different. We will marry. When I'm well. Children. You and I. I know you love me. I know you're waiting. When I'm well. No worry. You must not worry. He will understand. He's good, I tell you good, he is the best. . . ."

Armchair. Sitting. Riven, driven, filled with guilt. He had taken her, tricked her, seduced her; he had lusted after that supple flesh and was still lusting, although thank fucking

God, it was beginning to diminish. But it *was* therapy. He had helped, he had goddamned helped, opened her up, released her to orgasm. Christ, she was shooting off rockets, and even reported orgasms at home. And she was over the father hump. The male hate was dissipating, the personality was closing to whole; she *was* getting well.

". . . I love you . . . you love me . . . we will be together . . . live our lives together. . . . I will be your wife until I die. . . . I know not yet . . . not yet . . . you are waiting . . . to declare . . . to change my life when I am well . . . when I'm well. . . ."

When she was gone, he called the answering service. Only one message—Chris. To remind him. They were having dinner with the McKees at the St. Regis Roof. She would pick him up here at the office after his last patient. He hung up, looked at his watch. Time before the patient, plenty of time to settle down. He leaned back in the swivel chair, but remained unsettled. Guilt this evening was a heavy enemy. He was protracting the therapy and he damned well knew it. By now he should be working on the reversal of transference, but he hadn't even started because he was still in the throes of sex-lust; it was diminishing but he was still morbidly, trenchantly driven.

Reverse transference. Always difficult, but he had never been unsuccessful: he was a skillful practitioner. Reverse transference: untying the knot, cutting the cord, severing the patient from the psychiatrist. A gradual procedure, like taking an addict down from drugs. No cold turkey. Slowly, slowly—but he had never failed. He estimated three months for this final stage; he knew his power over her, his mind over her mind. In three months she would be free, and damn glad to be rid of him—but he was not yet ready to be rid of her. He pondered that, and determined a schedule. August. In August there would be the mandatory clean break: August was his vacation month. And then in September he would commence the reversal procedure and in November, discharged, she would go happily home to Tony Ashland and they would start making their babies.

And now, of course, a twist away, a need: rationalization. The couch had done wonders; the sex had opened her up and drawn her out, and when she lay there alone afterward, yapping, babbling, internalizing, rambling, that was all to the good, a catharsis, an analeptic expurgation, a powerfully therapeutic ego-exegesis, all necessary for this patient. But—was the sex necessary? And his psyche, contumacious this day, played devil's advocate and answered: no! He damned well knew he could have brought her out without the fucking on the couch, without his own self-indulgence. Example. The woman who was coming, his last patient, a lady of sixty-three, but strong and sturdy, whose problem, believe it or not, was essentially sexual. A good lay would do her a world of good, but would he take her to the couch? He wouldn't dream of it, would he? And damned well knew he would help without humping her. As he damned well knew he could have helped that other without humping, that gorgeous, white-skinned, irresistibly sexual beauty.

He lit a cigarette but, after a few puffs, killed it in an ashtray on the desk. Hell, she was lucky that, however fortuitously, Dr. Reuben Grayson had turned up in her life as the psychotherapist. Because *he* knew, he empathized, he himself had been child-molested; he knew of the subtle torture, the abominable secrets, the internal harborings, the sheer impossibility of heinous confession: he had not opened up until he himself had been in analysis. He knew of the weird anguish, the repressed panic—but his thing had been the opposite of hers. Where she had been male-violated, he had been female-violated; where she had been male-dominated, he had been female-dominated.

His mother. Ah, Mother. She was still one hell of a woman, Grace Grayson, designer of women's clothes, today the famous corporate president of Grace Grayson Creations, Inc. One hell of a woman, Grace Grayson, and too much for any man. Daddy Grayson had divorced her when Reuben Grayson was two years old. And had fled to Canada and never returned. Which had not fazed Grace Grayson, nary a whit. Rich even then, she had imported an English nanny to care for her boy-child while she was busy with her burgeoning activities on Seventh Avenue. Ah, that nanny who became surrogate Mommy: she had systems of her own for child care. When the little boy cried too much, she suckled him; took his tiny penis in her mouth and thereby pacified him. And as he grew, they bathed together—*their* secret: Mommy never knew. And when he reached puberty—he reached it early, he was twelve—nanny taught him to kiss pussy, and they lived together like that, in oral-oriented beatitude, until he went off to school and she went back to England.

"Which is why you're so great a cuntlapper," the analyst had said. "Eating a woman, unconsciously you seek to incorporate the woman, to *be* a woman. However you didn't turn out to be a fairy, I'll never know, what with no male influence, and a mother whom you venerated, and a nanny who was your oral lover."

She was still around, his mother, haughty and famous and active and never remarried, her residence a mansion in Mamaroneck where, living in, were two male secretaries (both of whom, he was certain, were screwing her), and the garage housed four Rolls-Royce limousines which required two sleep-in chauffeurs (who also, he believed, were screwing her). Quite a woman, Grace Grayson, president of Grace

Grayson Creations, which explained to Dr. Reuben Grayson why he despised weak-willed nothings like the beautiful Clare Ashland and adored dominant women like Christine Talbert, who he knew, he knew, would give him sons—

He heard the outer door open and close.

"Good evening," his patient said, and slammed the inner door and sat in the armchair on the patient's side of the kneehole desk, her bag in her lap.

He looked at her gravely, his eyes smiling.

"So?" he said. "How are we today?"

The rooftop of the St. Regis was lively and glittering and the McKees were lively and glittering, and he relaxed and laughed at Christine's quick-wit gibes and listened, always in surprise, to the McKees' in-gossip about show-biz famous names, and ate the marvelous food, and drank huge quantities of champagne (washing away guilt), and took Chris off to dance, and when they returned Rosie said, "You were the best-looking couple on the whole damn floor."

"Thank you," Chris said.

"When are you two going to do it the whole way?"

"Do what?"

"Get married," Rosie said. And laughed at them.

At home, at 330 East Thirty-third, they showered and went directly to bed. Lay there, accustomed lovers, not touching, the bedlight burning. "Tired?" she said.

"Rough day."

"We are going to do it."

"Are we?" Languidly. "What?"

"Get married."

"What?" Abruptly, he sat up.

She left the bed. Went to the living room. Returned with a joint, smoke drifting. Sat on the edge of the bed. "Fuck

Rosie," she said. "She thinks I'm strictly gay. That was woman-talk back there; she just couldn't resist a spiteful remark. But we *are* getting married, and we're going to have babies. Within wedlock. A traitor to the cause, aren't I?"

"Why so? Many in the cause are married."

"Not people who shot their mouths off like me. But I've been thinking, thinking, going crazy. Decision. I'm going to have to eat a lot of crow, but the hell with it, the hell with everything. We're engaged, Doctor."

"I love you," he said, and kissed the back of her neck.

"An unannounced engagement. You're not going to breathe a word."

"Not a word," he said.

"And a long engagement."

"How long?"

"Six months. I've set a date, if it's all right with you. December 15th."

"Sure," he said. "But question. Why so long?"

She smoked the joint. She said slowly, "I'm going to need time. Drop a word here, drop a word there, let it seep through. Reconversion requires a hell of a lot of explanation. It ain't gonna be easy. Many of the sisters'll be after me with the long knives—and this time with reason. A lot of them have been after me anyway because, kind of, I've been a star in the Movement, and you know how it is with stars; there's envy, there's jealousy, you're always a target. Could be, if the pressures get rough enough, I'll have to resign from *Flare*."

"Well, hell," he said, and chuckled, "you won't have to worry about starving. A husband *has* to support a wife. It's the law of the land."

"Male chauvinist piglet," she said.

And laughed. And he laughed.

They laughed. . . .

19

FRIDAY. Warm and lovely. The last Friday in June.

Tony had called that he'd be home early, about four o'clock, and was bringing Duncan McKee. Now, at ten after four, they had not yet come. On the bar in the drawing room she had set out bourbon for Duncan, Scotch for Tony, and ice, glasses, soda, and water. Her bag lay on a low table near a green velvet armchair; she was dressed and ready to leave for her session with Dr. Grayson.

The bell rang and she opened for them to enter. Duncan carried a narrow, dull-leather attaché case. She led them to the drawing room, gestured toward the bar. "Help yourselves," she said, and sat in the green velvet armchair and crossed her legs.

Duncan set down the attaché case, looked at her, smiled.

"Beautiful as ever," he said.

"Thank you," she said.

"Lucky Tony," he said.

"Yeah, that's me," Tony said.

They made drinks, drank.

"Clare," Tony said.

"Yes?" she said.

"How about Chinatown tonight? Dinner in Chinatown?"

"Love it," she said.

"Clare," Duncan said.

"Yes?" she said.

"I'm not intruding in paradise," he said. "I won't take up too much of his time. A half hour at most." He pointed to the attaché case. "A contract I want him to look over. Talked him out of my coming to the office. At the office, what with the frigging phone calls and all, it would take hours. I don't have the time today. Got to pick up Rosie at five. We're going to the country for the weekend. So, please believe—you'll have him back in half an hour."

"That's all right," she said. "I won't be here a half hour from now. Got to leave at four-thirty."

"Appointment with the shrink," Tony said.

"The shrink," Duncan said, and drank down his bourbon. "Boy, do I have some gossip about her shrink."

"With the McKees it's always gossip," Tony said.

"A ripsnorter," Duncan said. "But a heavy secret."

"Naturally," Tony said. "So—let's have it."

"He's getting married."

"Grayson?"

"Correct."

"To whom? Do I know her?"

"You know her. Christine Talbert."

"I don't believe it."

"Believe it."

"How do you know?"

"Got it from the horse's mouth."

"Who's the horse?"

"My wife. And *she* got it from the horse's mouth."

"Who's *her* horse?"

"Christine Talbert herself."

"But that one's against marriage," Tony said. "Lectured against it, wrote against it—"

"People change. They grow up, mature. They can shift their value judgments, can't they, Counselor?"

"But can they shift from dykedom?"

"Dykes have thumbholes. Ever hear of bisexuality?"

"I've heard, I've heard."

"Whatever, they're getting married. Definitely. Chrissie Talbert and Ruby Grayson are definitely, positively, absolutely—getting married. But hark ye, my friends—it's not yet for public consumption. So kindly keep the lips buttoned. Until they announce, it's supposed to remain a great big dark secret among intimates. I consider you people intimates."

"Well, hell, more power to them," Tony said.

"All right, that was my bombshell for today." Duncan grinned, took up the attaché case. "Let's go do some work now, Counselor."

They went into the study and closed the door.

She sat there in the green velvet armchair, her knees numb. Sat in the green velvet armchair, shocked, shriveled, deflated, beaten. Sat small, sick, aching, heartsick. Sat there in a confusion of inchoate wrath, rage, waste, defeat, despair, nausea drubbing at the pit of her stomach. Sat amidst the debris of ruined dreams, sat in torpor, sat numb, used, traduced, sat there silently howling. The son of a bitch; oh, the son of a bitch, the son of a bitch! The smooth, smarmy, vicious, venal son of a bitch, lasciviously after his hunk of flesh like all the rest, using her like before him *they* had used her, as her father before *them* had used her. But this one was the worst of all, a goddamned snake, the phoniest of all the horny phonies, the *super* phony, the master, the guru, the pedestal sovereign, the worshipped. Psychodrama, he had said. Therapy, he said. I will make you well—oh, the mean, slippery snake of a son of a bitch, the dirty fucking bastard. Letting her lie there, vomiting hope. Letting her tell of her dreams with him, letting her tell of love, letting her tell of their shining future together, and not once interrupting, not once contradicting, and therefore—may God curse his soul—he went along, affirmed, acquiesced, tacitly promising him to her when she was ready, when she was well.

She sat there, whirling. Dazed, bemused, benumbed. Until finally confusion began to abate. To be superseded by—incredulity.

She did not believe. Could not, *would* not, believe. What in heck to believe? A tidbit of gossip from gossipy Duncan McKee? Which he got from the horse's mouth, the notoriously capricious Rosie McKee? Which *she* supposedly got from the mouth of the beautiful bull dyke Christine Talbert? Who could be laying in new planks to support her public platform of heterosexuality? No, sir, I do not believe, and I will not believe, unless and until I hear it from *my* horse's mouth, Dr. Reuben Grayson.

But then, somehow: oh, that smarmy snake of a son of a bitch.

She looked toward the tall, ornate, antique grandfather clock, brass pendulum soundlessly swinging. Four-thirty-five. Stood up and almost fell back: her legs were numb. Reached down for her handbag and then walked, hobbled, needles still tingling in her legs, toward the door. Stopped. Stood for a moment. Walked back, stiffly. Stiff but not hobbled; circulation returning to her legs. Walked stiffly to the library and opened a drawer of the desk. Took out the pistol and closed the drawer. Placed the pistol in her handbag and snapped it shut.

840 Park. Basement garage. The Mercedes in place, the ignition locked. She walks slowly to the elevator, touches the

metal button in the stone wall. Waits, drawing breath deeply. Into the elevator and up to the twelfth floor. Looks at herself in the corridor mirror, smiles dreadfully, adjusts clothes. Walks rapidly now to 12-C. Opens, closes. Sees him in the inner room, there in the swivel chair. Enters, swings the door shut. Sits in the armchair on the patient's side of the kneehole desk, her bag in her lap.

He studies her. His face is placid, but his eyes are smiling.

"So? How are we today?"

"Are you going to marry Christine Talbert?"

Surprise beclouds the placid face.

"I beg your pardon?"

"Are you going to marry Christine Talbert?"

"Well, yes. Matter of fact, yes. But it's still a good way off, months." His eyebrows contract. He squints, pleasantly. "It's supposed to be a closed secret. For a moment there, you kind of startled me. I mean, how do you know?"

"I was told."

"By whom?"

"Duncan McKee."

"I'd have preferred to tell you myself. And in time, of course, I would've. All in proper time. Lord," he says, and flashes that smile, "there just *are* no secrets, are there? As Benjamin Franklin once said—"

But now his eyes are round in astonishment.

"No," he says. *"No."*

The first bullet pierces his forehead directly over the bridge of the nose. He sits there, blood trickling. The smile is frozen in his face, the eyes are astonished. The second bullet shatters the left eye. The socket gapes, ragged, red. Blood pours thickly now.

The right eye is still astonished as the smiling corpse topples from the swivel chair.

She stands up from the patient's chair, drops the pistol, closes the bag, turns and leaves.

* * *

He was in the drawing room, in shirtsleeves by the bar, shaking up a whisky sour, when he heard the door open and close, and a strange, unaccustomed wisp of fright coursed through his veins. What the hell? *Who* the hell? Nobody but he and Clare had keys, and she wasn't due home until at least an hour from now. He set down the shaker and went forward impulsively, bravely but stupidly, damned well knowing it was stupid, toward whoever the intruder.

No intruder. Clare. She met him halfway. And the wisp of fright congealed to fear. Something was terribly wrong.

"What the hell?" he said. "What's the matter?"

Her eyes were glazed, opaque, her lips wan, her face ashen.

He gathered her into his arms, held her, felt her trembling.

"What's the matter?" he said softly.

"I—I . . ." she breathed at his ear.

"What?"

"Killed . . ."

"Speak up. I can hardly hear you."

More strongly. "Killed. I killed the cocksucker."

Cocksucker. He had never heard that word from her.

Held her. Kissed her cheek. It was cold.

"Who? What? Whom did you kill?"

"Grayson. Killed the fucking son of a bitch."

And went limp, almost oozed out of his arms, her bag falling to the floor. He held her, firmly; heard her crying, sobbing, choking in tears. Held her, pulled her, dragged her, let her fall to a corner of the couch, and she sat there weeping, openly crying like a child, grimacing, fingers uncontrollably fluttering.

He took up her bag, found a handkerchief, gave it to her.

"Thank you," she said simply. Wiped her eyes, blew her

nose. "You're good, so good, only you. I love you, only you. There's no one else, only you. I dreamed up this other one, the son of a bitch, because I'm crazy. I tell you, I'm crazy."

"You're not crazy."

"Crazy, crazy, I'm crazy."

"Stop it!"

She was weeping again, dabbing at her eyes, tearing at the edges of the handkerchief.

He went to the bar, poured a brandy, gave it to her.

She sipped. "Drink it all," he said.

She drank it all. He took away the glass.

"What happened?" he said. "Tell me what happened."

"Killed him. I killed the snake of a son of a bitch."

"How? Why? What, when, and where?" Sat beside her on the couch, an arm around her. Drew her head to his shoulder. "Easy," he said. "Easy does it," he said soothingly. "I want you to tell me, step by step. Tell me all of it, step by step, from the very beginning right up to now."

She told him. All of it. Everything. Step by step. From the very beginning right up to now.

He was up, pacing, walking, and *he* was saying, "The son of a bitch; oh, these sons of bitches. About time. About time one of them got it." And the lawyer in him loved it. "Good girl, good girl," he said, pacing, grimly smiling, knowing she was free, as good as free; *he* would free her. And looked toward the antique clock, pendulum silently oscillating. A symbol. Like a symbol. Time goes on. Life goes on. Inexorably.

There was time, sufficient time to prepare her before they came. Oh, they would come, in a straight line, right to here. Grayson's last patient would arrive at quarter to seven and find him dead. She would call the cops, and the cops would do the easy check. The guy was not dead too long and the patient before the last patient was Clare Benton Ashland, as they could ascertain from his appointment diary. And the gun there on the floor was properly and legally registered in the name of Anthony Ashland. Soon, soon, soon enough but with sufficient time between, they would be here.

He crossed to the phone, called down to the doorman.

"I'm expecting policemen. They'll ask for me or Mrs. Ashland. Don't hold them up down there. Don't ring me. When they come, send them up here directly."

"Yessir."

He hung up. He had spoken loudly enough for her to hear.

"Time, time," he said. "Plenty of time before they come."

She sat there, limply in the corner of the couch, drained, no longer weeping.

"Did you hear me?" he said.

She nodded.

"Good girl," he said. "And don't you worry about a thing, nothing. Nobody's going to hurt you, nobody's going to harm you. I'll take care of it all, everything. A thousand percent. Believe me."

He brought her another brandy, gently took the torn handkerchief from her hands.

"Sip it now," he said, and smiled. "Just sit here and sip, rest, relax. And don't worry, please don't worry. The bastard got what he deserved. You just leave it all to me."

He was pacing again, the lawyer in him loving it. His uncelebrated *cause célèbre* was going to surface to open focus. A sensational trial would finally expose a subterranean devil-practice; a goddamned silent cancer lurking within the bowels of society would finally be cut open to public view. The goddam love-treatment rapists would begin to think twice before committing their easy assaults.

Sweet Jesus, all he had heard from parents and people, the sufferings caused by this hidden, screened, egregious form of rape, and now here it was come home to roost as a motive for murder. But the rat bastard had got what was coming. You heedlessly tinker with a bomb, it goes off in your hands. You want to challenge fire, then be prepared to get your balls burned off. You goddamned knew whom you were dealing with; I myself brought you Dr. Ira Warsaw's psychiatric report.

Facts. We have facts here. We have the goddamned facts, Your Honor.

A girl twenty-five years of age, a sick kid, twice an attempted suicide, now fighting for a life, struggling for survival, clawing desperately toward a plateau of normality. And so we put her into your hands, Dr. Grayson, your putatively capable hands: you were recommended as the best. We depended on you; you the healer, the physician. We depended wholly, totally, completely. And how did you return our trust? By violating her, you son of a bitch. Under the guise of therapy, violated her. Because you could not resist lust, and because it was an easy form of rape. You were young, handsome, rich, and on the outside there was plenty of cunt at your disposal. But it was easier in the office, wasn't it? There she was, a gorgeous young gal, and you had her in transference, a willing victim to whatever your word. In a sensational trial, we are going to open up the facts to the public, not only as her defense but as an out-loud warning to that fringe band of bastard rapists, the so-called love-treatment therapists who fuck their beautiful patients, only the beautiful patients, no matter that they further imperil a fragile psyche and no matter that they pollute a profession, a comparatively recent profession in the syndrome of this civilization, a profession under the constant artillery fire of the crazies, the conservatives, the pietistic religious, and the ignorant.

Sensational trial. It would be a sensational trial. It had to be. The woman at bar, under a homicide indictment, would admit to adultery. But standing up for her as defense counsel would be the cuckolded husband. Unusual? Damn right, unusual. It would pack the pews of the courtroom, and reporters would flock from far and near, even overseas. Anthony Ashland knew in advance. This was *his* business.

He paced. He paced in his drawing room.

She was as good as free right now. With her background, her psychiatric history, his plea of temporary insanity could not fail. No jury in the world would convict. But he would also file an ancillary defense, a secondary defense of justifiable homicide—a killing in resist of rape—and under the umbrella of that second defense he would be able to open up to the world the evils of the love treatment: the parochial, prurient, carnal violations on the couch in the office—and the bastard therapist was being *paid* for that. Under the umbrella of justifiable homicide, he would be able to bring in proper psychiatrists, people like Dr. Arthur Sawyer, who could testify about the proper procedures of the profession and about the fundamental moral and ethical interdictions. Who could explicate upon the meaning of transference, the inevitable dependent-love relationship, the subtle inflowing hypnosis, the veneration of patient to therapist, the eventual inability of a patient to distinguish between trespass and therapy as practiced by a satyr-psychiatrist. Once and for all, defense counsel would open to the world the invidious depredations of the love-treatment rapists who, under the guise of therapy, indulged their lusts upon victims-in-transference incapable of legal consent.

Free. Free. As good as free right now. No jury in the world would convict. Hell, he ought to know. This was now in *his* bailiwick and *he* was the expert.

He paced, restlessly paced, looked at the clock, looked at her, went to the bar, poured the ice-melted sour into a glass, drank, put away the glass, paced, and tried *not* to look at her.

The poor kid, the poor sweet kid; Jesus, would her sufferings never end? Soon there would be cops and the ordeal of arrest. They would take her down to a precinct house, mug her, print her, type out name and address and all the other necessary information, and then put her away in the slammer for at least overnight.

He would have to tell her. He would have to prepare her.

He paced. Christ, what an ordeal for this suffering kid, for that fragile ego. He would try to soften it, give her the good side. She would get the very best of treatment. He was the renowned Anthony Ashland and she was Anthony Ashland's wife. And he would call his brother, talk to his brother the big shot, the First Deputy Police Commissioner. She would get the best of treatment, the very best of treatment.

But what is the very best of treatment when you are locked in a cell with rats and cockroaches? He could not tell her that, he *would* not tell her that. Nor would he tell her it could be more than overnight; it could be until Sunday. Tomorrow was Saturday, a rough day to get at a judge. No question about bail; in these circumstances he would have her out on bail, no question. But before the affidavits were drawn, and before he could get to a judge to sign the order, and before the unwieldy machinery of law clanked into place—it could go into Sunday. Sweet Jesus, this poor sick kid locked into the steel and concrete of a vermin-infested cell.

He paced. He knew exactly what to do once he had her out. Immediately he would transfer her to Payne Whitney and place her under the beneficent auspices of Dr. Ira Warsaw. And she would stay there until the time of trial, unless Warsaw advised otherwise.

Paced. Looked at the clock. And then made a show of

standing before the mirror, closing his collar, adjusting his tie. He put on his jacket, picked up her bag, took the brandy glass from her hand, gave her the bag.

"Soon they'll be here," he said, and smiled as brightly as he could. "Want to put some makeup on?"

"Yes, thank you," she said. So quietly. Simply. It broke his heart.

She fixed her face, placed the bag on the floor.

He sat beside her on the couch, an arm around her, and talked.

He told her all he thought she should know.

"Do you understand?" he said.

"Yes," she said, and looked up at him.

He wanted to cry, he bit down against tears.

That sweet face, that innocent face. The ravaged eyes in that innocent face.

He kissed her forehead. He kissed her eyes.

"It's going to be all right," he said. "Believe me."

"I believe you."

"I love you," he said. "You're my life."

"You are my life," she said. "Please don't ever die."

And they were crying now, they were both crying.

"It's going to be good," he said. "I tell you, it's going to be good."

And knew he was talking truth; he *knew* it. Karma, the occult, precognition, whatever the hell: he knew it, he felt it; it was going to be good. This suffering child had finally reached crest; from here on out it was going to be good. And suddenly he remembered Dr. Ira Warsaw's words: *Life, experience, even hard knocks. The gradual, inevitable nurturing process. She needs to grow up, Mr. Ashland, and I do believe, in time, she will.*

Yes, Doctor, and this is it. Finally, inevitably, now in the throes of this ultimate experience, she is at crest. And she will come out of it whole. I know it, I feel it. Intuition, precognition, karma, occult—I know, I *feel!* She is over the top, over the hill.

"It's all going to be good," he said. "Believe me."

"I believe you," she said. "I believe—"

The doorbell rang.

Henry Kane

Henry Kane has written novels, short stories, screenplays, radio and television scripts: he has been published in virtually every language. A man of frightening energy, a native New Yorker, a volatile man of high humors and black despairs, Kane has been described by *Esquire* magazine as "author, bon vivant, stoic, student, tramp, lawyer, philosopher, a master of the massé shot on a pool table."